A Field Of Bright Laughter

A Field Of Bright Laughter

Connie Monk

PIATKUS

First published in Great Britain in 1992 by
Judy Piatkus (Publishers) Ltd of
5 Windmill Street, London W1P 1HF

The moral right of the author has been asserted

*A catalogue record for this book is
available from the British Library*

ISBN 0-7499-0123-3

Phototypeset in 11/12pt Linotron Times by
Computerset, Harmondsworth, Middlesex
Printed and bound in Great Britain by
Mackays of Chatham, Kent

Chapter One

Lottie could point to the day and hour when her dream was born. It was afternoon, the month was August and the year 1933. It was her tenth birthday.

And because the afternoon was so clearly etched on her memory, so was the rest the day, from the moment she opened her eyes, aware even in that waking moment of a feeling of anticipation. Then the reason for it dawned.

It's nothing to do with presents . . . Presents! Imagine if Mum and Dad have got me the bike. And as she imagined she crossed her fingers tightly. But it's not only because of presents, her thoughts rushed on, it's . . . oh, it's special. Already it doesn't feel like an ordinary day. She stretched to make herself as long as she could in her bed, arms held high.

There was the sound of bare feet padding down the stairs from the top bedrooms. There were four rooms on the second floor; two were slept in by the boys, one by Freda the maid who'd been with Kate and Rupert Bradley for the seventeen years of their marriage, and one still known as the playroom. Hearing footsteps Lottie sat up, waiting. The boys were on the way to wish her Many Happy Returns.

'Hush, boys, quietly. You come down the stairs like a herd of elephants. Your mother is still asleep, she had a very poor night.' That was her father's voice, his words pricking Lottie's first pure bubble of excitement. 'Before you go in to see Lottie, back to your rooms and get your dressing gowns on. You're too old to wander into her room in that state of undress. In any case, remember we have your aunt with us. What would she think to see you roaming about straight from your beds? Up you go.' A man rarely roused to anger, seldom heard to laugh, to his family Rupert Bradley's word was law.

'Right you are, Dad.' That was Michael. He was the elder of Lottie's brothers, nearly sixteen.

1

'Aren't you coming in too, Dad?' Ronnie asked. 'Don't you want to see Lot's face when she hears what you and Mum have got for her? If she has to wait for Mum to wake, you might have gone.'

'Indeed, I hope she'll sleep most of the morning. You tell Lottie to come downstairs and see me before I leave the house. And mind – no hinting that you know what it is.' He spoke in a whisper but, straining her ears, Lottie heard every word and smiled to herself. 'Quietly, mind. Keep your voices down. And warn Lottie about your mother. Any noise must be downstairs.'

'Mother's headaches' were something they'd all grown up with. At whatever time of day Kate Bradley took to her bed, there she'd stay until tomorrow, when she'd usually re-appear as if nothing had been the matter.

'Poor old Lot, does that mean she won't get her birthday picnic on the punt?'

'Let your mother get her rest. Sleep works wonders. But if she's not feeling up to it, Lottie will understand. There will be plenty of other days.'

Yes, there'd be other days. But they wouldn't be her birthday. Lottie listened as the footsteps retreated, her father's downstairs, her brothers' up. Ah, they were coming back! She was bolt upright, ready for them.

As instructed, they'd tied themselves into their dressing gowns. But their hair was still tousled; Michael's fair and silky, hanging over his forehead, Ronnie's a few shades darker, a good many degrees coarser and standing up on end. In features the brothers were similar, their father's gingery brown eyes and high cheekbones. In personality they were quite different. Somehow it always seemed to Lottie that their hair had been chosen specially to suit them. Michael, quiet, gentle, peacemaking; Ronnie, full of fun, always wanting to climb a branch higher up a tree than his friends.

'Happy birthday, Lottie.' Characteristically it was Ronnie who was first to climb on to the bed and push his package into her hands. 'Hope you like it. You'd jolly well better! All my own work.' A trinket box, the product of a whole term's woodwork lessons.

Her spontaneous bearlike hug told him what he wanted to know. Then it was Michael's turn. The small package had been wrapped with great care, he'd written his greeting on it in fine writing with a mapping pen and red ink.

'If it's not what you want, Mr Rogers said you can take it back and change it. But I thought it would suit you. You're into double figures, Lot, ten years old.'

The paper had been torn off Ronnie's gift with the same speed that he'd put it on. So now with Michael's she wanted to make the most of

2

the seconds as she undid each fold then went through the same procedures with the white tissue paper underneath. Finally she lifted the lid of the little cardboard jewellery box. A silver chain, and hanging from it a pendant that to the eyes of the three youngsters looked like amber.

'Whooo!' she whistled. 'Gosh, thank you, Michael, it's beautiful. And I'll be able to keep it in my box.' She looked at her elder brother with new respect. From her ten-year-old viewpoint, the gift had elevated him to the plane of adulthood. No longer did Michael have a few pence a week spending money doled out to him. Now on a Saturday afternoon he worked for Miss Blunkett at the kennels where she bred chows. The pendant must have cost him a fortune! And by their standards so it had. Carefully she placed it in the trinket box, closed the lid, her sigh of satisfaction clearly for both box and contents. Above her head the boys looked at each other with relief. Lottie's birthday had got off to a good start.

'Let's go down and find Dad. He's waiting to see you, Lot. But we've got to keep quite. Mum – '

'I know. I heard what he said.' Eagerly she jumped out of bed then, in deference to her father, put on her knickers and slippers. They crept down the stairs and she went to find him in the back lobby where he started to give his shoes a second polish as he heard her coming.

'Ah, Lottie my dear. Out here in your nightgown . . . why's that then?' She knew he was playing a game with her. 'Were you looking for me? Were you wanting me for anything special?'

'Dad, don't you remember?' But he did, of course he did. There it stood at the back of the lobby, a bicycle, a sports model, not like her old fairy bike that was too small. 'Dad, you know what today is!'

'Yes, yes, of course. Tuesday.'

He was teasing her. She was so happy it was almost too much. She hugged him, burrowing her face against his shoulder.

'Silly Dad. It's my birthday, you know it is. I'm ten.'

'Ten years old. My goodness. I'll soon be having to save up to pay for your wedding at this rate.'

'Silly Dad.' She grinned. She could feel her face beaming. Even though she held her teeth clenched together she couldn't stop her mouth smiling – and neither could she take her eyes off that gleaming new bicycle.

'What's that you're so interested in back there, eh?' Still he was pretending.

'Dad, the bike? What's it doing here?'

'Bike?' He ruffled her short dark auburn curls under the palm of his hand. 'You'd better see if the saddle's the right height. Wait though, you've got your nightdress on.'

3

'I've got knickers underneath, I'll tuck it in those. Let me just try it on the garden path, Dad. Isn't it a beauty? Oh thank you, thank you. It's the most gorgeous present.' As she gabbled she busily tucked her long skirt out of harm's way.

The boys came out too, and with his two sons Rupert Bradley watched as she wheeled the bicycle out of the lobby. Michael told her she looked like Sir Walter Raleigh with her puffed out knickers.

'Safer than looking like Wee Willie Winkie and letting her night-dress flap on to the spokes,' was Ronnie's rejoinder.

Oh, the joy of it! As she wobbled off on her maiden ride down the path by the side of the lawn, which during the summer was marked out as a tennis court, around the rose garden and beyond to the vegetable plot, her confidence grew. So much so that she carried straight on to what they rather grandly called 'the orchard' (eighteen fruit trees of various sort standing in a patch of rough grass). She zig-zagged from plum to apple, then from greengage to walnut before she finally tore back up the brick path to where the others waited. "Perhaps Mum will say she doesn't feel up to the picnic – perhaps I'll be able to go biking instead!" Too late her conscience prodded her telling her that was a mean thing to hope.

Only yesterday her Aunt Eva had arrived in England from Canada. This was her first visit since emigrating as a nurse soon after the end of the Great War. Lottie would love to have driven to Southampton to meet the boat. At one point a few weeks ago she'd heard her father suggest that the whole family might go by train. That would have been more exciting. But plans had been changed. He'd need the motor car to bring her luggage, so he decided that just the grown ups should go. They were to leave the house very early, so the family had been surprised to find their mother in her usual place at the breakfast table.

'What's happened, Mum? Isn't she docking today after all?' Ronnie had been the one to ask, both Michael and Lottie silenced by their mother's withdrawn expression, the eyes that told of recent tears. Ronnie was less sensitive to these things.

'I didn't think I could face hours on the road. Better for him to meet her by himself. She'll be all noise and chatter – my head wouldn't stand it.'

'Gosh, I wish I could have gone!' Lottie imagined the excitement at Southampton.

'Your Aunt Eva will be here soon enough.' And somehow her mother's tone put an end to the conversation.

Eva Bradley was Rupert's younger sister, but Lottie's interest in her was more personal than that. As long as she could remember

4

she'd heard her mother's: "Oh, but you're so like your Aunt Eva", usually said with exasperation when she was standing up for what she considered to be her rights and when her parents were being particularly unsympathetic to her desires. Somehow, in her mind, she and Aunt Eva had had an understanding of each other. Add to that the fact that Christmas never passed without a parcel arriving bearing gifts a little more attractive, clothes a little more striking, dolls a little more lovable, than they saw in the shops here.

As far as Canada was concerned, Lottie's only knowledge of it was what she remembered from one school term when it had been the country covered in her weekly geography class: the St Laurence River was frozen each winter until March; much of the world's grain was grown in the prairies (the book did tell her how much, but she soon forgot the facts and only knew that it was a lot); the land at what she thought of as the top of Canada was something called tundra which meant that it was horrid and cold; and Canada was just above the United States. Her interest in Eva had nothing to do with where she came from, everything to do with that often heard: 'That child's another Eva!'

It had been late evening by the time the car had arrived back from Southampton, a brief greeting had been all Lottie had been allowed last night before she'd been sent upstairs. But even in those few minutes she'd been disappointed that she hadn't immediately been struck by some resemblance to herself. Once in bed, she had soon lost interest in the visitor. On the eve of a birthday she had far more exciting things on her mind. Again at breakfast she surveyed her aunt and today disappointment gave way to something else. It was nonsense to say they were alike – but if that's what Mum and Dad thought, then there must be something. She wished it was true. Aunt Eva seemed to push everyone else in the room into the shade. It wasn't just what she said, it was the way she talked. It wasn't even her accent, it was because her voice was so full of life. When she laughed you felt it bubbled up from a great store of fun she knew about. Yet when she was listening to Rupert speaking, she listened with all of her, it wasn't the sort of superficial table chat that so many people went in for.

Silently Lottie observed her, surprised by just how right it felt that she should be here on this special day. But going back to being like her . . . they both had the same colour hair – although where her own was cut short and curled just where it wanted to, Eva's was long and sleek, anchored into a bun at the nape of her neck. They had the same colour eyes too. Not gingery brown like the boys, but darker, a richer shade. 'Conker eyes', the boys sometimes called Lottie. But there all resemblance ended.

Rupert told Lottie: 'I don't want you waking your mother to ask permission – you may take your bike and try it just up and down the avenue. Not quite to the corner, mind. And all three of you, take care of your aunt. It's unfortunate Kate is like this today.'

As he went out he closed the door almost soundlessly, but there was no way he could dull the noise of the engine. They heard him roar off down Sycamore Avenue. Eva assured the boys they had no need to worry about her, she had her trunk to unpack, and so the birthday morning got underway. Wheeling her bicycle out to the road, Lottie could hear the clatter of crockery as Freda washed the breakfast dishes, the sound interspersed with a trans-Atlantic voice. Then she put it all out of her mind and concentrated on the thrill of trying to look as though she were off on an errand, not a practice run.

Time melted. It must have been an hour or so later when Freda came out armed with two large shopping bags.

'Your mother has come down. You'd better go and let her wish you a happy birthday. And you'll want to be showing her how well you ride your cycle.' Then, head forward, a basket in each hand, she was off to town for the weekly market.

If Rupert had expected Kate to rest all the morning he was clearly mistaken. With a hint of lipstick and rouge she had camouflaged the evidence of her night. So well she remembered her own tenth birthday: a houseful of family and friends at Bullington Manor, a party with a conjurer to entertain the children. How different the day they planned for Lottie. A picnic on the punt – and Eva the guest! But the magic was the same for any ten year old and nothing was going to be allowed to mar it.

'Is your headache gone, Mum?' Lottie asked her after she'd duly admired both bike and rider.

'Much better, dear. I'm just going to start on the sandwiches, we'll have a lovely picnic. Take care not to go too near the corner. Some people drive their motor cars with no care for anyone but themselves.'

So what happened between then and Lottie being called in to lunch.

'Mum's gone back to bed,' Ronnie told her. 'Rotten luck, Lot. I suppose we could take the punt without her, just the four of us go.'

'Mum loves the punt picnics.' Michael looked anxiously at Lottie. 'Would it matter too much if we put it off a day? It seems mean for her to lie there feeling bad and hearing us all clear off without her.'

'I'd rather ride my bike.' But she couldn't help feeling guilty at the memory of her earlier wish for the day.

'I sure wish I could lay my hands on a bike,' Eva said. 'Suppose Kate doesn't have one?'

'Mum? No, she never cycles. Tell you what though, Aunt Eva, if you can get your leg over the crossbar you can take mine,' Michael offered. 'If Mum's staying home, Ron and I could hang around here, have a game of tennis or something.'

'Oh, boy, I'll get my leg over that right enough. Lottie, child, you and me are going to have a real great time.'

And so it was that Lottie set out on the road that led her to her dream.

The afternoon of the birthday a bridge was built between the child just ten and her relative who was a stranger and, in the eyes of one so young, already middle-aged. With a box of food stowed in Lottie's new saddle bag, she and Eva pedalled off.

'Oh, boy, but what fun! You know, Lottie, I've not sat on a bike since 1919. This is great! Is yours OK, are you comfortable with it?'

'It's great.' She found herself copying Eva's expression. 'Fancy, you can still ride really well. You don't wobble at all, after all those years.'

'Yep.' Clearly Eva was enjoying herself. Lottie could tell from the way her skirt was blowing and she didn't try to hold it down, and by the way she held her head with her chin jutting forward, as if she was eager to meet whatever the outing brought. 'And you should have seen the bike I used to have in those days,' she laughed, 'a fixed wheel job, sit up and beg handlebars. This one of Michael's is real dandy.'

The expression was new to Lottie. It suited the mood of the afternoon.

'So's this. Real dandy!' She took her eyes off the road long enough to beam her pleasure. In that moment she seemed to understand what her parents meant when they said: 'You're just like your Aunt Eva'. What a splendid birthday this was turning out to be!

Later, as they munched their sandwiches, sitting on a five-bar gate and watched by two baleful-looking heifers, Lottie's day chalked up another first. Never before had a grown-up talked to her as if they were equals. Sometimes Aunt Hester, her mother's sister, assumed a gushing show of interest, asked her hundreds of questions about school or riding or dancing, all the things she was expected to want to talk about; Lottie always found that uncomfortable and tried to escape. Most grown-ups treated her like they did all children, as if they were higher in the scale of values than household pets but far below grown-up human beings. Of the two, that was the better. But Eva was quite different.

It began when Lottie asked:

'Do you wish you were home for keeps, Aunt Eva? I heard Dad saying he thought perhaps you might come back.'

'Home? No, Lottie, I've been away too long to slot back into place here and to think of it as home again. A holiday's great. But to live here I'd have to have a purpose, something really pulling at me, something of my own.'

'There's us.' She was surprised to hear herself say it.

'Yes, there's you. My little "look-alike" niece.'

'Do you think we do?'

'Look alike? Not as much as I'd expected from what your father had written to me. I guess you're prettier than ever I was. It's not really what people look like that matches them up though, it's something in their genes. Oh, it's there right enough, in you and me.'

'You mean we think the same things are funny – '

'And the same things are important, unless I'm mistaken. Have another sandwich. There's one ham and one salmon. You can choose, it's *your* birthday.'

Lottie chose salmon, then before she took her first bite and before she stopped to consider whether it was the sort of question one should ask: 'It's a shame you're all by yourself, Aunt Eva. Don't you wish you'd got a husband and some children?'

'Yes, to both questions. I was going to be married, but that was during the war. He was killed in France when he was almost due home on his leave.'

'I didn't know any of that.'

'Not many people do, and those who did I dare say have mostly forgotten. I was a nurse. There were so many wounded men to look after. Being a nurse, making sure I was a good one, I guess that had to be my goal. If life knocks you down, Lottie – and make no mistake, it *will* knock you down somewhere along the line, not many folk get away Scot free – just make sure you jump straight back up again. Don't give yourself time to think, fix your sights on a goal and work at it.'

'Is that why you went to Canada? To find something different, like writing on a clean page with no smudges?'

'Yes, I suppose it was.' She was gazing into the distance, but Lottie knew that in her mind she wasn't seeing the gentle meadow. 'In the beginning it must have been something like that. I must have seen it as an escape route. You know, I can't really remember when that all changed, when I started wanting to be there because of what it was, not what I was hiding from.' There was a pause. Lottie waited. 'It's a fine country. It's a young country. You don't have to fit into a groove that's already been carved out years ago by someone else. No, that doesn't even start to tell you. And I can't find the words to paint a picture. There can be nowhere on God's earth quite like it. You have to breathe the cold winter air, crisp, pure, there's no other way of knowing what it's like. So dry that you don't realise just how cold it is. Frost bite is something that really happens once you get inland of the west coast. But that's only part of the time. You should see the Alberta sun! Nowhere else can there be a sun so big, so golden. No wonder the corn grows high. Then there's the mountains, the lakes. Last summer when I was on vacation I bathed in a hot spring lake. Just imagine floating in water that's tepid, warmer than tepid, under a clear blue sky, then looking around you at mountains topped with snow.'

Lottie felt inadequate, she couldn't find any words to show that what she'd heard meant something important to her.

'Even that doesn't start to let you see what I mean. Here – and don't misunderstand me, Lottie, I love England dearly but in a different way – here, man is supreme. The countryside is safe, you can wander where you will; there is no part of it where someone hasn't walked before you; and you can go anywhere.'

'But an awful lot is private, Aunt Eva. There are "Trespasser will be prosecuted" notices all over the place.'

Eva laughed. 'Oh, you might get a red-faced farmer waving a fist at you – or a bull making you run like merry hell. But man is supreme for all that. Over there, there's so much that's still wilderness, untamed. And you don't get cocky in bear country, believe me. Bears, moose, elks . . . the country belongs to them. It's humbling, Lottie, it makes you realise something about the scale of things. And that's good for us. It's so easy to get puffed up with our own importance, to see our own disappointments larger than life. When you stand in that vast silence, you see just what a *little* speck you are. It puts all your troubles in perspective.'

Lottie nodded. Still she didn't know the words.

'In my luggage I've got photographs,' Eva told her.

'You've not shown them.'

'Well, I guess other people's snapshots can be pretty boring. But I figure you'd like to share them.'

Again Lottie nodded. When she did speak the words tumbled out; she wasn't sure how to explain what she meant but it was important that she tried.

'Dad talked about you coming back to your roots, he thought you'd stay in England, but of course you won't. I can see you won't. And, do you know, I'm glad you're going back there. That's sounds horrid, doesn't it, but I don't mean it like that. It's just that you seemed so alive when you talked about it. It would be dreadful to leave all that.'

'You know what I think? All this business about hanging on to our roots – where in the world does it get us? Just think about it, Lottie. If

9

you get held by your roots, you never get anywhere. A plant needs good roots, sure it does, but if it's going to grow tall and strong it's got to reach up, upwards and outwards. That's the big difference over there. It's a young country. People like me, lots of them, who've come from other places and other customs. It's up to every single person to build – not with one eye on the way our grandfathers ran things. One of these days, when you're a few years older, you just come out and stay with me, see for yourself, get the feel of it.'

'Can I? I'll save hard. You said about having a goal. I'll choose that for mine.'

Eva lived in Calgary. To the west were the Rockies, to the east the great wheat-growing prairies. In geography lessons none of it had meant much to Lottie, but listening to her aunt was different: this was real. The photographs were only holiday snaps, amateurish, black and white, where could the magic be in those? Yet from Eva's descriptions she seemed to smell the heady scent of the red cedars in the west, hear the plaintive echo of the train hooter, breathe the crisp clear air in the Glacier Park where even in the middle of summer one was held in the grip of ice.

She was shown a flat grey picture where wheat and sky merged on an undiscernible horizon.

'It can't even start to give you the feel of it, Lottie. The corn is so golden, it ripples gently in the wind, as vast as the sea. And the sky, such a blue, with that huge, huge, sun.'

Lottie nodded. In her mind she saw it already. One day she's see it for real.

'. . . be a good thing when she clears off back.' The boys stopped talking when she went into the room. But she knew who they were talking about. The atmosphere in the house was prickly, Mum and Dad hardly looked at each other. Their room was next to Lottie's and last night something had woken her up. She'd kept very still and listened. Voices: Mum's voice sounding shrill and unfamiliar; Mum never shouted. Or was she crying? And this morning at breakfast she'd passed him his coffee without even looking at him; he'd taken it without his habitual 'Thank you, my dear'. Not a word, not even a glance passing between them. Last night Lottie had pulled the covers high around her ears and tried to pretend it wasn't happening. At breakfast there was nowhere to hide. Now the boys were blaming Aunt Eva, saying it would be a good thing when she went. But it wasn't her fault. She was about the only one who didn't seem all eaten up with hate.

There were other occasions that made their mark on her memory. Instinct told her it was better not to talk about their visitor to her parents, but turning a deaf ear to instinct she commented in a carefully conversational tone to her mother that Eva had told her about almost being married and then her sweetheart was killed.

'I didn't know about that, Mum. Wasn't it sad for her?'

'There was no reason why you should know. She has no business talking to a child about the horrors of that dreadful war.'

'But if there's something miserable like that, that's what families are there for. Didn't he have any people? You'd think they'd ask her to go and see them, wouldn't you?'

'Lottie, it's really not our business. And if you feel so sorry for her, it's much kinder to let it rest. Don't talk to her about it.'

Yet Lottie couldn't hear any kindness in her mother's normally gentle voice.

Then there was another occasion when Eva came back from town where she'd been shopping and called her into her room.

'See, Lottie, honey, I've got you a present. Well, I say "you", but I guess it'll be me as much as you who'll get the pleasure out of it. It's a money box. I'll put something in it to start the fund going for you. Saving for your visit, hey?'

'My Canada Box! Gosh, every week I'll put a bit of my pocket money in. Oh, thank you! Shall we decorate it? I could cut some pictures out of that magazine you gave me. Will you help?'

Together they pasted the pictures. On the front a maple leaf, on one side a view of Lake Louise, on another of Banff, and on the back a wild rose, the emblem of Alberta.

And after Eva's holiday was over the box stood as a visible sign of that bond they'd both been so aware of, a reminder of what had gone and promise of what was still to come.

Her parents encouraged her to save, never doubting that before long she'd see something she wanted to spend her money on. As for it being a fund for her one day trip to Canada, no one took that seriously. With Eva gone the shadow that had hung over the household seemed to have lightened; only Lottie wanted to hang on to the memory of her visit. The money box had pride of place on her chest of drawers. Each week from her fourpence pocket money at least one of the pennies was put into it. Any additional little windfall found its way through the slot and, as the years went by, birthdays and Christmasses added weight.

By then her parents' patience had grown short, with her silly talk about saving to go to Canada. It was time the child outgrew her foolish daydreams and gave more thought to school work! Typical of Eva to have filled her head with a lot of nonsense, was Rupert's view. Kate's wasn't as straightforward. Damn Eva! What right had she to come here unsettling the child? Hadn't she done harm enough?

'Is there any message for Aunt Eva? I'm just finishing a letter to her,' Lottie called over the banisters to where her parents were sitting in the drawing room.

'Haven't you homework to do?' Rupert looked up from his crossword to call.

'Done it, Dad. It was only botany. Any messages?'

'Not from me.' Kate's voice held no smile. Lottie could imagine how her lips would be held tight together as her knitting needles clicked, and how she would be breathing through her nose. 'I really can't think what you find of interest to tell her.'

Whatever it was, they never read Lottie's letters. The habit of writing to each other had grown from that holiday in 1933. Eva's replies were always passed round for the family to read and there was nothing in them Kate or Rupert could find to criticise. Yet, even though Eva didn't come to England again, Lottie seemed to them to grow more and more like her.

Never an academic, in the summer when she was sixteen she managed to scrape through her School Certificate, although even then she got far more satisfaction from winning the cup at the local gymkhana. That was in 1939, an autumn that saw an end to the old order.

Michael was already a Territorial. At the outbreak of war he was given his first stripe and became a full-time soldier. Two years younger at twenty, Ronnie enlisted in the Air Force. Only Lottie was left at home, cycling each day to a Secretarial College in Brimley, just as in the past she'd cycled to school there.

She longed to be older, to put on a uniform and be a person who mattered. By the time she was the magic seventeen years and three months required of her it would probably be all over. And now that the boys had both gone she could feel her parents tightening their hold on her.

'It's all right if I stay in town to go to the pictures with Celia tonight, isn't it, Mum? Fred Astaire's on at the Regal.'

'What time is it over?'

'It's over at ten to ten. Or if we go straight from college we'd see the end first, then the small film, and come out when it got round to where we went in. Then I could get out about half-past eight.'

Rupert pushed his glasses down his nose and looked at her over the top of them. Humour had never been his strong point. Now, what little of it he might have had appeared to have been destroyed by the boys going off to join in this war which ought never to have happened.

'Just remember you're only sixteen years old. You might like to call it a secretarial college or some such tom fool name but as far as I'm concerned you're still a schoolgirl. How many times do you need to be told?' He folded the newspaper, corners at ninety degree angles and edges straight, just as he did each morning, then stood up from the breakfast table. 'I'll not have you out after blackout time. So let that be the end of it.'

'What about coming home from college? That's after blackout. I do it every day. Do you want me to tell them I have to leave early?' Disappointment made her cheeky, she knew it would do her no good.

'Don't take that insolent tone when you're spoken to. You know very well what I mean. These days Brimley is full of goodness knows who – soldiers with nothing better to do than hang around looking for girls. You hear what I say? Straight home. You'd think you'd be glad to keep your mother company.'

'The soldiers are just the same as Michael and Ronnie. You wouldn't like it if people looked down their noses on them because they've got nowhere to go in the evenings.'

Kate chewed the corner of her lip. 'Don't argue, Lottie. Just do as your father says. I've got enough to worry about with two sons gone to war without you being difficult.'

'Oh, Mum, Michael's in Wiltshire and Ronnie in Lincolnshire, both of them safe as houses – and probably having a whale of a time. Better then they would if they'd stayed here, never supposed to want any fun.'

'Stop it, Lottie. That's an unkind thing to say. I don't know what's got into this house, ever since the boys have gone. You egg your father on, you know you do. And it's me who bears the brunt. You'd think it was all my fault.'

Lottie couldn't see what all that had to do with whether she could go to the pictures. Anyway her mother was being stupid, what had being *her* fault got to do with anything?

Rupert Bradley's glare was aimed at both of them, indeed it seemed to encompass the world in general.

'Now you've upset your mother! I can't wait here arguing. You've heard what I said. You're to come straight home when you finish your classes.' Then with a sigh that spoke as clearly as any words: 'I don't know what's the use of having a car out there in the garage and not enough petrol to make use of it.'

'You must have petrol in the tank, Rupert, you only spent your coupons the other day.'

13

'I'm quite capable of riding my bicycle.' Taking the newspaper with him he turned to go, leaving the two of them still at the table.

'Oh dear, another day got off to a bad start.' Kate looked at the closed door. 'It's this wretched war. But it's no use taking it out on me, anyone would think it was all my fault. It's as hard on me as it is on him, but he never thinks of that.'

'It was me, Mum, I got him cross.'

Unexpectedly Kate reached her hand across the table as if she was going to touch Lottie, then pulled it back.

'I'm sorry about Fred Astaire. Can't you go to the matinée on Saturday? It's just that he'd be worried, we both would. I know most of the soldiers are nice lads, no different from Michael and Ronnie. But not all of them, Lottie. The boys would agree if they were here, they wouldn't want you exposed to – well, you're too young to understand.'

'Of course I'm not too young! Of course I know what you're getting at. You think someone would try and get off with me – that's what they call it at college – pick me up.'

'Hush, Lottie. I don't like to hear you talking like it, it sounds so rough and coarse. When you're older you'll find that men don't look on things the same as we do. More of the animal in them. That's the danger, Lottie. You talk about picking a girl up. What a dreadful expression! Rubbish is something you pick up. Always remember, no boy would respect a girl he met that way. Bear that in mind until Mr Right comes along.'

For months Kate had had it on her conscience that she ought to try and steer the conversation in this direction. But how difficult it was. Lottie could surely help her, show that she was heeding the warning, understanding what her mother was trying to say, instead of sitting there with that rebellious expression on her face.

'Of course you're right, a lot of them are nice boys. But not all, Lottie, and we just don't want you getting caught up in that sort of thing.'

She inched her chair a little further under the table. She'd started on her oft-imagined heart to heart, now nothing was going to stop her, she meant to get it over once and for all.

'Not all the girls are the same as you, remember that too. They give their sex a bad name. Don't let yourself be tainted by it. "Get off", did you call it? Oh dear, what a way to talk! Time goes so fast, Lottie. A few more years and some nice young man will come along, one who respects you, wants to put you on a pedestal. You see, a man might want to play around himself, but when he looks for a sweetheart to respect, then he doesn't want one who's – who's given her kisses

14

perhaps, to other boys. Those aren't the sort men marry. Suppose your knight in shining armour rode in and found that you'd let other boys – what did you call it? – "pick you up"? It could spoil – '

'Oh, for goodness sake, Mum! I only wanted to go to the pictures!'

Eva heard all about it. Not particularly that one occasion but the fact that Lottie felt herself kept under lock and key, life going on without her. Pouring out her frustrations on paper was her safety valve; perhaps if her aunt had been living nearby, been part of wartime England, then she wouldn't have shared the honest outpourings. Lottie would have to have kept her own counsel.

It was late the following summer when as usual she passed Eva's latest letter to her parents to read.

'Now that you're seventeen, you'll be finding some sort of war-work, I expect. Your folk will miss having you at home, but I always figure it's the hallmark of a good upbringing when a young person can go out in the world and stand on her own two feet. It must give them such pride to picture the boys – and now it'll be your turn. I guess there's only one thing anyone can be sure of with a war, and that's that it'll mean sacrifices.'

Lottie could imagine the twinkle in the conker brown eyes, Eva knew that her letter would be passed around.

Kate read it. She made no comment but there was something in her expression as she passed it across to Rupert that Lottie couldn't fathom. Had it been anyone but her mother, Lottie would have read it as contempt. She felt uncomfortable. She must have imagined it.

'She's right.' Rupert folded the letter with his usual precision, and put it neatly back in the envelope. 'About the warwork, Lottie. Your year at the college is pretty well over and I chanced to talk to James Richardson at the club. He's in charge of Rampton's works here in Brimley. I want you to ask for a report of your work. I've made an appointment for you to go there for an interview. He'll actually see you himself, very good of him. He's doing that as a favour to me, of course, we've known each other twenty years or more. He will assess where he can best use you. Agriculture is warwork every bit as important as any other.'

'Rampton's! In Brimley? But, Dad, I've only got to wait seven more weeks and I'll be old enough to join the WAAF. That's what I want to do, you know it is. I'm not going to get a job in Brimley.'

Home on embarkation leave, Michael watched anxiously. He could imagine how Lottie felt, poor kid, she probably believed that you only had to put on a uniform for life suddenly to take on a new glamour, a new freedom. She'd learn! Or rather, she wouldn't learn, for there was no chance of her leaving home.

15

Only afterwards, when the two of them were alone, did he voice an opinion.

'Lot, Ronnie and I didn't have any choice. If we'd not joined when we did, then they'd soon have sent for us. If you work at Rampton's you'll be doing vital war work. There's nothing much more important than farm machinery.'

'I won't do it! By November I can volunteer for the WAAF. But if I'm at Rampton's they may not release me. I'll be stuck. Home by ten o'clock. Can't do this, can't go there. You don't know what it's like here.' Her voice croaked on the edge of tears, partly anger and partly disappointment.

'Believe me, there's no sudden freedom to be found in putting on a uniform. Anyway, even in November you can't just fill in the forms and go. You're under age. Dad would have to give his consent. And, Lot, now that you're the only one of us left, you do have a sort of duty to the parents, to Mum in particular. She looks so down in the dumps. You can't walk out on her. Land yourself a job at Rampton's and you'll be doing something just as useful as you would in uniform. And you can keep an eye on things at home too; that'll be doing Ronnie and me a favour. I'll probably be gone for ages now, maybe I won't have a home leave until the war ends. And look at the worry they have with Ronnie flying. Have you watched Mum's face when they read out the numbers of the fighters that have been lost? You can't run out on them as if you've only been waiting for the moment you're old enough to go. In any case, like I said, Dad would have to give his consent, and I bet he wouldn't sign the paper.'

Ronnie wrote to her in much the same vein.

As always Eva was her safety valve: 'I ought to stand up for what I want, other parents are in the same boat. It's just not fair, Aunt Eva. I remember you saying how wars make a mess of people's lives. If you've got a mess, then you have to sort it out. That's what you told me. But mine isn't even a mess, it's just nothing. School, college, Rampton's. I even get my bike out at the same time as I used to each morning. The war hasn't made so much as a dent in my routine!'

And back came the answer, unfailingly understanding – yet still fit for family reading: 'So you've got a job at the farm machinery place, Lottie. I knew you'd be doing something that these days they call "essential work". No one chooses what they'll do or where they'll go once they start war work.'

Lottie found a secret comfort in the comment. At least there was one person who understood.

Having a job of work made very little difference to her life at home. Her father was still positive the town was full of undesirables; her

16

mother's habitual headaches could be brought on at the first hint of friction. Headaches that led to tears, dizzy spells, more tears . . . And all the time the rebel inside Lottie was struggling to get out.

In the spring of 1942 fate took a hand. At Rampton's a directive was sent from their Head Office to all members of staff. The Brimley plant was to close. Manufacture of potato diggers and seed drills was to be transferred to Kingstaunton in the West Country, the location of the main works. Lottie and two more shorthand typists were offered accommodation in Kingstaunton House which had been taken over as a hostel for staff.

How contrary human nature is! It was on the morning that Lottie was leaving that she seemed to see her parents from a new angle. No longer were they her captors, coming between her and every chance of fun and freedom. How fragile her mother looked. And Dad . . . he always seemed so cross. Poor Dad. What a moment for her mind to leapfrog back down the years, to take her to the lobby where he was pretending to polish his already shining shoes, her bicycle new and gleaming just behind him. This morning when he stood up to leave, she held up her face to kiss him.

'Mind you behave yourself,' came his last instruction. 'Write often – at least every week. Your mother's going to miss you.'

'Oh, Dad.' She hugged him, rubbing her cheek against his shoulder. 'And what about you? Aren't you going to miss me?'

'Be a quiet house.' But he held her close for a brief moment. 'Bless you. Come home as often as you can.'

'This is it! He puts us down at the end of Union Place and we cut through there.' Tina, the girl who'd been sitting next to Lottie, was already on her feet, determined to be first out of the coach, keen not to lose a moment of the evening. It was already a quarter to nine, but with Double British Summer Time the sun was only just disappearing, West Street bathed in its golden light as it promised another warm spring day tomorrow.

Now everyone was jostling to get to the door, Tina leading the way and Lottie caught up in the crush.

'What time does the coach fetch us?' she asked anyone who heard.

'Dunno,' a tall girl propelling her forward along the gangway laughed. 'What time to you go back, Joe?' she shouted down the gangway to the driver.

'Eleven, from the end of the road here.' The driver sucked on his empty pipe. Be some hi-jinks in there with this lot, he chuckled silently to himself. Just look at them, all like to think themselves Betty Grable. 'You reckon you'll be on the bus tonight then, Sal? What's up? Losing your grip?'

'Me? Not flipping likely I won't be! It's Lottie – that's your name, isn't it? – she's new at Kingstaunton. It's her first week.'

Jo, Rampton's driver, looked at the pretty child, a worried frown puckering his brow. Damn it, that was all she looked; nothing more than a pretty child. In her cotton dress and flat-heeled sandals she'd look more in place in the classroom than racketing around in the Palais with a bunch of soldiers making up to her.

'Not been to one of these knees-ups before?' he asked her unnecessarily as she worked her way down the gangway towards him. 'Watch your step with some of those lads. A long way from home and out for all they can get – ah, and a bit more too if they can manage it. I'm told a bunch of Canadians have taken Everton Grange. I expect you'll get a new lot in there tonight.'

'Canajians? Cor, that'll liven things up.' Sal gave Lottie a good-natured shove. 'Let's show 'em we're not such stick in the muds as they've heard, eh?'

'Here, listen here.' As they came level with Jo, he put a hand on Lottie's arm. 'Like I said, we leave at eleven o'clock. But the bus'll be out here long before that. If you've had enough, I'll be parked right here where I am now.'

'I'll remember. But eleven's not late. I'm going to have a great time. Everyone says what fun it is.' And the thought that the soldiers would be from Canada added to her confidence.

'Get along and have a good time then. But watch those Cannucks. Got a bit more money to throw about than the Tommies have.'

Sucking hard on his empty pipe he watched Sal and her gang leading the way up Union Place. He could imagine the stuffy dance hall, the noisy music, the stirring of excitement as that bevy of beauties trooped in! Some of those sons of the Maple Leaf were going to think it was their birthday!

Taking her place in the line Lottie waited to pay her one and ninepence entrance charge. Outside the evening light had been filled with golden sunshine; this was like stepping into another world. A wide marble corridor with a cloakroom on one side where they again had to queue, this time to leave their coats in exchange for a numbered ticket.

'We can always dance together, that's what we do if any of us don't get asked,' someone said, meaning to sound reassuring.

'There'll be lots of partners, the driver said so.' Lottie never lacked confidence. She didn't consider the possibility that this evening might find her a wallflower! Just hark at that music! A quickstep was fine, but she hoped she'd get asked to dance by someone who could jitterbug.

It was as she went into the dance hall that she felt someone was staring at her. Surely that must have been what made her look to the far side of the room where he was standing by the bar, a tall, khaki-clad Canadian corporal.

'Care to dance?' It was a boy in Air Force blue who asked her. She turned to him with a smile. This evening was going to be such fun!

One after another partners presented themselves. In an 'excuse me' quick-step she danced with no less than five different people. Someone gave her a glass of cider. There was lots of laughter, lots of jitterbugging. But none of her dances were with the tall Canadian. Yet all the time she was conscious that he was watching her. And because she knew he was, and because he didn't ask her to dance, she kicked her legs that bit higher and threw herself with more abandon into the relentless tempo.

'Don't sit under the apple tree
With anyone else but me,
Till I come marching home.'

The crooner, a man too old for the forces to find a use for him, came to the end and the music stopped.

'Time you and me got acquainted.' She knew who it was even before she turned to look at him. 'Over here. I've put our drinks at a table.'

Chapter Two

Kingstaunton House was about two miles outside town. The tall Canadian kept his arm around her shoulder in the dark as if to guide her as they walked.

'Do you believe in Fate, Lottie?' Then without waiting for an answer: 'Lottie! Fancy calling you Lottie when you have a beautiful name like Charlotte.'

'What about Fate?'

'I figure it must have taken a hand, both of us landing up in this place – what's it called? – Kingstaunton. Arriving the same day. Now doesn't that seem like Fate to you? Sure must be some sort of design in it.'

She laughed, excited by his words. 'There were three of us who arrived at Kingstaunton from Brimley at the same time. You might say the same of any of us.'

'I might. But I wouldn't. Let's sit here. You say the hostel doesn't shut its door until midnight. We have a while yet.' He guided her to a bench by the roadside, its outline just visible now that their eyes had grown accustomed to the night.

'Neil O'Hagon, that's your name, isn't it? It makes me think of Ireland. But you speak as Canadian as any of them.'

'My great-grandparents came from Ireland when they were first married. I can't remember him but Great Gran O'Hagon – to the day she died, a real old lady, I reckon she was Irish at heart.'

'One day I'm going to Canada. I made it my goal ages ago. I've been saving almost as long as I can remember. I'll have to wait now until the war's over, but I shall go then. To Alberta. I have an aunt in Calgary.'

'Gee, now that's Fate again. That's no more than a hundred miles from home.'

'Tell me about home.'

Having already discovered at the dance that she didn't smoke, he didn't pass her his packet, just took a cigarette himself and lit it before he spoke.

'I wish I could – could really tell you, I mean. Jeez, but you gotta see it, get the feel of the saddle under you, sniff the air in the morning after the first frost of fall.'

'You don't live in a town?'

'You're darn right, I don't. There's me, then there's Craig – he's my cousin. There's Donald too. The place used to be run by my old man and his brother – both dead now. They sort of grew into looking after things years ago with their old man. Then when Pop – that's my grandfather, their old man – got caught out in an accident they took over. And I guess it was like that with Craig and me, we just grew into it. Never thought of any other way, at least not till the war came.'

'Looking after things? Not in town? Are your farmers?'

'Not like the pokey little farms we've seen here in England, all neat and trim with fields that look like squares on a chequer board. Back home we run things different, we got space. Mostly we rear beef cattle at Kilton Down. Each spring we turn our cattle free to roam on the range, soon as the snows go and the ground shows green.'

So he started to tell her. Minutes passed; he hardly seemed aware. As he talked she knew his spirit had returned to those wide ranges of home, but she didn't try to hold him back. Wide-eyed, she listened. She thrilled to the tone of his voice. He was part of the great outdoors. Cowboys belonged to the cinema, yet that's what he must be. Neil, his cousin, Old Pop as he called his grandfather, another man he called Donald, all of them men reared to a life that had nothing in common with the world she'd known at Brimley: a man's life.

'Go on,' she breathed when his thoughts drifted silently for a few seconds. It was as if all he told her was an extension of the dream she'd harboured so long.

'When the storms come unexpected . . . ' He needed no pressing.

Until tonight in her mind she'd seen Eva's Canada, Eva's Alberta. But this was different. Neil O'Hagon was part of that very Land of the Wild Rose. Until now he'd known nowhere else, no other way of life.

'I guess I know that range like I know my own face,' he said as he told her about round-up time, the searching for cattle, roping them. 'And the wild horses . . . ' Under his breath he laughed, remembering. 'Oh boy, but it takes some sort of rider to bring in a wild horse. Suppose you can't ride, Charlotte Bradley? Seems not many folk can here in England.'

'Indeed, I can. I've got rosettes and a cup to prove it.'

'Bet you couldn't sit a wild horse,' he chuckled. 'They don't earn us our living like the beef cattle do, but it's all part of the round-up. Catch a wild horse, bring it in with the lasso, see who can sit it longest.' There was something private in his soft laugh, she knew he was remembering things outside her ken. 'At the end of the day we have competitions, our own private rodeo. Keeping your seat on one of those critters – yep, man, but that sure does take some sort of a rider . . .' He drew in his breath through his teeth.

'You and your cousin – and Donald, you called him? – you all work together. Aren't there any women?'

'Working the cattle? Sure, there are one or two girls ride well enough to help with the round-up.'

'I mean at home. Do you look after yourselves?'

'Oh, those sort of women. Sure there are. And there's Old Pop too; he's had to hang up his saddle long since, I told you. Indoors women, that's what you're asking? There's Mom. Then Craig's got a wife, Eugene she's called. Got a youngster pretty well any time now. Donald's different, he's Mom's kid brother. Nothing wrong with Donald, strong as a buffalo and can work as good as any man I seen. But I reckon he won't be hitching up with a wife. Me, well, I got no regular woman, but like Mom says, it's time I had.'

Sitting side by side his arm moved from around her shoulder. She felt his hand on her waist. Then up, her firm breast resting against his palm.

'We ought to walk, it must be getting late,' she breathed as into her mind sprang a picture of her own home, of her parents. No one had ever touched her like this before. Of course they hadn't, she was on forbidden ground.

'Little Charlotte Bradley, I do believe you're frightened.'

'Stupid, of course I'm not. It's just, I don't want to be in trouble for being out when the door gets locked.'

'I'm not going to hurt you. I'll get you back in time. Relax.'

But how could she when his fingers were arousing such strange feelings in her.

'Look at me,' he whispered.

'It's dark, I can't see you.'

'I can see you . . . your eyes.' While one hand still did these previously unknown things to her, with the other he moved his finger down her forehead, down her nose, her mouth, her chin. Then his lips found hers, gently as if he were coaxing an untamed animal.

'Yes, you're right. We must walk or I'll not take you back to that place at all.'

As they stood up he pulled her to him. With his hands on her buttocks he drew her close. She felt him hard against her. She'd had

23

no experience but she wasn't ignorant. His unspoken message was clear.

What she read into that message stemmed from her own innocence. He'd talked about Fate bringing them together – he'd talked about it in a soft Canadian voice.

It was half-past midnight by the time she climbed into her narrow bed. Sleep was miles away. Sitting upright in the dark, her bottom lip between her teeth, she went over all he'd said, all he'd done to her. Her own hand became his as she remembered. Her body was awake, eager for what would one day happen to her. He'd wanted it to be tonight, wasn't that what his silent message had told her? Neil O'Hagon, a man from the range, a man who could master a wild bronco, could lasso a running steer, his light brown hair bleached by sun and wind, his blue eyes clear and far-seeing. Nothing soft about him, he was a real man from a man's world, toughened by a tough life.

If Rupert and Kate Bradley hadn't kept her on such a tight rein she might have viewed her evening differently. But she'd had no casual boyfriends; until tonight no one except family had kissed her. Fate, Neil had called it. Lying down, she smiled a secret smile.

The next evening he met her outside the gates of the hostel. They walked; they drank cider in the Packhorse; they stood with a group around the piano while one of the customers thumped out songs they could all join in:
'You are my Sunshine,
My only Sunshine,
You make me happy,
When skies are grey . . .'
and
'We'll meet again,
Don't know where, don't know when,
But I know we'll meet again some sunny day.'

'You're not used to men are you, Charlotte?' They were walking back to Kingstaunton House when he said it. For a moment her confidence took a nose dive. Had she done something wrong? Did he find her dull? Was he disappointed in the way she was?

'I've known lots of men .I mean, there's Dad – and I've got two brothers. Their friends, uncles, cousins.'

'Sure you got a family – but I wasn't meaning them. Boyfriends, men who've dated you. You remind me of a young foal, not broken in. You're ready to shy at the first unexpected move.'

'Of course I'm not.' And as if to prove it she moved closer as they walked with his arm around her. Neil had broken in too many young horses to make the mistake of pushing her.

24

That was the beginning of May. Already a letter had gone off to Eva telling her about the Canadian who'd found his way into Lottie's new freedom. Yet, when she wrote home, she said nothing. She'd brought her bicycle to Kingstaunton and she persuaded Jo, Rampton's driver, to let Neil borrow his. That opened fresh fields to them. During those May evenings of Double British Summer time they rode for miles. In her new freedom Lottie was falling in love, falling further each day. She lived for the moment, not questioning tomorrow but somehow sure that, whatever it brought, the joy she knew today would be a part of it.

Then came the evening when, as she pushed their bicycles to the gate of Kingstaunton House where he waited, his greeting hit her like a physical blow.

'I just heard – seems we're being shifted out.' Deep in her heart she must have known that one day it would happen, but she hadn't let herself imagine it, she wasn't prepared. 'God knows where to, but I hear it's likely to be tomorrow.'

'Oh, no!' He saw the sudden fear in her brimming eyes and the way she bit the corner of her trembling mouth.

'Hey, hey, honey, I'll be back. Maybe we're not going that far. Hey, don't look like that, Lottie.'

'You must be going far. They wouldn't move you all just to send you somewhere nearby.'

'Here, hop on your cycle. Let's get clear of this place.'

They knew just where they were going. Lottie didn't want to talk. It was easier just to pedal as hard as she could, heading towards Clinton Wood and the brow of Madlock Hill, one of their favourite spots. The last quarter of a mile the hill became very steep, their cycles had to be pushed; but the view and the privacy made it worthwhile. The 'top of the world', they called it. To her it was more than that, it was their own world, where nothing could touch them.

For some way they rode in silence, then as the lane grew steeper got off and continued the climb on foot. Not quite to the summit of Madlock Hill he put out a hand and turned her handlebars to steer her towards a track into the wood.

'Here, let's stop right here. I like the look of this mossy patch. And it's time you and me had a talk.'

'I'm sorry, Neil, for being a misery. And on your last evening.'

'My last evening here – but not *our* last evening.' Their bikes propped against a tree he sat down, tapping the ground beside him. She dropped to her knees at his side. She was ashamed. Their last evening and she was being a misery. Turning away from him she looked through a gap in the trees towards distant Exmoor, a scene

25

they'd viewed so often these summer evenings but tonight misted by her tears. When he reached to pull her towards him she was unprepared. She toppled sideways. Somehow she was lying on her back, Neil close beside her and anchoring her down with one khaki-clad leg. Far, far away they could hear a rumble of thunder. The day had been still and airless; now, as if to welcome the approaching storm, a ripple of breeze stirred the roof of leaves above them.

All these weeks Neil had been gentle with her. He's read her moods, had known she'd wanted him every bit as much as he had her. And because he'd been the one to think for both of them, so her confidence had grown.

This was their last evening. Tomorrow he'd be gone. She ached with love for him, with longing to make these hours last for ever. She was bursting with love for love's sake. All her yesterdays were forgotten, for her there was no tomorrow. Nothing but this moment, the two of them together. All the poetry she'd ever read was alive in the movement of those leaves overhead, and every love song she'd ever heard rang in her ears. She cried out – in agony or in ecstasy? Distant thunder rolled across the sky. She gloried in the sound of it, as much part of nature as the movement of their bodies and the hard ground beneath them.

And afterwards she held him close in her arms, hearing the first splashes of rain on the leaves that sheltered them.

'Now you're mine.' His soft Canadian voice was all part of the wonder. 'Mine. Branded like the cattle.' He could have chosen no better words; it was as if in his mind she already belonged to the wide ranges of home. She wanted to shout for joy. She was his. He loved her. That thought was quickly followed by another: her parents, all their veiled warnings, the shame they'd feel if they could see her now, lying on the wooded hillside, their little girl, her skirt around her waist, her virginity gone.

'Jeez, Lottie, my Charlotte, I've made you bleed. I ought to have gone easy with you first time. Did I hurt you, honey?'

'I wanted you to hurt me. It was right for it to hurt.'

He laughed softly, ruffling her curls.

'Funny girl. I never had a real maiden before, not till now. Oh boy, this woman is mine, no one else's. Just mine.'

Her first wild joy melted.

'You mean you've done that before – with other women?'

'Why, honey, I had my first dame when I was fifteen. Don't look at me that way. These things are different for men.'

'I don't see why. Don't you have to be in love?'

He grinned.

26

'Reckon it helps. It's never been like this time, that I can tell you. Being in love must have figured in it somewhere.'

Her spirits soared again. Yet she couldn't help remembering the men she knew in Brimley, her father, the boys, their friends; men who would put their women on a pedestal, wasn't that what her mother had said? Ah, but Neil was different. He'd lived hard, he was a real man. Anyway, if there had been other women, they were all in the past. Now he had her. His woman, branded, just his.

Still lying on her back, she watched him as he dressed, pulling on his trousers, tucking in his shirt.

'You've got nice legs,' she told him with a grin.

'Yours aren't so bad, either. Pull your skirt down and cover yourself up or I'll surprise myself just how much of a man I can be.'

She wished he would. The first time she hadn't known what to expect, the second she'd be ready. But there was no second. A flash of lightning was followed by a crash almost overhead. Never shelter under the trees in a thunderstorm, she'd always been told. This evening there was nowhere else, but she had no fear. With Neil nothing could frighten her.

The next day seemed endless. Had he left yet? Where would they be going? When would she get a letter? It was Wednesday, one of the twice-weekly jaunts to town to the Palais. Usually she went on the bus and met Neil there. But this evening the last thing she wanted was a dance hall. Instead she set off for a solitary ride. She'd pedal along the quiet lanes, remembering. Branded, like the cattle. His. Turning out of the gate she meant to follow the same route they had yesterday, she wanted to re-live every moment.

'Hi! Hi there, Lottie!' And the sound of boots pounding the road after her.

'I thought you'd be gone! What's happened? Aren't you being moved after all?' Her brown eyes shone with happiness.

'Search me. I'm only a humble corporal. Let's just make the most of having a bit longer together, eh? Can you get me Jo's bike? Let's get off into the country, shall we?'

And of course they did. After last night's storm the world was washed clean, the air clear. And if the ground was still damp, neither of them cared.

'Are you going tomorrow? Or are the plans all changed?' she asked as she knelt, spreading out his battle dress top.

'Maybe. Perhaps we'll have a bit longer. Each night is a gift.' Already he was unbuttoning her blouse, then he slipped his braces from his shoulders. Neil didn't intend to waste time. Talking could come later.

27

His haste excited her, and yet she wanted to savour each step, sure what the end would be. Unclasping her bra she let it slip and, naked to the waist, knelt before him, hardly daring to breathe, not quite looking at him. Her body was known to no eyes but her own. Could he know just how much this moment mattered?

'Say something,' she breathed. 'About me. Say something.'

Instead he pushed her backwards on to the jacket, holding her down. Her excitement was tinged with a fear that he could so easily have dispelled with a few tender words. But Neil was a man of action, not words. He was also a man of experience gained with a series of women in the twelve years since he was fifteen. Lottie was lost. He held her in the palm of his hand; she was his woman, confident that they held the secret of the universe.

On the way back to Kingstaunton they stopped at the Cherry Tree Inn. There were other Canadians in there, their western voices were like music to her ears.

'I thought you said the boys from Everton Grange were moving out?' It was Susie Bond who came into her cubicle late that night, Susie who'd come with her from Brimley. 'There were crowds of them at the dance. No one I spoke to knew anything about a rumour that they'd been going to leave.'

'I think it was cancelled.'

'You watch out, Lottie. If your folk had let you go out the same as anyone else, you'd have learnt: you can't always believe all a chap tells you.' Susie had only lived two years longer, but into that time she'd packed a good deal more experience. She felt responsible for Lottie, who was such an innocent.

'Don't be daft. It wasn't as if Neil was fed up with seeing me, just the opposite. He was waiting for me tonight. So why would he have pretended to be going away? You don't understand, Sue. If I tell you something, promise it's a secret.'

'Go on, then.' Susie braced herself for anything.

'Neil and me . . . Susie, I expect I shall marry him. Well, I say "expect". I'm sure I shall.'

Thinking about it afterwards, Lottie couldn't help feeling that her announcement had fallen flat. She wished she'd kept her secret to herself.

In August she was to go home for a week's holiday.

'I wish you could get some leave, Neil.'

'Sure, honey. I want to meet your folk. I want to tell them that I'm going to take their daughter away from them one of these days.'

28

She was chewing her thumb, not quite looking at him.

'Lottie?' he prompted. 'You figure they won't like the idea of me for a son-in-law, is that it?'

'Of course not!' Did she say it just a bit too vehemently? Who was she trying to convince, herself or him? Of course the family would love him, they'd see him just as she did – different from the people they knew, stronger, braver.

'Heck, honey, it's not anyone's business but ours. You're under age, that's going to mean we'll need you old man's consent. I'll be a model of good behaviour.' He laughed. 'Cheer up, honey.' Then his expression changed, the laughter faded. 'What's he going to have against me, anyway? A soldier fighting the same cause. Reckon my record's as good as anyone's your folk might fancy for you. I'm not some idle waster who's happened to have raped their daughter. Anyway, what the hell. In time they'll get used to the idea. I love you, you're my woman, and I 'm going to take you back home. No one's going to stop me. Don't you forget it – and don't you let anyone tell you different.'

She nodded hard, tramping down the memory of the years when she'd not been allowed out at night for fear of marauding soldiers.

'Can you get leave?'

'I'll put in for seven days. But whether I get it . . . ' he shrugged. 'At any rate, I'll manage a thirty-six hour pass. That'll give me time to meet your folks, let them see I want to make an honest woman of you.'

She tried to laugh, but what had happened to the glory of those summer evenings? Going home made her feel soiled, guilty. If only she'd told them about Neil in her letters. 'I go for lovely bike rides.' (How could they have known from that that she didn't go alone?) 'The view from the top of Madlock Hill is stupendous.' (But what view would they have seen? Their daughter lying in the arms of a Canadian?) Now, without preparing the ground, she was producing a stranger.

They wouldn't understand . . . And in that she was right. They didn't.

On the day before she was due to go home she sent a telegram. 'Bringing Neil O'Hagon. Important you like him. Lottie.'

That should give them notice not only to have one of the boys' rooms ready, but why it was she wanted them to meet him. It did. And it put them on their guard. When they saw him the stand they took was reinforced. Bad enough that Lottie, after only a few months away from their care, should bring a strange man home, a soldier. But far worse, he was a Canadian, part of the idiotic notion she'd always had about the place!

Saturday afternoon Rupert would normally relax, cut the grass, weed the vegetable garden. Today, though, he hadn't changed at lunchtime from his office suit and Kate was wearing a silk dress. Their garb set the tone for the visit; their guest was to be held at arm's length, the atmosphere to remain formal.

'You're from Alberta, you say? You must find things different here. My sister has been in Calgary for some years and I know from her one and only visit home she'd become accustomed to ways very unlike our own.'

'Sure, things are different.' Neil was impervious to the chill in Rupert's voice so apparent to Lottie. 'My folk came from over here, you know. My great-grandparents were from Ireland.'

Kate managed to convey that she looked down her nose without actually doing it. 'Really?'

'Yep, the old lady was real Irish. You folks been there?'

'Ireland?' This time it was Rupert's unsmiling voice that answered. 'I'd hardly call Ireland "over here". No, we've not been there. I can't say I've ever felt any desire.'

'Oh, Dad, please don't take that tone. Please be friendly,' silently Lottie begged.

'Lottie's got a reason for bringing me to meet you. I guess you must be waiting for us to tell you. Me and Lottie, we plan to get married.'

'Come now, my dear chap.' This time Rupert blustered, thrown off his stroke by the approach. 'Time enough to think of all that when she has had more experience of the world. Get the war over before you think that far ahead, make sure you come through it safely.'

'No, Dad, we don't want to wait. We want to be married now. Suppose he gets sent overseas? We don't want to wait.'

'Don't talk nonsense. You're eighteen years old, no more than a child.'

Kate was watching from one to the other. So far she'd said nothing.

'I'm not a child! Only a week and I'll be nineteen anyway. Can't you see, I'm different, I'm grown up?'

'Don't you take that tone with me! If this is what racketing about with Canadians does to your manners, then it's time you found yourself more suitable companions.'

'Lottie,' Kate was twisting her fingers together, tears weren't far away, 'tell me the truth. Oh dear, what a question to hear myself ask! Look me in the eye. Have you been doing anything you're ashamed of?'

'No, I haven't.' The gleam in her eyes was defiant. What she'd done had been right!

'Thank God at least for that.'

'Neil and I are going to be married. Please, Dad, don't ask me anything else. Please just agree.'

Rupert ignored her, didn't even look at her. Neat, orderly in thought and speech, that was the father Lottie was used to. Now his tone was uncontrolled, a nerve twitching at the corner of his mouth as he glowered at Neil.

'And you, what have you got to say for yourself? You march in here, a stranger – not the sort of person we're accustomed to. What do you expect us to do? Welcome you? Tell you to help yourself to our daughter? Well? Speak up, man, have you nothing to say?'

'Sure I have.' How could he sound so calm? 'I've told you, Lottie and me mean to get wed. I can understand you and her mom don't like it. It means I shall take her long ways away. But there's no one going to stop us. And if you want her to be happy, she'd be better to have your blessing than to go without it. Be better for you too in the end.'

'Insolent young pup!'

'Why it is everything always goes wrong? Every time I look forward to something . . . ' Kate gave way to her tears, her hands on her temple. 'All these weeks I've been here on my own, evening after evening, always picturing Lottie coming home. Now it's all spoilt.'

'Mum, please try and understand. If you'd only talk to each other – try and know each other – '

'It's because he comes from Eva's damned country. I suppose you've told *her* all about it! Never a word to us, oh no, what do we matter! That blasted woman – ' Lottie had never heard her mother speak like it. All the weeks she and Neil had been together she'd built a picture in her mind of taking him home, the family welcoming him. She'd tried not to acknowledge how unlikely it was. If only they had more time, if only they could get to know him gradually. But time was one thing no one had these days. Perhaps next week, perhaps next month – soon he'd be gone. Kate was letting her tears roll down her cheeks. She didn't wipe them away, she didn't turn her head, her misery was there for all of them to see. Even the way she stood, her shoulders slumped, was evidence of it.

Neil felt in his pocket for a packet of cigarettes, held it first to Kate then to Rupert, only to be ignored. So he put one in his mouth and lit it. That he might have said 'Do you mind if I smoke?' didn't cross his mind. Lottie saw it as another black mark. She cringed with shame for him, and for herself too that she could wish he'd acted differently. Such a small thing, yet from the way her mother bit hard on her knuckle, the way her father's mouth turned down in angry contempt, she knew they'd noticed. How could they be so mean-minded? She slipped her hand into his. Like a cornered animal she glared at them.

Kate made an effort, which was more than Rupert did as, taking the paper, he marched off to the garden.

'Mother's coming this afternoon.' She dabbed her eyes as she spoke. 'We invited her before we knew about any of this. She's staying a day or two, especially because you're here, Lottie. I don't want a word said about this. At least you can do that much for me. I'll tidy my face. We don't want her to think anything's wrong.'

'Anyway, Mum,' Lottie had the parting shot as her mother went to 'tidy' her tear-ravaged face, 'I don't know what you're crying about. Whatever happens you're not going to lose. If I marry Neil you'll come to love him, I know you will. And if Dad won't give his consent, then it's my life that's ruined, not yours.'

'Stop it, Lottie. You know that's not true. I just want you to be happy. Try and see it my way – ' And sniffing into her handkerchief, she started up the stairs.

Sitting tall and erect in the back of the station taxi, Lavinia Matheson arrived. Even in these days of war and shortages, she always brought an air of occasion to her visits. Hearing the engine, Rupert went out to greet his mother-in-law. (Could it be that her visit had had something to do with his gardening clothes being upstairs in his wardrobe still?) Opening the taxi door for her he helped her out, touching her cheek with a kiss that showed more homage than affection. Then Kate hurled out to embrace her, relieved that Rupert hadn't needed reminding that the taxi driver was waiting for his fare.

Over her daughter's shoulder Lavinia's sharp eyes were looking for Lottie.

'Hasn't she arrived yet?'

'Yes, she came an hour or more ago. Come inside, Mother. How was your journey?'

'An hour ago? And not here to greet me!'

'She's in the orchard, she couldn't have heard the car.' Kate had always been aware of her mother's special affection for Lottie. 'Mother, she's brought someone with her. Before you meet them I'd better warn you – '

'And a young ruffian he is too,' Rupert put in. 'We seem to have no influence, perhaps she'll listen to you.'

'She always does and I always listen to her too. What makes you say this friend of hers is a ruffian? No pips on his shoulder, is that it?' Her eyes mocked him. Silly ninny! How Kate could have been so stupid I'll never understand if I live to be a hundred. Humdrum, full of nothing. Bah! Only thing worth while he's ever done is fathering those children and from the look of Kate sometimes I shouldn't think she got a lot of pleasure out of his part of it.

'A corporal in the Canadian Army,' Kate whispered. 'That's the attraction, Mother, a wretched Canadian.'

'I'll sit in the garden. Run and tell her I've arrived, Rupert.'

Rupert 'ran'. The first time he'd been brought into the presence of tall and beautiful Lavinia Matheson he'd been in awe of her, and twenty-five years of marriage to her daughter had done nothing to change his attitude. Silently he resented what he saw as the Matheson assurance, the confidence that grew from the family's two centuries at Bullington Manor, the suspicion that he was tolerated but not liked, and certainly not respected. Now, though, as he went to tell Lottie her grandmother had arrived, he smiled wryly to himself. *She'll* soon send him packing, he anticipated, certain that this time his autocratic mother-in-law would support his own views.

But it seemed he was wrong. An hour or so later he could see the three of them, Lavinia sitting erect on the wrought iron garden seat, Lottie cross-legged on the grass at her feet, and Neil O'Hagon, the sleeves of his khaki shirt rolled up, sprawled full-length on the lawn. He couldn't hear what they were saying but the conversation was clearly a three way thing; the old lady was talking, listening, nodding, laughing – and the Canadian's voice rose above the others. It seemed as if she was actually drawing him out, encouraging him to talk.

As the day wore on the first tension eased. Neither Kate nor Rupert could be openly hostile to the visitor in the face of Lavinia's attitude. There was no more talk of an engagement, for Kate had made it clear she wanted nothing said in front of her mother. As Neil only had a thirty-six hour pass and Lavinia would be there until after he'd gone, the atmosphere relaxed. Lottie's spirits started to rise. More than once she felt her grandmother's gaze on her, on her and on Neil.

'It'll be all right,' she told him the next day as he prepared to leave, 'Grandma likes you, you can tell she does. I've seen the way she watches. Mum said don't tell Grandma.' She chuckled. 'You can bet there's not much she needs telling.'

How easily she slipped back into her old place at home. Neil gone, and Lavinia, there was just herself and her parents.

'It's as if you've never been away, Lottie. You've no idea how dead the house is without you and the boys.'

She and Kate were picking the last of the broad beans for supper.

'I was imagining at breakfast what Dad would have said if I'd told him I was going to Brimley to the cinema this evening.' Lottie giggled.

'There's nothing wrong in trying to protect you from – from – all that sort of thing. Look where your newfound freedom has got you. Don't do anything silly, Lottie. There'll be other young men.'

'I shall marry Neil.'

'And what sort of life do you think you'd have? Eva's filled you head with a lot of rubbish about the fine way she lives. You forget, she's in a city. This place Neil talked of – Kilton Down, he called it – it's miles from civilisation. Can you see yourself roughing it? I can't understand why Mother didn't try and make you see sense. And I'm frightened. If he were a nice upright lad, someone we could feel you're safe with so far away from home, someone who would hold you in respect . . . Lottie, promise me – '

'Hush. Listen,' Lottie held up a finger, 'someone talking to Freda. We have a visitor. Oh, wow, look who it is!' Dropping her bundle of beans she tore up the garden path and hurled herself at Ronnie.

'I didn't say anything. I wasn't sure if I'd wangle my leave pass, but when Mum said you were going to be home I put in for it, hoping. I've got seven days. So has Barrie, so I brought him along. That's OK, isn't it, Mum? We've got our ration cards. This is Flight Lieutenant Barrie Miles – a good mate of mine.'

Kate's pretty face was flushed with pleasure. Lottie home, now Ronnie too. And this young friend, what a nice-looking young man. He might have come in answer to her prayers.

'Of course you're welcome, Barrie. There's nothing I like more than to have the children bring their friends. All fall to and see how many more beans you can find. I'll go and help Freda make sure your rooms are ready.'

That was on the Tuesday. Lottie returned to Kingstaunton on the following Sunday. Five days of summer and three young people with nothing to do but enjoy them. Punting, hiking, helping Curtis (the man who came four mornings a week to look after the garden), the three of them together going to the Majestic Ballroom (with Rupert's warning to Ronnie to 'See to it that you take care of your sister'). Kate tried to smile the remark away. Far better to let Barrie have a free hand! There was no doubt that he was taken with Lottie, and no wonder. These last few days she'd looked so pretty, so smiling and happy. Kate began to put the shadow of Neil O'Hagon out of her mind.

'Dad, we've not talked any more about Neil. I shouldn't have sprung

34

it on you so suddenly, I ought to have told you about him weeks ago. But I know you and Mum worry. Now you've met him, and you could see Grandma liked him – well, when he comes home with me again, things will be all right, won't they?'

'This week you seem to have lived perfectly happily without him.'

'Of course this week has been just great, with Ronnie home. And Barrie's nice too, of course he is, he's Ronnie's friend. But that's got nothing to do with me and Neil.'

'I thought I'd made my views clear. I'm not having you throwing yourself away on an ill-mannered cowboy, and the sooner you understand it the better for all of us.'

Lottie clenched her teeth hard. Why did it have to be like this? For a second she remembered the feeling of queuing on the high diving board and waiting her turn to jump, knowing there was no other way. He couldn't say no if he realised she already belonged to Neil. 'Now you're branded, you're *my* woman, you belong to me.' The words echoed in her mind. Yet here at home they thought she was still a child, playing games of falling in love. They didn't even begin to understand.

She heard her mother come into the room; she heard the clock on the mantelpiece chime two; she heard Ronnie and Barrie playing tennis on the court they'd marked out again during the week. Seconds ticked on. No high diving board had ever held the terror of this!

'I didn't want to have to tell you . . . I thought you'd be upset.' How low her voice sounded. She was surprised at herself that while her heart thudded she could sound so calm. It took all her courage, but she had to make them understand and see that she knew just what she was doing. 'Mum, you said that no man wants a girl who's let other men – you know – touch her.'

'What the devil are you saying?' She could see the corner of Rupert's mouth twitching. 'I want the truth. Has that swine tried to tamper – '

'Stop it! Why do you have to speak about him like that? You make everything sound beastly!'

'Lottie,' Kate's colour was high, 'so it is beastly if it's like that – it's shameful, degrading! No man would subject a girl he respected – ' She floundered, out of her depth. 'You swore to me you'd done nothing wrong. Now are you saying you lied?'

'I didn't lie. I haven't done anything wrong. What I did was right. So now you know it all. I belong to Neil. And I'm glad!' More even than her words, what hurt Kate was the defiance, the triumph in her expression.

Rupert was a man who shied from emotion, yet now he lost control. Taking Lottie by the shoulders he shook her with all his might. It was as if, once started, he couldn't stop himself.

'You little whore!'

From outside came Barrie's call: 'Forty: thirty.' It seemed the only sanity left.

'Leave her alone! Stop it! You'll hurt her!' Kate turned on Rupert, her voice shrill. 'And if that's what she is, you know where she gets it from! You know who's to blame. Leave her alone, damn you.' Often enough Kate cried, but not like this. This was hysteria, sobbing taking over where words stopped.

Rupert let go, his arms hanging limp. The fight had gone out of him. Lottie felt helpless as she looked from one to the other.

'Oh, Mum, don't cry like that. I've got to go in a few minutes. I can't leave you like this. I oughtn't to have told you. But you've got to see why I want to marry him. And you mustn't blame Neil. I wanted it to be like that.'

'Are you pregnant? Is that what you're saying?' Rupert's voice held no colour.

'I don't think so. But I might be.' Then, chin held high: 'And if I am, I'm not ashamed. I'd be proud.'

'Oh, dear God!' Kate snorted. 'What did I do to deserve it? Haven't I put up with enough? I can't take any more.'

Just for a second Lottie was angry. Wasn't that just like Mum? Always turning everything as if it were designed specially to make *her* suffer.

'Dad . . . ' To look at him, grey and defeated, hurt her. Had she done this to him? But it wasn't fair. Love should bring joy. 'Dad, I know what I'm doing. I love him.' She put out a hand to touch him, but it was as if he didn't notice. 'Please, Dad. I've got to go, but how can I leave you like this?'

'You give me no choice. Tell your Canadian I will give my consent.'

'I don't believe it . . . I can't believe it!' Kate was quieter now, her wild outburst seemed to have drained the strength from her.

Lottie looked from one to the other of them. She ought to be elated, she'd won her own way. Yet where could the joy be in this? She saw the one brief look that passed between her parents. Scorn, contempt, dislike . . . what was it she read in her mother's eyes? In his there was failure.

'You'll come to love him, I know you – '

'Go and get your case. It's five to three. Your taxi will be here. You mustn't keep the man waiting.' Rupert took the folded newspaper and went out into the garden.

Chapter Three

Before there could be a wedding there were other hurdles. Since Neil was serving overseas, it seemed that his Commanding Officer had almost as much authority as Lottie's parents. By the time final approval was granted and the licence in Neil's hand it was the end of September.

And it was then that Lavinia Matheson stepped in.

'Oh dear, I don't know what to think.' Kate looked up from the letter she was reading. 'It's from Mother. She suggests that Lottie should be married from Bullington. She says she's already written to her about it.'

'This is her home, she should be married here!' That was Rupert's first reaction, quick to see the offer as a reflection on the home he provided. Kate might not have heard him, her mind was away at Bullington Manor, time and place slipped back a quarter of a century. 'Of course, your mother means it generously.' Rupert had never been able to stand out against Lavinia. 'Perhaps, Kate, we should be glad to accept. The less the locals from around here satisfy their curiosity about the sort of match she's making, the better. If you're able to tell people it's to be a family occasion and so naturally your mother wants it to be from the Manor, that should stop the gossip before it starts. Yes, it's a generous offer.'

'Mother's not offering out of generosity. She's always been the same about Lottie. Hear what she says: "It means a great deal to me that memories of the Manor go with Lottie into her new life. It may be selfish of me to want her wedding to be at Newton Dingley but I've written to her suggesting it. Those first days of a marriage are times one never forgets. That's why I've offered them the use of the East Wing – let her remember the Manor, not some unknown hotel that's meant nothing to her." She can write that to me! My own mother! Wanting Lottie to have her precious memories. What about me? Doesn't she care? Or has she forgotten? The East Wing . . . '

'Kate, it's all a long time ago. Can't we be grateful for all that we have?'

Ignoring him she folded the letter away. When she spoke her voice was hard. 'At least that young ruffian will realise that this place isn't all there is to Lottie's background. He'll see how out of his depth he's swimming when he comes to Bullington.'

It was more than two hundred years since Egbert Matheson had commissioned the building of Bullington Manor, but if the family ever thought of its history they looked back beyond Egbert, to his father Giles. But for him all their fortunes might have been very different.

Giles had been the fourth son of the Reverend Charles Matheson, vicar of Newton Dingley. His elder brothers had slotted suitably into Army, church and law; Giles slotted into nothing, a rolling stone who would gather no moss on his downhill slide. When he'd announced his intention of going to the New World his father had set him on his way with a small purse of sovereigns and very little hope for his future.

For a long time they heard nothing from him. They imagined he must have fallen into the same sort of company in the New World as he'd kept in the Old. In that they may not have been far from the truth, but what they didn't know was that he'd had a windfall at the gaming tables and, for once, had had the sense to move off before he lost it. He'd been gone from Newton Dingley for three or four years when a letter came telling them that he'd moved south from New England, and become involved in the tobacco growing business. Then had followed another lapse of two or three years before news had come that he now owned a large plantation and was about to be married. More time, then tidings that a son had been born, Egbert Matheson.

Giles had never harboured any thoughts of coming home. When he'd died Egbert, then thirty years old, had inherited one of the largest plantations in the southern states. He was a man of substance – he was also a man with a yearning to see the land of his roots. So, in the year of his inheritance, 1737, he'd installed a manager and sailed for England. He'd intended it to be a tour of discovery, nothing more. In London he'd met and fallen in love with the daughter of a tobacco importer. In 1739 he'd married her and laid the foundation stone of Bullington Manor. It had risen as a vindication of his one-time wayward father, evidence of the verdant moss that had clung to the rolling stone.

Since then other Mathesons had left their mark. Before the end of that century Egbert's son had added a West Wing to the south-facing house, and laid the foundations of the East Wing. Next had come the formal gardens in front of the building, a contrast to the rolling parkland that dropped away to the Lake.

During the First World War the family had moved into the East Wing, giving the rest of the house to be used as a Military Hospital. But that was long ago, it was a period Lottie had seldom heard mentioned and never by her parents. Once when she'd been staying with Lavinia she'd stumbled on the subject, she'd even remarked that no one had ever mentioned any of it to her.

'There's a lot of wartime that's better forgotten, Lottie my dear. They weren't all happy times. Much better to let the ghosts rest.'

Lottie hadn't been satisfied, but she knew her grandmother well enough to ask no more. And the last thing she wanted to do at home was upset her mother by reviving memories of unhappy wartime days.

The date of the wedding hadn't been arranged, Neil was having difficulty over his leave. Then, just before the end of September he telephoned Lottie at Rampton's. His leave form was signed. Seven days commencing the following weekend – embarkation leave.

She travelled to Bullington by train with Neil and Johnny McMinn, a fellow Canadian who was to be best man. Kate and Rupert arrived, accompanied by Freda. In Sycamore Avenue she was almost part of the family but here she was handed over to the housekeeper and taken to the servants' quarters. Not that she resented it, indeed it added kudos to her position; she noted every smallest detail in the household arrangements, storing them in her mind to regale her friends with. They wouldn't know about the running of an establishment like this, how could they, all of them in ordinary places the same as she was herself. Ronnie came from Lincolnshire bringing Barrie Miles. Other members of the family made the effort where they could at such short notice, drawn by a combination of curiosity, family loyalty and a genuine fondness for Lottie.

From the open doorway of the little church in Newton Dingley Lottie looked at the assembled gathering. A gathering of Mathesons . . . and when would be the next time the family gathered? Where would she be then? Her mouth felt dry.

There was Aunt Hester looking so tall and proud, the only relief to her navy blue ensemble a white ostrich feather swathed around the brim of her hat. Alistair her only son with a major's crown on his epaulet; he had never seen his father who'd been killed on the Somme. Next to him was Uncle Charles, her mother's brother. There used to be two brothers, Charles was the younger. Jonathan had been killed in 1917. It must have been the sight of so many people in uniform that made Lottie remember the photograph of him on Lavinia's writing desk, and from that thought came another . . . the time would come when Bullington Manor would belong to Uncle Charles.

Her gaze flew to her grandmother sitting next to Kate. What a moment to imagine a day when she'd no longer be in her regular place in the front pew, the head of the family, the doyen of the village. Was it the finality of the step she was about to take, a step that would carry her away from all these people who'd been part of her life? Was it the sight of Neil in his battledress with two stripes, a soldier every bit as much as Colonel Charles Matheson? Perhaps it was a combination of all these things.

In sudden panic she looked at Rupert and for answer felt her hand taken and tucked through his arm. But he didn't look at her, his face showed no expression. Her cousin Luke, a Pilot Officer and Charles's younger son, winked at her as she moved up the aisle; his brother Christopher, two years older and two promotions ahead, sent her a look of encouragement. The family were seated on the left hand side of the small church. On the right were people from the village, staff from the Manor – except for Freda and she had firmly insisted she belonged to the bride.

Lottie felt torn. When Neil held her hand in his and made his vows, all her doubts melted. What she was doing was right, all the other was just natural nerves. 'As nervous as a bride', somewhere she'd heard the expression. And what about Neil, did he feel the same, surrounded by strangers, binding his future with hers? Her fingers clung to his, she felt the answering pressure. Then she became aware of her mother, only feet away, crying, not just sniffing into her handkerchief but really crying. Rupert stood helplessly by, his daughter given away. Lottie sent a fleeting glance in the direction of the front pew, ashamed that her paramount emotion was anger. Mum, you're trying to spoil everything. Well, you're not going to! That quick glance met Lavinia's, and for a second it lingered. Tall, proud, still a beautiful woman, Lavinia Matheson sent her a silent message. Love, trust, confidence, support – all those things that had never failed her through the years.

'I pronounce you man and wife . . . ' It was done. With her hand in Neil's she moved towards the vestry. Lottie Bradley had become Charlotte O'Hagon.

For more than twenty years Lavinia Matheson had been a widow, matriarch of the family. Today in the way she welcomed Neil she set the tone. Let them say what they liked to each other and out of her hearing – and she had no doubt that they would! – but as long as they were under her roof they would treat him as Lottie's choice of a husband should be treated. Excluding the bridal couple, there wasn't one of them who failed to receive her silent message. Lottie was grateful to her for giving them such a lovely wedding, but that the family should be friendly and hospitable to Neil she accepted without question. As for Neil, he'd left the ranch and the life he loved to come and help win this war; he was as good as any man – and better than most! What difference if a man had rings on his sleeve or stripes, wore a cap decorated with gold braid or a simple forage cap? War was a fight that had to be won, then they'd all get on with proper living again.

There hadn't been a school holiday when Lottie hadn't spent weeks at a time at Bullington with Lavinia. Until now, though, she'd never slept in the East Wing. Already it was late. At Kingstaunton the bus would be on its way back from the Palais. In the fading light she'd taken Neil to the lake. As they'd wandered back in the darkness of a moonless night they'd heard the sound of departing cars. Even those of the family who'd stayed for dinner with Lavinia had been leaving, shielded headlights from the taxis hardly casting enough light to follow the curve of the long drive. Lottie had felt like a child playing truant, not being there to wave the family away. But this was her honeymoon!

Stretching full-length in the huge bath, lightly she moved her soapy hands round her breasts, then down her slim body, holding her palms against her flat stomach. Mrs Neil O'Hagon, wife of a Canadian rancher, one day mother of his children. Her mind jumped of its own accord to Eva, to that August when her dream of Canada had been born. And soon it would happen. She wouldn't be a visitor, guest of a few weeks; she'd belong, her children would grow up speaking with that accent she'd grown to love.

And thinking of that accent she heard: 'Hey, wife, have you drowned?'

'Coming,' she laughed. She'd chosen her nightdress with such care, but now she pulled it quickly over her head and ran her fingers through her curly hair.

He was sitting on the edge of the bed, wearing just the trousers of his pyjamas.

'Well?' His eyes teased, telling her he was aware of her scrutiny.

'I was thinking – I've seen you lots of times without your trousers, but never without a khaki shirt.'

'Now that's a real romantic way to warm up for your wedding night. Come to that, I've seen you – well, never mind how – but never in a

41

nightgown.' He came to stand in front of her, his hands on her shoulders. 'You look taller, kinda regal.'

'Me? Regal!' She laughed, buffeting her head against his shoulder. 'But I like it. Go on, say some more nice things.'

'Guess I'm not the sort of guy to say nice things to a dame, not for the sake of inflating her vanity.'

'Not even a little? After all, it is our wedding night, I'm due a bit of spoiling.'

'You'll get all your dues.'

So they bantered, but there was much that was serious just under the surface. With only three days between now and his going, the emotion they felt underlay every teasing word.

She slipped her arms around his neck, and all the jesting was gone. Instinct must have been her guide, for afterwards she could never remember how it was that her carefully chosen nightdress came to be no more than a pile of satin around her ankles. She did remember pulling the cord of his pyjama trousers. Then she was lifted into his arms and carried like a baby to the bed. They'd made love on the brow of the hill, they'd made love in a disused barn during a rain storm, at dusk in a hired punt under the sheltering tent of the branches of a willow tree, in the dark and disregarding the "Keep off the Grass" signs they knew were there in Kingstaunton Gardens where the railings had gone into the melting pot to make guns; they'd made love in the sunshine and in the moonlight. But tonight was different, these weren't stolen moments with one eye and one ear on guard against intruders.

Neil must have been thinking on the same lines.

'Charlotte O'Hagon. Jeez honey, my wife, my ol' lady.' Fascinated she watched the way his Adam's apple moved in his neck. 'Lottie, my Lottie . . . wish I was clever with words. So full of things I want to say. What was it, there in that little church? To love and to cherish . . . don't know how to say it to you.' His voice was tight, emotion had to find an outlet. Words weren't his way.

'Don't say it. Show me. Love me.' She pulled him towards her.

'Sure, didn't I say it? With my body I thee worship.' She gave herself up to the wonder of being one with him, man and his woman, woman and her man, united, belonging. Afterwards, as they lay breathless, they were still uplifted by the wonder of what had happened to them.

'Oh, boy,' he panted when he had enough breath to speak, 'this is my wife.'

She knew the moment had come to tell him.

'Good thing she is, too.' Her voice was soft, full of happiness. 'She's going to have your baby.'

42

His eyes shot open.

'How come? How do you know?'

She chuckled. 'The usual way – answering both questions.'

'Lottie honey, you never hinted. I ought to have noticed, counted up. Are you feeling OK? When did you know?'

'I should have – you know – a few days before we went to Brimley. That's nearly seven weeks ago and still nothing's happened. So I think it must have been somewhere end of July, beginning of August. Take me to about March.'

He moved off the bed to kneel on the floor by her side.

'I can't believe it.'

'Aren't you glad? You don't sound it.' For a moment she was frightened. There was something unfathomable in his expression.

'Glad? Not just that. Glad's what you feel about ordinary sort of things. I feel – I guess I feel small, sort of humble. Can you understand?'

He reached out a hand and laid it on her.

'Right there, in that flat belly of yours, a person. And I put it there. Ours. Another person. Another O'Hagon, eh? Your belly'll swell and I shan't be here. You'll feel it inside you. Ours. And I gotta leave you honey, like that and all on your own.'

'Shan't be on my own.' She forced herself to smile. 'I'll have the baby, getting bigger each day.'

He leant forward and rested his head on her stomach, then on her groin. She felt his lips as he kissed her.

The following Tuesday he reported back to base and she returned to Kingstaunton. He didn't know when they were to be shifted but his last words to her were: 'This may not have to be goodbye. Don't let's say it. Not until we have to. I'll come tomorrow evening if I can.'

He didn't. And when the girls reported back after their next jaunt to the Palais, they said the Canadians had gone.

Kate read Lottie's letter a good many times during the course of the morning, so many times that she must have known it by heart. A grandchild! She didn't feel a bit the way she'd always thought of grandparents. Perhaps no one ever did. She sat down on the dressing table stool in her bedroom and peered closely into the mirror. No lines. She looked again, even had the grace to smile at her own dishonesty. Almost no lines, she corrected. Fancy, of all of them, it was she who would be a grandmother first.

As a child at Bullington Kate had been the youngest, the delicate one, protected and cared for by the rest of them. Jonathan had been the eldest, followed a year later by Hester, and eighteen months later still by Charles; then a gap of four years before Kate had arrived. Small, dainty, delicate, timid, but with a sweetness that made them all her willing slaves. For a minute now she indulged in memories, let her mind wander back to years that in retrospect seemed cloudless. But today's news soon pushed everything else out of her mind. Now that that wretched man had been sent overseas Lottie would be theirs again, things would be like they used to be. But better, much better. She would come home, not to rush off and spend each day at work but to be here, company in the house. Imagine! They'd be able to make tiny clothes together, get the old crib down from the loft and re-line it; the next months would be so happy. And after that, a baby. Tiny, trusting, watching you with innocent love . . . What a good thing the wedding had been at Bullington, people wouldn't remember the exact date like they would if they'd attended. End of March . . . well, first babies were sometimes late. March could be April – and Lottie wouldn't be the first to have an eight month baby. Beyond that she wouldn't look. It was wicked even to harbour such thoughts about Neil O'Hagon, but now that he'd gone off to fight, who knew what might happen? Wars brought casualties. Fate might sort everything out for them in a way that would bring ultimate happiness.

Daydreams behind her, she went downstairs to her writing desk.

'What news! I'm so looking forward to these winter months. You will be home, we shall plan and make. No more long evenings on my own while your father is out with his ARP Warden duties. Of course, to start with we'll keep our secret to ourselves, you know what people are like for working things out and spreading gossip.'

With the end of her pen held between her teeth she considered what she'd written, imagined Lottie reading it – then tore it up and started again.

'Your news has made us very happy. With so much for us all to look forward to, more than anything we want you to come home. Let your father and me be part of the preparations, and let us share the joy and love a baby brings just as long as we are able.'

To Lottie her letter came as a sign of acceptance. She'd go home. Through her they'd come to see Neil as she did. All the harsh words would be forgotten and everything would be all right again. So, with trust in the future – the immediate future at home and the long-term future when the war was over and she and Neil could start a life together – she came back to Brimley.

Although she'd undrawn the blackout curtain, the night was dark. Lying in bed Lottie gazed around her at the room that had been hers as long as she could remember, the outline of the familiar furniture gradually taking shape as she became accustomed to the darkness. Her old room, her single bed, and although she couldn't see any of it, her gymkhana cup on the mantelpiece, three certificates for dancing framed and hanging above it, a trinket box that Ronnie had made for her on the dressing table, the Canada Box on the chest of drawers. Home. Nothing was changed. She might have stepped right back into yesterday. How easily she'd slipped back into her old role, almost as if nothing had altered. They hadn't mentioned Neil, hadn't even enquired about him. How silly to go on as if nothing had happened. As if to prove to herself just how different she was from the child her parents still tried to think her, she gently explored the changes in her body, felt the hard tightness of her enlarged breasts.

Her parents were forgotten, she was back in the East Wing. Word for word she could remember telling Neil about the baby. With flat palms and spreadeagled fingers she held her not-so flat stomach. Alone in her childhood bedroom she seemed to hear Neil's words: 'Your belly'll swell and I shan't be there.' The house was quiet, her parents had gone to bed, no one stirred at this time of night in Sycamore Avenue. Under her sheltering hands something moved . . . hardly more than a ripple . . . but there was no doubt. The baby! A living thing. She wanted to leap out of bed and draw the blackout curtains so that she could add this stupendous piece of news to her letter; but something told her she shouldn't leap anywhere, these minutes belonged to the baby, to the new life that was waking in the tiny limbs. She laid perfectly still, waiting for the miracle to happen again.

It had been important to write to Neil tonight. If only he could have been here, been part of the atmosphere that had welcomed her. But she couldn't hide from the truth – had he been here it wouldn't have been like that. She didn't blame him, it was their fault. But once they came to see how happy she was, how faithfully she wrote to him and he to her, then they'd stop doubting.

'There's a delivery of white wool coming in at Currie's, they'll have it for sale Tuesday morning,' Kate told her after Rupert had left them still at the breakfast table next morning. 'I've got some coupons. If they'll let me have enough for it I thought I'd make a pram set. We could go in together, Lottie, and you could choose the pattern.'

'Don't use your coupons, Mum, not if you're getting short. I've got all my special baby ones.'

'No, we'd better not, not in Brimley. Anyone I've spoken to about you expecting, I've said May, the end of May. You wouldn't have had extra coupons issued yet. Even at that, I can imagine them going home to count out the weeks and wonder how you managed it. Oh dear, Lottie, this could have been such a happy time, if only you'd married some nice young man, one who wasn't planning to whisk you and the baby so far away.'

'I don't see what we have to tell lies for. I was pregnant when I got married, but Neil didn't even know. He wanted to marry me, it wasn't as if Dad made him. Anyway, it's no one's business. I'm having a baby and I'm glad, it's the best thing that's ever happened to me – well, that and Neil.' She wanted to hurt her mother, to punish her.

'Well, if you have no shame for yourself, at least you might think of me. You're showing already. Perhaps if you got a good maternity corset . . . they can work wonders, you now.' Then, meeting the look in Lottie's eyes, she said no more.

There were good days and there were bad. The good ones followed no particular pattern, or if they did then Lottie didn't know what it was; but a bad one was inevitable if the morning post brought her a letter from Neil.

It was two days before Christmas when Freda brought in the collection of cards and letters she'd picked up off the doormat.

'Post's early today. I see they got a new girl bringing it round, bit quicker on her feet than that fat Jennie Cummins was. A lot for you this morning.' Then peering hard at the top envelopes: 'Well, it got here, more by luck than anything I'd say. That one's for Lottie – but I'll give them all to you.' She put the pile down by Rupert's plate and disappeared to the kitchen to fetch the breakfast, this morning consisting of scrambled dried egg on butterless toast.

When Lottie came into the room a minute later she found her parents both examining the envelope, a look of distaste on Rupert's face and of pain on Kate's.

'For you, it seems. From Canada. Certainly not your aunt, so it must be one of your husband's cowboy acquaintances.'

Lottie slit the envelope with her knife, then turned to look at the signature. Molly O'Hagon. Back to the beginning, careful that her face gave no sign of how difficult it was to read, how the outlandish spelling meant that many of the words had to be guessed at. Loyalty to Neil made it important no one should guess at his mother's illiteracy – and loyalty to Neil made her ashamed that she should be so conscious that there was something to be hidden.

'Who's it from then, dear?' Kate wanted to know. 'Some child, perhaps?'

'You know it isn't. It's from Neil's mother. She sounds nice. She's pleased about the baby, says she'll make things. Says she's looking

46

forward to when we're there. It's always been a family place, you see. Neil's Dad and then Neil himself, they all grew up there. Eugene, that Neil's cousin's wife, she had a son just a month or so ago. Mrs O'Hagon says ours will be great company for him.' (In fact she'd said 'he'll' be great company, but Lottie preferred to overlook that.)

'Scandalous!' Rupert lowered the newspaper, the corners of his mouth pulled down as if he were confronting something unsavoury. 'Just look at that wretched letter. If that's the best the woman could manage, can't you imagine what she must be? Yes, look at it. Now see your own mother. The child's two grandmothers!'

He didn't intend to give Lottie time to argue. As he spoke he'd been folding the paper. Now he touched Kate's cheek with his in what passed for a kiss, and left them.

'Oh dear, oh dear, he talks like that, but it's me who's going to be left alone when you go. I won't even think of it. It's way in the future, it might never happen – '

'What do you mean? Can't you understand even now, Mum, Neil and I know what we're doing. We're going to make a good life together.'

'No one can say what they're going to do. You forget, I've lived through another war before this one.'

'That's wicked!'

'I didn't say anything wicked. I simply said none of us can ever be sure. Look at the air raids there've been, anything can happen to anyone.' But Kate knew very well it hadn't been air raids she had in mind. Lottie was young, she'd get over it, she'd find another husband, someone suitable, when the boys all came home . . .

That was the day Ronnie arrived home on leave for Christmas. In the evening Rupert was on warden duty. Lottie and Ronnie found an old game of Happy Families in the drawer, a game from their early childhood and one that no one had touched since. It must have been excitement at both of them being home, or perhaps a touch of Christmas already walking abroad, but their contest turned into a riot of noisy, boisterous laughter. Working on the white pramset, Kate listened. If only Michael were here too. If only all three of them were home and this beastly war over. But if it were, then Lottie would be going. Just for a moment Kate's fingers were still. Staring into the flickering flames of the fire she let her imagination go unchecked: the war over, the boys home, Lottie and the baby still here with no thought of going to that ignorant woman . . .

It was the 28th of March. One of the drawers in the chest in Lottie's room was full of clothes for the baby; another was full of cot sheets

47

and terry towelling nappies. For a confinement not expected until May, things were in a remarkable state of readiness! Kate knew that May was out of the question, but soon they'd safely be into April. She was grateful for each day that went by.

'Our young Lottie looks a bit wan today,' Freda remarked as Kate worked at the kitchen table, rearranging last week's flowers to try and make them last a few more days.

'I've not really seen her. I couldn't face breakfast this morning – I expect you noticed.'

'Got one of your heads?'

'Behind my eyes. I can feel the tension, just waiting to catch me.'

'Ah.' Freda took 'one of Kate's heads' in her stride without much interest. 'Over a fortnight since she heard. That's the tonic she needs, a nice letter. Probably worried and not sleeping like she needs to.'

'Who of us does these days? I know I don't. Lie awake hour after hour, worrying, frightened even to think ahead – yet if I don't picture the day when they're home again, it's like tempting fate.'

'Can't ever be like it was, Mrs Bradley, and that's for sure. Not with our Lottie gone away.'

'That's the best I can do with these.' Kate surveyed the flowers. 'Perhaps I'll take a little walk to the shops, the air might do me good. Do we want anything?'

So it was that she wasn't home when the telegram arrived.

With fingers that felt useless as cotton wool Lottie tore the envelope.

'Want me to take a reply?' the telegraph boy asked.

She shook her head. Reason wouldn't accept. There must be a mistake. She slumped down clumsily to sit on the second stair, holding the sheet of paper in front of her and reading it again. Words . . . they were clear enough. But they couldn't be right. Not him. Standing up she held her hand to her back. Today it felt as though someone had hit her with a hammer.

'Mum! Mum, where are you?'

'Gone out for a breath of air. Who was that at the door, love?'

'Freda, look, the boy brought it.' Her face crumpled and hot tears were running down her cheeks. The telegram had stripped her of all her newly acquired maturity. She was a little girl again, a little sister.

'Oh, dear God,' Freda whispered. 'Oh, your poor mum, it'll break her. Better get your dad home. Let him be here to tell her.'

'Mr Bradley isn't available, I'm sorry. Can I give –'

'Where is he? Where can I find him? This is his daughter, it's urgent.'

48

'Oh dear. Well, I don't know if I do right to disclose his client's address . . . he'll be back in an hour or so.'

'Where is he?' Lottie's voice was tight, that was the only way she could hold it steady.

'All right, I'll tell you. Oh dear, she's not going to like it. He's at Armitage House with Mrs Hetherington. She won't like me telling anyone. I'd telephone him for you if I could, but Mrs Hetherington refuses to have one in the house. She won't like it if she knows I've told anyone she has her accountant with her.'

Lottie replaced the receiver. What to do next?

'Did you tell your poor father?' Freda hovered in the kitchen doorway.

Her question, the helplessness of her tone, told Lottie just what she had to do.

'He was out. I know where to find him. When Mum comes home don't say a word, just go on as if nothing's wrong.'

'As if nothing's wrong, you say! Oh, Lottie –'

'Don't – don't even think. Just try and pretend. I'll get Dad.'

It said much for Freda's state of shock that she didn't query that Lottie should set off on her bicycle, didn't even ask how far she had to go. Sycamore Avenue lay to the west of Brimley, Armitage House to the north, hidden from the road by a high wall and tall wooden gates. Lottie set off, pedalling hard, her thoughts concentrated on reaching her father. It was months since she'd ridden her bike . . . she must hurry . . . how hard it was to turn the pedals . . . I'm hurrying Michael, oh no, it can't be true, not Michael . . . Her aching back was a searing pain now. Must hurry, must get Dad.

His car wasn't outside Armitage House. Perhaps he'd not arrived yet. Perhaps he'd been held up on the way, they hadn't said how long he'd been gone. She'd call at the house and tell Mrs Hetherington she had to take him home.

The front door was answered by an elderly servant.

'Yes?' Not a promising welcome.

'My father is coming to see Mrs Hetherington. I have to speak to him. It's urgent, important – '

'And who might you be, young lady?' At the sound of voices Mrs Hetherington appeared, clearly not pleased to have a caller.

'My father, Mr Bradley, is coming to see you. I have to speak to him. I tried to contact him at the office, he must be on his way.' Then she remembered she mustn't get the girl in the office into trouble. 'I made the girl tell me where he was, she didn't want to, but it's – it's – when he comes I have to send him straight home. There's been a telegram – '

With a nod, Mrs Hetherington dismissed the maid. 'I'll have to speak to him,' she grumbled, 'I'll not have some chit of a girl broadcasting my affairs. Anyway he's been gone from here some minutes.' Then, looking more closely at Lottie, 'You should be home where someone can look to you.'

The pain that had been so violent was lifting. Lottie's spirit was coming back.

'Where is there a telephone?'

'At the corner of the road. I'm not having one of those things in *my* house. If anyone wants to speak to me, then let them have the courtesy to come to my door.'

Down the drive, through the great wooden gate, on to the bicycle . . . she must get the message to him before that pain came again. Yes, he was back, the secretary told her. Then the relief of hearing his voice.

'Dad, don't say anything. Just listen.'

And typical of Rupert, he did just that, listened and then said simply: 'I'll go straight home.' He seldom used the car these days, the meagre ration of petrol made it impossible except for essential business visits. As no public transport went near Armitage House, today was one of the rare occasions he'd driven into town, so now he could get home quickly. Putting down the receiver Lottie leant against the side of the telephone kiosk. Memories of childhood chased through her mind and, at the forefront of all of them Michael, gentle, understanding Michael.

Now there was no need for her to rush, she wouldn't get on her bike again. She was frightened to get on the saddle and force the pedals round. This time yesterday if she'd felt a pain like it she would have been eager, not for the agony she knew she had to go through but for what it was leading to. Today belonged to Michael. She wouldn't even let the memory of the pain into her mind. All her thoughts were of him, and what must be happening at home now with Mum and Dad.

But it came again. It took her breath away, leaving her bent double, her head on the handlebars. The road was empty. In the residential area no one was about. Just give it time, grip hard and give it time, it would go away. It did. But for how long? There was no hiding from it, pains like that could only mean one thing. It was her baby. In a few minutes it would happen again. There was no room in her mind now for anything else.

As it eased she tried to collect her wits. Hurry, hurry, she must hurry. How long did babies take to be born? Supposing she was all alone out here in this deserted road, what would happen to her, what

50

could she do? As soon as the contraction relaxed she raised herself on to the saddle. Hurry, that's what she had to do, get as far as she could before it happened again. Perhaps she'd get home first . . . oh no, not so soon . . . she *had* to get home. Still on the long, hedge-lined road she stopped, balanced with her foot on the raised verge, her body bent over the handlebars. She realised she must be crying, she tasted the salt of tears. Michael . . . 'Missing' would have left room for hope. 'Killed' . . . At the pain's worst it filled her world. Only as it lessened she reaslied that hers must be nothing compared with what his must have been. Then to the next stage, strength enough to turn the pedals. Houses. She was back where there were people, soon she'd be home.

'Watch out!' someone shouted. She didn't know who, she didn't know why. The pain was there again, she was on the ground, faces were peering down at her, people talking, voices that grew more distant . . .

Chapter Four

'That's a good girl, you're doing well' . . . 'Just rest a bit' . . . 'Now we're ready, now we'll try again' . . . It seemed to have no beginning and no end. Just as she'd not been able to hold off the early contractions, so they took control of her, growing all the time stronger, the periods of abatement shorter.

Hours ago a message had been telephoned home. The baby was to have been delivered in St Almo's Maternity Home. Lavinia had made herself responsible for all the expenses and Lottie had been shown around, talked to some of the nurses, and generally been given the feeling that she was to be made a welcome guest there. But like a fool she'd lost control of her bicycle and hit the kerb in Mandrake Road. She had no clear recollection of the next few moments, just an awareness that people were bending over her. 'Better get an ambulance,' one of them ordered, 'from the look of things the only place for her is hospital. Race against time with this baby if you ask me.'

And how long ago was that? She'd felt herself lifted by experienced hands, somehow a stretcher was bearing her weight. 'Where were you going, duckie?' someone called. 'What about the bike?'

'Sycamore . . . 14 Sycamore Aven – ' A mask was held to her face. Thankfully she drew in her breath. The scene receded from her. But not for long. Once in the hospital she was a pawn at the mercy of a band of nurses, no part of her was her own. Not that it mattered, she was beyond caring. In one of her clearer moments she was aware that time had marched on. Afternoon, evening . . . Michael . . . With each moment of clarity the realisation was there. Tears of weakness rolled down her cheeks, for him, for herself, for Neil so far away, for the world her baby was so loath to enter. Those lucid moments became less clear and less frequent. She no longer had any idea of time.

It was halfway through the next morning when the white-coated people who ruled her world decided to put an end to her battle.

53

'We're going to give you an injection, you won't feel anything else. That's it. Good girl. Now leave it all to us.' All! Could there be more? She heard their words, she even believed she answered.

When she opened her eyes she'd been moved to a small, sparsely furnished room. Daytime. Sun was streaming through the window. Gingerly she felt for her 'hump', her fingers touching tight binding where it had been.

'Nurse!' With all her strength she shouted.

'Mrs O'Hagon, it's all done. You have a beautiful baby. A little girl. Just perfect she is. I gave her her bath myself, she's a wee treasure.'

'Where is she?'

'I'll tell her her mum's waiting for her. Let me just give you an extra pillow first. We'll make you comfy so that you can hold her.'

'Another O'Hagon growing in there. I put it there.' The memory of Neil's words brought him so close as the nurse put the bundle into her arms then left them to get acquainted. Yet when Lottie looked down on the tiny form so new to the world all thought of Neil vanished. The blue eyes gazed up at her, unfocussed and innocent. Born of her flesh, hers to love, to guard and to guide. Part of her own body, part of her own soul. Hot tears overflowed, love and fear combined in the emotion. It was a physical thing that gripped her, arms, legs, chest, a hollow ache. This tiny person, what would life do to her? Please God, make it be good for her always, please, please . . . Mum, how can you bear it? Was it like this for you when you looked at him, your first baby? He always loved you so much . . . Oh, Mum, what can you do, how can you bear it?

She'd had a hard time. The white-coated medic diagnosed it as an early attack of post-natal depression. An injection would ensure a good night.

By morning she was sitting up in bed, a blanket bath behind her, and wearing one of her own nightdresses. From the answers to her enquiries she pieced together the picture of the person who'd brought her case. Freda.

In the afternoon visitors were allowed. She wanted just to see her mother. What she felt defied words, but she was sure that once they saw each other Kate would be as aware as she was herself of this new understanding. By now she was on the ward, her bed at the end furthest from the door. People were queuing up in the corridor waiting, then at a nod from Sister a young student nurse clipped the doors wide open to let them stream in. All around her proud young mothers were sitting erect, trying to look as glamorous as they'd seen on the movies. Still she watched the empty doorway. Reaching out to her mother in silent sympathy, Lottie expected visible signs of the trauma of these last days. Perhaps she was too broken spirited to come at all. But still Lottie watched.

It was another ten minutes before she heard a step she recognised. Kate's once blonde hair was a mousey brown now, but today, just like every other day, it had been combed with care, curling neatly around the brim of her hat. The seams of her stockings were as straight; shoes, handbag and gloves all the same tone of grey; single strand of pearls, pearl ear-rings, these things were second nature to her.

Yet, as she bent to kiss Lottie, there was a new aloofness.

'Mum – ' And suddenly Lottie didn't know what to say to break the barrier. 'Oh, Mum – '

Kate looked down the length of the ward with distaste and before she drew a chair near to the bed, pulled the dividing curtain to give them what privacy she could.

'I spoke to the Sister. She says you had a bad time, but you're doing very well. Of course, it was the fall. Everyone seems to have heard about it. You must have swerved into the kerb and been thrown from your bicycle. Freda tells me the whole road is concerned. But of course, people have known you all your life. A fall like that – well, no wonder the baby started before your body was ready. Of course you had a difficult time.' She spoke fast, not quite looking Lottie in the eye. 'Mrs Murdock spoke to Freda this morning. She says a seven month baby is sometimes stronger than an eight month.'

Lottie almost argued. But if this was the way Mum wanted it, what did it matter?

'She looks strong, Mum. Here she is! Nurse Drew's bringing her for you to hold.'

Wrapped like a papoose, arms securely anchored by the imprison-ing shawl, only the small head was visible. Kate cradled the bundle. Silence. What memories must be crowding into her mind. Lottie ached with pity. Mum always cries, tears and headaches . . . now it's as if she's made of stone.

'Mum, we'll call her Michelle.'

'No!' For the first time the armour was down. 'What are you trying to say? He's gone, so fill the gap?' She held her jaw painfully rigid, she took in great gulps of breath, but she wouldn't cry.

'You know I'm not. We can't, we wouldn't if we could.' The un-named infant was thrust into her arms where it turned its head to nuzzle against her. 'The gap's there for me too, for all of us. It's just that,' she looked helplessly at the baby, 'oh, Mum, I do know, *now* I do know, for you it's – it's – ' Her voice trailed into silence. But this time it was an easier silence. Her message had been understood.

'We'll call her Katrine, same as you.'

'Another Kate.'

Lottie's hand rested gently on the tiny, warm head. 'She'll be Katie.' Katie O'Hagon, she added, but only silently. These last few days had brought Lottie a long way.

Kate could share her grief with no one. Least of all with Rupert.

'I do think Mum's a bit hard on the old man,' Ronnie said. Home for forty-eight hours' leave, he and Lottie were gardening, the pram, covered with net to keep off cats and insects, in the shade of the orchard.

'I don't think she can help it, Ronnie. You know how easily she used to cry. Always there were tears if anything upset her. Now it's as if she's cut off from everything, happiness and hurt too.'

'Yes, I know. But, after all, it's just as rough on Dad. She was always cool with him. I say, doesn't that sound awful? It's Mum and Dad we're talking about.'

'It's true enough. And he doesn't make it any easier. He buries himself in that damned newspaper, he runs off to the ARP Post the moment he's swallowed his tea, he's as frightened as she is of showing any feelings.'

'You know what I think? I think they ought to have a great tumbler of whisky or vodka or something, anything that would knock them off balance. After all, Lot, if they can't share this with each other, then what sort of a future have they? They won't always have us about the place. One of these days it'll be just them.' And following that train of thought: 'How's Neil enjoying Italy? You get letters OK?'

'You know what the post is like. Sometimes I have to wait a couple of weeks, then I get letters every day for a while. I wouldn't say he's exactly enjoying Italy, but he's well.' She reached to touch the wooden handle of the hoe he was holding. 'I heard this morning,' she added, but didn't enlarge on it. She simply needed to hear herself speak about the letter that was upstairs on her pillow.

'. . . not often I dream, but last night it was clear. Honest to God, Charlotte, it seemed like you were flesh and blood. You and me, we were back home standing by the corral. I could even hear the sound of hooves as if the animals were treading the hard earth. It all seemed clearer and louder than real life, you know what I mean? I tried to touch you – funny things happen in dreams. Didn't seem odd that one minute we were standing next to each other and next minute I was going to move over on to you, both of us flat on the ground. There you were – honest, Lottie, just thinking about it now, how you were, now – well, reckon you know. I reached out, and you weren't there. That's what it was woke me up. Sure was in a state. Could have cried like a kid. Never wanted you so bad, Lottie. Seeing you so clear, back home, my wife . . . '

A yell from the pram put an end to the conversation, and the next day Ronnie returned to his station. He believed the medicine that Kate and Rupert wanted was something that would knock them off balance, take down the barrier that held them apart. And certainly one did. It had been Kate who'd suggested they should move into separate rooms. 'My nights are so restless,' she said. 'It's because I'm trying not to wake you. Would you mind? I'll sleep better if I don't have to concern myself for anyone else.' And years of falling in with her every whim had led Rupert into the spare room.

Whisky and vodka were unobtainable and even if the cabinet had been full, neither Kate nor Rupert would have taken that sort of medicine. Lottie stood on the sidelines, there was nothing she could do. Only Katie, with her first dawning of intelligence, had any power of healing. It was Kate who had her first smile. There were moments when Katie held the whole of her attention, left room in her mind for none of the misery.

Then, on the very day that the highchair had been brought to the table for the first time, came something that must surely knock Rupert and both her off balance. A telephone call from Barrie Miles, leader of Ronnie's squadron. He wanted to tell them himself: Ronnie's plane hadn't come back after a mission this morning. There would be an official telegram, but he wanted to speak to them, to tell them that a search was still going on. Ronnie had been reported coming down over the channel. Men were often picked up, a lost plane wasn't necessarily a lost pilot . . . 'Something to knock them off balance' – wasn't that what Ronnie said they needed?

The wall between them was strengthened, every hurtful misunderstanding of over a quarter of a century went into the building of it.

The clock on the sitting-room mantelpiece struck eleven. Only Lottie was still up, everyone else had gone to bed and turned out their lights. It was two days since that message from Barrie. Since then the telegram had come – then nothing. As if to hide from what they couldn't accept, she knew that her parents hadn't even told Lavinia. 'Missing' left hope. None of them were brave enough to go beyond.

A tap on the window pane. Whoever could that be? For one wild moment she expected Ronnie had come home. Whoever it was must know there was a baby in the house, must have wanted to make as little noise as possible. She switched off the light and opened first the curtains, then the window.

57

'Who is it? Is it you?'

But it wasn't.

'There's news. You won't get word till tomorrow, so I came straight away.'

Barrie Miles had come fifty miles on a borrowed motor cycle.

'What have you heard?'

'He's back, Lottie. He's wounded, but he's back. In a hospital in Dover.'

In the dark she heard his whispered words as he swung his legs over the window sill and came into the room.

'Tell me about him.'

Before he answered he closed the window and the curtains, then switched the light back on. Ronnie had been picked up some ten miles off Dover, unconscious, in an inflatable, with serious burns to the lower part of the body. That's all he knew, that and the fact that there was no danger to life. Ronnie would come back to them.

'Go in the kitchen, Barrie, start to make some toast or something. You must be starved. I'm going to tell Mum and Dad.' Tell Mum – then tell Dad? Or Dad – then Mum? As she went quietly up the stairs she felt they were so distant from each other as the two poles. Someone had left the bathroom door open, she knew by the ray of moonlight that shone on to the first floor landing. She must shut that before she could put the light on. Somehow in the dark she slipped, not hurting herself but making enough noise to bring Kate and Rupert into their respective doorways. Regardless of the bathroom door, Kate switched the light on.

'Mind that blackout!'; the Warden in Rupert ordered.

'He's been picked up.' Lottie got to her feet and closed the bathroom door. 'Ronnie – he's in hospital in Dover. We shall hear tomorrow. Barrie's downstairs, he's come specially so that we'd know straight away. He's got burns – on his legs, Barrie thinks – but he's going to come home again.' Her parents seemed incapable of speech, and Lottie incapable of stemming the torrent of words that tumbled out. 'Barrie's downstairs, I'm finding him something to eat before he drives all that way back. Are you coming down to see him?'

Rupert moved towards the stairs, then looked at Kate. All these weeks she'd encased herself in ice. Now it had melted. She was drowning in it, trembling as if with ague. Clinging to the doorpost, she buried her head against her arm. The tears must have been waiting for just such a moment. In her relief she sobbed. With his arm around her, Rupert steered her into her room, their room until a few weeks ago. Tonight she leant limply against him. She didn't share, neither did she fight.

58

A howl from Lottie's room told her they'd woken Katie.

Five minutes later it was a domestic scene in the kitchen. The highchair had been brought from the dining room and Katie lowered into it, beaming her delight at this sudden turn in events. She was given a crust of toast to chew, a new taste and one she approved. The cupboard could produce nothing festive enough for the occasion: a tin of baked beans on butterless toast was the best Lottie could do, but for them both this was a feast of thanksgiving. And then, as she washed the dishes and he dried them, she suggested he might stay the night. She had no qualms about offering Ronnie's room where Kate always kept the bed ready in case he came on unexpected leave. This time yesterday she couldn't have done it, it would have been tempting fate. But tonight the fear was gone. Gratefully, Barrie accepted.

Ronnie's road to recovery was slow. Whether he'd fly again no one would predict. He was transferred to a hospital in Sussex where he stayed for months. The burns to both legs had been extensive. 'Reckon Jerry tried to cook me,' he said with a studied cheerfulness that he was far from feeling.

It was just before the close of the year, as 1943 gave way to 1944 and the expression "Second Front" was on everyone's lips with no one knowing where or when – or even if – it would come, that Barrie was grounded from operational duties. He was made a flying instructor at a training station only a few miles from Brimley. He fell naturally into the habit of spending much of his off duty time with the Bradleys. Or was it the O'Hagons? Either way, Kate decided it was time she had a few days with her mother. She liked to imagine that with her away, Lottie and Barrie would have plenty of opportunity of slotting into a comfortable domestic scene.

Telling Lavinia about Barrie's proximity to Brimley, Kate smiled a secret smile of satisfaction.

'It'll make it easier for Ronnie when he comes home to have a friend nearby,' Lavinia agreed, but she wasn't blind and there was no one who knew Kate as well as she did.

'He comes to us even without Ronnie being home. You did like him, didn't you, Mother?'

'I usually like the children's friends, why should I not like him?'

Kate moved nearer to the great fireplace where the log blazed. Did Mother know just how lucky she was living here at Bullington? At home they were allowed just a few sacks of coal. Freda tried to eke out the fuel by burning rubbish – and what a nasty smell it made sometimes! Here, there was never a shortage of wood, their own wood, taken from their own trees.

'Of course you like him, we all do, and welcome him to the house. But, Mother, it's not us he comes to see. It's Lottie.' Lavinia gave her a searching look but said nothing, so Kate plunged on. 'She gets on so well with him, she has done right from when Ronnie first brought him home. And as for him . . . truly, he's quite smitten, I can see it. Just think, wouldn't it be wonderful! Little Katie loves him too, and he's as natural as can be with her. Rides her on his shoulders as if she were his own. When it's all over, what better – '

'Kate, I don't know whatever can have got into you. You're forgetting: Lottie has a husband, Katie has a father.'

'Forgetting! As if I can ever forget for a single minute. Don't ask me how I know, just believe me. It's over for them. That man she married won't come back.'

Anyone other than Lavinia might have felt the chill hand of Fate at Kate's words. She was made of sterner stuff. There was something about Kate's manner, the shifty expression, that wasn't right, wasn't normal. Leaning forward, she reached out her hand. For a moment it put her in mind of her riding days, times when she'd had to soothe a frightened mount.

'You can tell me, Kate. Never mind Neil and Lottie, there's something else. What is it, my dear? Surely you can trust me? Is it to do with Rupert?'

'Rupert? What could be to do with him?' The idea of Rupert having any influence on what troubled her was new to Kate. Just as if the years had rolled away she was home, her family ready to listen and protect. What a relief it was to talk about it. 'It was my punishment, that's why I lost Michael.'

'No, child, don't ever say that. Remember I've been through it, I know what you suffer.'

'You don't. You can't. What guilt could you have had? Night after night I prayed, let something happen to that wretched man, anything to get Lottie out of the dreadful entanglement. Men get killed, that's what I said, men who matter, good men with families dependent on them. So let it be him. And you see what happened? Men get killed, let him be one of them. You don't get anything without paying, even God makes you pay. So I've paid. It's a sign, a promise, that He'll give what I asked.' Her eyes were wide. This was how you must feel when you'd been to the Confessional, cleansed, absolved.

'You say losing Michael was your punishment? No, Kate my dear. If there's any punishment it's something between you and your conscience. It's not for us to decide who lives and who doesn't. And what sort of a God do you think we have, one who sits up there on high waiting for us to give our orders or draw up bargains? You have grief for losing Michael, but never guilt.' Kate didn't answer. In silence they sat for a minute then Lavinia asked: 'Lottie never hints that she has any regrets?'

'Lottie's not likely to tell *me* how she feels. But I keep my eyes open and to see the three of them together, Lottie, Barrie and my darling little Katie, it breaks my heart to think of what she has before her if that man comes back.'

It would have gladdened her heart if she could have looked back to Sycamore Avenue that same afternoon. Barrie had arrived an hour or so before. While Kate and her mother were sipping tea by the side of the roaring fire at the Manor, he was on all fours crawling around the sitting room with Katie astride his back. Her blue eyes sparkling with excitement, she laughed until she had hiccoughs.

Over those months it was so easy for Lottie to let herself slip deeper into the friendship Barrie offered. Winter days indoors, then, when spring came, outings with him carrying Katie carried high on his shoulders. Nothing could ever fill the gap Michael's going had left; Ronnie was only gradually moving towards the time he would be fit enough to come home. Her thoughts were on a future that had no clear shape, its only reality those letters she watched for each morning; from whether or not she saw the spidery slant of Neil's writing her day took its colour. But Barrie was always her support. He was somewhere between the brothers who'd been part of yester-day and the man who was her tomorrow.

Even when the time came for Ronnie to leave hospital, home for a long recovery period before returning to duty (whatever duty he was finally decided fit for), nothing changed between Lottie and Barrie. Their relationship had gone far beyond his being her brother's friend. And if she hadn't known it already, the way Katie would rush to him would have told her.

And what of him? Based at the RAF station, did he come so often because he liked to be part of a civilian household? Did he see them as his family, no more than that? Lottie wanted to believe that was the truth, that those occasions when she'd chanced to glance at him unexpectedly she imagined the way he was watching her. He was good company, a cheerful companion; never by a single word did he hint that he wanted more from her than the easy friendship they shared. And if her conscience told her she wasn't being fair, an hour in his cheerful presence overcame her doubts.

Kate watched and said nothing. She began to let herself weave dreams that Lottie would change her mind about going to Canada. After all, she'd fallen in 'so-called love' before and let that dreadful, coarse Neil O'Hagon take what he wanted from her. What was to say

61

she wouldn't do it again with Barrie? Of course there would be gossip, but what was gossip compared with keeping Lottie and Katie at home? And Barrie was so suitable, just the sort of man she would have chosen for Lottie.

Summer and the Second Front at last. For weeks there was no news of Neil, then letters started coming through. His Division had been moved, he was in France. By this time Ronnie was in Lincolnshire, transferred to a ground branch; and by this time, too, Katie was walking, shadowing Kate wherever she went. Life must have been like this for so many people in so many homes up and down the country, everyone playing a waiting game, filling the days with trivia because the things that mattered were out of reach. Lottie, pushing Katie into town, would see a queue for tobacco. It would be the highlight of the morning to acquire half an ounce of her father's favourite kind; making sure Katie was kept quiet while the news was read on the wireless; ITMA, the nation's favourite programme, sets switched on and families gathered ready to laugh, for laughter was as necessary as food.

'You know, Lottie, I'm quite happy to put Katie to bed if ever you want to go out. All your old friends can't have left Brimley.' Purposely Kate suggested it when Barrie was there.

He threw an appreciative look in her direction before he suggested to Lottie: 'That sounds a good idea. You've got a friend here at any rate. If your mother doesn't mind, what about a ride down to The Crown? We could try our luck to see if they have anything we can drink, eh? Or we could go to the pictures. I could borrow Ronnie's bike, couldn't I?'

Later, when Rupert came back from the ARP Centre, he found an unusually good-humoured wife waiting for him. She'd never told him what she hoped, but that hadn't stopped him watching and working things out for himself. That was something their marriage had accustomed him to.

'We don't have to worry about Lottie if she's with Barrie, there's no need for us to wait up for them.' He sensed it would please her to hear him pair them off like that. Since the night they'd heard Ronnie had been rescued, he'd been back in his half of the marital bed. Tonight she'd looked really pleased to see him when he'd come in, been excited to tell him the youngsters were out. Even now she seemed agreeable. He'd undress in the bathroom. He knew his Kate hated them peeling their clothes off in front of each other. "Men should have dressing rooms," she'd told him often enough. When he got back into the bedroom she was sitting up reading. How pretty she was. He wasn't good enough for her, never had been. But she was his wife. Gentle, delicate Kate. Tonight her brow was smooth as a girl's, no sign of a headache. He may have been allowed back to share the bed, but never had she been as warm towards him as this; as for him, there was no hiding his eagerness.

'I'll put the light out, shall I?' He ignored her book.

'Yes, if you like. But, Rupert, open the door wide before you get into bed. I want to make sure I can listen for Katie.' And a minute or two later, her voice no more than a whisper: 'No, you shouldn't – not with the door open. Suppose Freda hears.' Then, as an afterthought: 'You don't mind do you?'

Yes, he did mind. He minded her cool, casual tone. In the dark he could say what he never would in daylight.

'I'm not some tradesman at the front door. "Not today, thank you. Perhaps if you call another time?" All right, you want to listen for the child. I'm only your husband.'

She pondered his words. 'I'm sorry if you're upset. If you really want to, then you'll have to push the door across first. Leave it just ajar – '

'Never mind. Let's get to sleep.' Rupert's moment had passed.

He was soon to learn that what put that sweet smile on Kate's face had nothing to do with him. It had to do with the evenings Lottie spent with Barrie, evenings when she was left in charge of her darling Katie.

Then early in the spring of 1945, Kate's dreams were shattered. The war wasn't over, but the end was in sight. Somewhere on the horizon was the first glow of a new dawn – and translated into more practical terms, even the blackout was a thing of the past.

It was the end of March, two days before Katie's second birthday. Hearing the click of the letter box Lottie went eagerly to pick up the post.

'Just one. For me. It looks official. I wonder what it is?'

Katie objected to her breakfast being disturbed. Rocking backwards and forwards in her highchair, she clamoured: 'Mamam, more, more,' orchestrating her demands by drumming her newly shod feet against the edge of the table.

'Shall Gran give you your breaky? Come on, sweetheart, open wide for Granny.' And as Kate spooned porridge into the rosebud mouth, there was no way she could prevent that wild surge of excitement. An official letter! She didn't find the courage to put into words even to herself exactly what it was she hoped, but surely she was entitled to something.

She wasn't the only one without the courage to let herself imagine what the envelope contained. Lottie's fingers were stiff as she haggled at the envelope and took out the single sheet of paper. Then the first fear melted, was overtaken by an emotion that must have been buried deep inside her waiting for a moment like this to swamp her. She saw it all with unbearable clarity: home, all this; the shaft of morning sunlight that fell across the breakfast table, brightened the pattern on the wallpaper, and highlighted the colour of the fireside rug; the portrait that hung over the fireplace looking grand and out of place in the little dining room, yet to all of them part of home, proof of just how lovely Kate had been at eighteen years old; Mum and Dad so often not quite meeting each other's eyes. How could she bear to leave it all? For two and a half years this letter must have been what she'd waited for; for half her life it had been her goal. But in those first seconds none of that mattered, she couldn't think beyond all that she was leaving.

'Well?' Kate prompted.

'It's about Katie and me going. You can read it.'

'What nonsense. Why, the war isn't even over yet!'

Lottie shook her head.

'The 18th of April. Not quite three weeks. Oh, Mum . . . '

Her future had no shape. With something like panic she looked at her parents. Rupert said nothing, but she couldn't bear to watch him. Kate pushed the letter away without even glancing at it.

'It's nonsense, I tell you. You can't go out there to those dreadful people, take this precious little soul to strangers! You don't know them' – she hated even saying the name – 'Neil wont be out of the Army.. The war isn't over. Perhaps he'll not get home at all. Rupert, don't just sit there, can't you say something? Can't you do something to make her see sense?'

'Mum, that's a wicked thing to say – about Neil and the war! And it can't be long before Hitler gives in, look where the troops are. Mrs O'Hagon is looking forward to having us there.'

Kate had taken Katie from the highchair. She was holding her in her arms, rubbing her face against the fair curls, not attempting to check her silent tears.

'And you?' Rupert had found his voice. 'You, Lottie? One hardly gets the impression you're overjoyed?'

'Of course I am. Well, I am – but not to leave here, not to leave you and Mum – and Ronnie and Grandma –'

'And what about Barrie?' Kate gulped. 'You must see how he feels about you just as clearly as we do. You could be so happy with Barrie, he would make a lovely father for my little treasure.'

'She has a father already. Oh, Mum, don't make it harder.'

'That's it! Isn't it always the same. Everything's always *my* fault. First Michael, now you – and my little angel here. Other women have grandchildren,' she wept, 'I've got nothing. Nothing.'

So often her self-pity had angered Lottie, but not today. Today she could easily have wept with her. Instead Katie took up the chorus, insecure with her grandmother's tears falling on her. Soon the old antagonism would be there, the scathing remarks about the O'Hagons, the slur on her family that she could have married Neil at all. But as she looked up from reading her orders she saw just the hurt in their eyes. However unjust they'd been she knew it was because they loved her, because they were frightened to face her going away from them. It had happened to her before, as she stood on the brink of marriage, this feeling of being part of a family, of belonging with the people she'd loved all her days. Neil didn't even enter into the pain that tore her.

Strangely it was when she was with Barrie that she breathed life into the image of Neil. Of them all, Barrie was the one who understood. She didn't ask herself why she was so sure, for if he were honestly no more than a carefree and heartfree companion, how could he comprehend the sort of love that was to tear her away from them all?

'Once the fighting ends, I expect they'll soon send the Canadians home. It won't be long, will it, Barrie? Do you honestly think it's nearly over?' They were walking together, not going anywhere in particular but keeping out of the way so that Kate could have the bedtime hour with Katie alone.

'I believe it will be. And the powers that be must believe it, or they wouldn't send a boatload of brides ahead of their husbands.'

She chuckled. 'You make it sound like a cargo of cattle.'

But he didn't laugh. 'Lottie, you're happy? Tell me the honest truth. Now that it's come, is it what you want?'

'I hate the leaving part of it. I think I'm frightened of it – not frightened of being there but of saying goodbye here. I want to be there with Neil, I want all the things we planned. Mum and Dad are wrong when they say I made a mistake. I didn't. Truly, Barrie, I didn't.'

He nodded, he even grinned at her. In his Air Force blue, his cap battered and worn, the outward sign of a flying veteran, he was a dashing man. He seemed to her to embody everything she was leaving, with all the traits of a good-natured Englishman.

'Promise me one thing, Lottie? No strings, no ties.'

'If it's something I can.' For a second she was frightened of what he would ask of her. 'Promise you what?'

'If you find things don't work out – '

'But of course they will!'

'Yes, of course they will. But humour me. If ever they don't, no matter how you feel about sending to anyone else, promise you'll tell me. I shouldn't say this to you. If you weren't just about to clear off, I wouldn't say it. But fool that I am, I've fallen in love with a married woman. One who is crazy about her husband.'

Hadn't she known it? Hadn't she tried all along to believe it wasn't true? She laid her hand on his arm. She didn't pretend not to understand what he was telling her.

'You haven't promised me. Do that for me,' he prompted.

'I promise. But, Barrie, it's because you've spent all your spare time with us. Having you has meant so much to me, I've been selfish. I never thought – I'm sorry.'

'Oh no, never be sorry. You've given me so much pleasure, you and Katie.'

When he pulled her gently into his arms she didn't resist. He kissed her forehead, he moved his chin against her hair. Then he let her go. That night he didn't come back into the house. And the next day he telephoned to say he wouldn't be able to get away. She, her mother and Katie were going to the Manor for two days, and after that she had so little time left he thought it would be better if he didn't come to Brimley. But he promised her that when she'd gone, especially until Ronnie got home, he would keep an eye on things for her, see her parents were behaving themselves and looking cheerful. Dear Barrie. So many times that had been her thought.

On the 18th of April a taxi took them to Victoria. Lottie's luggage had already been collected by the railway wagon, all she had with her now was one suitcase and Katie. On Victoria Station she saw other groups like themselves. Was it like this for all of them? Everyone determinedly cheerful, no one daring to look the truth in the face and recognise that today was goodbye to everything that was familiar.

Identities were checked. She was told which compartment she had to go to. This was it, this was the moment. She hardly dared look at her parents.

'You mustn't worry, Mum. I'll be fine. And I'll write ever so often, I promise. When the war's over and things settle, perhaps you'll come and visit.' Oh, but what a silly thing to say! As if they would. To Kilton Down, to Molly O'Hagon. 'And I'll come back and see you.'

'Take care. Lottie, if you don't like it – come home.' That was the nearest Kate could come to saying goodbye.

'This is your compartment. Better get in.' Rupert opened the door for her. Then he took both Lottie and Katie into an embrace that held all the emotion he couldn't express. Not knowing what was going on, Katie was frightened and as he released them she whimpered: 'G'an. Me up, G'an,' holding her arms towards Kate.

They were in the train, the doors were slammed, the shrill whistle pierced the air, the guard waved a green flag.

'G'an . . .' One last call. They were moving. From every compartment heads were hanging out of open windows, handkerchiefs being waved, faces pressed to closed windows.

The train snaked slowly out of the station.

Chapter Five

For days the great railway train carried her westward. In the beginning the constant rhythm as the wheels covered the track was an
important background orchestration to the changing scene, for to
start with there was plenty to take the attention of these young
women fresh from war-torn England. Montreal; Ottawa; on through
Ontario. Places Lottie had read about and dreamed about. Soon she
became so used to the sound of the wheels that she hardly heard it at
all. But the plaintive wail of the whistle echoing through the night,
that was surely something that would stay with her for ever. In it was
the heartbreak of farewell, the nostalgia for yesterday, even the fears
of a tomorrow that daylight wouldn't let her acknowledge.

Was it the same for all of them? Were they all lying awake just as
she was? By morning they'd wear the cloak of confidence, and the
smile on *her* face would be as bright as any. It was only now, hurtling
through the alien darkness, that she had nowhere to hide from her
doubts. But that wasn't fair. Of course she had no doubts. Soon Neil
would be home, soon they'd be at the beginning of their proper life
together.

And now, in the loneliness of night, how many hours behind her
would they be at home? What would Mum and Dad be doing at this
very moment? What would the time be in Brimley? Seven? Eight?
Evening . . . She imagined Kate sitting with her knitting, listening to
the wireless: ITMA, Bandwagon, programmes that almost every
household had woven into its existence through the years of blackout. And Dad, would he be with her? Since there'd been no need for
him to go to the ARP Centre he'd mostly stayed late in the office . . .
perhaps Barrie would be there, "Keeping an eye on things, seeing
they were cheerful".

Katie stirred in her sleep, flung her arms wide and muttered, half
waking. Drawing her close, Lottie felt the sweet warmth of her. That

love that flooded through her was no passive thing. Cradling Katie to her, her arms ached with tenderness. This tiny person put all her trust in her. Here in a world full of strangers, she was Lottie's to protect, to guard. In her sleep the little girl laughed. What dreams were chasing through her mind? Already at two years old she had a consciousness that Lottie couldn't share. And what was that she said as she chuckled? 'G'an' . . . that's what it sounded like.

Oh, Katie, I've taken you away from them, Lottie whispered silently. You'll never really understand how much they love you. Soon you won't even remember them, they'll be just names to you. I'll make it up to you, I'll take care of you . . . but them? Please God, please don't let them be empty without her. Strangely it wasn't whether or not Kate and Rupert were miserable without *her*, their own daughter, that saddened her so.

Thunder Bay . . . Winnipeg . . . Regina . . . shouts of 'Goodbye, good luck' as they shed their fellow passengers, each with her best foot forward to step into her new life. Saskatoon . . . The very vastness of the prairie removed Lottie from England far more than the thousands of miles she'd already travelled. She'd seen nothing like it. Neil had told her; Eva had told her; but words couldn't convey the flat terrain, a land that seemed to stretch to the horizon and beyond. Yet, seeing it through the train window, she was held apart from it; it was a view, a strange land, like a picture from the page of a geography book. Then, at first imperceptibly, but soon with certainty, the landscape changed. Alberta! She was in Alberta! All her dreams were focussed on these last hours of her journey. Now even the long hoot of the whistle had lost its melancholy, it held a new excitement.

'Look, Katie,' she whispered into the tumbled, fair curls, 'this is where we're going. Oh, look, far away you can see the first hint that we're coming to the mountains.' This time she spoke aloud. Throughout the long car the spirit of anticipation stirred. Some of them had to journey on, through the Rockies, as far as Vancouver. But for Lottie this was almost the end of the track.

By the time she climbed down the steps on to the platform and heard the cries of 'Goodbye, good luck' following her, fears and doubts had given way to a new confidence.

'Lottie!'

At the sound of that voice she forgot she was supposed to be scanning the crowd hoping to recognise whoever had come from Kilton Down to meet them. She was wrapped in Eva's bearlike hug. The years melted away. This was the moment she'd put her pennies into her Canada box for, had dreamed of for so long. Only Katie disapproved of being squashed between them and didn't hide the fact.

'We're over here. We're all together.' Then, lowering her voice: 'Lottie, they're good people.'

Her words ought to have warned Lottie not to be put off by what she saw. Instead she took it to mean that she'd feel at home with them. Eva steered her towards the couple waiting at the back of the platform.

It's a mistake to build pictures of people in one's mind, but it's a trap everyone falls into. From Molly O'Hagon's childish letters Lottie had imagined her to be round and rosy, her face creased in an every-ready smile; she'd pictured her plump form encased in a dazzling white overall. Surely this wasn't the mother-in-law who'd embroidered cushion covers and sent them to her, who'd knitted matinée coats for Katie? Molly towered above all the women and most of the men; in height she must almost have touched six foot. Wearing khaki drill trousers – trousers made for a man, and one whose girth matched his stature – and heavy lace-up boots, from the waist downwards she might have been one of the farm hands. But today was no ordinary day. Molly very seldom travelled the hundred or so miles to the city and that alone would have made it special; more than that, though, today she was meeting Neil's wife, making the acquaintance of her grand-daughter. So she'd honoured the occasion as she thought fitting by donning her best blouse of pink satin festooned with various coloured flowers of some unrecognisable variety. Her hair was pinned tightly into its accustomed bun and her head topped with a wide-brimmed straw hat designed to give shelter from the sudden early summer sun but with no eye to appearance. What a moment for images of her own family to crowd Lottie's mind – her mother, her grandmother, Aunt Hester!

'This is Mrs O'Hagon,' Eva told her, 'and Craig, Neil's cousin.'

'Howdy.' It was the man who greeted her. Craig, the cousin Neil had always spoken so highly of. Again Lottie realised how wrong she'd been to build pictures in her mind, for she'd expected the cousin to be an older variation of Neil while this man bore no resemblance to him. Shorter than Molly by three or four inches, he was thick-set and gave an impression of solid durability. She felt that nothing would fluster him. Today they must have left home early, perhaps that's why he hadn't shaved. Yet could that stubble have grown in just those few hours?

'Hello,' she answered, holding out her hand. He seemed not to notice.

'I'll go rustle up your luggage.'

71

So she turned to Molly and this time her fingers were crushed in the firm grasp of the large, work-roughened hand.

'Guess we were lucky being noticed by Eva here. Don't know if we'd have picked you out as Neil's choice of a wife, else. From your letters I had in mind someone bigger.' She looked Lottie up and down and added: 'Ah, well.' It seemed she had to make the best of a poor deal.

In her left hand she still carried a placard bearing the single word: 'O'Hagon'.

'This is how I came to talk to them.' Eva indicated the sign.

'That was a clever idea.' Lottie smiled at her mother-in-law.

'We O'Hagons may not be a handsome lot, but we're not short on intelligence. How else would you have recognised us – or us you? Here now, that child's heavy, let me take her. First girl child Kilton Down will have known. Takes a real man to sire a girl child, that's what folk say. Let's have a look at you then, see if you have anything of young Neil in you.'

Katie didn't think much of the idea of being handed out to this burly stranger and opened her mouth wide to proclaim her feelings.

'She's tired, everything's strange to her.' Lottie held her arms to take her back.

But Molly didn't give up easily. In a minute Katie stopped shouting and, thumb in mouth, surveyed her captor.

'Take a good look honey. Ol' Molly, she ain't so bad now, is she?'

While this exchange went on between grandmother and grand-daughter, Lottie and Eva shared a silent glance. 'They're good people' Eva had whispered, and now Lottie hung on to those words. Of course they were good people, they were Neil's people.

'We got a drive ahead of us, but before we set out Eva here is taking us for a meal. Guess you want a chance to talk to your aunt, and we all need feeding. Can't do a drive like that without good food inside us.'

How Kate would have cringed with shame could she have seen the party being led to the table at Eva's habitual eating house. Eva, striking, smart, self-assured; Lottie wearing the best she had so that she'd make a good first impression; Katie as pretty and adorable as any two year old; Molly . . . dressed as she was she'd have been out of place anywhere; Craig looking as though he'd be more at home in some western saloon. A giggle threatened Lottie as they took their places and a highchair was brought for Katie. Yet there was no humour in the rising laughter. Indeed she was ashamed that she could be embarrassed by Neil's family.

Lottie left the ordering to the others. The very word 'steak' had become no more than a memory at home. As for 'steak and lobster', she felt she was stepping into a new world of luxury.

Gosh, imagine Mum and Dad with a meal like this in front of them! The thought sprung into her head at the sight of the plate: the eight ounce steak, the lobster, the jacket potato filled with crunchy, crumbled bacon and seasoning. The side salad was crisp and fresh; the drinking water ice-cold. She couldn't remember ever having seen such a meal, and wanted to enjoy every mouthful, yet how could she forget the Sunday joint that would fit onto a saucer, how could she not think of the millions of homeless people in Europe who were actually hungry?

'Something we don't often get to eat – lobster. I'll make do with a twelve ounce steak to go with it,' Molly said as she passed the menu to Craig.

'Bring me a sixteen ounce steak, rare as you can make it. I'll skip the lobster.'

If Lottie needed evidence that she was in the New World it must surely have been the sight of the O'Hagons' plates! Yet they neither of them attacked their meal with greed, nor were they troubled by thoughts that to much of the world this would be a feast. It was simply that ekeing out food was something beyond their experience. Eva couldn't really understand either, yet she came nearer to it. Perhaps memories of that other war prompted her.

'If Kate and Rupert could take a peek at you, honey, they'd be thrilled to see you get your teeth into it. So eat up. You've got a long drive ahead of you.'

Mealtimes were never given over to conversation at Kilton Down. They were occasions to stoke up for the hours ahead, like putting gas into the truck at the filling station. So now, as Lottie and Eva talked, Molly and Craig concentrated on the job on hand, chewing their way silently through every morsel, finishing by mopping up the meat juices with their bread. Then, their tanks re-fuelled, they were ready for the journey and within an hour the truck was heading out of the city, Craig at the wheel, Molly and Lottie by his side, and Katie soon giving up the battle and sleeping on her mother's knee.

'Kilton Down's given over to beef cattle, not like the land out there.' Calgary was far behind them when, with a nod of her straw-hatted head, Molly indicated the distant flat horizon. The edge of the prairie.

'Yes, Neil told me,' Lottie answered. 'So much sky . . . '

Neither of her newly met relatives attempted to answer her. Sitting between them on the bench type seat of the truck, she felt them exchange what Freda would call 'a look'. In all directions the horizon was far away. Overhead the blue sky told of approaching dusk, the darker hue in the east, the gold in the west. Soon it would be evening.

73

Soon she would be in Kilton Down.

It was morning when Lottie had her first real view of Kilton Down, for it had been dark by the time they'd arrived. Now, in the early light, she climbed out of bed and moved quietly to the window, not wanting to wake Katie and perhaps disturb the household. But she needn't have worried. Already Craig's wife, Eugene, was outside in what they called 'the yard' pegging out a line of washing. Lottie looked at her watch. A quarter past six! Then Molly appeared from behind the house, carrying a large empty pail which she put down with a clatter. No creeping about there!

For a moment Lottie was undecided. By now Eugene had come indoors. The sound of drawers being opened and closed, a cupboard door slamming, pinpointed her as being in the kitchen. Along the wooden passage outside the bedroom, Lottie heard the rush of small feet. That must be the boys, Earl who was just three, and Mickey, a hefty twenty month old. They'd been in bed last night. This morning Katie and her cousins would get acquainted for the first time.

As quietly as she could Lottie opened one of her cases and took out her jodhpurs, then thought better of it, laid them carefully over the end of the bed and rummaged through the neatly folded garments until she found her old corduroy slacks. She'd take her things and dress in the bathroom, leave Katie sleeping. Small chance of that! At that moment the pounding of those small feet again, whoops of excitement as the boys romped in the passage.

'Mum . . .' Katie's blue eyes were wide open. She turned on to her knees and started to climb out of bed.

'Go on then, go and say hello to your cousins. Hold on a second, let's take that nappy off. Can't let the boys see you in a nappy, can we?'

Then, that done, Katie was off.

'Dere's boys!' Eyes like organ stops she looked back at Lottie, making sure she was aware of this wonderful discovery.

From the bedroom doorway Lottie watched them. Three children, suddenly silent, each surveying the other two. It was Mickey who made the first move. He staggered back to the room he shared with Earl and returned astride a small horse on wheels.

'Me . . . me on hossey.' Katie beamed. Always if Katie asked for something with that smile, it was given to her. When Mickey ignored the request she was puzzled. As far as her baby mind could reason, she supposed he'd not understood. 'Off.' She gave him a gentle shove. 'Tatie on hossey.'

But Mickey thought otherwise. He rushed along the passage, looking back over his shoulder with a triumphant grin. It was because

74

he wasn't looking where he was going that he crashed into his mother as she came to collect them for breakfast.

'Me hossey.' Instinct told Katie her best approach was through a grown-up.

'Sure, Mickey'll let you ride on his horse, won't you, Mick? Off you get, let Katie have a go.' She backed her words by lifting him off and giving him the handle to push it back to Katie.

'S'mine!' His face was red with determination. Who was this stranger to come here demanding his things?

'Sure it's yours. Just let Katie have a ride.'

He knew he was beaten. With a face like thunder he pushed the horse up the corridor, and when he got almost to Katie he lunged forward then let go of it so that it knocked her off her feet.

For a second there was silence, then the air was rent with her screams as she tumbled and his screams as the flat of his mother's hand came smartly across his fat little backside. But Eugene took children in her stride. Mickey chastised, she lifted Katie on to the saddle of the horse, totally ignoring the noise they were both making.

'Shouldn't hang around in your nightgown,' she advised Lottie, nodding her head in the direction of a half open door at the end of the passage. Only the movement of a shadow told them anyone was there. 'Donald.' Silently she mouthed the one word. Then went on: 'Don't worry about Katie, she and the boys'll soon find their own measure. If they fight a bit, they'll get over it. Kids understand each other.'

There was something reassuring about Eugene, Lottie thought as she bolted the bathroom door behind her. From the look of her, her third child couldn't be more than a month or two away. Bearing and rearing children seemed to be what she was here for. As Lottie dressed, her mind dwelt on what she knew of the older woman. Neil had said that she came from a neighbouring ranch known as Upper Reach, the eldest daughter of Carey Clayton. When her mother had died at the birth of the Claytons' ninth child, Eugene had been eighteen years old. Looking at her today, Lottie could understand just how it was that she'd stayed single to care for the others. Had Craig wanted her and waited for her all those years, or had familiarity finally steered them towards marriage? She'd been in her mid-thirties when she'd come to Kilton Down, but it seemed she was intent on making up for lost time. Soon she'd have her third child, making three in five years. In appearance she was a plain woman, her complexion pastey, her eyes set too close together in her broad face. Yet she exuded a feeling of safety and stability. Lottie was aware of it. The children must have been too. A smack had been administered on

Mickey's bottom, it had been accepted with no hard feeling; even Katie, who Lottie realised now had been all too used to getting her own way with no one to compete with, fell in with the idea of taking turns. Her ear to the bathroom door Lottie smiled at the childish babbling that was going on now in the passage. Peace had been restored, the young stranger still in her nightdress had been accepted by the boys, and Eugene had returned to the kitchen and the clattering of pots and pans prior to feeding her brood.

Lottie's optimistic nature took it as a sign that boded well for the start of her first day. She'd write a long letter home, she'd tell them Neil's mother and Craig had met her, she'd tell them about how happy Katie was going to be with the boys, she's reassure them that she'd been welcomed. Only behind all those thoughts were others she wouldn't let herself acknowledge: she'd add no clear descriptions of her in-laws; she wouldn't paint a word picture of the domestic scene.

'You were out in the yard early, Mrs O'Hagon,' was her smiling greeting to Molly. 'I was creeping about not wanting to disturb anyone, then I looked out of my window and you and Eugene were both in the yard already.'

'Got better things to do than lie abed. Indoors women, that's what I've heard young Neil call us. Plenty of work to be done outside though, even for women.'

'That's it,' Old Pop croaked, spitting into the log fire that heated the bread oven. 'Foreigners ain't gonna be any good around these parts. With their fancy gear and red lips. Young Neil'd been better to stay home, done a man's job. Marching off and fancying himself a hero, picking up with dames from foreign parts.' Another direct hit to sizzle on the burning log underlined his sentiment.

'Now then, Pop,' Molly winked at Lottie, 'you can't pretend you won't appreciate having a pretty young girl come waiting on you.'

'Pretty is as pretty does,' mumbled the old man.

Lottie's spontaneous but silent rejoinder was that, in that case, there was nothing pretty about *him* with his carping and unfair criticism of people he didn't know. And there was certainly nothing pretty about his unshaven and unkempt appearance nor yet his filthy habits. Ignoring him, she turned to Molly.

'Anyway, Mrs O'Hagon, there must be jobs I can take on? Things I can do to help.'

'Perhaps, like I say, you can give Old Pop some company. He's not such a misery as he makes himself out to be. Now, ain't that so, Pop?'

'S'pose you think 'cos you got me stuck in this danged chair thing I got to put up with anything you women want. This is what happens, young woman, when you live longer than your usefulness.'

'Nonsense,' Lottie sparked, 'there are more ways of being useful than doing a day's work.'

He hadn't expected her answer and he looked at her more closely. Then he sniffed and turned his shoulder on the pair of them, making much of hand-rolling a cigarette and tearing off the end before he lit it.

'How often does the post get delivered, Mrs O'Hagon?'

'Either Mom or Molly, which you like. The mail, you say? On a Monday. Not right to Kilton Down. If we've got mail to send we have to take it to Radley. We drove through it on the way home last night, about seven miles back. I pointed out the school house to you, remember? The mail comes in round about noon on a Monday and the outgoing gets taken.'

'Just once a week?' She couldn't believe it.

'Just once a week?' Old Pop mimicked. 'Perhaps we ought to tell the mail man we have a red lips English dame here, used to better ways. Perhaps he'd ride out and put her letters through the door – '

'That's a job I could do.' To his disappointment, Lottie ignored him. 'I could ride in to Radley on Monday's if you've a horse I could take.'

'Sure we have. You're used to horses?'

'Trit-trot, trit-trot,' the old man chuckled to himself. 'You want to have a word with Donald, he'll sort you out for a horse to ride.' He threw Lottie a mischievous glance, and this time when he spat into the flames she knew he did it purposely, hoping to offend her.

Oddly enough, it didn't. In that teasing look she recognised a sense of fun that his grizzling tones belied. He was a dirty and hostile old man, yet those brown eyes of hers told him as plainly as any words that she understood his game and was prepared to play.

Molly was busy cutting a great slab of beef into strips. Waiting for her attention was a pile of vegetables to be prepared and follow the meat into the huge iron pot.

'I'll do those, shall I?' Lottie picked up a knife.

'No, better you don't.' Molly's big hand was held up to ward her off. 'We all have our jobs, we know just what we have to do. You can keep an eye on Katie, or take a walk and have a look around the place. Didn't you say you had letters to write? Things here will be different from the way you've had them back there in England. Reckon if you want to turn into being a good wife to young Neil, the best thing you can do is watch Eugene and me and learn. Back home, do you help your Mom? Neil told me in a letter you had a servant in the house.'

'Freda. She does most of the cooking, but of course Mum can cook . . .' And Grandma? She thought of Bullington Manor, the respect

77

the staff had for Lavinia and she for them, the gracious way of living . . . so far away . . . gone like a dream. 'I'll go and write my letters. I'll do them in my bedroom. Or perhaps I'd better sit in the yard where I can watch the children.'

'They ain't gonna come to harm. Kids learn better to look after themselves if we give them freedom to do it in. If there's trouble, I'll hear them hollering. Anyway, Eugene's outside cleaning out the pigs. You go write your letters, tell your Mom and Pa you got here, Give them my respects and tell them when the war's through, there's a welcome for them if they care to come visiting.'

A snort from Old Pop might have meant anything.

Alone in her room she pulled the wooden chair to the dressing table, then dug into her half emptied trunk to find her writing paper.

In those first few days it would have been so easy to give way to homesickness. From this distance life in Sycamore Avenue was seen from a new angle. Her old feelings of frustration and resentment were forgotten, buried somewhere beneath the warm knowledge of care and protection; the atmosphere of aloofness that Kate held between herself and Rupert had no place in her memories. Looking back from the isolation of Kilton Down Lottie imagined the home her parents made as serene, unchanging. Taking her place at the rough wooden meal table here, how could she help in her mind's eye seeing the dining room at home, the bone china, the silver cutlery? It had all come from Grandma Matheson (and Grandpa Matheson too, but Lottie couldn't remember him). Perhaps Rupert saw it as a constant reminder of Kate's changed lifestyle, but to Lottie it was just one piece in the jig-saw that made up the background of her years.

To acknowledge any criticism of these people seemed to her like a criticism of Neil. So, with determination, she forced herself to see only what was good. Molly: bluff, tough, prepared to make the most of what Lottie was certain she considered Neil's foolhardiness. Eugene: if anything bluffer, tougher, insensitive to what was beyond her own experience, yet a woman who'd never have a mean thought. Old Pop: dirty, uncouth and unkempt, his mind as warped as his crippled body; like Molly, he considered Neil a fool to have lumbered himself with a 'red lips furriner' for a wife, but unlike Molly he said so. Craig: a man of few words, but Lottie sensed that if she needed a friend she'd find one in him, for Neil's sake rather than her own.

Only Donald remained an enigma.

'Pop said I ought to ask you, Donald,' she found him alone in the yard, 'is there a horse I can ride? He said you'd know which was the best one.'

It was the morning of her second full day at Kilton Down. Yesterday she'd only seen him at the meal table – and that was something she tried not to think about. The O'Hagons made a serious business of eating, but Donald surpassed them all. The meat stew had been served direct to the plates from the huge black saucepan, then battle had commenced. No knife and fork for Donald, but a spoon to shovel the food into his mouth. From the early recesses of memory Lottie had remembered her father bidding her: 'Don't speak with food in your mouth.' Donald didn't actually speak, but he made a constant singing noise, opening his mouth wide to each chew. Like the rest of the family, she had concentrated on her food, her eyes downcast.

'Old Pop said come to me? Well now, jus' fancy . . . ' He moved nearer to her, she felt dwarfed by the size of him. He was enormous. Tall, broad, thick-set, a giant of a man. But, huge though he was, his great head was out of proportion with the rest of his body. Leaning over her he laid his hand on her shoulders. She wanted to draw back yet something prevented her. He wasn't like the others. He was a simple man. What was it Molly had said about the O'Hagons not being short of intelligence? Perhaps the rest of them weren't, but there was something strange about Donald.

'Lottie, can you spare me a moment?' It was Molly's voice from the doorway of the house that rescued her.

'Yes, of course. I'll see you later, Donald.' She ducked away from the hand that still rested on her shoulder.

'Saw you talking with Donald out there. Ought to have told you about him right out when you got here. You mustn't be frightened of Donald, you'll have nothing to fear from him. And work! Could outwork any man I ever seen. But, poor boy, bit empty in the head, can't think things out for himself. Give him a job to do and he'll go at it till you have to stop him.'

'It was the horse. Pop said I should arrange it with Donald.'

'Pop's got the devil in him. Yes, *you*,' she turned to the old man as she spoke, 'you're a wicked ol' man.' But there was too much affection in her tone for Pop to be upset. Instead he chuckled to himself. 'Well, I see Donald's saddled up a horse for you. How well do you ride? You had experience?'

'I've ridden since I was not much bigger than Katie.'

Molly sniffed, somehow conveying her doubts. 'Don't know whether horses in England are the same thing as out here. All dressed up in your fancy gear, trotting along. I know – I seen it in a movie once.'

'You can't believe all you see in the cinema.'

She'd show them what she was made of! That was her objective as she mounted. It seemed they were testing her, and the horse was in league with them. It stood docilely enough while she mounted and settled herself in the saddle, almost as if it were fooling her into misplaced confidence. Only then did battle commence. But she was ready for it. Try as it might, it wouldn't throw her.

She'd mastered frisky horses before and told herself this was no different. It was important. She felt her whole future depended on proving herself. In the yard Molly stood watching, Lottie knew rather than saw. Out of the corner of her eye she noticed that Eugene had brought Old Pop to the door. Close by her side stood Donald, his mouth open. She felt the nearness of all of them, but her concentration was on the sherry-coloured mount. Again it stood on its hind legs. She gripped with her knees, silently sending up a plea that she'd not be unseated. In that moment it was partly for herself, for her own future here, that she felt it important; but it was more than that. *She'd* show them that a 'red lips furriner' wasn't going to be conquered. Molly's remarks about English riders trotting along in their fancy gear still rankled. Sherry, as mentally she'd christened her mount, stood still, breathing hard. She stroked his neck while her knees told him clearly who was the boss. Then, digging in her heels, she started him forward.

'I'll be damned . . . ' She heard the admiration in Molly's voice. Riding out of the yard she felt she'd scored a point – in fact, three points: one for her own pride, one for her homeland, and one for Neil. Her immaculate jodhpurs may have been looked on as fancy dress, but this morning she'd shown the family there was more to her than they'd expected.

She rode away from Kilton Down, thoughts of the O'Hagons soon dispelled by this new freedom. The feeling of the saddle under her, all around her silence except for the sound of the horses hoofs on the hard ground. Oh, the joy of it! Presently, she halted Sherry. She sat quite still gazing up into the clear sky where, high above, a solitary goshawk hovered. The hawk surveyed its territory, drifted lower, circling; it paused; it hung; it swooped to bring sudden death to some creature out of Lottie's sight. She'd seen such things happen at home, always she'd hated it. Yet today the bird, the unseen animal that had given him a good dinner, the horse that obeyed her will, herself the only human, all were part of the dream that had been woven into the fabric of her life. And, more than that, this was Neil's home, Neil's land.

From that day, Sherry was hers to ride.

It was the journey each week to Radley for the mail that made Eugene suggest that Lottie should learn to drive the truck.

80

'No use me offering to teach you, not just at the present time.' For any day now the newest O'Hagon would put in an appearance. 'Would you take her out, Craig?'

'Sure I will,' he agreed. Then to Lottie: 'Up to now you've had good Mondays, but you wait till the wind blows its dust storms off the prairie – you'll be glad to be in the truck.'

Donald watched them, looking from heavy-featured and heavy-bodied Eugene to Lottie, so trim in her well-cut jodhpurs. Not that he analysed his thoughts, but he let his open mouth turn up into a smile as he compared the two women.

'Be more use here once you can master that truck,' Molly told her.

'Soon Eugene will be busy with a new baby. It'll mean me leaving Katie while I'm out learning. Will you mind?'

'Chil'en get on with their own lives here at Kilton,' was Molly's answer to that, 'and all the better without our eyes always on 'em. You take the opportunity while you can. In a while Neil'll be home and I reckon he'd be glad to see you'd managed to master a vehicle when it's time to meet him.'

Lottie imagined the scene: the crowded railway platform, Neil's look of pride when she climbed into the driver's seat.

'I wanted to learn at home, Dad taught both the boys as soon as they were old enough. But when it was my turn there was no petrol. If you'll teach me Craig, I'll be glad.'

A chortle from Donald. But no one seemed to notice.

They must surely have seen how eagerly he helped her into the driver's seat that same afternoon. Did his face show appreciation for his pretty niece-by-marriage? Did it show excitement for her that she was to learn a new skill? Or had the way he laid his huge hands on her to do with some instinct in him that he wasn't quite 'of this world' enough to follow through? She didn't let her eyes meet his. She was ashamed of the only half understood fear she had of him. He couldn't help it if nature had made him simple, she ought to treat him with the same friendly acceptance that he had from the family. But she couldn't. So often when she thought she was alone she'd find he was nearby, saying nothing, just watching. Only when he suspected she was aware of him did he amble away, moving with that unco-ordinated rolling gait of his.

'I want you to get the feel o' the gears,' Craig was telling her. 'Put your left foot hard down on the end pedal, that's the clutch. That takes the drive off the motor, let's you move into another gear. Slam that door, Donald. You can watch if you want, but don't stand close.'

Like an obedient child the big man did as he was told, moving back into the yard. For an hour Lottie went through the motions of travel,

81

going no further than round and round the ranch house. The truck went forward, backward, turned, stopped, re-started. In Brimley, with people and traffic (even wartime traffic) to contend with, she could never have learnt so fast. At the end of one hour she and the truck were friends.

And so began a series of daily outings with Craig.

It was ten days after Lesson No. 1. She was dressed in her jodhpurs ready for her weekly ride to Radley.

'I'll come with you to get the mail,' he told her. 'You can drive the truck, it'll be practice.'

It was a beautiful summer day, she'd looked forward to her long ride. Even so, she didn't want to sound ungrateful.

'It'll mess up your afternoon. I like the ride, truly, on a day like this. Anyway, do you think you ought to go so far? Eugene's not feeling too good. It might be the beginning.'

They were on the wooden verandah. Even Old Pop had been pushed outside to enjoy the sunshine.

'Hark at the woman, her and her fine English ways.' He chewed a plug of tobacco as he looked Lottie up and down. 'Holy diddle, girl, if the man says he's coming with you, then it's not for you to say he ain't.'

'Sure, Pop's right,' Eugene agreed. 'Before you go, Craig, you'll sort Donald out for the afternoon's work, won't you?'

The remark seemed to have an underlying meaning. Lottie was puzzled, but her mind was already moving ahead to her first proper drive on the highway. When Craig sent Donald off the check the drift fencing on the far side of the range, she knew he'd be occupied until late evening but thought nothing of it. Another ten minutes and she and Craig set off towards Radley, two small boys and one girl waving them goodbye.

'This is great!' Today she didn't feel like a novice; today she was out on the highway, she was driving to a destination. On the outskirts of Radley they passed the town's tall elevators, then the school where one day Katie would go. With a honk on her hooter she turned the truck into Fourth Street, feeling that every eye must be on her. They passed the chapel with the Manse next door to it, the drugstore, the bank, then with a jolt came to rest outside the Trading Post which doubled up as general store and mail depot.

Craig said he was going to wander down the street to talk to Dougie Osborne at the ironmongers while she did the shopping Molly wanted and saw to the mail. The only post to be sent was her own. The O'Hagons weren't letter writers.

82

Passing her the envelopes she'd come to collect, Digby Bint, the old man behind the counter in the Trading Post, looked at her over the top of his spectacles.

'Seems the post's all for you. Ain't so much as a picture postcard for any other of 'em out at Kilton.'

She hurried back to the truck, hoping to have time to read at least Neil's thicker than usual letter before Craig came back. His words brought him very close. A smile hovered as she read: ' . . . yet now that I'll soon be home, honey, the waiting seems worse than when there was still fighting. Home, and with you as part of it! Gee, but Lottie, there can't be a guy coming back from this war as proud as I shall be. *My* wife, the prettiest girl in all Alberta . . . Times I get scared, I should be on my knees thanking whatever God there is for making you love me. Never run out on me Lottie. Whatever I am is all for you.'

She read her letters from home. Today there was one from Brimley, one from Ronnie, one from Lavinia and one from her cousin Luke. She skimmed through them all, somehow warmed by their never failing support. Then she put them in her pocket to be saved for later, and went back to the slanting hand that was the pivot of her waiting days. Still there was no sign of Craig, but she was content with her thoughts.

When he did appear it wasn't from the ironmongers, but from the Men's Club where he'd been playing pool.

'OK. Head for home,' he said as he slammed the truck door. No explanation why he'd kept her waiting so long; no apology. Normally she would have been infuriated by his natural assumption that being a mere woman she had no right to expect any. Today, with that letter in her pocket, she gave no more thought to Craig than he did to her.

From the time they left Kilton Down until they returned must have been about three hours. Lottie drove back into the yard with a glow of satisfaction. She hadn't mentioned to Neil that she was learning to drive, she was going to surprise him when she went to meet him. This afternoon had been an important stage in her progress.

'Run someone down?' Old Pop greeted her. 'Is that what's been keeping you?'

'Of course I didn't. I did all right, didn't I Craig?'

'Ain't got much to show fer yer afternoon,' the old man treated them to a gummy grin, 'not like Eugene. Better git in there an' meet yer new son, Craig. Got a pair o' lungs on him sounds healthy enough.'

Craig didn't wait to hear more.

'But we've been gone no time . . . Is she all right?' Lottie remembered the twenty-four hours it had taken Katie to make her debut.

'Sure she's all right. Why shouldn't she be all right? Comes from good breeding stock.' He looked at Lottie out of the corners of his rheumy eyes. 'She ain't been ill. Only dropped her young, the way women was made to do it, afore things got so fancy and they liked to think of themselves as medical cases. Cattle out there on the range, they manage for themselves. You reckon women less than the cattle in the fields? Is that how it is back in your country?'

He'd succeeded in one thing: he'd managed to take the joy out of the triumph of her afternoon.

Eugene stayed in bed for three days, then the house seemed to be back to normal with the exception that there was a new mouth to feed – at all times and in all places. Sometimes on the wooden rocking chair on the verandah, sometimes at the meal table, even standing by the stove stirring the porridge, it was all one to Sean; like the rest of the O'Hagons he was being reared to take food as a necessity of life, fuel for his boiler. Lottie sometimes thought of the precious moments when she'd nursed Katie. How could Eugene know the enveloping bond that tied her to that new life when feeding time was no more than this?

'Katie is thrilled with the idea of a tiny baby in the house,' she wrote home to her parents. 'He's to be called Sean. Three boys and Katie! Can't you just imagine how spoilt she'll be?' All of it was true – and yet none of it was. It gave no picture of the rough and ready household. And never did her letters hint at the enigma that was Donald.

In Europe the war was over. In August came the end in the Far East. After nearly six years peace had come. Soon Neil would be home. That was the thought at the forefront of Lottie's mind, intermingled with a plan that was forming: she'd persuade him to build them a house of their own. It could still be on Kilton Down, that was his home, but they'd have their own place. They'd not sit to table with Donald shovelling his food and opening his mouth as he chewed; they'd not have Eugene suddenly pulling up her blouse and lifting out her heavy bosom, squeezing the nipple so that the milk oozed then pushing it into the searching mouth – for after Sean there was sure to be another as soon as nature allowed. They'd use proper china, shiny cutlery; they'd talk to each other and make mealtimes something to look forward to.

Happily she dreamed of what she was so sure would lie ahead.

He'll be home by the autumn, she told herself. 'Fall' was what the others talked about; to her the golden days between summer and winter were still the autumn. Soon she had to accept that round-up

84

would come and go before the Red Letter Day arrived when she would drive to meet him.

The third Monday in September was a wild day, the fall wind blew straight from the prairie.

'Craig said Rosie rode in yesterday,' Eugene told Molly.

'To help with the round-up? She ain't been by for these past three years.'

'Guess she figured the war's over now, time she got the lie of the land again. Maybe she hadn't heard – ' with a nod of her head in Lottie's direction.

'Maybe. Did Craig take her on?'

Eugene laughed. 'He put her in the picture, told her the fellas weren't home yet. She didn't wait. Got her boy with her.'

'He must be ten years or more now. Ah well, good job she cleared off.'

'Who's Rosie?' Lottie asked.

'A half-breed Indian woman. Rides a horse like I never seen. Comes by some years to give casual help with the round-up. Lives out on the settlement. Hark, there's Sean . . .' And Rosie was forgotten.

'Is there any mail for Radley? I thought I'd take the truck. I'm fine on my own.'

'Nothing from me. Guess we're not the letter writers you are. But if you've got the truck you might take my boots in to Abe Wilkie and ask for new bottoms on them.'

While Molly fetched her boots Lottie stood looking out of the window. Swirls of dust were being blown, then they lost strength, almost disappeared before a fresh gust of wind would shriek and give them new strength to go on their mad way.

'I'll take Katie. She'd like to come in the truck.'

'You don't need. She's fine here. Did Craig say you're ready to go on your own?'

'He never has to tell me what to do now. He didn't say because I didn't ask him. Do you want to come for a drive, Katie?'

Katie danced with excitement. 'Me'll det my toat. Me come in truck wivvu.'

Lottie was confident. It was only seven miles and almost empty miles at that, no harm could come to them. She set off smoothly, drew to a halt lined up perfectly with the sidewalk outside the Trading Post. She took the boots to Abe Wilkie and he said he'd do them straight away to save Molly waiting a week. Give him an hour, do the other things she had to do, and he'd have them ready for her to take home. So she went to the Trading Post, left her mail, collected one letter from Eva, and bought a jacket for Katie. Abe must have had other callers to hinder him, for it was late afternoon by the time the boots were done. But at last they were ready and set out on the homeward journey. While the wind picked up a sheet of paper lying in the middle of the street and carried it high to wrap it almost to the top of a telegraph pole, she pulled the starter and drew gently away. Between her and Katie a smile passed. They both seemed aware of this new freedom.

How funny the truck felt; rough, lumpy. It was dragging to one side. It must be her imagination. She drove on, trying to ignore what she didn't understand. The buildings of the town were behind her now. A dust-devil billowed towards them to hit against the windscreen.

'Mummy, Tatie don't like it.' She covered her ears.

'It won't hurt us, we'll soon be home.' Could it be the wind that was making it so difficult to keep going straight? Then just as suddenly as it had whipped up, so for a moment the air was still, the howling gone. From the front of the truck there as was an unfamiliar sound: 'Kerflump . . . kerflump . . . '

Only now she realised how ill-founded her confidence had been. She stopped the truck and climbed out. Memories of things she'd heard her father and the boys say teased the back of her mind: 'A pancake' . . . 'must never drive on a flat tyre'.

With new abandon the wind tore at her, standing her hair on end. She held down the front of her skirt; the back of it blew high.

From inside the truck she heard Katie shout: 'Mummy, Tatie don't like it. Wanna go home. Tatie don't like it.'

Chapter Six

'It 'cratches!' The flying dust stung their faces. Katie buried hers against Lottie's skirt.

'I'll carry you. Here comes the big wind again. Whoosh!' Lottie felt as if her teeth were coated with grit, and even though she turned the battle against the wind into a game, yet her eyes were almost closed as she strode forward. How far were they from Radley? More than a mile and Katie was heavy. Soon they'd come to the tarmac highway, but as far out of town as this the road was merely what they called 'graded' – a dirt track that each spring was raked to level out the pits and ruts left from a winter of snow and frost. Once they reached the streets of town the wind wouldn't pick up all this dirt to hurl at them. Still she managed to keep her voice bright. Putting her feet down firmly she marched along, stepping out in time to the song she made up as they went:

'Here we are, here we are, marching back to town,
Our poor car, our poor car, it has broken down,
We'll find a man to sort it out.
Here comes the wind, so "whoosh" let's shout,
We'll sing our song and march along – '

'Can we give you a ride into the town? Where are you making for?'

For all her cheery singing, only a moment ago in her imagination Lottie had seen a Radley that was deserted, the filling station closed, the shop doors bolted by the time they reached there. Now suddenly she wasn't alone any more and hope bounced back. There was relief in her smile. At first glance she saw two things: one, the driver was a woman, second the car was different from any she'd seen before. From the driving seat forward it was a saloon model, but the rear seemed to be that of a van with double doors at the back for loading. All that flashed through her mind as she answered.

'I need to find someone to look at the truck. The front tyre is flat as a pancake.'

'You mean you cannot change a tyre? But it is simple.'

As the stranger spoke Lottie looked at her more closely, her interest aroused as much as anything by the voice. The woman's roots weren't in this country any more than Lottie's own. But neither was she English. Mid-European perhaps? There was an assurance in her manner that made Lottie conscious of her own ignorance. A competent woman, and a good-looking one too in an austere way, with her brown hair pinned into a coil at the back of her head. Her hands rested on the steering wheel – strong, capable, well cared for hands. There was arrogance in the way she spoke. She was a woman used to steering her own ship and in the direction she chose. But Lottie needed help, so bit back her answering retort. Of course she too would find it simple to change a wheel if she'd ever been shown how to do it! But at this moment what she wanted was to get herself and Katie to Radley.

'Shall we take them to Radley, or are you going to fix it for them?'

The child who asked the question was sitting in a wheelchair and now Lottie understood the reason why the back seats had been removed and the roof heightened. The driver opened the passenger door and threw her parcels to the floor beside the wheelchair so that Lottie and Katie could get in. Nothing vanlike about the comfortable bench seat in the front.

The child in the invalid chair was quite beautiful. Lottie guessed her to be seven or eight years old. Her golden-brown hair was in deep waves, the fine tendrils at the front in tight curls still a hangover from baby days. There was no evidence of any physical disability, yet clearly she couldn't walk or why would she have to travel in this hybrid of a vehicle?

'It's kind of you to give us a lift,' Lottie said, settling a quickly restored Katie to kneel on her lap and gaze at the unusual sight of someone sitting in a chair inside a car. 'There must be someone at the filling station in Radley who will drive out and do it for me – or even telephone back to Kilton Down so that my brother-in-law will ride out and rescue us.'

'If you have a spare, then I will easily change it. I said to you: it is a simple thing to do.'

'I've only just started driving, you see . . . '

'Even so.' Her tone said more than her words.

Lottie felt herself to be as useless as Katie or the child in the back of the car.

'Marthe can do most anything.' The little girl spoke with pride.

'Me's Tatie. Who's you?' Except for certain letters, Katie was speaking clearly now.

'I'm called Ginney. My proper name's Virginia, but you can call me Ginney, same as folks do.'

One word would have done Katie, she was swamped in the long explanation. As is the way with the young, they silently observed each other and accepted what they saw. It had taken more than half an hour to walk from the truck to where they were picked up, but the return journey seemed no distance. Determined to learn, when they stopped Lottie got out to help. Already she was imagining herself casually telling the family that she and another woman driver had changed the wheel!

'You are not from here,' the stranger said as she wound the jack and lifted the off-side of the truck from the ground. She wasn't asking; it was a statement. 'Are you a visitor or an immigrant? I can tell because you have the accent.'

For a second Lottie was lost for words. To be told she was not 'vrom' here and that she spoke English with an accent!

'I've come here to live. My husband is from Kilton Down. But of course I'm English. And you?'

'I am from Hungary. I came here even before the war started. I have made it my country.' As she talked she loosened the nuts and released the wheel. Eager to be part of the job Lottie bowled the spare round to her and took the damaged one to fix to the back of the truck, all the time watching, noting just what had to be done. 'I should tell you my name. I am Marthe Kopamony and the child is Ginney McFee. We live out at Higley Creek on the easterly road out of Radley. You were lucky we happened along your way.' She had learned the English language in Canada, her expressions were theirs, yet no Canadian called the war a 'vor' not yet Canada their 'count'ry'. 'The wheel is on. You lower the truck, I will tighten the nuts then you may go home. We must, too. I have a supper to cook. I never keep Ramsey waiting for his meal.'

'That's your husband.'

'Well, no, not really husband. I have been with him for many years. I was there when the wife still lived there. One man, then another. She was – ah, how can I say it? – she was a cow, that's what she was. Even men on the ranch, right near her own home. Loved to be flattered.' Lottie had a feeling that all this had been bottled up inside Marthe until just such a moment. The man Ramsey looked like waiting for his supper this evening. 'I saw it all. But I knew he – Ramsey – he didn't care. Why should he want what was given out so cheap? Not he. He has more sense, more pride. Then there was the accident. She took little Ginney riding on her horse with her. Ginney was just two. It was to show off. She loved to ride and that day

89

Ramsey had a dealer out there with him, arranging to buy a new combine. So she carried on, knowing she made a pretty picture, she and the little one. Then over the fence she goes, once, twice. Ramsey shouted to her. Madness with a baby. I started out to let her hand Ginney down to me. But she took the jump again.' She bit her lip, remembering. 'Until that day Ginney was running around as fine as any other.'

'And the mother? She was killed?'

'Holy jeepers, she was surely not killed! Not hurt. Things in the house were bad, Ginney taken away for months in hospital. Next time Jeanette – that was her name – next time she got a fella Ramsey told her: Stay home and behave, or clear out and stay gone. She cleared. The house was brighter without her. I'd give a lot to see Ginney run and play same as any other girl, but even as we are, we're a happy enough house, her and Ramsey and me.'

'She sounds happy.' Lottie smiled, listening to the giggles coming from inside the other car where Katie had climbed into the back and the two had bridged the gap of the years that separated them. 'Perhaps we'll see each other again? I hope so. I come in each Monday to collect the mail. Until Neil, my husband, is demobbed I'm living with his people at Kilton Down.'

'If you've ever got time on your hands, drive out to Higley Creek. I'd like you to make a visit with me.'

And Lottie decided that when she had the opportunity she'd make that 'wisit.'

' . . . took Katie with me in the truck when I went to Radley to collect the week's mail. It was great. I do believe she knew what a milestone it was – *me* let loose behind the steering wheel on the highway. Would you believe, when we went to set out back to Kilton Down' (she felt the small white lie was justified, there was no point in mentioning the desolate, windswept walk back towards town) 'I found we had a flat tyre? Over here you don't have tyres, Dad, did you know? You have tires. Anyway, I was just going across to the filling station to get someone to come out and fix it, when along came a car driven by a Hungarian lady. She knew just what to do. I do too now. Together we changed it. Don't you think I deserve a Brownie point, Dad? This person, Marthe Komaromy, has been here since before the war. She's very nice, I'm sure you'd like her.

'She asked Katie and me to drive over and see her. There's a little girl of eight who was crippled in an accident when she was smaller than Katie. When I go visiting, I'll tell you all about it so that you can picture everything. Katie and her new friend got on very well. She is talking more all the time. I have your picture in our bedroom and she always says goodnight to you . . . '

Strange how talking to an immigrant from Hungary could have given her this hunger for home. She knew the picture she painted wasn't entirely the truth, but if she told her mother that she supposed Marthe was living with Ramsey but not married to him then it would be just one more thing Kate would hold against the entire Canadian nation.

She wrote her letter on Monday night. There was another week before it could be mailed.

'We haven't seen much of the men while they've been getting the cattle in.' Lottie spoke into the silence of the kitchen. As if to remind her of his presence, Old Pop cleared his throat with gusto and spat on to the burning logs.

'Dat nasty thing,' Katie told him as if he didn't already know it.

'Don't turn your head, Katie, I want to trim this bit at the back. There!' Carefully she laid a curly lock on a piece of paper. 'We'll send that home to Mum.' Such a thought would never have entered her head had she been living six hundred miles from Brimley instead of six thousand.

'Fall's their favourite season of the year.' Molly looked up from sewing patchwork squares for a bed cover to go on the youngest O'Hagon's bed. Her hands were as large and strong as a man's, no one would expect them to produce such delicate stitches. 'All through round-up they reckon to start a bit before can-see and not quit till a bit after can't-see. Ain't that so, Pop?'

'Yep, that's the way it al'ays was.' He chuckled at his memories, puffing contentedly on his pipe. 'When I was courtin' Alice I remember having a crack at my ol' man about it, thought I had better things to be doing with my time. He tol' me: "Dunno what you got to grumble about. Days is gettin' short now, jis you 'magine the hours you'd be riding out if we did the round-up in the summer!" Ain't got no answer to that one.' In the comfort of a fireside seat he was in a reminiscent mood. 'More to a round-up than a work-a-day chore. Got to get them in right enough, look on them critters as a pile o' dollar bills, that's what my ol' man used to say, and it's true enough. Every one of them, down to the last calf, gotta get 'em rounded up. Leave 'em out there and you might as well take some of them dollars and melt 'em away on this fire.'

'I don't see how you can ever find them all. It's so vast, they can get anywhere.' When Old Pop was in one of these moods Lottie enjoyed him. He was part of the old West. Cantankerous, uncouth, sarcastic, he could be all those things and usually was, but he had a courage that she respected – and hidden away he had a sense of fun too which just occasionally she glimpsed. Now she lifted Katie down from the chair. 'That's OK. Off you go and play with the boys. Neil said you get to know the places they hide, Pop?' she encouraged him to talk.

'Yep, get to know right enough. Have to search out ever gully, every creek bed. Now this year ain't been bad. Craig tells me he got high hopes of the auction if prices hold. Wouldn't wonder they'll be back by tonight, Craig's never been a man to hang about once auction's done. Yep, I reckon this year they'll have done good. It's been a fair season to round-up, gives a man an easier task. Many a time the storms have come before this.'

'It snowed last night. They were finished just in time, I suppose.'

'Can't call that snow, girl! Get a proper blizzard, winds giving drifts, and the cattle hold out any place they can get protection – then o' course there's no track to follow, the snows cover right over. But I tell you, we've had some high times out there at round-up.' By now he was talking more to himself than to them. 'Holy diddle, watch that Sam Willocks. Never saw a man lay his lasso around the heels of a runaway steer so neat as young Sam Willocks could.'

'I wish Neil could have been back in time for this year's. He used to talk about it to me, said they have their own competitions – especially with the wild horses. A sort of private rodeo.'

'Season o' the year, right enough. Then off to the auction. And I reckon young Neil wouldn't like missing that. Craig was al'ays the one to hurry home. Jeez, yes, Neil'd like to get himself over there to that auction.' Was the look he gave her malicious or was he teasing? 'He al'ays could – how's it you smart talkers would say it? – extract all the juice life had on offer. How's that, eh, Molly? I'm learnin'. Mus' be having a young lady in the house with her fancy talking.' Easing himself in his seat he passed wind and sighed with satisfaction, his rheumy old eyes turned on Lottie with a wicked twinkle.

What did he have to spoil it for? Pretending she'd not noticed, she carefully picked up the piece of paper with Katie's hair on it and went along the passage to her bedroom where she put it safely in an envelope.

The cattle had been brought in, the breeding herd fenced in the corrals near the ranch house, the rest driven off to auction, Craig, Donald, two regular cowhands and the others who were taken on casually, riding with them. Today was Friday; they'd been gone since last Tuesday, perhaps by tonight they'd get home.

Last night had brought what Lottie looked on as a fall of snow – although apparently Old Pop hadn't thought much of it. Only a foretaste of what was ahead, enough to cover the ground with what, by the light of dawn, looked like a film of gleaming ice over the frosted land. By mid-day it had gone, even the resultant mud in the yard had dried away. It wasn't yet October. How many months stretched ahead when they'd be thrown together indoors like this? But soon Neil would be here. Just hold on to that. When he came everything would be different.

Lying back on her bed she steered her thoughts back to those magic months she'd had with him. Think just of *him*, pull back from the memory of the view from the top of Maddock Hill, the scent of the English lanes, the beery smell in the Packhorse, the tinny tone of the piano as they'd all stood around it and sung. She shied, too, from thoughts of her old home: the feel of the door handles, the creak in the fifth stair on the flight up to the attic where the boys had slept, the sound of her father mowing the lawn on a Saturday afternoon and the sweet smell of the grass, the ping of the tennis balls against their racquets, candlelight dancing on the white damask tablecloth and glistening on the silver cutlery. The last years she'd been at home never haunted her in the way her childhood did. And yet she was afraid to take out her memories and look at them. Only to Michael did she willingly let her spirit stray. Somehow he was still near her, still part of a yesterday that was gone for her as surely as it was for him.

Think just of Neil. It was for him that she'd said goodbye to all those familiar things. Soon he'd be with her, and all the magic would come back. Again she controlled her straying mind. 'Mine, branded like the cattle . . . ' Like the men were doing, bringing in the cattle, branding them. Neil wanted her to be part of his world. And so she would be; so she was. Things would be different when he was here with her . . . and again the future gave way to the past, but this time a past she'd shared with him. A few wonderful months, then for three years she'd been without him. Longing surged through her, excitement that was a physical thing, making her jaw ache, her blood tingle in her veins.

She ought not to let Old Pop bother her. She seldom argued with him. When he behaved like he had just now she knew it was a bait to make her rise. She'd seen the twinkle of victory in his eyes as she'd turned to the door; he'd know now that she was hiding in her room and chalk up another point scored to his credit. It wouldn't be like that when Neil came. She'd have a proper place to fit into in the household. Yet, in this place, what did it mean to be part of the household? Like Eugene, constantly breeding, happy in her daily drudgery? No, of course not. It hadn't been like that at home. She

93

and Neil would show them what a proper partnership could be, a husband and wife two equal partners. And, unexpectedly, a picture sprang to mind of Kate and Rupert. From this distance it was so much more comforting to remember the good times, the happiness shared by all the family – like the way they'd all watched her as she'd received the cup at the gymkhana or Christmas with all of them gathered around the piano while her mother played carols, her father turned the pages of the music, and they all sang, even Freda coming to join them.

Perhaps in her heart she knew that her reminiscences were painted with more gentle hues than they merited, that they were no more a complete picture than the letters she sent home.

Getting up from the bed she took out her writing pad from the drawer in the nameless piece of furniture that doubled as dressing table and chest of drawers.

'Dear Grandma . . . ' She needed to reach out to someone. Of course she'd sent letters to Bullington Manor over these months, letters much like those that had gone to Sycamore Avenue. Today's missive started in the same vein: with just the same pride as she'd written home earlier in the week, now she told Lavinia of her solo trip to town in the truck; then a description of the first snow of winter. '. . . once it really starts, I suppose we shall be under each other's feet for months. They're good to Katie and me. Please, Grandma, don't imagine we haven't been made welcome. Neil's Mom is a great character. Not a bit feminine, as tough as anything, except when she has an embroidery needle in her hand. But there's a difference between being tough and being coarse. I remember the day Aunt Eva met me on the railway station, before I even saw Molly (that's what I call Neil's mother) and Craig, she whispered to me: "They're *good* people." I expected that to mean they'd be easy, the same sort as us. Silly really, because they couldn't be, could they? Whatever anyone is is what their life has made them – and here they've had to be tough as leather. I respect Molly – she really is a thoroughly *good* person, and Eugene too. But I'm not a bit their sort of woman. I suppose they see I'm not, that's why they won't let me be responsible for any of the chores. I've not said any of this to Mum, she'd worry, and think I meant I was regretting coming here. And that's not true. When Neil gets home everything will be different, they'll understand that he and I are proper partners. Molly and Eugene take it for granted that they wait on the men; not just preparing meals and doing the clothes and cleaning – I'd do that willingly. It's more than that, something you have to experience to understand. It's as if they look on themselves as somehow inferior, themselves and I expect me too because I'm what

94

they would think of as *just* a wife. Wait till Neil gets here, we'll show them! They'll see that I can work as hard as anyone, but a wife is a partner not a chattel!

'I feel much better now that I've written all that. Like sharing a trouble – except that this isn't a trouble, it's just something no one here would understand until they see what a proper team Neil and I are. Once he's back everything will be just perfect . . . '

Her pen rushed on, her outpourings went to five sides of paper and at the end of it she felt much better. Better enough to send a short note home enclosing Katie's curl. She sealed the envelopes and put them in her drawer ready for next Monday's trip to Radley.

The ranch house at Kilton Down was a long, single-storey building, the verandah running the full length and reached by three wooden steps from the yard. The bedrooms all fronted the verandah, their doors opening on to the corridor where the children often played. They were there this afternoon; the game was 'round-ups', Mickey riding his wooden horse and Katie and Earl charging along the corridor at a great speed on all fours. It was a noisy game, but noise was part of the O'Hagon lifestyle. Mickey had seen his father use a lasso. He knew just what he was doing as he twirled and aimed his dressing gown girdle in an attempt to catch the runaway 'cattle'; Katie only knew it added to the fun, so she shouted and scurried with as much gusto as the others.

Outside in the yard a truck door slammed. The men had gone on horseback, the Kilton Down truck was in the shed. Maybe they had a caller, but the O'Hagons weren't given to social visiting. Marthe Komaromy perhaps? Lottie went to the window, half expecting to recognise the hybrid car.

'See ya, Bud, and thanks for the lift!'

Neil! She flung open her window but he'd already leap up the three steps and disappeared into the kitchen. Would he come straight through here to find her? She didn't wait to see. Three boisterous children seemed intent on getting in her way as she pushed past them. Then she swooped down on Katie to carry her to meet her father.

'Down.' The little girl wriggled. 'We's busy. Down!'

'Come and see who's here. Katie, he's home!'

In the kitchen everyone was talking at once, Old Pop's face creased in a beam of pure pleasure, Eugene standing up from her low nursing chair with Sean hanging on to her nipple, nothing interrupting his steady guzzling. Molly had dropped the patchwork quilt and with both hands firmly on Neil's shoulders was inspecting him as if to reassure herself that he was returned undamaged.

'. . . said they were coming right by the place, seemed too good an offer to turn up.' That was Neil, explaining how he'd come to get a lift home.

'A few days sooner and you'd have been in time for the auction. They'll be home tonight.' That was Eugene.

'How's it been? What sort of a year?' It was Old Pop he asked.

'Pretty good, weather held out real kind.' Old Pop sat that bit straighter. 'Holy diddle, but dang me, what a day it's turning out to be!'

'Neil . . .' Lottie's voice cut in.

'Hi, honey.'

'Down. Me's playing wiv boys.' Katie had no time for any of them.

'Let her go,' Molly said. 'There'll be plenty of time later for them to get acquainted.' Of course, she was right, Lottie knew it, but she was childishly disappointed. 'Never seen you so smart in your turn out, boy. Did the Army give you this suit of clothes?'

'Sure they did, Mom. Took away my old khaki one and gave me this. Never had much use for a good suit before, but –' As he spoke he held his arm out to Lottie, somehow inferring that, with her, his life would need a 'good suit'. Their first moment together and here they were with Old Pop watching them, missing nothing. Neil's lips covered hers. She could feel his mouth opening, his tongue moving on her lips. That his family were watching didn't bother him. It was a kiss that should have been private, she wanted to cling to him, she wanted the moment to be just their own. Old Pop spat into the fire.

'How's she been?' Releasing Lottie, Neil grinned at the others. 'This woman o' mine – how's she been without me here to keep her in order?' He was joking, Lottie knew he was. Yet there was an underlying seriousness. 'You never said, Mom, when you wrote me, you never said whether you thought she'd do?' It was the sort of question that needed no answer. 'I mean to go have a look around the place, maybe ride out for an hour. I'll go take off my suit.'

He steered Lottie towards the door. She wished she hadn't glanced at Old Pop at just that moment. He didn't say a word, but one look at his face was enough for her to know what he was thinking as he watched them go.

'I want you to see Katie.' Still within earshot of the family Lottie said it. It was as if she needed an excuse to go with him. In that moment she hated the others.

She wanted to be alone with Neil, to find the man who had been hers. It was silly to wish he'd arrived wearing the uniform she'd been familiar with, the cloth whose feel and smell she could remember. How could Molly and the others have been so impressed with this dreadful suit he'd been given? Never had a good suit before! No tailor would have fitted a jacket so badly, the waist too loose and the sleeves too short for his long arms. The back was creased from where he'd been sitting in the truck, and the trouser legs too.

They didn't interrupt the children's games, but went into the bedroom and closed the door. As if his family could make any difference to them . . . She reached out her hand and touched his cheek. She felt his lips on her palm. The suit was forgotten. This time she clung to him; as he kissed her her moment was complete. He was home and their lives stretched ahead of them. They'd served their time of purgatory, they were out of the darkness and facing the sunshine.

The suit was hung away, the white shirt and brown tie with it.

'We ought to go back to the others,' she whispered as, clad now only in underwear, socks and shoes, he held her against him.

'You're my wife, aren't you?' Between his words he kissed her neck, her throat; she could feel his teeth. She knew how Old Pop would look at those marks. 'Heck, honey, ain't I due a husband's welcome home? Anyways, you can't send me out like this. Look what you've done to me. I'm horny as hell.'

The words excited her. It was an expression she'd never heard, in keeping with the way he pushed her back and half rested against the bed, half knelt over her. There was no finesse in the way he held her skirt out of the way and pulled the wide knicker leg to one side; she wanted no finesse. As he entered her and her legs gripped him, a suspender pressed into her thigh. It hurt. It was part of the urgency. She held him closer, taking his weight and glorying in the pain, in the force of his movements. In the second it took to flash through her mind she thrilled that he wasn't like the men who'd peopled her life at home, suits made by the bespoke tailor, gracious manners; he was strong, hard, tough, a man who needed her. Somewhere down the corridor a door closed, Eugene called to Molly, Molly answered. Was there nowhere to be free of them? Damn the family, damn anything that came between her and him.

Outside in the corridor a battle royal started over Mickey's horse. Katie was screaming. For Lottie the spell was broken.

'It's Katie. Perhaps she's hurt.' She raised her head to try and listen.

With eyes closed and teeth clenched he appeared not to have noticed. She listened as Eugene read the riot act and marched the children out to the yard to play in the fresh air.

'Mummy, where Mom? Mom in dere.' Katie rattled the bedroom door handle. She suspected there were things going on; she hadn't cared for her mother being so excited about a strange man. And if Mom was in there, so was he. She'd seen them go in. 'Mom!' And another vigorous waggle of the handle.

'Your mom's having a rest right now. Go play with the boys. Presently she'll come and see you.'

Lottie heard it all. Neil gave no sign of hearing any of it. The suspender pinched. She found herself frightened to move in case the bedsprings creaked. The children were on the verandah now, running up and down near their window. The ghost of another occasion haunted her, Maddock Hill and she with her skirt pushed up around her waist, just like it was now. Forget the movements in the house, the voices, the curiosity. What did any of it matter? This was Neil, her darling Neil. He'd come to her, wanting her, loving her. Her mouth sought his.

That night Craig and Donald came home. At Kilton Down there was no six o'clock bedtime for the children as Katie had been used to at home. Sometimes they'd gone by the time the men came home, sometimes supper was earlier and they all came to the table together. Tonight supper was held back.

'The boy's first night home, we'll wait and have a meal together,' Molly said. 'Craig never hangs around, they'll be back.'

'Don' know what he'll be missing, eh, Neil?' Old Pop winked a wicked wink.

'Reckon I'd rather be here,' Neil answered.

'Now then, Pop, that's enough nonsense.' Moll's voice told the old man to let the subject drop. So he contented himself with putting a screw of tobacco in his mouth and setting his hard gums to work on it.

If there were hidden meanings they went over Lottie's head. Neil's answer had been sufficient to fill her cup of happiness. At what point some of the happiness spilled out she didn't know but when, with Craig and Donald home, they all sat down to their meal, the glow of it had faded. So often it was at mealtimes that this feeling swamped her. She was made aware that she was an outsider. Donald shovelling in his food, his loud crooning as he chewed, was always an indication that he was content. Tonight though he went one stage further: he got up from his seat, walked around to Neil and patted his shoulder.

'M'boy,' his big face wore a permanent smile, 'see, it's m'boy.' Then to Lottie who sat next to Neil: 'Always been my boy. He told you?'

'That's it, Donald.' Neil patted his hand. 'Sure I've come home for keeps now. Go and eat up your supper. Then you can tell us all about the auction, eh?'

As obedient as a child Donald went back to his own place, taking up the shovelling where he'd left off. Only every now and again he'd stop chewing and stare at Neil. There was such adoration in his eyes that it hurt Lottie to look at him. No one ought to show his heart to the world so clearly.

She'd never been comfortable with Donald. So often she'd found him watching her, standing half hidden and peeping; on one occasion when she'd pulled her bedroom blind she'd come face to face with him through the window. But because he was so patently pleased to welcome Neil she had a greater tolerance of him tonight.

Knives and forks scraped on plates – or in Donald's case a spoon scraped on his for Molly always chopped it up before she passed it to him. Lottie and Neil had had plenty of meals together. She knew how he always cut his food then put the fork into his right hand to raise it to his mouth. Her parents had frowned, it had been just one more Canadian habit for them to object to. What would they say if they could see the O'Hagons at home? Serving dishes were unheard of. Faced with a piled plate they cut their food (as if they were getting it ready to feed a dog, had been her first thought), then with a fork and with thick hunks of bread, the battle was on. Her meals in England with Neil had been times to talk, the food secondary to their time together. Here he was the same as the rest of them. No one spoke until the last morsel had been wiped up with the bread.

'That was good, Mom. Haven't enjoyed a meal like that since I left home.'

Lottie put her knife and fork together. She kept her eyes lowered, ashamed of the sting of tears she wouldn't shed.

A haze of tobacco smoke hung in the air. Around the table the four men sat, a bottle of whisky passing from one to another. Molly had already gone to bed.

'Don't wait up for us, you girls,' Craig said, lighting another cigarette and preparing to settle for the sort of evening he enjoyed. The cattle auction was the culmination of a year's work. There's be no need to ride off before first light tomorrow morning. Added to that, Neil was home. It was four years since they'd gathered around the table together like this.

'I might as well wait for you, Neil. You could even offer me a drink. I want to hear all you have to say too.' Lottie pulled a chair to the table next to his.

She could see they were all surprised. Old Pop held his tongue between his gums as he watched, looking from one to the other; Donald frowned, his fingers drumming on the table; Craig turned

99

helplessly to Eugene who'd put her knitting away as soon as he told her to go to bed.

'Why don't you come on, Lottie? There'll be talk that ain't no good for your ears time these fellas get going.'

But it was Neil who had the last word.

'I'll be with you in a few minutes. I want to have a while with these guys first.' He softened his dismissal by pursing his lips and planting them on the already fiery mark on her neck. Old Pop's tongue waggled in merriment.

Lottie went to bed alone.

From the kitchen came the noise of ribald laughter. 'A few minutes' Neil had told her. She lay wide awake for an hour, waves of sound carrying along the corridor, male voices talking, shrieks of laughter, the crash of a bottle falling to the ground, more laughter, singing, talking, laughter . . . She pulled the covers over her head.

It was much later when he followed her. Wide awake and still smiling he lurched into their room, closing the door with a crash as he leant against it.

'Jeez, honey, but that was some night. You know,' he dropped heavily to sit on the edge of the bed, 'while I was away I used to worry about Old Pop, I was real scared he'd not be here waiting when I got home. He's a great guy, isn't he?' He turned to look at her, squinting as if he had trouble in focusing. 'You didn't answer me. You don't like Old Pop, is that it?'

'Don't be silly. You sounded to be having a good time out there.'

'Sure we were. I had more than four years of war to tell them about. Holy Jim, but what a laugh we've been having.'

'I wish you'd let me stay.'

It wasn't even worth an answer. He tore off his shirt and vest in one go, stepped out of his trousers, pants, socks and shoes in another, throwing the lot on to a chair, then climbed into bed.

'You've forgotten even to clean your teeth,' she reminded him, hating the smell of stale whisky.

'Now what sort of a welcome is that? You never made me go and scrub up when we were up there on – what was it called? – Matlock Hill? Madlock Hill? Remember it, Lottie?' Even the whisky didn't matter now as she moved closer to him.

'But there we belonged just to each other,' she whispered. 'I know I shouldn't mind sharing you with the others. I just felt sort of like an outsider.' Hearing the words tumble out, she was ashamed.

'Not now you won't be, honey, not now I'm back. Charlotte O'Hagon, my Lottie, you belong here with me, you're part of Kilton Down same as the others are. But you're mine, and oh God but

100

you're beautiful. All those hundreds of nights I've wanted to touch you like this – and like this –

"Yes, yes.'

Giving, taking, belonging, just as she'd dreamed, yet surely no moment had ever been like this. All the anxiety, fear, misery, loneliness, longing, of the years they'd been apart, were washed away. Afterwards as he lay gently snoring at her side, a whiff of whisky on every breath, she smiled into the dark night, content and sure of all she had. His family loved him too, of course they did. What sort of a mean spirit did she have that was jealous of letting them have the crumbs from her table?

Hark, what was that? There was a movement in the corridor outside their room. Lying very still she listened. She heard the click as Donald closed his bedroom door.

Chapter Seven

Lottie had been sure that things would be different in the house once Neil was home. And so they were, but in a way she'd not even considered. Katie had been a happy child, her days filled with fun. Now her bottom lip was all too ready to pout; she became possessive over her toys, hating to share; she screamed at the slightest tumble.

And another new habit: in the middle of the night the bedroom door would open and in she'd come. Without a word she'd climb into bed by Lottie's side. Instinct seemed to tell her that she mustn't speak. If she risked rousing the man she'd been told she had to call Daddy then her mother would be lost to her again. So silently she'd cuddle close and within a minute or two would be sound asleep. Careful not to wake her Lottie would carry her back to her own bed and in the morning she'd not even remember it had happened, or if she did she probably thought it was a dream.

In Radley an Ex-Servicemen's Club was formed and, on its opening evening, Neil took the truck to town. This was great! To him, and to most of them, it seemed like the climax of the years they'd spent in Europe. Reminiscences of the good times, no mention of the bad; beer laced with whisky; the room getting warmer, the talk looser, the stories riskier; tales of women they'd loved and left, hoots of laughter; whisky with water, whisky without. Faces got redder. One young stalwart who wasn't the man he'd thought himself to be, was borne homeward, held up by two others. One after another they left, all of them (except perhaps that one who was beyond thinking) conscious of a glow of well-being. They'd fought the fight, they'd proved themselves, and because of that common experience the camaraderie they'd known was still theirs.

Neil was one of the last to lurch off towards his truck.

'Christ, but it's cold!' He spoke to himself as he fumbled to switch on the engine, then changed his mind. For a while he sat, the window

103

closed, his breath condensing on the glass. Ought to get home. He'd start just as soon as the bloody road kept still. Fresh air, that's what he wanted, and opening the window he took great gulps of it. Success this time. The road ahead was stationary, the engine fired, he was on his way.

Not a mile down the road he stopped. 'Christ, but it's cold!' Again he said it, his whole body shaking. Just in time he opened the door and leant out.

And so went his journey home – his and a good many of his companions, not that any of them ever mentioned to each other how that first evening of the Club ended. But Neil's wasn't finished yet.

Lottie heard the truck return. Why didn't he come indoors? She got out of bed and went to the window, just in time to see him climb out, slam the door behind him, then stand leaning against the vehicle as if the distance to the house was too much for him. Careless of it being ten degrees below, she pulled on boots and coat then went outside to help him.

'Lean on me, you'll be all right.'

'It was the cold. Was fine at the Club. Not drunk. Never get drunk.' He glowered defiantly at her as they came across the verandah and into the kitchen. Did she dare accuse him of not holding his liquor? It seemed she didn't. He could read nothing but concern in her expression, so he relaxed, letting her guide him to the armchair where Old Pop spent his days.

'I'll make you a hot drink. You ought to eat something perhaps.'

He shook his head, his eyes closed.

'Don't fuss. God, girl, can't a man have a drink without being fussed?'

His arrival must have disturbed Katie.

'Mummy! Where's you? Mummy!' And the sound of bare feet running along the corridor.

'I'm here. Hush, pet, I'm here.' Before they woke the entire household she opened the kitchen door and Katie rushed to her. 'Daddy isn't feeling well. Don't make a noise, love.' How warm and sweet the little girl was to hold. Arms that hadn't quite lost their baby plumpness gripped tight around her neck.

'Go to bed. Never mind me.' Neil's tone belied his words. 'Just see to her. If I'm sick it's my own bloody fault.' His glazed eyes glowered resentfully at both of them. 'Isn't that what you're thinking?'

'You know I'm not.'

'He 'mells nasty,' Katie observed.

'He isn't well. Come and let me tuck you in, Katie.'

She stiffened, suddenly suspicious, frightened of being left. 'Why you's got your coat?'

'I'm not going anywhere. Only because I was cold. I'll take it off when I tuck you up snug.'

'No, no bed.'

From deep in his belly Neil belched. Into Lottie's mind sprang a picture of Old Pop sitting in that chair . . . Cuddling Katie to her, she carried her back into her bedroom.

'No. Wanna go in yous bed.' Katie lay rigid, ready to scream. In the next room the boys slept. Next to theirs was Donald's room. Molly, Eugene, Craig, Sean, Old Pop . . . soon all of them would be awake at this rate. 'Mummy, stay wiv me. He all cross.'

Donald lumbered down the corridor. He put his great head around the open door.

'I was watching – out o' my window. I saw you out there in your night things. You get warm, I'll help the boy to his bed.' He looked at her with his mouth hanging open, but this time his eyes weren't empty. He was excited. She pulled her open coat around her, feeling naked before his gaze. 'Done it before when he's got pissed. I know how to help him.'

She looked away, avoiding his eyes.

When he'd gone she slipped off her coat and boots then got into bed with Katie, listening all the time to the sounds from the kitchen. It seemed Donald did know what to do. Shuffling footsteps in the corridor making for her bedroom, the clump of boots being taken off, the low tone of his voice but what he said she couldn't hear. Silence. Soon Katie slept, only she lay wide awake.

No one mentioned the night, perhaps no one except the three of them and Katie had heard it. Or had they? Old Pop's expression mocked her – but then so it often did.

Neil showed no sign of a hangover. It might have been remorse though that made him pay extra attention to Lottie and go out of his way to play with Katie.

The next day came a change in the weather. Winter loosened its grip.

'It feels quite different. Do you think it's the end of winter?' It was the voice of optimism rather than logic. Winter couldn't be gone so soon.

'Hark at her!' Old Pop jeered. 'Ain't you heard o' the chinooks back there in England? For all your lady ways, don't seem you've got much learning.'

If Neil had been indoors he wouldn't have said it, only his sly look would have left her in no doubt what he thought of her question.

'Chinooks? I may have. Yes, I'm sure I have. But what are they.'

105

'Winds, girl, winds that blow down these parts, east o' the mountain range. Protects us from some o' the winter. You'll see how the snow goes. But sly as the devil is the ol' chinook. When night comes, down goes the temperature. By morning you have to watch your step or you'll be down on your arse on the ice out there.'

'Even so,' Lottie wasn't going to have her spirits put down, 'you can feel the promise in the air.'

The chinooks held. It was a few days after the opening of the Ex-Servicemen's Club that she and Neil rode out together over the winter landscape. In the early hours it had been like a skating rink, but now the horses had a firm foothold, there was magic in the air. Wasn't this just what she'd dreamed of? She knew he was proud of the way she handled Sherry. She felt her happiness was complete. At home Katie was playing with Earl and Mickey, while here she was galloping with Neil under a winter Alberta sky. Nothing else had any place in her mind.

'Remember you asked me how I knew where to look for the cattle, how I knew where they sheltered?'

'I remember. Oh, Neil, I remember ever single bit of it.'

'Sure, honey, and so do I. Here, see this overhang of rocky ground? This is a favourite place.' He swung himself from his saddle and reached up to help her to the ground.

'It'll be a favourite of mine too. You and me, here, no one else for miles.' An exaggeration but she didn't care. In this moment she felt that everything was larger than life – this wonderful country, her own happiness at being with Neil, the beauty of a day in winter that held the promise of all she was sure their life would be.

'My Charlotte O'Hagon, I ought to go down on my knees and thank whoever it is who's god o' this universe. I don't deserve you. I'm an ordinary rough sort o' guy. Sometimes I get sick with fright. One of these days you gonna tell me you realised what a bum I am. If you ever left me, I swear – '

'Don't Neil, don't spoil all this by even talking about it. I love you, you know I do. Why, we've got a whole future waiting for us. We'll build a place of our own, Neil – '

'You mean you want to leave all this?' He looked at her in disbelief.

'Of course not, not the ranch. But we ought to have a home of our own.'

'What for? There's plenty of room back at the house. The boys get on OK with Katie. It would be crazy. When I'm away – the auction or maybe just with the guys at the Club – you'd be alone nights.'

'We're a family, you and Katie and me. We ought to run our own place.'

'Well, we'll have to give it a bit of thought when the snows have all gone. Right now, honey, all I ask is us being here together.' With his hand under her chin he tilted her face up to his. And when he looked at her like that she was lost. 'You're getting cold,' he said gently as he finally released her. 'Wrap that scarf around your head, keep your ears warm as you ride.' As he helped her to mount she felt loved, protected. The thought of a home of their own was forgotten.

The wind changed, more snow came, it froze, the frosts lasted through nights and days alike; then the chinook came again, the sly chinook, beguiling them into believing winter was on the wane.

'There's a dance at the Club on Saturday,' Neil said. 'How's about you or Mom seeing Katie to bed, Eugene? You'd do that so Lottie could come with me, eh?'

'As if you've any need to ask, son. Eugene's got plenty to see to, but Katie and me get along easy enough.' Which was true. Molly never talked down to any of the children. Noise didn't bother her, they would shout as much as they liked when they played; but one word from her and they obeyed. She gave them the same sort of respect as she would an adult, and small as they were they seemed to understand it demanded fair play from them in return.

When Saturday came Lottie got ready with all the excitement of a debutante at her coming out ball. The last time she'd been dancing had been with Barrie in Brimley. She remembered cycling home, he on Ronnie's bike. She remembered the fun they'd always had together, the certainty that he'd always be there. Dear Barrie. She'd worn this very same skirt and blouse, a russet brown skirt cut on the cross of the material so that it swirled out as she twisted, and a pale apricot blouse. What was Barrie doing now? she wondered. Sometimes her parents mentioned that he'd been to see them, but now he would be out of the Air Force. How much for granted she'd taken him. Had he really been in love with her, or had it been a fantasy because he'd needed someone to love and she'd monopolised his time so greedily? She twirled around, delighting in the way her skirt stood out in a circle.

'Do it again.' Neil's voice surprised her. 'Oh, boy, do you look pretty! Mrs O'Hagon, there won't be a dame there to compete.' Obligingly she spun round again. 'Hey there, not so fast. Legs that go right up to your . . . oh boy, for ten cents I'd not go to the dance at all. I can think of better things – '

'Oh no you can't!' she laughed. 'We're going to dance and dance and dance.'

'Like at Kingstaunton, eh?' He was wearing his 'good' suit and white shirt. 'Hey, Lottie, what do you think about this tie? It's the one they gave me, but I got a real nice one somewhere. This is a bit dark, isn't it?'

With his ill-fitting brown pin stripe suit he was wearing a bottle green artificial silk tie.

'What's the other one like?' It could hardly be worse!

'Somewhere in here. Ah, here it it. Mom gave it to me for my birthday one year. Hardly ever had cause to get dressed up, so it's good as new. See, it's bright. Wouldn't you say that was better?' Mauve and orange stripes on a red background.

'I think I prefer the one you're wearing.'

He looked disappointed but assured her: 'Well, guess that's it then. If you think this one looks good, then that's the one for me. Say, though, but what a fine-looking couple we make.'

She thought so too. Not for anything would she give a hint of her opinion of that dreadful suit. In the mirror their reflections looked back at them, brown eyes looked at blue eyes, the message that passed between them saying more than any words. Lifting her hand he planted a kiss on the palm and then curled her fingers over it.

They could hear the music as they parked the truck in the yard at the back of the Club.

'It sounds a super band.' She could hardly wait to get inside.

'Band? Where would we get a band from out here? Old Syd Heinnerkin plays his fiddle, Jim Mahone his piano accordion – but that's for barn dances. Tonight we got the big band sounds on records. But we've got a good selection, real first rate stuff.'

Any disappointment was short-lived as they went into the brightly lit room where already couples were quick-stepping. As they walked through the doorway he took her arm and they joined the throng. People called out to Neil, said 'Hi!' to her as if she were already a friend, simply because she was his wife. It was going to be one of those magic evenings, and she was intent on living every single second of it to the full.

At the end of the first hour she was even more certain. At the end of the second she was still dancing every dance, but as they congared around the room she realised Neil had disappeared into the adjoining bar. However, that dance over he was back with a whisky for himself and something he called a Prairie Queen for her. She didn't ask him what it was, she was thirsty.

He took the glasses back for a re-fill and while he was gone a middle-aged woman moved over to her from where she'd been standing with the man in charge of the gramophone.

'You have Prairie Queens before, Mrs O'Hagon?'

'Is that what it is called? No. But dancing makes you so thirsty – '

'Just take a tip. They can knock you right out. One won't hurt, but steady if you're not used to them. Don't mind me warning you, do you?'

'No, of course not. A good thing you did. I'd hate to get blotto the first time Neil takes me amongst his friends. Isn't it fun?' Although, when she came to think about it, she hadn't seen the older woman dancing.

'That's my man – Keith Bollam – him doing the records.' And as if he knew their attention was on him, the sandy-haired man turned their way. 'Served four and a half years. Mentioned in dispatches.' She wore her pride in him as prominently as he wore the medals pinned to the pocket of his checked shirt.

When Neil brought their drinks Lottie took a sip then put the glass on a ledge for later.

'Let's dance, Neil. Look, some of them are jitterbugging. Let's shown them!'

Neil was tall and lithe. Lottie was supple. They both had a sense of rhythm that simply couldn't go wrong. Dancing had played a part in their first days together and now, after all this time apart, as they moved in unison, rocked, kicked, twirled and stamped, the years of separation might never have been.

'Jeez, but that was great!' Neil drew in his breath to whistle through almost closed lips. 'I need a beer. How about you, honey?'

'No, I've still got mine, thanks.'

'Looks like a crowd in there. Plenty of folk wanting to talk to you, you'll be all right.' His tone told her just how proud he was to be showing her off to his colleagues and their wives.

She sipped her Prairie Queen, watching him push his way toward the bar. The music had started again, her foot was tapping.

'Care to dance?' someone asked her.

Oh yes, she cared to dance all right. Through the open doorway into the bar she could see that Neil had already been served. He was one of a group, none of whom showed any sign of hurrying back. Out here couples danced, occasionally two women together; no doubt their husbands or boy-friends were in the same place as Neil.

It must have been more than an hour that Neil kept her waiting but Lottie was never brought to the stage of being partnered by one of her own sex, neither did she miss a dance. A red-headed young man who told her his name was Ginger was leading her in an exaggeratedly passionate version of the tango when she found herself pulled out of his hold.

'Get your coat.'

109

'Hey, fella, what's buggin' you? She ain't doing you any wrong.' Ginger sprung to her defence.

'You keep your hands off her.' Then, to Lottie, 'You heard what I told you.'

'Neil, don't tease.' She couldn't believe what she was hearing. He couldn't be serious! Or was he? Her heart was banging and her mouth felt dry with sudden fright as he pushed her towards the door.

'Hey, fella, calm down,' she heard Keith Bollam say as she walked blindly towards the cloakroom.

'You can keep your bloody nose out of it!'

Oh, Neil, don't, please don't, she begged silently. I mustn't cry – I won't let myself start to cry. Why's he got to spoil it all? Pushing her arms into the sleeves of her coat, she tried not to hear the music. Music, that's all it was now. No happy voices, no laughing. They'd wrecked it for everyone. She clenched her teeth tightly together. She'd wait outside in the dark night, wanting just to get away, to hide her shame at what he'd done. As she went into the yard she was aware of a different sound from inside, as if a chair had been knocked over. She didn't know what it was; didn't want to know.

One stark unshaded electric light bulb illuminated the wooden porch that led on to the yard. Already in the truck she turned at the sound of the door being slammed. Neil's thunderous expression was made worse by the trickle of blood that ran from his nose. He was a big man, the muscles in his arms like steel rope; if he walked away looking like that, what could have happened to someone in the hall, young Ginger or middle-aged and be-medalled Keith, someone who'd done no more than fight her corner for her? She was ashamed – for Neil and for herself too. It had started as such a happy evening. Consciously she pulled her thoughts away from those early hours. Tears were near the surface still, but they came from nervous shock rather than unhappiness. It was easier to shelter behind the anger she whipped up against him. He read it in her expression as he wiped the blood with the back of his hand.

The way he drove the truck was a reflection of his mood, starting with a jolt, turning out on to the street with hardly a glance.

'"Bring your wife," that's what the guys said, "let's meet your English bride." Well, they met you. Carrying on like any floozie they might have picked up in the dancehalls overseas. Christ, but how do you expect me to behave? Was there another woman there who showed herself off like it?'

'And what did you expect. That while you propped the bar up with your cronies, I'd sit and wait?'

'Plenty of other women there, other wives. Suppose you reckon yourself too good for them, is that it? Kicking your legs about. Christ, woman, every man in the room could see your stocking tops. And what they couldn't see they imagined. Jeez, but I know how a man's mind goes. I took you there, made you get decked out in your best. Thought I'd be the envy of them all. Holy arse'oles, how they'll be laughing!'

'Shut up! Don't talk like that, I hate it. Anyway I don't understand what you men here expect of your woman. I don't even understand you. We went there to dance, to have fun . . . ' Careful, careful, mind that crack in her voice. She clenched her teeth.

That's when he drew to a stop right in the middle of the ungraded road. A bright moon shone down from the clear sky. Tonight the temperature was already twelve below. Even in the truck they could see their breath.

'I'll tell you what we expect of our women.' His face was close to hers, little more than a white disc, but she could see the blood on his upper lip. 'I'll tell you to look at Mom and Eugene, at those wives in the hall tonight. Was there a single one of them who showed their husbands up like you did? Those men there, same as me, we've been in dancehalls back in your precious England. Dammit, we've all known which ones we could be sure of. Didn't call themselves whores, but they were there for the taking.'

'Well, I'm nobody's for the taking! Not yours and not theirs either. That's all you want, someone to cook and clean for you, breed for you, put on their best frock so that you can get the credit, a body in your bed to roll on top of – '

She cried out at the sting of his hand on her cold cheek.

'Bitch!'

'If that's your idea of marriage, it isn't mine. Damn, damn!'; She gritted her teeth, but it was no use, she couldn't hold back the tears any longer. 'I'm not a possession, I'm a woman. I've seen how it is for Eugene; for her, I suppose it's the way she likes it, she's happy. But not for us, Neil.' Her words tumbled out, there was no stopping them. 'You know that I'm not what you just said. I wasn't flirting, I wasn't showing off. I'm *me*, the same as I was in Kingstaunton, the same as I was at Bullington when we were married, the same as when – '

He interrupted her, his voice low, toneless, defeated. 'You wish you'd never come out here. Is it me? Is it the place?'

'Of course I don't wish I hadn't come,' she gulped, groping in her pocket for a handkerchief.

It was as if they'd expended all their anger in that outburst. Now as he drew her gently towards him she rested her damp cheek against his. With her hankie she wiped the blood from his face. Neither of them talked. They felt too bruised.

111

Her words came back to her later, to her and to him too, as alone in their dark bedroom, he eased his body over hers.

'Say you didn't mean it,' he whispered. 'Lottie, I love you. Tell me you know it. If you stopped wanting me there'd be nothing. Honey, honey, you only said it to hurt me, that's the truth, isn't it?' His hands were on her forehead, holding her hair off her face. She could tell they were trembling.

For answer she moved her hand and guided him to her.

'It's the same for me. If you didn't want me . . . I can't bear to think. Forgive me. Love me, just love me.'

The evening that had started so well had carried them on to hopeless despair, they'd plumbed depths they'd never touched before. Tonight there was a new tenderness in their passion, they reached out to fresh heights.

In the fall the cattle had been brought in, most of them taken to auction, only a breeding herd kept. But now the months of feeding them hay with supplements that had to be brought from the dealer in Radley were over, and it was time to turn them loose on to the range. Nature would do the rest.

There can be no time of year like spring for awakening feelings of nostalgia. Hanging a line of washing in the yard, Lottie thought of the garden at home. By now the snowdrops would have given way to hyacinths, their heady perfume filling the air; under the trees in the orchard would be a mass of golden daffodils like jewels in the long grass. People would be cycling out from town to the woods, carrying home baskets full of bluebells and primroses. Ted, the elderly gardener-cum-handyman, would have dug the vegetable plot, the seeds would be planted, the packet carefully skewered into the earth at the end of each row. She smiled as she pictured her father, so methodical, so exact. And at Bullington, in the grounds of the manor, the great chestnut trees would soon be coming into flower; on the lake the ducks and drakes would be swimming, each followed by a new family. Grandma, smart in that way that was especially her own, would walk down the long sloping lawn to the lakeside seat to feed them. So often they'd gone together to feed the ducks.

Lottie shut her eyes and held her face towards the hint of warmth in the sunshine. Supposing a kind fairy were to appear, tell her that for half an hour she could be anywhere, with anyone of her choosing? Conscience nudged her; she ought to choose Brimley, be at home with Mum and Dad and Ronnie. But with make-believe good fairies you couldn't hide from the truth: she'd like most of all to be at Bullington with Lavinia. At home she'd have to be so careful. She

112

mustn't say anything to give them cause to believe they'd been right and she wrong. Because that wasn't so! Of course she was happy, gloriously happy, with Neil.

It's not that I want to pour out a pile of troubles, that's not what I want Grandma for. It's just to see her, to describe it all to her – perhaps most of all just to see her, to make sure that she isn't changing. Being with her never alters.

And just as suddenly as she'd shut her eyes, so she opened them, blotting out the sudden picture of a Lavinia who *was* changed. Of course she grew older, her hair quite white, her ringed fingers bony, the skin too loose. But her spirit never altered. She wrote regularly to Lottie, not replying as such to any little confidences, but making it clear that she'd read and understood.

Today was Monday. Amongst the bundle of letters to take to Radley was one to Bullington.

'I'll take Katie – the boys too if they want to come,' she told Eugene. But it seemed the boys didn't. Katie was pulled both ways: a ride to town usually meant a candy bar from the Trading Post, and quite often too she saw Ginney, 'M' friend', as she proudly talked of her to the boys; but the barns held great appeal, there was still hay and straw to be rolled in, and doing a job with Aunt Eugene always turned into something they enjoyed. Katie wasn't old enough yet to realise that the satisfaction came from the fact Eugene worked with them, and at the end they could all be proud of what had been accomplished.

However, today the almost-spring sunshine must have tipped the scales and together Katie and Lottie set out. As always they sang what they'd come to call their 'Monday Song.'

'We're zipping along to Radley,
Taking the mail to the Trading Post.
We want to get there quite badly,
Monday's the day we like the most.'

One verse was as much as Katie could master, and one verse said it all. Monday was the special day of the week, not only because of the giving and receiving of letters, but often they met Marthe and Ginney. Monday was the one day Lottie got away from Kilton Down. In the truck she felt she had the freedom of the road, even though in fact she knew every foot of the way and Radley had few enough shops to attract her.

'There's her! Look, Ginney's car!' Katie was first to notice the hybrid parked ahead of them down Second Street near the Knox Presbyterian Church. The habit had formed that Katie would keep Ginney company while the shopping was done, when they'd each get a candy bar for their patience, so today as always Lottie let her through the vanlike door at the back then left them to amuse themselves. Usually she met Marthe either in the Trading Post or nearby, one could hardly miss anyone in Radley! But today there was no sign of her. As she went from one shop to another she glanced back up the road towards where the cars were parked. It half registered on her that a man was hanging about nearby, but she was too busy looking out for Marthe to give him any thought. Today, her weekly supply shopping done, she had to match up some knitting wool for Molly. The only assistant was serving a long-winded customer, then had to unpack a fresh supply of wool to find the shade code Lottie needed. It was ten minutes before she came out. One more call to make and then she'd go and see the children, ask Ginney if she knew which stores Marthe had gone to. The man was still standing on the sidewalk close by the car. Something prompted her to keep an eye on him as she went to buy Old Pop's tobacco. He wasn't doing anything wrong, she couldn't accost him.

Hurrying back up the street to them, she opened the passenger door of Marthe's car. Ginney looked up from the story she was reading aloud.

'Hi, Mrs O'Hagon'.

'Ginney,' she said in hardly more than a whisper, 'has anyone tried to speak to you girls? There's a man hanging around – it's just, you wouldn't let a stranger get in the car when you're left, would you? He's probably quite all right – '

'You meaning me, ma'am?' The softly spoken voice came from immediately behind her. 'Ginney can vouch for me.'

'You talking about *him*?' Ginney giggled. 'He's not hanging around, Mrs O'Hagon. That's Dad.'

Lottie felt uncomfortably embarrassed.

'I'm sorry, Mr . . . ? I don't think I've ever heard your name. Whatever must you think of me, planting Katie in your car, then accusing you of – I'm not even sure what. I was just frightened – two children on their own . . . '

'My name's Ramsey, Ramsey McFee. Marthe told me that you usually left the girls together. Ginney looks forward to it. I've finished all I came to to town for but I didn't get in to wait with them. I think they were enjoying themselves better on their own.'

'I'll collect Katie if you're waiting to get away. I only have to go to the bank now. Isn't Marthe in town today?'

'No, I had to come in so I said I'd fetch the mail home. Don't bother to drag Katie to the bank, I'm OK for time.'

114

'Oh Dad, Dad!' Ginney knocked on the window. 'I only just remembered: Marthe gave me this, said she'd written down something she wanted from Mr Wilke's drugstore.'

'I'll wander up with Mrs O'Hagon here and collect it. Drugstore's right next door to the bank.'

The first thing Lottie had noticed about him was his voice, unhurried and positive. Now she looked at him more closely. His dress was much the same as any other local man's: tough work trousers, checked shirt, leather coat, wide-brimmed hat with a deep well in the crown. As he walked away from the car she saw the smile he gave to Ginney, a smile that came from his brown eyes and only hinted at pulling at the corners of his mouth. In reply Ginney beamed, then turned back to the story and her anxious audience.

'It means a lot to her to have your young Katie come and sit with her.'

'Katie's too young to be much company, but you should hear her boasting to her cousins about "m' friend".'

This time there was no mistaking his smile.

'That's great. But you see from Ginney's point of view it's the one thing she's really lost out on, having the chance to look after someone else, being made the one to be responsible.'

'You know, I'd not thought of that. She's such a sunny child – so normal, unspoilt.'

'Yep, she's great.'

'She reads well. But she doesn't attend the school here? She can't do, she's always with Marthe on Mondays.'

'We take her in to Brian Haggerty three mornings each week. Maybe you've heard speak of him? About the time the O'Hagons were going through the school he must have been Principal. Been retired since before I came to the district. Some ways she gets as much learning in those three mornings as she'd get in five in a classroom. But there's no making up for the companionship she's missing. Here's the bank. Sure glad to have met you, Mrs O'Hagon. It's not just Ginney looks forward to the companionship, but Marthe too. She tells me she's asked you to visit. If you can get around to it, she'd appreciate it.'

'I mean to. Neil hasn't been too happy about me taking the truck anywhere I'm not familiar with, not in the bad weather. I've only been driving since the autumn. Did she tell you she rescued me when I had a puncture?' She smiled, remembering.

'Marthe can do most anything.' It seemed the McFees were of the same mind on that.

115

'My f'end was waiting,' Katie announced when they got back to Kilton Down, 'my f'end Ginney wiv the man.'

'I met her father today. He'd brought her to town, Marthe hadn't come,' Lottie explained.

'All the years he's had that woman living there, wouldn't you think he'd have married her?' Eugene spoke to the room at large. 'I remember my pa talking about the McFee affair. Just about all the district knew tales of Jeanette McFee and the way she carried on. Disgrace to him, she was. Went off with some fella and that was the last we heard. Except that he'd got the foreign woman still living there. Had her eye on him way back then, or that's what Pa used to say. 'Course we lived nearer to Higley Creek than you do here, we would have heard more about it all.'

The gossip wasn't news to any of them, no one bothered to answer and the affair between Ramsey and Marthe was forgotten. That Lottie had met him didn't even cause a ripple on the pond. The following week it was Katie who told them: 'De man was wiv my f'end.' Even Old Pop didn't merit the information worthy of interest.

The dance had given Lottie an idea of what was expected of O'Hagon women, an insight into something she didn't want to acknowledge but could never forget; perhaps it was the lack of interest in her casual meeting with Ramsey McFee that helped draw a veil over that evening.

Last week all she'd collected had been a letter from Eva. This week the mail boat must have come in. One envelope from Brimley with the two separate letters, just as they'd always sent to her when she was at Kingstaunton, just as they'd written their letters to the boys. She could picture it all so clearly. She'd read them later, as she would the one from her grandmother. That's what she always did, shutting herself in her bedroom. If she scanned through them here in the street she'd spoil it. On a third she recognised her cousin Luke's handwriting, then there was another with a Vancouver postmark – she knew must be from one of the girls she'd travelled out with. All those she pushed into her pocket for later. There was one more. It was over a year since that night she'd said goodbye to Barrie. In all that time he hadn't written, and she hadn't looked for any word from him. She was surprised to find just how pleased she was to hear from him now. The letter had to go in her pocket with the others as she and Marthe stacked their shopping away and Katie was transferred back into the truck.

Driving out of town her fingers kept going to the envelope until finally curiosity got the better of her. Half way home she drew to the side of the road and opened it up.

116

'Why we stopped, Mom? Have we broken?'

'Do you remember our friend Barrie?'

'De man wiv Ginney?' Clearly she didn't.

'No. In England. You can't remember? Granny and Grandad, you remember them, their picture's in your room? You don't forget them, Katie?'

'Kiss picture,' Katie assured her. But that was all they were to her, a picture in a silver frame, Kate's parting present.

'Listen, Katie, listen to what he says!'

Obligingly, Katie listened.

Chapter Eight

What had she said? Old Pop's rheumy eyes accused her, his tongue gripped hard between his gums; Eugene looked from one to the other, uncertain what to expect. It was Molly who spoke.

'The boy won't like it. Can't understand what sort of a friend it can be, writing to you like you're a free woman. He knows you're a Mrs.'

'Of course he does.' Lottie laughed, still confident they'd somehow misunderstood. 'He was a guest at the wedding. Neil met him. Why, pretty well all through the war he used to spend all his free time with us.' It was at this point that Donald came in. 'But isn't it sad? All the miles Barrie must have walked with Katie on his shoulders, all the hours he spent romping with her, and would you believe it, she doesn't even remember.'

'You do, though,' the old man's tongue waggled, a sure sign of excitement, 'gave you plenty to remember did he, this young Barrie?'

'Now then, Pop.' Molly put her hand on his shoulder. He was enjoying himself at someone else's expense, and when that happened he never knew when to stop. 'No one's accusing Lottie of misbehaving with this young man. All I'm saying is this: you're a married woman, Lottie, ain't the thing at all to get letters from men not even part of the family, 'specially men you've had time with without your husband. Perhaps customs are lax amongst your folk, but that's the way of it here at Kilton Down – and you'll find Neil thinks same as we do. If this man wanted to write to you, then he should have addressed his words to the both of you, Mr and Mrs.'

'Can you see Eugene here getting letters from some man out of her past?' Old Pop wasn't going to give up that easily.

'You're talking nonsense.' Lottie pushed Barrie's letter back into her pocket. 'A family friend, someone I've known for years, why should he write to Neil? They wouldn't even recognise each other. But they'll have the chance to know each other. Barrie is coming to

119

Calgary, that's what I was starting to tell you, that's why he's written. He's a flyer, you see, he's going to work with an air freight company.'

Donald said nothing, just turned to look at each of them, his big head nodding or shaking according to the way the discussion went.

Eugene hated arguments. 'We can't blame Lottie because she got a letter. Right, like you say, Mom, the proper thing would have been to send it to the both of them,' she soothed, 'but when she writes back she can explain to him, make sure next time that's what he does. Just give the letter to Neil to read, Lottie, share it with him, that's all you need to do.'

'Not so sure.' Molly frowned. 'None knows the boy better than I do. Anyways, he's not so different from any other fella fresh to having a wife – you can't count those years before you came out here, that was no marriage – '

A guffaw from the old man. 'Holy diddle, no marriage, and there she was with this young English flyer.' The situation brightened up his dull day, he meant to make the most of it.

'Hush up now, Pop. Nothing wrong with the way Lottie carried on while Neil was away, we're not suggesting there was. Just that young Neil'll see it like any other man would. His woman belongs just to him . . . ' Then, finally closing what Lottie saw as a ridiculously petty discussion: 'You bring the stores from town that I told you, Lottie?'

On that Monday Neil didn't come home with the others.

'Doug Rogers drove by and picked him up,' Craig explained. 'Went straight out to Radley to that club of theirs. I walked his horse home, seeing it saved him coming back here for the truck. Doug'll pass this way later, he'll drop him by.'

On the evening of the dance Lottie had expected that Neil's behaviour would have spoilt things for him at the Club. But it seemed that the men accepted his jealousy, the skirmish, the bloody nose, and whatever it was that his opponent had suffered. He'd gone right back there as if nothing had happened. Since then though he'd not taken Lottie with him.

On this night he'd not yet returned when Katie cried out in her sleep and Lottie went to her. Sitting on the edge of the bed, the little girl again asleep, she listened to the sounds of the house. One by one the family were going to bed. Doors were closed, lights out. She crept from Katie's room and went to her own. Only once had he been as late as this, she thought, uneasily: on that first evening that the Club had opened. With her ears attuned for the sound of Doug's truck, she undressed.

There was the motor now. The door slammed . . . yes, he was crossing the yard. With no one for him to stop and talk to, he'd come straight in here to her. So she climbed into bed. But it seemed she'd not been the only one waiting and listening. She heard Donald's door opening, heard him hurry along the corridor outside her room. There was no mistaking his stumbling footsteps. He must have gone to see if Neil needed help. 'I've looked after him before when he's been pissed.' Tonight though there'd been nothing in his step to suggest that he'd had too much to drink.

From the kitchen came the sound of voices. Minutes passed. Fancy staying out there chattering with Donald at this time of night! She got out of bed and very quietly opened the door of her room, trying to hear what it was that kept them. Too late though, already Neil was coming along the passage, Donald close behind.

'So you heard!' Neil pushed her back into the room and closed the door, leaning against it, reaching to switch on the bedroom light.

'Heard what? I couldn't think what was keeping you. I looked out to watch you come in – '

'Heard what he was telling me, that's what. That you got a letter from your boyfriend.' There as an ugly twist to his mouth, his eyes were full of hate. 'No wonder you're so keen to get to Radley on Mondays. Writes often, does he? But now of course it's different.' He came to stand over her, his face only inches from hers. 'This time you put up a show of surprise: "A friend from home" (spoken in an exaggeratedly English voice). Following you over here, is he?'

By now she knew she'd misjudged the straight course he'd taken from truck to door. He was not as drunk as on the other occasion, but even so she turned her head away from the smell of whisky on his breath.'

'I don't know what Donald told you. It's Barrie, you remember him? I've got the letter in the drawer here, I put it for you to read.' Her heart was hammering. In this mood Neil was unpredictable. Already the rest of the family must have heard his loud voice. There was no privacy.

Now as she pulled the drawer open to get the letter he was just behind her; his hand reached out, not for the envelope, but for a cardboard package he recognised as containing contraceptive jelloids.

'What the hell are you doing with these things? Have you ever used them?'

'Of course I use them, Neil, one of us has to see we're careful.' As his voice got louder so hers seemed more controlled.

'Who the hell do you think you are to tell me what I should do? Christ Almighty, you're my wife! *I'll* be the one to decide if we don't want children!'

121

'Of course we want more children. And, Neil, we'll have them too. But not here. When we have a home to ourselves we'll have more babies. You missed so much with Katie, but next time it'll be different. There'll be just us.'

'This is my home, this is where my work is, and you bloody knew it when you married me. Ain't things smart enough for you, is that it?' With his eyes half closed he peered at her, his face close to hers. 'Three sons Eugene's given Craig already. And I been watching, waiting – and all the time you been getting ahead of me with those bloody things. Did you use them with your friend Barrie too while I was at the war?'

Her action was spontaneous. Her hand lashed out, leaving the marks of her fingers on his face. And as if my contrast, into her mind came the memory of Barrie, her final farewell to him in the garden at home, their one short embrace.

She was unprepared for Neil's next move. He pulled the letter from its envelope, without so much as glancing at it. From his pocket he took his lighter and before she could stop him orange tongues of flame were reaching out from the bottom corner of the paper, leaping, stretching.

'You drunken fool!' She tried to get it from him, but he held it higher, waving it out of her reach. Only when it scorched his fingers did he left it fall, and ground the charred remains into the wooden floor.

'I wouldn't remember him, that's what you told them. Well, you're wrong. And you know why I remember him?' Now his hands gripped her shoulders. She tried to struggle out of his grasp but it was useless. 'You think I didn't notice the way he looked at you, wanted you for himself, just like *she* would like to have had him for you? Smarmy sod . . . one of the "boys in blue", one of the heroes of the air with his wings on his pocket and his squadron leader rings on his cuff. Would have fitted in with the rest of them, that's what *she* would have liked, wouldn't she?'

'Who? I don't know what you mean. You're drunk. Don't grip me like that, you're hurting.'

'Oh, yes, you do know who I mean, and you know it's true. That mother of yours who looked down her aristocratic nose on a soldier who didn't have pips on his shoulders.'

'And where would you have put them if you'd had them, with a chip the size you carry there already?'

'Christ, but sometimes you're bitchier than your old lady.'

Why did he have to be like this? Her stomach was tied in knots, her throat felt tight. Only anger could protect her. They glared at each other, their eyes full of hurt.

'I don't want to talk about them, not now. Just leave go of me, can't you?' Her voice was low. She was frightened that if she raised it she'd lose the control she fought for. 'I don't know what Donald told you, but there was nothing in Barrie's letter.'

'And what about all the time I was away fighting? Is that true, that he was with you? While we common bloody soldiers won the war, he was swanning it at home with your lady mother, keeping company with *my* wife?' His eyes half closed, he glowered at her. 'Well?'

'He was stationed near Brimley after he was grounded. Of course he spent his time with us.'

'Just like "of course" you didn't tell me. Walked miles together? Bicycle rides too? Just like Kingstaunton, eh?' His sneering expression made it impossible for her to tell him why she hadn't written about Barrie in her letters. Perhaps, too, she wasn't even sure herself what the real truth was about her silence. She'd put herself into his position, tried to imagine how *she* would have felt to know that somewhere overseas he was sharing the experience of his war with a girl who was part of his life at home. But tonight it was suddenly impossible to try to explain. The way he'd spoken about her mother and her family was holding them apart.

'When you're sober, you might talk more sense.' How small and cold her voice was. She was almost frightened to open her mouth to speak, her jaw ached from being held rigid. 'I shall sleep with Katie, she's already cried out once. If I'm with her she'll settle.'

'Oh no,' he was breathing deeply, 'no, you won't. If I say you'll stay here, you'll stay here. Right here . . . ' Before she knew it she was pushed back on to the bed. With both hands he gripped the silk of her nightdress at the neck. She heard the material rip. She wriggled to get free but he held her down with his knee. 'Now where will you run to?' From neck to hem it was torn. His eyes devoured her, though not with love. Lust, anger, a need to overpower her, to prove himself her master, these were the things she read in the look that travelled over her. The knee still anchored her, that and one hand now while with his other he unbuttoned the front of his trousers.

'No! Please, no. Not like this. No!' She crossed her ankles, she bit his hand. All that her struggling did was to add fuel to his strength. Roughly he forced himself on to her while she lay spreadeagled, hardly able to breathe. She bit her lip hard, hating him. How could he do it to her? He was hurting her.

Oh, but what a moment for her to remember that other time, there on the brow of Madlock Hill. 'Honey, I've hurt you.' And her reply: 'I wanted it to hurt.'

Tears stung her closed eyes. Her body felt raw – used – unloved. And as he pounded at her he snorted, grunted; he was doing it

123

purposely, it was all part of that act of mastery. She knew that in seconds now it would be over for him. She mustered her strength and chose her moment to throw him off her.

'You're not a man.' Her heart was banging, she was gasping for breath now that at last she could get air. 'You're just an animal!'

Rolling from the bed she stood up, her ruined nightgown hanging open. He was silent, his head buried in the pillow. And in that moment she heard a sound that was familiar: footsteps in the corridor, then Donald's door being quietly closed. He'd listened! She looked at Neil sprawled on the bed still in his working clothes, even his boots. Her husband. For him she'd sacrificed everything familiar. (Later she'd perhaps be honest enough to admit that there'd been much she'd wanted to be free of.) Now she slipped her arms into her dressing gown and tiptoed towards the door, switching off the light as she went.

'Christ!' Hearing, she stood still, rooted to the spot. 'Oh, Christ!' He was crying, sobbing helplessly. 'Didn't mean . . . just . . . couldn't help . . . ' He was struggling from the bed, groping out to reach her. In the dark he found her and knelt at her feet, clinging to her, his head pressed against her. 'Don't leave me, don't go.' Crying so that he was barely able to form the words.

Not five minutes ago she'd been shaken with the intensity of her hatred for him. Not that was swept from her mind, even the memory of it gone. Whatever self-inflicted hell they'd made for themselves tonight, it had been for both of them. She dropped to her knees too, holding him close. At last her own tears won the battle and she gave way to emotion that had no words.

'Lottie, what've I done to you? Love you so much.'

'It's all right, we're all right now. Hush, hush.' Who was she comforting, herself or him, as they rocked in each other's arms? 'You've got to trust me too. Love's no good without trust.'

'So frightened. Frightened someone'll take you away from me. Things I said – about your family – there's part of you I can't reach, don't you see? Christ, but I want all of you.'

She'd recovered quicker than he had. It was years since he'd cried, and now he couldn't stop trembling.

'We've got to be honest.' She rubbed her cheek against his as she spoke. 'If I said to you that I wanted all of you, that you mustn't love your mom, your family, Kilton Down, you can see it's just not possible. If you could change like that, just stop caring, then you wouldn't be the man I love. The things I left at home – '

'Ha! "Home"! Is that what you still call it?'

'The things I left in England, they're sort of knitted into me, of course they are, and that's the me that you got to know in Kingstaun-

124

ton.' She felt drained, wanted to steer them away from emotion. 'Anyway, it was Barrie's letter that started all this.' Consciously she made her voice friendly, as if none of the last half hour had happened. 'He's really Ronnie's friend. It would have been the same with any of their friends if they'd been stationed nearby. He was glad to have a home to come to – but more than that, after I'd come out here and with Ronnie still away, Barrie visited just the same. Mum often mentions it in her letters.' There was no suggestion in her manner of the pictures in her mind; heads down as they cycled home from the pictures; the undemanding companionship as they'd tramped the hills, Katie astride his shoulders; the echo of a voice in the night: "If things don't work out . . . no matter how you feel about sending to anyone else, promise you'll tell me." And: "Fool that I am, I've fallen in love with a married woman."

'Still went calling, did he? Yeah, and I'll tell you something else – I bet the welcome he got was different to the one they held out to me.'

'Perhaps they were scared too, Neil. They knew you threatened them and Barrie didn't.'

He didn't answer. They moved away from each other, both wanting now just to forget.

'Neil,' she whispered into the darkness later as they lay in bed, 'don't let's talk – not about all that, not any more – it's just that . . . you know what I heard? It was Donald, outside. He must have been listening, must have known how you – ' She didn't finish the sentence, frightened to dig into memories so new.

'You don't want to worry about Donald, he don't reason things out too well.'

'He watches me, I know he does. You say he can't reason things out – I think that's what frightens me.'

Neil was weighing her words.

'No need. Just make friends with him, that's all you got to do. You got nothing to fear from Donald. I tell you, he ain't like the rest of us.'

'But he creeps about, watches, listens – '

'Not much else for the poor old guy, is there? He's always been real fond of me. Maybe you might just keep out of his way for a day or two. If he figures you treated me rough . . . ' He turned his back, settled comfortably, and almost immediately she knew he was asleep.

For a long time she lay awake. Home, Bullington, her people, Barrie, the feeling of soft rain, summer holidays and the sound of waves on the shore, games of tennis in the garden, the boys charging down the attic stairs on the morning of her birthday, Eva and the birth of a dream. Then Barrie, what life might have been had she not met Neil . . .

125

'Lottie, here a minute,' Neil called her out into the yard the next morning, out of earshot of the rest of the family.

'You'll be answering your fan mail. Just remember, that guy might have been welcomed into your folks' home, but there's no way he will be here.'

'That's dreadful! He's been my friend and Katie's, he'll be your friend too.'

'Like hell! Jeez, but don't you know anything? Men don't work that way.'

'Not again, Neil. Please. We said it all last night.'

'Sure we did. Lottie honey, I couldn't take another night like that. I know men. If you had a body like a sack of turnips and a crop of acne on your face, you're telling me this guy would have come chasing out to Canada?'

'Depends how good a job he's been offered, I'd say.' Then her conker-brown eyes teased. 'Anyway, I expect if I had a body like a sack of turnips and that crop of acne, you'd have left me where I was in the dancehall in Kingstaunton!'

'You're darned right I would.' This time he laughed too. The words seemed to draw a final line under the incident.

It was soon after that that two things happened to alter the regular pattern of their days. The first stemmed from a Monday when, arriving in Radley, they could see no sign of the hybrid car.

'They'll soon be here,' she tried to cheer crestfallen Katie. 'You'll have to come with me to the stores until they arrive, we'll watch out for them.'

Not a happy outing as Katie's bottom lip made clear.

'Hi there, Mrs O'Hagon.' She recognised the voice even before she turned.

'Mr McFee, hello. You've come instead of Marthe? Katie was miserable, she thought she wasn't going to see her friend.'

'Just Ramsey, let's cut the Mr. And Marthe speaks about you as Lottie. Do you mind if I do too?'

'I'd much rather,' she smiled, aware of Katie's change of expression too as she peered up and down the street for that familiar car. 'Where's Ginney?'

'I'm afraid her Mondays are tied up now. She used to go to Mr Haggerty three mornings a week, remember I told you? Now, for personal reasons of his own at home, he wants her in the afternoons on Mondays, Tuesdays and Wednesdays. That means no more trips to town for the mail. I have a message for you, for both of you. Marthe says won't you come to Higley Creek for the day? She suggested Thursday but I guess she'd fall in with any day you want.'

126

'Thursday will be lovely. Hear that, Katie? A whole day with Ginney on Thursday. Can you explain just how I get there?'

'Sure. See here, I've drawn out a map for you. You needn't come all the way to Radley. Turn off to the left about mid-way, heading straight on about four miles. You'll come to a lake, Hermit Lake, maybe you know it? See, I've marked it. Just beyond you'll get a right turn and then another two miles or so and a road crosses. If you can give me some idea how early you can get there, I'll be waiting on that cross-road and lead you in.'

'Are you sure you don't mind?'

'Sure I'm sure.' How silly that a smile from a man of forty should suddenly put her in mind of a shy lad. 'I'll guide you back to the house then I'll leave you girls. They've been looking forward to your visit. Not many folk come calling. Of course, not every woman can handle a car and we're a long way out of town.'

The following Thursday Ramsey was good as his word. He was waiting at the cross-roads, he led the way back to Higley Creek, then with a wave of his hand, drove on to the yard where he left the car – not the hybrid, this four-wheel-drive vehicle put her in mind of the Jeeps the Americans had used during the war. A few minutes later she heard the sound of horses hooves as he rode out to whatever day's work he'd interrupted to meet her.

The McFee home was very different from the ranch house at Kilton Down. Here there was no eating in the kitchen, the food doled straight from saucepan to plate. Here the wooden floors were polished, the rugs regularly shaken so that no dust dulled their patterns, the chintz covers on the chairs as fresh as the curtains at the windows.

'Who else is there here except the three of you? Who helps you in the house?'

'To care for the house is a joy to me, I want no other woman polishing these windows and interfering in the way I do things.' Marthe gazed around her, her expression putting Lottie in mind of a loving mother admiring her talented offspring. 'Outside – that's not for me. The home is my kingdom. Would you like to see all the rooms? Do you like homes? But of course you do. Didn't you tell me, you plan one day to move into a place just for yourselves? That is good. That is as a family should be.' Even though by now Lottie was used to her voice, it still fascinated her. It seemed to encapsulate Marthe's vigorous personality; she didn't shout, yet she spoke with force in that accent that set her apart from anyone else. 'Ginney, I am taking Mrs O'Hagon to look into the rooms. You are to take care of Katie. You have all your crayons and the books. You may each eat an apple if you wish.' And it seemed that they both 'vished'. Then, the

127

door closed on the children: 'This is what is good. To leave them. There is years between them, but they are friends.' She actually said 'vriends'. But then Katie talked of 'my f'end'. What difference how they pronounced it, friendship there certainly was between the eight year old and the three year old.

The tour of inspection showed that every room in the house was sparkling with loving care. Marthe showed her 'my room' – no frills here, but then Lottie would have been surprised to find any – then Ginney's, as feminine as any little girl might dream of.

'This is Ramsey's.' Lottie felt she was intruding; she took only a quick glance. Just long enough to see the polished rosewood furniture, folkweave curtains with counterpane of the same material thrown over a double bed. She was glad to shut the door and turn to bedroom number four. In all there were six, even the spares looking ready for use. There was no doubting the truth of what Marthe had said: caring for the house was a joy to her.

It was only driving back to Kilton Down late in the afternoon that Lottie's thoughts wandered to those two rooms, Marthe's with her single bed, Ramsey's with his double. Did they keep up appearances for the sake of Ginney? As Eugene had said, why weren't they married? Then she pulled her curious mind back into control. Whatever their reasons it was no business of hers!

Thursdays became Higley Creek days. And for Katie the reason for going to Radley no longer existed, it was more fun to stay at home and play with the boys. So those were the two alterations in the pattern of Lottie's days, a trip to town on her own on Mondays and a visit to Higley Creek on Thursdays.

'That young fella, the one you got the letter from, has he come over to Calgary yet?' It was Old Pop who asked her. The whole family was there, the only sound the scraping of forks on plates as they stowed away their food. Now even the forks were stilled. 'You never said except just the once?'

'Get on with your supper, Pop. Ain't any business of yours what letters Lottie gets from England.' Molly glared across the table at her father-in-law.

'I don't know, Pop,' Lottie lied, 'it's too far for him to come visiting. I doubt whether he'll contact me.'

The tip of Old Pop's tongue trembled in his enjoyment of the moment. Then, meeting her glance, he shut one eye in a broad and mischievous wink. She hoped her cheeks didn't look as warm as they felt, or all of them would know she'd not told the truth. Realising how Neil felt – and being sure how he's behave if Barrie came here – she'd

128

torn up her first spontaneous reply. But the following Monday she'd mailed a letter to him telling him how glad she was about his new job, giving him Eva's address in case he wanted a local contact, explaining that Kilton Down had no spare rooms so she wasn't able to invite him, but when she could get to Calgary she'd let him know so that they could meet.

The Monday that she'd collected his answer there had been a short and violent thunderstorm. Vivid lightning, crashing thunder, but what rain there was had splashed in separate, heavy and well-spaced plops. She'd left the truck outside the chapel at the other end of the street and, coming out of the Trading Post with the mail, had eagerly torn open the envelope. A rumble of thunder almost overhead, then down came the rain!

'Here, jump in, you'll get drenched.' Ramsey had opened the car door as he'd called to her.

'Thanks. I'm parked at the end of the street.' Settling by his side in the car she'd looked at the two sheets of paper in her hand, the ink smudged.

'I guess letters mean a lot. You've got a family back home? I mean a close family, parents? Sisters maybe?' He'd taken out a cigarette packet and offered it to her.

'No thanks.' Then as he'd put it back in his pocket: 'But you have one. They all smoke at Kilton Down, it's just that I don't like the taste.' But instead he'd taken out his pipe and started to pack it with tobacco. 'My father smokes a pipe.'

'Ah, so you have a father? And a mother?'

There was something very comforting about a man smoking a pipe, she'd always thought so, and that afternoon with the rain dancing on the roof of the car and Ramsey contentedly puffing at her side, she'd thought so again. How easy it had been to talk to him. And he'd listened as if he honestly wanted to hear about her home, the evenings of black-out, the years of growing up with Michael and Ronnie. She'd talked about the day Katie had been born, about how she'd suddenly understood her own mother. Ramsey McFee was a stranger yet she'd told him things she'd never spoken of to a single soul. Afterwards she'd wondered why it had been so easy to talk – and why suddenly she'd felt it so necessary. Perhaps it had been something to do with the storm, the two of them enclosed in a world of their own, water flooding down the street, rain hammering on the roof; or more likely it had been because somewhere in his past he'd known unhappiness, his marriage had gone wrong, his wife had been unfaithful, his daughter hurt. Even today, she'd supposed, as the clouds had moved away and the sun suddenly broken out, there must

129

be obstacles that stood between him and Marthe, some reason why they had to make this pretence and couldn't live honestly together, Mr and Mrs McFee.

She'd laid out Barrie's letter on the back seat of the car. If she'd folded the pages away they would never have been readable even when they'd dried. As the rain eased and the sun cast its first rays, she'd picked up the two still wet pieces of paper.

'Pity you opened it, it looks a real mess.' He'd sounded really concerned. 'It must have been one of the hardest things to get used to here, only having mail once a week.'

'Yes. But there aren't the disappointments. I know each Monday I shall have something. Watching each morning for the postman to come up the road so often ends in just seeing him pass the gate.'

'All the same, to wait a week then have it almost too smudged to read – '

'This isn't the only one. I've got the others in my pocket. I never read them until I get back. Sort of save them up, knowing I've got them. Like if you've got lots of money in your pocket you don't need to spend; it's only when you haven't that you see things you want.'

He'd smiled, blowing out an aura of pipe-smoke.

'This one's different. It's from Barrie.' She'd sensed a change in his manner – or had she imagined it? 'It's not like you think. But that's why I'm not going to take it home with me. I was reading it so that I could get rid of it before I went back. They thought like you did. Even Neil was – was – well, I suppose he was hurt. But it was so silly. Barrie is a dear, I'm very very fond of him. The silly thing is that that's not the sort of thing you can say to your husband.'

It had been the sort of thing she could say to Ramsey though. He'd prompted, but never probed. When it had come to Neil's part he hadn't even prompted, neither had she told him. She'd been surprised by the way the family had reacted; been shocked by Neil's attitude. Listening, fitting the pieces together and mentally adding those that she'd left out, Ramsey had been surprised at none of it. He'd known the sort of people she was dealing with. 'Good people' had been Eva's opinion; he might have said the same. But he'd met enough of their sort to known the way their minds worked. And there'd been another piece of the puzzle he'd been sure about too: Barrie wouldn't have spent all his off-duty hours with Lottie unless he'd been in love with her.

No one asked her whether she saw Marthe Koparomy in town now that Ginney had to be taken to Mr Haggerty on Mondays. And she'd learnt her lesson: she didn't mention the occasions when she chanced to meet Ramsey. The O'Hagons had what she considered silly, narrow-minded ideas, they'd read into the meetings something that didn't exist. There was only one man for her and that was Neil. As for Ramsey, he belonged to Marthe and to Ginney.

Yet, during those months of summer, a friendship was growing. It made no demands; it gave no heartache. Until she came to know Ramsey she'd not realised just how much she'd missed a kindred spirit. Despite the difference in ages between Lavinia and herself, that's what they had always been, kindred spirits. And then there'd been Eva.

As long as Lottie had been in England, this special aunt had been cognisant of all her hopes and disappointments; she'd been entwined in dreams of the future too as childhood had given way to adolescence. Last summer Eva had suggested they spend some of her leave together, but with each letter from Neil Lottie had expected to hear when he was to be demobbed, so the idea had come to nothing. This year though it was to be different. Neil was home. When Eva planned her leave she arranged for a week at Kilton Down in June and a fortnight in California in August.

Molly's welcome was genuine. Lottie's aunt would be treated as a member of the family.

But the visit didn't materialise. Eva suffered a minor car accident, wasn't hurt, but decided she'd wait and come later. And Lottie wasn't as disappointed as she would have expected. Somehow she'd never been able to imagine Eva at Kilton Down.

All through those years in England Lottie had poured out her heart in her letters, all her hopes and dreams, feeling no sense of betrayal in what she wrote, for always associated with Eva had been the dream that had started so long ago – life in Alberta, the land Eva loved.

In the last year Lottie had grown wiser. If the castles she'd built in the air had no substance on the rolling range of Kilton Down, it was because happiness can never be handed out, ready-made and all embracing. She'd found plenty of moments of carefree joy, riding with Neil, learning to swing a lasso, putting Sherry to a jump and hearing the shout of praise from him that she wanted; or lying in his arms, enveloped in a peace that came from their shared content. There were times when her happiness stemmed from Katie: the tilt of her head as she laughed, her determination in handling a huge broom as she and the boys helped in the yard. There could never be unadulterated pleasure in those moments, though; her happy pride was bitter-sweet. Katie was robbed of a family who loved her. Letters home described how the baby they'd lost was growing into a merry little girl – but letters couldn't carry the sound of footsteps that had

131

changed from the rush and stumble of a two year old to the firm light tread of a three year old; letters might tell that she could sing in tune now but there was no way of conveying her eagerness as she carolled. These days it was a Thursday song:

'We're on our way to Higley Creek,
We go on Thursday every week.
We don't care if it rains or snows,
We don't care if the north wind blows,
Ginney and Marthe are waiting for us – '

Lottie was no poet. On their second visit when the song had been born, a last line had eluded her until in desperation she'd sung: 'More 'an that we don't give a cuss.'

And so it had remained, to be sung with gusto as they covered the miles. Coming home there was a slight variation:

'We're coming home from Higley Creek,
That's were we visit every week.
We don't care if it rains or snows,
We don't care if the north wind blows,
Ginney and Marthe were waiting for us
More 'an that we don't give a toss.'

It wouldn't be long now before the threat of those snows would become a reality.

'Can smell it in the air. Soon be fall.' There was eagerness in Neil's voice. From far away he'd dreamed of round-up time.

There was an atmosphere of anticipation in the house too; this year with Neil home Lottie felt herself caught up in it. Casual labour was being taken on, the fences of the corral checked and any damage made good. Kilton Down was ready for its 'season of the year.'

'There's excitement everywhere, you can't help getting caught up in it even if you aren't going to ride out and help get the cattle in. They have taken on extra labour.'

At the sound of people riding into the yard she looked up from her weekly letter home. The men had been out since first light, they weren't expected home until evening. But that was Neil's voice. Going to the window she looked out.

Lowering herself from her saddle as easily as he did was a woman. Lottie was reminded of the olive-skinned people she'd seen from an Indian settlement area a few miles west of Radley. She had hair as black as jet, anchored at the nape of her neck by some sort of a band and hanging sleek and straight to below her waist. Riding behind them and still mounted was a young boy, as dark as the woman. Although he remained in the saddle, Lottie was sure his movements would be just as agile.

132

Eugene must have looked out of a window and seen them too.

'Hey Mom, take a peak. It's Rosie and the boy.'

In the back of Lottie's mind a memory stirred. Last year hadn't she heard them talk of someone called Rosie, someone who'd ridden in looking for work with the round-up? But last year she hadn't stayed.

In the kitchen Old Pop heard and looked up from the chair where he spent his days. His eyes were bright. His tongue was clamped firmly between his gums, the tip waggling with anticipation.

Chapter Nine

'. . . hoped after she heard last year how things were, she might have kept away. Have to watch out with that boy – ' Hearing Lottie come into the room, Molly cut off in mid-sentence.

'Who are the visitors?'

'It's the woman, Rosie, and her son.' Eugene gave her the bare facts.

It was Pop who took up the tale. Chewing on his tobacco and settling more comfortably in his chair, hc was prepared to enjoy himself.

'Casual help for round-up. You heard them saying they been taking 'em on. Rosie, she been coming here for years, since before she had the boy. Not a man out there can catch a running steer sweeter than Rosie – never seen her for myself, but you ask young Neil!' He anchored his tongue as he chortled. 'Not been these past few years.'

'She did look in last year, Pop, but I reckon it was too late, they were fixed up for men.' Again it was Eugene the peacemaker. Molly said nothing but plainly she was worried as she stood at the window watching the three in the yard.

'Are they from the Indian settlement?' Lottie asked. Could that be why Molly was uneasy about them being here, was it something to do with the rules for employing people from there?

'She's not pure Indian. Rosie's a half-breed. Ain't her race that bothers me. See, he's bringing them in. Wouldn't you think . . . ?' But she didn't elaborate. The others must have understood. Eugene nodded, looking as worried as Molly; Pop chortled then spat on to the fire, the sizzle of a direct hit adding to his enjoyment of the situation.

'I've brought Dylan to the house, Mom, same as we always used to,' Neil said as he led the way in. 'Rides good enough to be out there with the men, eh, Dylan? Just got an inch or two to grow first.'

135

'Rosie taught me to throw a rope – I'm not some kid has to be minded,' the boy argued.

What a handsome child he was! Hair was black as his mother's, but not heavy and sleek like hers. The way it curled belied his Indian ancestry, just as did his startlingly light blue eyes. Yet his skin was as dark as hers, and he had that same feline grace in his movements. Lottie took all this in at a glance before she turned her attention to the woman. Seen at close quarters she was older than she'd seemed dismounting out there in the yard. Mid-forties perhaps, older than one would have expected to be mother of this child.

'You'll keep him at the house, Mrs O'Hagon?' She turned to Molly. 'I'll pick him up when the light gets too bad to work.'

'Hadn't expected you round here this year, Rosie. Thought you'd be done with Kilton Down.' Then Molly seemed to dismiss Rosie, and instead turned to the boy. 'But you're welcome enough here, Dylan. Same as you always were. Old enough to be useful too. Got plenty I'll be glad of our help with, boy.'

Lottie might not have been there for all the notice anyone took of her.

'Neil, aren't you going to introduce me?' There was a smile in her voice. She didn't begin to understand the undercurrents, but she was aware of them and so must Neil be. If he brought people to the house, then let him see that at least in her he had support.

'Sure. This is Rosie, she helps get the cattle in. Rosie, you heard about Lottie, out from England?'

'Your wife.' Rosie's black eyes mocked him as she said the words he appeared to have avoided. She clasped the hand Lottie held to her. 'You're about what I expected from what I'd heard.'

Lottie laughed. 'That might mean anything! What's he been telling you?'

'There's nothing secret around these parts. Dylan's OK with you then, Mrs O'Hagon?' This last addressed to Molly.

'I told him so.' Molly had spoken to the boy in the same way as she did the other children; she never fussed over them, never talked down to them, but met them as equals she was prepared to get on with. Now, turning away from him, she addressed herself just to Rosie: 'You been working some other place these last years. Ain't no wisdom in coming back looking for times that are gone.'

'Hey now, Mom, Rosie here is worth two men. Round-up wouldn't be the same without Rosie.' Only for one brief second did Lottie suspect that her remark had thrown Neil off-balance, then the grin he gave his mother told her that she must have imagined it.

136

'That it wouldn't,' Pop chuckled. 'I reckon there's no living things moves too fast for Rosie to bring in. Dang these old legs o' mine, what I wouldn't give to be out there with you, boy.'

Neil and Rosie were keen to be off. A minute later Lottie watched them ride out of the yard. Not many women handled a horse well enough to help at round-up, that's what he'd told her when first he'd talked about it. But he'd made no mention of Rosie, the woman worth any two men.

'Now then, you kids, there's all those logs to be sorted and got under cover.' Molly believed in keeping small hands occupied.

'I'll help them,' Lottie offered, looking at the mountain of sawn logs that had been brought home and tipped in the yard.

'Yeah, best you do. Some of that wood is too heavy for them,' Eugene agreed. 'Dylan looks strong, but give me a shout if you want me. You know how they get stored – in the long shed, smallest easiest to get at. Got to get it under cover before the snow comes or we'll be in trouble.'

A bright September, the satisfaction of working outside, the smell of freshly hewn logs, the sight of small children staggering under the weight of the wood, the knowledge that Neil was out there on the range doing his favourite job of the year . . . all these things added to Lottie's growing contentment. There would be days when she'd only see the other side of the coin, when she'd know that if she lived amongst them all her days she'd never become what the O'Hagons expected of their women. It was different with the children. Today she felt herself in tune with them, and with the blue-eyed half-breed Indian boy.

'Careful, Dylan,' she called out to him, seeing him with the axe in his hand. 'You'd better leave the chopping for the men. Let's sort out the logs that are small enough to go straight on to the fire.'

'I'm not a kid!' He spoke with such assurance, the three young ones silently watching, giving him new respect. 'I've chopped the wood for years.' The way he wielded the axe proved his words.

'Come on, Katie, don't slack off,' she heard Earl say a few minutes later.

'I's busy watching, I's seeing Dylan.'

Sitting cross-legged at a safe distance from the axe she watched him, her blue eyes wide with admiration. Three and a half years old, already Katie had found her first hero.

On that first morning Dylan had resented being left at the ranch house. He was used to freedom, that's the way he'd been brought up. Back at the settlement, often Rosie would be gone all day and he'd be alone, or sometimes he'd ride off and be gone all day himself and she never bothered. He hunted and fished, brought as much into the house as she did herself. Dylan considered himself a man already. No wonder he objected to being left in a house of women, children and one old man.

By the time Neil told him his mother was waiting in the yard ready to ride back to the settlement, he'd forgotten feeling ill-used. All day he'd been busy. Mrs O'Hagon ('the old one' as his eleven-year-old mind thought of Molly) had piled is plate with a man-sized dinner and told him he'd done a man's job and earned it.

'We'll be expecting you in the morning, boy,' she said as he was leaving. 'By first light your mother will be out there, so you come right along in and take your breakfast with the rest of us.'

He nodded. He was actually looking forward to coming again! Then: "Bye, you lot,' to the three children. "bye Lottie.' All day they'd worked as a team. But he'd been the most important, he'd been the only one with the axe.

The others shouted their goodbyes; Katie followed him out to the yard to wave as he rode away into the darkness.

'Trouble with you is, Pop, you can't get off that skinny old butt of yours and do a job of work,' Molly read the riot act to him. 'Sitting there all day long scheming how you can amuse yourself by stirring up a bit of trouble for someone else. You're a wicked old man, that's what you are.' Hard words, but her tone took the sting out of them.

'Bet you ten cents it's true. That lad of yours was never one to waste his time with a woman playing tiddly-winks.'

'Sure thing he wouldn't be your grandson if he did.' Pop took that as a compliment. 'Anyways,' Molly went on, 'things are different now and no good'll come of you trying to rekindle life back into dead ashes.' Then, seeing Lottie and her 'team' coming towards the house: 'Hush up, now, she's coming. And don't you let me hear you making trouble.'

'Still say what I've said from the start, he should have found a wife from our own sort. Not some foreigner just because she's got a pretty face.'

'Oh, so you do give her credit for that much?'

At that moment Lottie came into the room. His 'Acch!' wasn't exactly an answer, but that and the way he looked from Molly to her and back again told her that she'd interrupted something not intended for her ears.

Pop knew when he was beaten. He got his own back in the only way for him. He cleared his throat, once, twice, again, took aim and fired.

'You're first home,' Eugene greeted Craig a couple of days later, an evening when low cloud had hurried dusk towards night. 'Rosie hasn't collected Dylan yet.'

'You know what those two are. Rosie brought in a stallion. Oh boy, was that horse wild!' He laughed. 'Reckon I'm getting old, I left 'em to it. Jeez, but that woman sits a horse like she's glued to it. They're down by Ketonee Bottom, they'll not be long.'

'You mean to tell me you rode away and left a wild horse?' Eugene raised her eyebrows. 'What's gotten into you, fella?'

'Like I said, must be getting old – or hungry.'

Hearing the conversation, Dylan had put on his leather coat.

'If they're down at Ketonee, I'll got meet Rosie. We know the track they'll take,' he said. 'I'd like to get a look at the wild stallion.'

'They'll not let you try it, boy, don't raise your hopes,' Molly told him. 'Donald's not home yet. He's not with them?'

'No, there's just the two of them. I think Donald was over Deep Cut way.'

Lottie could see no connection, but Craig showed no surprise at the question. Molly nodded, satisfied.

'OK, boy, you ride out to meet your mom. We'll expect you in the morning.'

An hour later Neil arrived home.

'Rosie's waiting for Dylan out by the corral. Where he is?'

'Been gone from here for ages. Rode out to Ketonee when Craig told us you'd fixed up your own private rodeo. You mean he never got there?'

There was a silence.

'Donald not back?' That was Neil.

'He was out Deep Cut way, Craig told us. Not the same track,' Eugene answered.

'You better go tell Rosie Dylan's gone, she can't wait out there all evening. You came up from Ketonee, you ain't been some place else on the way? Checking they were all fenced in, maybe? That could have put you off the track.' Molly was worried.

'I'd best go tell her. I'll ride back with her, see he's all right.'

'Perhaps he's lost the track in the dark,' Lottie put in, imagining the boy wandering on the range.

No one answered her.

It was as Neil opened the door to go back out into the night that Donald appeared.

'Where you been working, boy?' Molly greeted him before he had time to get through the door.

'I been along Deep Cut way.' His mouth hung slightly open in a smile. Round-up was his favourite season too.

'Yeah,' Craig sounded relieved, 'didn't I say?'

It seemed to Lottie less important where he'd been than whether he'd seen Dylan. If the boy wandered from the track he might be anywhere.

'Have you come across Dylan anywhere?' she cut in.

'No! I never seen the boy! No!' His empty eyes were full of fear – or was it cunning? 'What you all looking at me for? Tell you I never – '

'I'm off to ride back with Rosie.' And Neil disappeared into the night.

'He could ride for miles if he's once lost the track.' Of them all it was Lottie who was most concerned for the Indian boy.

'He won't come to any harm.' Craig pulled his chair to the table, an indication that he was ready for food. 'Saying a boy like Dylan could get lost on the range is about like saying a fish could die of drowning. Between here and Ketonee, I don't see how they could have missed passing each other.'

Old Pop ground his gums, then smacked his lips, eyes alive with mischief.

'You don't? Bet you ten cents – '

'Stop meddling and let me get you to the table. If Neil rides right home with Rosie there's no knowing when he'll get back, and he won't leave her till he's seen the boy's safe. Now, Donald, sit to the table if you want your food.'

'I never seen him – honest, Molly, I never been near – '

'Of course you haven't. We knew you were at Deep Cut, we knew you couldn't have seen him. Stupid suggestion.'

Sometimes Lottie thought that the longer she was here, the less she understood them. Pop winked at her across the table.

'Ever ridden that way at all, have you? Ever gone down there to Ketonee Bottom?' He turned to her, his eyes wide and innocent. In this mood he was harder to fathom than when he was openly hostile. 'Many a year since I've been down there, many a year since I been any place but my danged chair, but you ought to take a look round that way. Nice old cabin we used to have out there, glad of it for the shelter on many an occasion.' Lottie noticed how Molly glared at him. He must have noticed it too but he pretended not to.

Neil was gone two hours or more, but when he came back it was to report that Dylan was safely back on the settlement, waiting there when they arrived.

'Fancy then, must have gone straight past each other,' Pop muttered, hardly audibly. Then, aware that Lottie had heard him, he whispered to her: 'Take yourself down there sometime.' His suggestion was loaded.

140

'Where's that, Pop?' Neil had apparently heard him too.

'Down where you been, out Ketonee way. I been telling Lottie about it. Al'ays was a favourite of mine.' Then seeing the look Molly threw at him, 'Back in the days before I was nothing but a burden to the house.' He slumped in his chair. But Old Pop's eyes always said more than his words. He'd been playing his favourite game, trying to stir up trouble. He knew it, and he knew that Molly knew it too. Now the baleful glance he turned on her silenced her. 'Time I was in my bed and out of the way of you young folks. Will one o' you boys give me a hand? Sad thing it is, to be past being any use.'

'Get along to your bed, you old rascal,' Molly's voice was affectionate. Somehow it banished the undercurrent that Lottie hadn't been able to understand.

'Dylan going to ride me! Mom, Dylan going to ride me! Me wiv him on his horse.' Rushing in from the yard, Katie's words tumbled out at such a rate, each one fell over the last.

'Reckon she'll be safe?' Eugene looked worried. 'He's only a kid himself.'

'Safe with Dylan? Of course he will. She rides in front of me and he's as good on a horse as anyone I know.'

'Dylan, Mom!' Katie jumped up and down with excitement. The wonder of it was beyond belief.

In the yard he was waiting. Surely a three year old was young to feel such hero worship! Katie followed him like a shadow and he treated her with endless patience.

'You won't go far away from the house, will you, Dylan? And no jumping! Promise me no jumping.'

'You don't need to worry. I'll promise if you want me to. But you know I'll take good care of her, honest I will. Katie won't come to harm.'

Today amongst the stores on Lottie's list was a twenty-eight pound sack of flour. It was as she stooped to lift it on the truck that Ramsey's car drew level.

'Hold it! Don't you lift that. I'll get parked then stow it on for you.'

Certainly it was heavy, but she'd meant to grit her teeth and do it herself. Pleased that he'd come, she waited for him. They didn't always meet on her Monday trips, probably some weeks he didn't bother to collect his mail until later. As for her, she was always at the Trading Post in time for her outgoing letters to be bagged for collecting, then she waited until the incoming bundle had been sorted so that she could take anything for Kilton Down.

Effortlessly Ramsey lifted the sack aboard.

'Mail man hasn't arrived yet. If you've brought anything you're still in time,' she told him.

'No, I haven't. If he's not been yet, you've got an hour or more to wait. Digby Bint takes best part of that to get it sorted, time he's tried to figure out who folks have been getting mail from.' She'd come to know that soft chuckle of his. Some people laughed boisterously, as if everyone around them was welcome to join in their mirth. But not Ramsey. Lottie felt that of all those who made a journey to the Trading Post on Monday afternoons only she and Ramsey shared the joke of how Digby Bint scrutinised each envelope.

'Too many postcards to be read and we'll be here all afternoon,' she chortled. 'Or aren't you waiting to see if you have anything?'

'I'm in no hurry. And you? Have you done all you came to do, except for the mail?'

'Yes. I drove in to town quite early. With Dylan there I don't have to worry about Katie. He's the Indian boy. I told you about them before, remember?'

'Then leave the truck where it is and let me take you out to the river. The fall colours on the trees are a sight, right down the banks. Maybe last year you didn't get around to seeing. If I remember, you'd only just started taking the truck out.'

'I'd like that.'

And so she did.

'Hold your nose! Don't breathe!' he said as they sped along the track towards what was known as the 'cut backs', where the river rushed and tumbled at a level far below. 'A skunk! Whew! Did you see it, run over back there?'

What fun it was, both of them holding their noses, hating the stench, yet enjoying the sharing of it. And what made it even better was that she was free to enjoy his friendship, there was no fear of his reading more into it than she intended. At home he belonged to Marthe; at home she belonged to Neil.

The leaves were like burnished gold, the river untamed as it tumbled on its way, sparkling in the sunshine, from this height the angry white waters holding no terror. The afternoon was turning into one of those special times, hours that she wanted to keep locked safely in her memory where she could draw on it later.

Driving back to Radley she thought of the letters that might be waiting. The trees, the colours of autumn – here on the 'cut backs' or at home by the lake at Bullington, was it so very different?

'In the grounds of Bullington Manor – that's where my grandmother lives – there's a lake. The elm trees around it are magnificent.

142

At home autumn is later than fall here. The leaves would hardly be turning yet. I wish you could see it there, smell it, the damp earth by the water's edge. And the ducks . . . ' She drifted into silence.

'Don't stop. I want to know what it was like.'

She frowned. '"Was"? You said "was". And for me that's true, isn't it?'

'That you won't go back there? But why not? The world is getting smaller all the time. Another few years and ordinary people like us will fly across the Atlantic. There'll be no need to take days on a train, then even longer on a ship. Of course you'll go home one day, Lottie. You and Neil will take Katie to see your people.'

'Neil?' She bit her lip. 'They didn't understand each other, that was the trouble. Because he was different from the people they knew, from Michael and Ronnie's friends, from Barrie – you know, I told you about him – they couldn't see below the surface. He's *good*, but all they could see was that he hadn't got the veneer of manners they thought all important. I shouldn't talk like this. It's as if I'm seeing faults in him too, and criticising them.'

'It's no such thing. It's that you're understanding him, and them too. As times goes on, when they accept he makes you happy, then all the rest won't count for anything.' They were getting close to town, in a few minutes she'd be back in her truck and gone from him. 'You were telling me about the place where your grandmother lives? But we're almost back. Tell you what, next week bring me some pictures. Your folk, your home there in England, your brothers. You must have pictures.'

'You can't really want to see – honestly, do you?'

'Honestly, that's why I'm asking. My friend Lottie has roots I can't put a picture to. Whatever people we are today is what yesterday made of us. And I want to know, I want to be able to see for myself.'

'I'll bring my album. Gosh!' It hurt him to see such open pleasure in her eyes. 'Oh, gosh, fancy you wanting to see. I've got a lot, you'll wish you'd never asked me!'

It was only after she'd left him and she was speeding along the graded road back to Kilton Down, leaving a trail of dust behind her that she realised how one-sided the arrangement was. His past was a closed book to her, except for the story Marthe had told her about the wayward Jeanette. She couldn't possibly probe, yet for him to question her had been so natural, she'd welcomed his interest. Perhaps it had to do with his being so much older than her? She was sure Marthe would prefer to be his wife than living like they did, there must be some reason that held him back from marrying her. He kept his own counsel. Probably he encouraged her to talk of home because he was kind, because he could tell how much she missed it all and he was sorry for her. Wondering about it sent a pale cloud over the anticipation she'd felt for next Monday.

As soon as they met on Monday her doubts vanished. They left her truck just as they had last week and drove out of town, this time not to the 'cut backs' but along Fourth Street until it was taken over by a straight ungraded track that looked as though it would run on forever. The sun was a great golden sphere, the land flat.

'You feel you could just drive on and on. Where does it go?'

'No town. It's just a rough track, not even graded.'

'If time had no meaning, if we could stop the clock, like with a stop watch, and then just keep driving, don't you feel as if way out beyond us we'd come to the land of the prairie?' With her album on her knee, she held her face towards the sun, eyes closed, taking a great gulp of fresh air. 'It even smells different.'

'No skunk this week.' He smiled. 'We'll stop along here, shall we? Pity we haven't the power to make time stand still.'

Out of the car he threw his leather jacket down over a crop of coarse spear grass.

'Sit on that. Save your legs getting scratched. Wait while I light up, then I want to meet this family of yours.'

'Oh, Ramsey, I wish you could.' She sat on his coat, clasping her drawn-up knees.

'Could be they wouldn't have taken any better to me – or any other guy from out here – than they did to Neil. Could be anyone from so far away would have been the same, they'd have resented all things Canadian, seen a threat to their hold on you. You and me, we've each got a child, we ought to understand. Could be we'd be just the same, don't you think?'

'Maybe that was part of it – all things Canadian. There's Aunt Eva . . . ' It was some time before she got around to opening the photograph album. The saga of Eva had roots that were deep, going right back to 1933, the August afternoon of her tenth birthday. 'But it must be Canada, it can't just be that Mum was jealous of any affection Dad had for his sister. It's hard to explain, but I know it wasn't that. Sometimes she seemed eaten up with hate for Aunt Eva – but she was never – never – sort of loving towards Dad.'

'Could she have resented Eva's life out here, her professional success?'

'Mum? Heavens, no. She doesn't approve of working women.'

'Open your book. Introduce me to your past.'

She'd been at Kilton Down for far more than a year. In that time her album had assumed an importance in her life that it would never have had but for the thousands of miles that divided her from the soil of her roots. She'd never shown her pictures to the O'Hagons; partly because they'd not taken any interest in her family or her life at home, and partly from a reason far more complex. The book was kept in the drawer in her bedroom. To take it through to the kitchen, have them pouring over old family photographs there, would have seemed a betrayal of her parents. As for Neil, he knew it was in the drawer but preferred to ignore it.

Sometimes she'd pointed pictures out to Katie: 'Who's that? You know, don't you? That's my mum, your gran. You used to love her, Katie.' Or: 'See that house? That's called Bullington, that's where my grandma lives. One day we'll go there, shall we?' Katie would smile obligingly, then slip down from the bed where they'd been sitting. 'Gotta go, Mom. Boys waiting.'

Today was different.

'Some of them are quite old,' she told Ramsey. 'Grandma sorted them out for me to bring. This one was taken during the Great War, my parents on their wedding day. That's Grandma. When I first learnt to ride it was at Bullington. I spent a lot of time with her. She always rode side saddle, back as straight as a ram rod.' Her big dark eyes were suddenly full of tears.

'You gave up a lot when you came out here, Lottie.'

She blinked hard, determined not to let him notice her moment's weakness. 'I did what I wanted to do. Neil never painted a picture rosier than it was. I wouldn't have things any different.'

'Sure you wouldn't. Even so, you still gave up a lot to get what you wanted.'

'I just hate to think they'll all change. We all do, all the time. But when we're with people, we don't see it. I want everything to stay like I knew it. I hate to think they'll get old – and Grandma, what'll happen to her?'

'Ah, look at this!' He pointed to a picture of a young Lottie wearing jodhpurs and hacking jacket, sitting astride a piebald pony.

'That's me when I was eight. I remember because it was on my birthday.'

'Eight . . . same as Ginney.'

Her eyes were fully of pity. 'Loving a person and not being able to help . . . '

'Hey, what's the matter with us! A sunshiny day, a book of memories – happy ones too, no one takes photographs of the miserable times – and here we are weeping on each other's shoulder. Tell me which this is, Michael or Ronnie? Oh, and say, just look at this! Lottie in a gymslip. Isn't that what you call it?'

That afternoon the mail had been sorted (including the reading of any postcards) for almost an hour before Lottie collected the bundle for Kilton Down.

Every hiding place had been searched, every stray animal brought back. The branding iron had done its job and the stock been sorted so that the breeding herd should be retained and the rest driven off to auction. Despite a thin covering of snow over the ground, or more likely drawn out there because of it, Katie, Earl and Mickey were in the yard making a pretence of sweeping. In fact Katie was more interested in watching for Dylan; usually he arrived long before this.

'I wouldn't even suggest it if I thought she'd pine,' Lottie pleaded, watching from their bedroom window, 'but, Neil, just look at her. She's fine with the boys. She'd understand – and Eugene and your mom would look after her. I'm as capable of riding it as you are.'

'Dammit, I've told you, no. Auction ain't no place for a woman, nor the makeshift living we shall have. Not your sort of woman.'

'I've been to the Cattle Market at home, I've seen auctions,' Lottie argued.

'Cattle Market at home! Jeez, honey, you don't know anything about the kind of show this'll be. Don't you see? It's the climax of the season. And what kind of a woman do you think they'd take you to be? You think I'd let my wife be looked at like she's some saloon Moll for every drunken cowboy to ogle and try and get his hands on?'

She could see he wasn't even taking her suggestion seriously.

'There are women who drive the herds in, you've told me so yourself. I bet Rosie goes. If she can, I don't see why I can't. Please, Neil, I want to see how it all works. I want to be part of what you do.'

'And I've said you can't come. Hey now, honey, don't glower like that.' His eyes teased, he raised her face to his. 'Say goodbye to me nicely. Do you think I like leaving you? Honey, you're not "other women", you're *my* woman.' He pulled her down to sit on the bed. 'Lottie, I know there's plenty enough I haven't done right by you with, shacked up here with the family, no place of our own. Things'll be different, I promise you they will. It's been a good season. Looks like the sale'll bring in the sort of money we need. Soon as spring comes round we'll mark out our ground and build somewhere for our own.'

The auction was forgotten. Anyway, why had she supposed Rosie was going with them? Of course she wasn't! This morning Dylan hadn't come to the house, she must be back in the settlement with him. Willingly Lottie raised her lips to his.

'How soon will you be back?'

146

'Soon as ever I can. Thursday night, I should think. Yeah, pretty sure we shall. Tell me goodbye so I've got something to remember.'

'Neil O'Hagon,' she laughed, 'I can read you like a book.'

'And it's a book you can't put down. True? True? Go on, own up.' His voice was soft, teasing, tempting. At just that moment she looked towards the window.

'Did you see? Donald! Watching us! He's gone now. Neil, you will take him with you, won't you? He doesn't stay behind?'

'Sure he rides with us. But, honey, I told you over and over, Donald's not a man to go peeping after the women. Just leave him, Lottie, he can't help being the way he is. He's not responsible like other folk.'

One thing Donald was responsible for was stopping Lottie 'telling Neil goodbye' in the way he'd intended. The moment was lost.

A few minutes later the three men were ready to set out on their long ride, driving the cattle. Heavy sheepskin coats, canvas bags of food, billy cans . . . they carried everything they would need down to dry kindling wood so that they could build a fire in a world white with freshly fallen snow.

'Rosie not going this year?' Molly asked as they were leaving.

'Sure she is. Can't picture Rosie missing the auction,' Neil answered.

'And the boy? Always used to come and bed down with us while she was away.'

'Getting too old to want a minder,' Craig said.

'Boy's growing up.' Donald nodded his head as he gave his opinion. 'Be riding with us?'

Behind his back Molly looked at the other two and shook her head.

'Seemed happy enough here with us, but you can't cage a boy like Dylan for long. Reckon he'll be glad of his freedom. As able to fend for himself as those critters you turn lose out there on the range. But tell him, if you see him – there's a place for him with us if he wants it. Fits in here, no problem to anyone.'

Old Pop winked at Lottie. 'Fits sweet as a kernel in a nut, danged if he don't.'

Soon they were gone. From the verandah the others could just see them riding away, Donald in front, the other two following.

Molly looked uneasy. 'I'll be glad to see them back again. Once the auction's over, they get in those saloons. Just hope they remember to keep an eye on young Donald.' 'Young Donald' would never see fifty again, but to his elder sister who'd always felt responsible for him the years made no difference. Only once during the days they were away did Dylan call and that was to bring a hare he'd trapped.

147

On the Thursday they went to Higley Creek as usual. The days since Monday had seemed long and empty. The knowledge that this evening Neil would be home gave Lottie a warm glow of anticipation. Before the weather finally broke they'd ride out, decide whereabouts they would build . . .

'I am glad for you, Lottie,' Marthe said when she heard their plans. 'A home just for yourselves is important. It is the foundation for everything in a family.' She threw another log on the open fire. The living room radiated comfort. 'When Ramsey collected the mail on Monday he found there was a letter for me,' she changed the subject. 'You take it for granted you get mail. But me? I am not so lucky. In other ways, indeed, I am very lucky. But not for mail. This was from Lazlo, my cousin. He was in the Hungarian Army when the war started. I have never heard all his experiences, only that he was a prisoner. He was in an American hospital, then Red Cross sent him to the British. There is nothing for him in this new Hungary, he will never go back there. When the war ended, first he was in England. Now, his letter tells me, he is in New York. He hopes to stay there, to work and to make America his country, just as I have made Canada mine.'

'That's marvellous, Marthe. I know it's still a long way from here, but you'll be able to take a holiday there. You must be dying to see someone of your own family.'

Standing behind Ginney, Marthe lifted a warning finger, shaking her head and pointing to the child. Lottie understood the message.

'Perhaps he'll get here to visit you.'

'It costs more dollars than Lazlo could find. He must get work, make a place for himself in a strange country before he thinks of holidays. But one day he will come. I am happy for the thought of it. Lottie, can you help the girls with clearing their games from the table? I will take the Cheese Strata from the oven and let it stand for five minutes and then we will have our lunch.'

No more was said about Cousin Lazlo.

That day the Kilton Down truck headed for home, their voices chorusing that they'd 'Been on a trip to Higley Creek', earlier than usual. If Neil happened to get back before he'd expected, Lottie wanted to be sure to be there.

The air in the beer parlour was hazy with smoke, the drink flowed. No one was anxious yet to take the last stage of the ride home. Those from Kilton Down weren't the only ones to have returned from the cattle auctions. Tonight saw the end of one season, the lull before the start of the next. Or, perhaps, truer, last night had seen the end of the

148

season, the hammer fall on the final bid. And what a night it had been! Foreshortened by the customary celebrations and, for Neil, Craig, Donald and three equally inebriated strangers, spent in a sparsely furnished room designed to house no more than two above the saloon where they'd spent the evening.

On these annual trips Craig always kept Donald with him, but until this year Neil had found a bed elsewhere. At the onset of the evening Rosie had been with him. Craig had watched his cousin, wondering which would win: the Indian woman who'd clearly had no intention of relinquishing her hold, or the thought of Lottie waiting at home. After a while Rosie had moved off to join another group, her black eyes following Neil as he sat with his elbows on the bar, seemingly content with male company. Round-up time, Rosie belonged to Kilton Down; but that was only a few weeks of the year. She knew men from all around the district and beyond. It was Neil she wanted, though, Craig was certain of that. Even if she'd lost the battle, the war was far from over.

This morning none of the men had been their brightest and best. If breakfast hadn't been a tempting thought, none of them had admitted to it. As if proving themselves n front of each other they'd attacked the food. By the time they'd set out for the ride home it had been after ten o'clock.

Whatever Rosie's night had brought, it had left no mark on her. But then, nothing ever did. From a distance she might have been taken for a slim young girl as she'd swung herself into her saddle with natural grace. Her olive skin had a leathery look, criss-crossed by a network of fine lines so faint that it was only when one came close that they showed at all; her startlingly white teeth were strong and even; her expression inscrutable; her strong hands slim and long-fingered, the white nails a perfect almond shape that would be envied by many a woman who might give more thought to such things than ever Rosie had. As they'd covered the miles towards home she'd ridden at the back of the little group; she'd been quiet, but then that was her way.

By dusk they'd only another mile or two before they reached Radley, and only then had she moved forward to ride with Neil. Craig had watched. He'd felt uneasy yet hadn't been sure just why. He'd seen Neil nod in agreement; but agreement to what? Then Rosie had returned to her place bringing up the rear of the party.

With no cattle to drive before them the homeward journey never took as long, and today they hadn't even stopped to eat. Outside the beer parlour when the men had dismounted and tied up their horses, Rosie hadn't attempted to join them. Craig had raised a hand in brief farewell, Donald had done the same, nodding his head and smiling emptily at her departing figure. Only Neil had gone straight inside, finding three seats and waiting for Jake Malone, the keeper of the beer parlour, to make his way round with a loaded tray of full glasses replenishing the empties.

'I'm only staying for the one.' Craig took his seat.

'What's up, man? Got the whole evening before us. You down that one and you'll change your mind.' Neil poured the better part of his half pint of golden nectar down his throat. 'Brother, but I needed that! Jake, how's about coming this way again?'

All around them men had the same idea: the consumption of cold, sparkling beer. The atmosphere here was very different from the saloon where they'd spent yesterday evening. This was a beer parlour, a drinking den for men who sat four or five to a table, working their way steadily through the half pints Jake carried to them. Craig stayed long enough to drink two.

'I'm not coming straight back,' Neil told him.

'Rosie? You mean now, almost home, and you're off to Rosie? Don't be a – '

'You got it wrong. It's not like you think. There's something bothering her, something she wants to talk over. Damn it, don't look like that. She needs advice, she's got no man there with her. Tell Lottie I'm riding out to the settlement when I've done here, but I'll not take long.' And as if to show he didn't mean to be moved, Neil lit another cigarette and signalled to Jake.

Craig looked worried. 'She could just as easy have asked me. But did she? Course she didn't. Watch out, that's all I'm saying. Nothing so dangerous as a dame who thinks she's had the brush off.'

Donald never jointed in a conversation, but heard every word even if often he wasn't quick enough to follow. He always understood the tone. Now he watched them, looking first to one then the other, his mouth not quite closed and his head nodding.

'You're talking balls!' Neil took a swig of beer, putting his glass down on the table with a firmness that indicated he didn't mean to be told. 'But if that's the way you see it, then I'll take Donald along. Will that satisfy you?'

Donald's mouth opened even wider in a look of pure pleasure while his head nodded frantically.

Thursday evening . . . at every sound Lottie listened, expecting to hear the excited voices of the moneyed revellers returning. When finally the door opened only Craig came in. In the family's greeting it seemed to her they all talked at once. How did the cattle sell? Did they get proper beds to sleep in?

150

Above the clamour she made herself heard at last: 'Where's Neil? Is he still seeing to the horses?'

'He'll be following pretty soon. I rode on ahead.'

'You left Donald behind with Neil?' Ever anxious, Molly wouldn't settle until he was home. 'What's keeping them?'

'They'll be here soon. We stopped for a beer, then he's riding out to Rosie's. Said he couldn't refuse her, she had some sort of problem worrying her.'

'Good for him! I bet she has, too,' Pop chortled.

'Donald's gone along as well, Pop,' Molly fixed him with a look aimed at curbing him, 'you just heard what Craig said. I'm glad I made that pot of bean soup. The boys'll all three of 'em be hungry.'

Lottie felt uneasy. How was it Old Pop could so easily do this to her?

An hour went by. The old man was taken off to bed. Another hour. Eugene rolled away her mending and said goodnight, Craig followed her. Then Molly, first going out to the verandah trying to strain her ears for the sound of the riders returning.

'Pity Craig left Donald,' she muttered. 'Don't like him being about like that . . . ' Then seeing Lottie's puzzled expression: 'Been a busy week. Easy for him to do too much. Can't think what Rosie can want with the pair of them all this time.'

At last they'd all gone to bed. Alone in her room Lottie still didn't undress. In fact with the window open she even slipped her arms into the sleeves of a jacket. She couldn't settle. The night was cold. She felt the bite of frost on the air. Clouds scudded before the crescent of a waning moon. She strained her eyes to peer into the darkness, and her ears to catch the first sound of the returning riders. At last she heard someone coming, a single horse being ridden hard. It must be him – but then where was Donald?

The rider came across the yard, as near to her open window as the verandah would allow. A stranger, an Indian with black hair tied at the nape of his neck.

'You Neil O'Hagon's woman?'

'Yes. Where is he? What's happened?'

'You to ride with me. There's bad trouble.'

151

Chapter Ten

Holding her hurricane lamp, Rosie glanced around the hut where she and Dylan stabled their horses. Just her own was there, fed and watered for the night. Satisfied she came out and closed the door. So Dylan hadn't come home. Maybe he was staying at Kilton Down. Wherever he was, he was capable of fending for himself. He'd learnt to set a trap as soon as he'd learnt to ride a horse, hunting, fishing, building a fire and cooking whatever nature provided, these things were second nature to him. Now he was eleven years old, the couch in the corner of the log home he shared with Rosie was still his bed. But if the moon was bright, the night warm, who could blame him if he preferred to find his own supper and sleep under the stars? Certainly not Rosie, many a time she'd done the same thing herself. There were times too when she wanted the single room of their cabin home to herself, a curtain dividing him from her and her visitors gave her no privacy at all.

So tonight she was pleased to see by the absence of his horse that he wasn't at home. Before Neil arrived she must light the fire, make the place warm and welcoming. She'd been away for three nights and four days, it would need a good blaze to make the room feel lived in again.

The first thing she saw on going into the cabin was that a log fire was burning in the stove. She frowned, standing on the threshold, holding her hurricane lamp high.

'Dylan!'

No reply, no sound. It wasn't the way she'd planned, not knowing whether he was home or away. But for the moment she had more to think of than the boy. Another log on the stove, a bottle of wine and two glasses on the table, and she was ready for Neil. Dylan had probably gone off to check his traps, he often didn't come back until very late. She listened intently. A rider was coming now. It must be Neil!

Unhooking the lamp, she carried it to the door to give him light to tether his horse.

It was Dylan, and she was annoyed at the turn of events.

'Can you smell the supper?' he greeted her.

'I didn't know you were here.' Which was hardly an answer.

'Oh, I've been around. The fishing was good yesterday. Can't you smell them smoking?'

'Dylan, food will have to wait. You can please yourself, but I've got no time for supper. I have some important business to discuss with Neil. He's coming soon – I don't want you here.'

One thing Dylan had inherited from his mother was that inscrutable expression. Perhaps he would liked to have had a mother glad to find him waiting, perhaps he had kept his smoker going since first light to please her with a feast of hot smoked trout, perhaps he would prefer to have had the place to himself, to come and go as he pleased. Or perhaps, living as they did in a cabin comprising one long room, he'd grown used to being turned away when she had company. He didn't argue, he showed no more sign of disappointment at what she said than he had shown pleasure in seeing that she was home. Without a word he turned and rode away toward where, in the darkness, the tripod of poles stood, a frame for the thatching of green boughs and grass that made the smokehouse for the fish. His movements had all the feline grace of his mother's and, also catlike, his eyes had the ability to tune themselves to night. Unerringly he reached for more green wood to add to the fire, the smell of its smoke and the fish arousing hunger pangs. Whether he meant to wait for Neil's visit to be over or to eat by himself out here in the night he gave no sign.

Smoking fish had been part of his early training, as necessary as riding a horse. The tripod frame stood permanently on the edge of a bank of trees fifty yards or so from the cabin. Dylan fed the fire with fresh wood. His horse was nearby, tethered to a post, restlessly stamping every now and again on ground that was covered with a thin coating of snow.

The sound of approaching hoofs told him that Neil had arrived, he saw by the light of Rosie's lamp that Donald was with him. But they weren't all going into the cabin. The big man was being left outside with the horses. Dylan could have called out, invited Donald to share what warmth there was over here by the smoker, but some instinct prevented him. Instead he stayed as still as he could so as not to attract attention to his presence. There was no disguising the smell of the fish, but the smoker might have belonged to any one of the cabin dwellers. Through all those days of round-up he had taken his meals

154

at Kilton Down; now he had five fine trout smoked and ready to be eaten. He was ashamed that he didn't call out to Donald to come and share his supper. He wasn't even sure what it was that stopped him.

'What's the trouble, Rosie? What did you want to talk to me about?'

'Why did you bring *him*?' She nodded her head in the direction of the door. 'Afraid to be alone with me?'

Never been feared of a dame yet.' Something in his laugh gave her confidence. He wasn't as much at ease as he pretended.

'Let's have a glass of wine first.' Already she was pouring it, not giving him a chance to refuse her. 'I drink to *us*, to all we've shared and all that is for us to share still.'

'Rosie, I didn't come here to talk about us. Sure, we shared plenty. But you know, same as I do, it's finished. Four years I was away. For me and for you too, life went on. Don't let's pretend different. Other men, other times . . . now hasn't that always been the way with you and me? No strings.'

'I'm not wanting strings, I never have. We've never been together because we were tied with strings. It's been because we wanted it that way. Other men, other times, like you say. And for you, other women. None of that has made any difference to you and me. Neil, we've had good times.' As Rosie topped up their glasses she came as near as she ever did to smiling. 'Remember the first? Half boy, half man. Real virgin, but knew just what it was you wanted.' Now she was serious, her black eyes pleading. 'And didn't I know too? You were mine. That's true, isn't it? Oh, that was years ago. There've been other women, of course there have, and I wouldn't want it any different. But I was the first. For a long time it was me, always me. And wasn't it good? Don't I know just how to make things right for you? Of all those women, has there been a single one, even your English bride, who knows what you like as well as I do? No, of course there hasn't!'

'Shut it, can't you! I told you, all that's over. OK, you were the first dame I had, OK we had it good. But no more, can't you understand?'

'You saying you turned into a man who never looks at a woman because he'd got a gold ring on his finger?' Her eyes were full of scorn. 'You? All that time you were soldiering are you telling me you never had a woman except her?'

'I'm not telling you anything. Christ, Rosie, it's not your business if I bunk a different dame each night. You were my first – and always we've had it good. But that's it – done – finished. This isn't what I came for. You said you wanted to talk about something.'

She turned her back on him, moved towards the stove. Her long fingers were fumbling at the buttons of her leather jerkin, then her

155

thick woollen skirt. When she faced him again, he would see the pale olive of her naked breasts.

'Stay with me,' she whispered. 'We'll make it like it always was, like it always can be. You want to stay, you want to have me, I know the way it's good for you . . .'

'Rosie, I can't stay here.' Yet he moved towards her, drawn against his will. 'Sure, right now it's what I want.' He swallowed, his Adam's apple too large for his throat. 'Jeez, but you know what you're doing to me.' Almost under his breath he said it, she stood as still as a statue only her eyes betraying her. 'Just talking to you – ' He pulled himself up, looking away from her. 'No! No, it's no use. Donald's just outside. Do your shirt up. If that's all you wanted me for, then I'm going.'

'I had to lie, how else could I have got you here? Send Donald home. Make some excuse. Say you're waiting to speak to Dylan when he gets home.'

'Where is he? Do you think he's been staying at Kilton?'

Her manner changed. She seemed to be weighing something up in her mind. 'You're fond of Dylan, aren't you? It's about him I want to talk to you.' Still she made no attempt to re-button her shirt. Instead she sat on the rumpled couch that was the boy's bed, then lay back on the dirty-looking cushion he used for a pillow. 'I suppose I'm too old for you now. I suppose you look at me and wonder how you ever wanted me . . .'

'You know that's not true.' The flame of the hurricane lamp flickered unevenly, it's light was fading. 'The lamp's going out.'

Her lips curled downwards, she gave a mirthless laugh: 'Like yours for me.'

'Rosie, my lamp for you will never go out. But I got a wife and kid waiting a few miles down the track. Thing's have got to be different for us.'

She didn't answer. The flame wavered, setting the shadows trembling and dancing on the wooden ceiling. In the silence he looked around him at this cabin he'd accepted for so long without a thought. For the first time he noticed the muddle, the squalor. Into his mind came a picture of Lottie.

'Long before you had a wife, you had me.' Her voice was low. 'Long before you had a daughter, you had a son.'

'Christ! You never hinted . . . I was only a kid . . . you had other men . . . I never supposed . . . Christ!'

'Where do you think he got those eyes? Not from me. You never supposed! You were – what – fifteen? My virgin lover. And like you say, there've been plenty of others.'

'*My* son. Jeez . . . ' Suddenly even Rosie wasn't important. His son, a boy who knew the range as well as he did himself. His son, soon grown to be a man, to work with him, to fall as naturally into the job as he had himself. But if *he'd* never suspected, what of the others? What about Mom? Pop? Craig? 'No wonder he fits at Kilton – what was it Pop said? – sweet as a kernel in a nutshell. My son! It's where he's got to be, Rosie. You ain't going to stop me taking him. I can give him a good life, a life with a future at Kilton. It's his right, and mine.'

'And what about me? Don't I have rights?' Her eyes were closed as she lay, hands behind her head, her shirt still open. 'I've done my best, taught him all I could. He'll never starve if he has the land and the forests to live off.' Neil watched her. Into his mind came memories of so many hours of love with her, but in all of them he'd never felt as moved as he was gazing at her now. In the flickering yellow light of the lamp he could see the fine network of lines on her face. Then she opened her eyes, looking directly at him, no hint of what was going on in her mind. 'You've got a wife, you keep telling me so. Go home to her if that's what you want. Dylan is mine, I'm his mother.' In one movement she sat up, swung herself off the couch to stand in front of Neil. Her look defied him. 'He doesn't belong to you or to Kilton Down, and he never will. Do you think I'd have you brush me aside and take him? Never! He's your son, but you'll never take him!' Like a cornered animal she confronted him. 'Done with me! All over – finished. Cast me off like a worn out glove. Me! The woman who taught you what love can be between a man and a woman. If that's how you see it, you can get the hell out of here. "You never supposed",' she mimicked his tone. 'You'll never prove it either. And even if you could, you couldn't take him from me. I'm his mother.'

Again her mood changed. Somehow he found himself sitting on the couch, Rosie forcing his legs apart and kneeling close to him, her arms around his waist. 'He's yours and he's mine. For now just forget him. Later we'll talk. Later . . . ' With her back to the fading light she might have been no different from the woman who'd guided him in to the wonders of the love they'd first shared so many years ago.

His hand that moved to her breast wasn't quite steady. Excitement surged through her. Hungrily she started to unfasten his buttons. He was hers. She lowered her head – and just at that second the lamp went out, throwing the room into darkness and breaking the spell that had so nearly bound them.

If Neil told Donald to stand and wait, then stand and wait he would. Only after a few minutes did he discover that by moving to one side of the window he could peep around the edge of the lowered blind.

There was one beacon that lit Donald's world and that was Neil. In years he'd been adult when Molly had had a son, but years hadn't left their mark on Donald. With the simplicity of a child he'd loved his nephew. As Neil had come to adolescence he'd loved him still. Half understood feelings had stirred in him for the boy who was growing fast towards manhood.

Molly had seen things that made her uneasy. It was no use trying to speak to Donald, it might do more harm than good.

'Neil, son, time we had a talk. About Donald.' She'd found her twelve-year-old son alone in the shed and, not knowing quite what she had to say, had plunged on: 'You know how it is with him? We can't blame him always for the way he behaves. Very fond of you. If he'd been different he'd have taken a wife . . . ' Having got so far, she floundered.

'Mom, I know what you're trying to say. Don't you worry about Donald, I can handle him.'

All that had been a long time ago. Neil, with a healthy appetite and natural attraction to the opposite sex, had never condemned his uncle. He'd grown up accepting that Donald could never take a full part in family life, he'd seen the way the great head would nod or shake as he tried to keep up with what was going on around him; so in his own over-simplified way Neil had come to understand the physical frustrations brought about by the vigorous and healthy body of a man coupled with the simple mind of a child.

Tonight, when Donald had heard that they were to ride out to the settlement together, he'd been in seventh heaven. His reasoning didn't go beyond the plain fact that Neil had said he could go with him. Now, watching through the strip at the side of the blind, his pure happiness was dulled. Inside they were talking, Neil and the Indian woman, and not smiling talk. Something was wrong. Then they moved out of his narrow field of vision. It took Donald's slow mind a few frustrated minutes before he had the idea of peeping at the other side of the blind. Yes, there they were, Neil standing by the couch, the woman was on it, lying back. Holy cow! Bitch! Bitch! Alone with Rosie the sight of her naked breasts would have frightened him, but this was different, because his emotions were knitted to Neil's. He knew just was Neil was feeling. Go on, take her, the bitch! Go on, boy.

He trembled with excitement that was mixed with hatred for her. Seconds ticked by as he watched. Now she was standing up, looked like she wouldn't let him have it. The bitch, she can't refuse you. Go on, boy! His huge hands pressed against his own body. Yes, Neil was on the couch now, sitting with her close between his legs. Donald's

158

breathing was heavy, desire and excitement almost more than he could bear; he groaned as he worked towards a certain oneness with Neil. Rosie's head went down. And in that second the fading light of the lamp flickered and died, cutting him off from them, leaving him alone out here in the night.He cried out, half sob and half curse, the sound immediately followed by the frightened neighing of a horse not far away.

Down the track, there he was, the boy Dylan crouching by the smoker! Donald's eyes were getting used to the dark now. Blundering, panting, still half crying, he ran towards him. Some premonition of danger had warned Dylan not to attract Donald's attention, but he wasn't prepared for this. As he started away Donald anchored him from behind in one vicious, powerful movement, tearing his clothing. Dylan was no match. With Donald's hand clamping his mouth, he couldn't even cry out. Passion was adding to the huge man's strength. He pressed his body against Dylan's, he snorted and grunted, the noises he made adding to the boy's terror. Dylan did the only thing he could: he bit hard on to the imprisoning hand, taking Donald by surprise, then with the agility of a cat he ducked, twisted, and was free.

'Leave the lamp, we don't need a light.' She clung to Neil. He shook himself free.

'For Christ's sake, Rosie, I told you – I've got a wife. Can't you understand? I don't want you, damn it.'

Roughly he pushed her, toppling her to sprawl on the floor. In one swift movement she was on her feet, facing him. It was no more than seconds before she spoke, but to both of them the silence seemed interminable, his words and violence hanging in the air.

Then Rosie spoke, her voice harsh and shrill.

'Who will she believe, you or me? Who will she believe when I tell her I've been your mistress for years? That you came here tonight because you can't do the things to her you do to me?'

It was a short jump for his passion to turn to uncontrolled rage. 'You whoring bitch, I'd kill you first.'

Suddenly everything happened at once.

Rosie was shouting: 'I'll tell them I'm the mother of your son.' Then, laughing wildly, 'I'll say you've always known it.'

Neil's answer was a stinging blow on her cheek. They were hardly aware of anything outside themselves, not the logs slipping on the stove and sending flames to illuminate the room, not Dylan rushing in nor yet Donald pounding after him.

Rosie was the quickest to turn the moment to her own advantage.

159

'I've told you – no!' she screeched. On the wall she kept a hunting knife. Now she grabbed it, holding it threateningly towards him. 'Go home to your wife!' Then, taking in the impact of what Dylan was running from: 'Don't you touch that boy, you filthy half wit!'

Wildly she wielded the knife, unprepared for Donald's strength. Her hold on the knife was lost. Now he held it. Neil had never seen him like this. 'I'd kill you' he'd said to her, and in the heat of the moment he'd felt he could. But reason would have stopped him. Reason had no influence on Donald. His face contorted, he intended to defend the one person he truly loved.

'Give me the knife,' Neil ordered. But the flame had died as quickly as it had burst into life, the room was dark now. There was a skirmish, a chair crashed to the ground.

Dylan rushed out into the night.

He'd seen plenty of fights, but he'd never been as frightened as he was now.

'Help! Please, someone come! Help!' He was crying as he ran along the track in the direction of their nearest neighbour.

'What's happened? Is it Neil?'

The Indian answered Lottie in a loud whisper. 'No light in Rosie's. Don't know what happened. The boy Dylan came to us. There is a fight. A bad fight. You ride with me.'

'I'll come and saddle Sherry. It's not Neil. Neil's not hurt?'

'Man's a madman – '

Some of her own fear faded. The trouble was to do with Donald and, whatever else she might doubt, she could always be sure that no harm could come to Neil from him.

'Trouble?' It was Craig. From his room next to hers he'd heard voices. Relief flooded through her.

'At Rosie's. I don't understand . . . something to do with Donald. I'm going to ride back.'

'We'll take the truck. Leave your horse, drive back with us.' What a relief to hear Craig's quiet command. His calm put Lottie to shame. Why hadn't she thought of the truck?

But the Indian refused. 'I ride.'

Craig wasted no time. Already he was back in his bedroom pulling on his clothes, telling Eugene to listen in case Katie woke. As he smoothed out the problems, some of the drama faded.

'The one they call Neil has been hurt,' the Indian told them as they got into the truck. 'Someone's ridden to Radley for the doctor. Dylan said there was a fight. It's a knife wound. I rode straight for the wife.' He pointed to Lottie.

160

Who could have done it but Donald or Rosie. Donald would never hurt Neil, nor yet stand by and watch anyone else hurting him. Whatever Rosie had done, it couldn't be serious, she hadn't the strength to fight two men.

'Is Dylan there? He's not hurt?' Craig called as the Indian started his homeward ride.

'The boy is frightened. He is with Lillian, my woman. The big man's crazy.'

Craig started the engine and within five minutes of the rider galloping into the yard they were on their way to the settlement.

'Damn it!' Craig muttered, more to himself than to Lottie. 'I should have stayed. Or else I should have brought Donald home.'

Listening, she understood so much that had puzzled her. 'Not got any use for dames,' Neil had told her. She remembered all the times she'd mistrusted Donald, not understanding any more than that he was simple.

'That must have been what the fight was about,' Craig went on, not stopping to ask himself whether she followed his train of thought. 'Rosie must have taken a knife. I guess Neil got hurt trying to get it from her.'

Already Lottie's first fright was lifting. A struggle for a knife might have led to a badly sliced hand. But the doctor was coming, he would dress it, it would soon heal. And, unacknowledged, was another thought: after this, Neil wouldn't be so keen on running after Rosie. Riding through the night it had taken the Indian an hour to reach them. Driving back was far quicker, but not quick enough. In the settlement people were standing about in groups. No one bothered that more snow had started to fall, covering the footsteps and the tyre marks leading to Rosie's cabin. The truck drew up and they climbed out. The door was closed, the room in darkness.

No one spoke. The air was full of the smell of smoking fish. Silently the snow fell.

Craig pushed open the cabin door, then shone his torch into the deserted room.

'Holy . . . ' he whispered.

Coming close behind him Lottie looked too. On the wooden table a bottle had been overturned, the dark wine spilled to drip to the floor. Blood, bright red from a fresh wound, had spread, the contrasting colours blending.

'Where's everyone gone?' Lottie heard Craig ask.

'We had to fetch the law,' a woman explained. 'They've both been taken in, Rosie and the big man.'

'And Neil?' This time it was Lottie. 'Didn't the doctor come? Where's Neil?'

161

'Took him off in the ambulance to the hospital. The boy's with Lillian Kitawan.'

A sudden gust of wind blew icy cold, swirling the snow in a mad dance.

'Stop here, Craig. Let me walk the rest of the way.'

She'd been up all night, they both had. Craig didn't like the thought of putting her out of the truck a mile from home.

'Just a bit further, Lottie.' But he understood what she was running away from. 'I'll still get back first. I'll break it to them . . . '

The night couldn't have been easy at Kilton Down either as they'd waited, not knowing what trouble Donald had got into. Firstly they would have been awake, listening for the truck to get home, not knowing whether to expect Neil and Donald with the others or whether they'd be riding. With each passing hour they must have grown more anxious, more fearful.

'If I'd brought Donald back with me, of if I'd gone with them to the settlement, none of it would have happened. I was uneasy. I said to him to watch his step, nothing got more spite than a woman who's had the brush-off . . . damn it, Lottie! It's no use pretending. I've known for years about Neil and Rosie – we all knew. But that was before you came. It was different, you got to believe that. Could always get what he wanted from Rosie. But not since you been here with him. Honest, Lottie, you got to believe I'm telling you the truth. I watched them together at round-up – but I swear to God, he'd done with her. That's why I didn't trust her – '

'Don't, Craig! I don't want to hear it.' She didn't want to hear, didn't want to think.

He stopped the truck.

'You got to hear. Ain't fair to Neil that you don't. He was never a man could go without a dame – but till you came along, he never wanted a wife. You just hang on to that, for I stake my life on it. Like with the trip to auction – this time wasn't like other years, this time he bunked down with Donald and me.'

'Stop it! I don't want to know.'

'You *got* to know. It wasn't like that, Lottie. Wouldn't be fair to him if I didn't make you understand. Then, when he said he was going to her shack, that there was something she wanted to discuss, wanted his help with, I warned him he was a fool. Didn't like it that I doubted him, I could see he didn't. That's why he said he'd take Donald. Reckon we both thought that would make it OK. I ought to have had more sense. God knows what happened, but if I'd kept out of it he would have gone on his own and he'd have been home now.'

162

She didn't answer. He was touched by the sight of her. Into his mind flashed the memory of her on the railway platform the day they'd met her, eighteen months ago. She'd looked like a child. The night had taken its toll; perhaps the months here at Kilton had too.

'I'm going to walk. I just want to walk. You tell them.' She climbed out of the truck and turned to him, meaning to reassure him that he could leave her. All through the night she'd seen nothing outside herself, hiding from emotions she couldn't face, not even considering that anyone else was involved. Dear, kind Craig. And back at home, Molly, waiting for the brother she'd always shielded, waiting for her son . . .

The truck drew away, leaving tyre marks on the thin covering of frozen snow. To the east the colours of dawn promised that soon the sun would be up, the pale gold Alberta sun of fall. Lottie looked up at the clear sky of the frosty morning. Friday morning. Only four days since they'd ridden away. The season of the year, didn't they call it? Back by Thursday . . . now it was Friday. And Neil would never come back.

'All the fault of that danged war. If he'd stayed home he'd never have got hitched like he did. What he and Rosie did was no business o' nobody's. But for that wife, he could have taken his pleasure with Rosie same as always – '

'Shut it, Pop,' Craig cut in.

'That's it, all turn on me. No one takes account of what you say when you get too old to matter. What I'm telling you is the truth. Anyways, if young Neil hadn't wanted Rosie to himself, why do you think he left Donald outside?'

'They'll have to be an inquest, Aunt Molly.' Craig ignored him. 'They'll tell us just as soon as they can fix the time with Mr Abercrombie.'

'William Abercrombie, the Coroner? You mean they'll be asking questions. Putting Donald in the witness box?'

Craig shrugged helplessly.

'There's only Donald and Rosie. It must have been an accident. Even Rosie couldn't have meant to – ' He didn't finish the sentence.

'Well, one of 'em will get the blame.' Pop's wrinkled face puckered. 'Better if that Hitler had given him a bullet, made a hero of him. That way we'd not have had *her* in the house as a reminder. A good boy . . . always a good boy.' Old Pop wept. This time no one told him to shut it.

The next Monday Lottie didn't go to Radley to collect the mail.

163

Home had never seemed so distant. If they had loved Neil, if they could have felt real sorrow, then she could have turned to them. Now their dislike of him held them away from her, the barrier insurmountable. Neil had been killed. Hadn't her mother's scarcely veiled hope been that that would have been his wartime fate? He'd escaped the armies of Adolf Hitler. It had taken Rosie, his half-breed mistress, to bring him down. At the thought of her, misery was swamped by rage. Anger made tears impossible. Lottie was eaten up with misery and hatred.

She did get as far as taking a sheet of paper and starting: 'Dear Aunt Eva, I must talk to someone, someone who knows the ways here and will understand – ' Then she tore it up. How could Eva understand? 'They're good people,' she'd said. But recognising that and understanding life here were quite different.

'Dear Grandma,' she started again. It would have been easy to pour out her heart to Lavinia, but had she the right? No. She couldn't do it. It wouldn't be fair to burden her with something she was powerless to help. A year ago Lottie might have, but she'd come a long way in that time and never so far as in these last few days.

So on Monday there was no mail to take and she shied from reading the never changing letters she knew would be waiting for her from home. Ronnie settling to civilian life and, to his mother's delight, on the brink of an engagement to Millicent Gower. That Millicent's father was a barrister made her suitable as a daughter-in-law, but the fact that her uncle was a one-time Member of Parliament who had been elevated to the peerage was sugar on the cookie, if Kate had needed it! Normally Lottie would have been able to smile when she read between the lines; so far from home she'd remembered only what was good. Now it hurt to remember at all.

At Kilton Down there was grief. Molly's face told of sleepless nights: she'd lost a son, the boy she'd had such pride in, the man who was perfect in her eyes; but her sleepless nights came from a worry that haunted her . . . Donald. Years through which he'd turned to her more and more. What must he be going through? How much could he understand? She was helpless, but he wouldn't realise that. All he must know right now was that he was on his own, lost, unloved. Molly's mind was never free of the worry.

Then there was Pop. He'd been old for a long time, old in years and infirm in body. Losing Neil had broken his spirit. Far from its bringing him and Lottie closer, it set them ever further apart. In Pop's mind there was one simple cause of blame for all that had happened, and it rested with 'the fancy-talking red-lips' Neil had married. But for her, he'd have gone off as usual to Rosie, come home after with no harm

164

done. Not that the old man could understand how it had all come about. Rosie had got him to the cabin – so what was she doing taking a knife to him? And when Donald came home it wouldn't be any use asking him, he got more barmy ever day.

Eugene found work to do out of doors. Perhaps when the inquest was over, when Donald was home, Molly at least would find healing in tears that now she was too frightened to shed. Perhaps then they would find a way of reaching out to help each other. But for the present they couldn't look that far, each protected in an armour of silence.

Lottie couldn't stay in the house. Instead, with Katie in front of her on the saddle, she rode out on Sherry. Not to Radley, not to anywhere, but taking some sort of comfort from the empty landscape. The snow had melted. Today the clouds were low, the wind had lost its bite. Tomorrow they had to go to the inquest. Beyond that her mind didn't go.

'We've got a visitor.' Molly saw a car draw into the yard. This time last week she would have said it with interest, been ready for such an unexpected turn of events as a caller. Now she had interest in nothing; merely performed her tasks and hardly spoke. Life had brought her plenty of problems. Donald had been only the first of them. After eight years of marriage she'd lost her husband; she'd been the only woman in the house, caring for them all, including a father-in-law soon to become crippled and cantankerous. One knock after another she'd taken in her long stride, a woman of such even temperament that nothing could throw her off balance. Until this. Neil . . . her boy.

'Who is it?' Eugene came to her side to look out. 'Why, Mom, that's the man McFee from Higley Creek. News gets around. We got to face up to folk.'

'I got things to do. You talk to him.' Out of character for Molly to take flight shutting herself in her bedroom, just as it was out of character for her to sit on the edge of the bed, her large hands limp in her lap, her shoulders hunched.

'Mr McFee?' Eugene opened the door from the kitchen as Ramsey came up the three steps on to the verandah.

'I only just heard when I was in Radley. Is Lottie here?'

Old Pop pricked up his ears.

'I don't know where she is. She took her horse and went off with Katie.'

Ramsey took the shiny orderliness of his own home for granted. That had been the way his mother had run an establishment in his youth. Marthe had been at Higley Creek for years and her standards were high. At Kilton Down the women worked hard, there was no dirt, but it was doubtful if the house had ever possessed a tin of polish. The floors were scrubbed, a line of underwear hung near the fire to air. He couldn't imagine Lottie in the setting of the room he saw over Eugene's shoulder. Into the wall a series of pegs were screwed and on each one hung two, or sometimes three, coats, hats, oilskins. All that in the room where they cooked and fed.

'Ain't you coming in, young man?' Old Pop called.

'You'd better come in and speak to him. Pop don't get many callers.' Eugene led the way.

'Come asking for Lottie, did I hear? How is it you're a friend of hers then?'

'Haven't they talked about us? Katie and my daughter are great friends.'

'Oh, they talk about *her* right enough. Thursdays is the day they visit, isn't that so? Some woman you got there – ' He felt Eugene's glare. 'No business of mine. Seems she and Lottie are taken up with each other.'

'Sure, it's made a big difference to Marthe having Lottie come visiting. She didn't see many folk.'

Old Pop shrugged. Eugene knew exactly what he was implying. Apparently Ramsey didn't.

'So this Marthe, you call her, she'll be missing Lottie if she goes off back where she came from?' Chewing on a quid of tobacco he was enjoying himself.

'She talks of going back to England?'

'I never said that. But I fancy it'll be what she'll do when things are settled. Nothing for her out here. Ain't no use to Kilton Down with her fancy ways and high flown – '

'Pop that's enough.,' Eugene's hand held his shoulder as if she could physically keep him in check.

'I guess after what's happened, we have to make allowances,' Ramsey said, but from the way he spoke it was clear that he made none. 'But if you ever take that attitude to her, I hope you're ashamed of yourself.'

'Ay-ya-ya,' Pop expostulated, 'coming in here, a stranger, taking that tone to me! Because I'm old, that's what it is. One day it'll come to you too. You'll be no use no more. How would you like to be sitting in this chair all day, a burden no one wants?'

'Mr O'Hagon, have you ever stopped to imagine how she must have felt, coming out here to a strange country? And now she's lost her husband, lost all she'd hoped for for the future. If you'd try and put yourself in her place, you might find you had less time for self-

166

pity.' Then to Eugene: 'I'd hoped to see Lottie. Tell her I called, will you? And here's the mail. I picked it up in Radley.'

He was glad to get out, to drive away and leave Kilton Down behind him. It wasn't so easy to put the thought of Lottie out of his mind. He'd never known much about the O'Hagons, but there were plenty like them – rough, tough, honest, hard-working. Eugene was their female counterpart. But Lottie . . . What was that the old man had said about her going back to England? And who could blame her if she did? She'd told him about her aunt in Calgary. Then there was that flyer who wrote to her. The O'Hagons were never told about those letters and somehow it pleased Ramsey to know he was the only one who shared her secret.

The room in the Courthouse was already crowded when they arrived.

'Right down at the front, Craig.' The last time Craig had spoken to Jim O'Hara had been in the beer parlour last Thursday, today he was doing his civic duty as Court usher. 'We kept four seats.'

'Only three of us, Jim. Eugene stayed back home with Pop and the kids.'

'We're fetching the boy in. Mr Abercrombie's instructions.'

Their conversation was carried out in whispers. Heads turned to watch as Lottie, Molly and Craig were guided to their appointed places. There were loud whispers of 'Hi there, Molly' from one or two groups, but she seemed not to notice. As they sat down a familiar figure leant towards Lottie. 'Howdy, Mrs O'Hagon. Get your mail safe yesterday?' It was Digby Bint from the Trading Post. She'd know that he had an unquenchable thirst for other people's business. Somehow it was reassuring to see him there. It held her to a reality outside this place. Then Dylan was brought in. He sat down in the seat they indicated, but didn't once look towards them. Craig whispered something to him. He nodded, but still looked at a patch on the floor just ahead of him, as if by not seeing the scene around him he could remove himself from it.

'Everyone stand,' boomed Jim O'Hara in the voice he kept specially for such rare occasions as this. Then, homage paid to his office, and for the benefit of a room full of folk he knew: 'On your feet. Here they come.'

Mr William Abercrombie, the District Coroner, led the way. Slightly built, his grey hair thinning to show a white scalp, he was clad in a brown pin striped suit. For one moment Lottie's mind flew to Neil's 'good suit'. No, no, think of something else, of how confused and frightened poor Dylan must be, of Molly, of anything except what hurt too much to contemplate. Over his half-moon spectacles

167

the Coroner viewed the assembled crowd. Then he sniffed, word-lessly managing to convey his disapproval of such blatant curiosity.

He was accompanied by two officials and followed by Rosie and Donald, each of them escorted on either side. Rosie walked with her head high, looking neither to left nor right, not even acknowledging Dylan. Donald let himself be led forward, an air of helplessness about him. Whereas purposely Rosie stared ahead of her, Donald looked down at his feet, his shuffling gait something familiar in an alien world.

'This inquiry has been called to see into the incident which oc-curred on the evening of Thursday last, when Neil O'Hagon was injured and found to be dead when Dr Marshall here got to the scene. So first I'll call on you, Dr Eddy Marshall. If you'll just tell the Court the cause of death.'

There wasn't a person in the Courtroom who didn't know the cause of death every bit as well as Dr Marshall did. He read out the medical report, the approximate time of death, while they waited restlessly. A stab wound, that's what the doctor meant. Why waste time on technical jargon they didn't understand? The Indian woman had been Neil O'Hagon's mistress for years, there'd been plenty of speculation when he'd come back from the war with a bride. So let's get on with it, let's hear what she dug the knife into him for.

'I call upon Rosie Kitashee.' At Mr Abercrombie's words they sat up, prepared to enjoy themselves.

'Rosie Kitashee,' thundered Jim, although she was within touching distance. 'Put your hand on the book and read this.'

Her face remained expressionless.

'Then you better just say after me – I, Rosie Kitashee, do solemnly swear . . .'

'Now then, Rosie, you just tell me in your own words what happened on Thursday evening.' The swearing done, Mr Abercrom-bie sat back and waited, the case already opened and closed as far as he was concerned. Like Craig he'd always thought there was nothing more dangerous than a woman who'd been given the elbow, and that's about what young Neil O'Hagon had done when he'd brought that pretty little English piece to Kilton Down. Ten minutes and his part in the case would done, she'd be put in the cooler until they carted her off for the Judge to settle. Accidental death he could deal with – not a happy thing, not a happy thing, in a community where he knew the folk like he did here – but murder, that was a different ball game. And no one fell on a knife by accident.

'We'd been to the auction,' Rosie started, her voice low yet every word clear. 'Coming home, Neil told me he wanted to come and see me, there was something he wanted to talk to me about. He said it was about the boy Dylan, about his future. It worried me, sir, now that he had a wife – there she is in the front row – '

'Just tell your story. You say he wanted to talk to you about your son?'

'Yes, sir, about Dylan. So I agreed. I couldn't refuse, he had rights.'

'Rights?'

'Same rights as any father.'

Chapter Eleven

There was silence. For seconds, not so much as a stir of movement. Lottie stared straight ahead of her. Had they known? All this time, had Molly and Craig known? Gradually life was coming back into her numbed senses. Dylan . . . those light blue eyes . . . the way Katie followed him. Had they all known, all of them except her? Old Pop? Was that why he looked at her so cunningly? Why he hated her? And Neil? Oh no, not yet. Later she'd think about that, not yet, not here. She tried to swallow but her throat was so dry. 'I had my first dame when I was fifteen' . . . and there she was! Rosie, the mother of his son. Behind her the stillness was breaking, first a whisper, something that could have been a titter, more whispers.

'Silence!' Such a commanding roar from Mr Abercrombie took every by surprise. 'I'll not have this noise. Any more and I shall get Jim O'Hara here to clear the Court. We are here on serious business. Now, Rosie, I understand the deceased wanted to talk to you about – er – '

'About his son.' Rosie's chin was high, she defied anyone to doubt her word. 'Why do you think they've come crowding in this morning? Because they've known I was his mistress, because they've suspected the boy was his.'

'I understand the reason for your agreement that he should visit. Beyond that, the Court is not concerned. Just proceed with your account of the evening. I believe Donald O'Hagon accompanied the deceased?'

'Neil left him outside. And I'll tell you why. He thought it would be just the same as before he had a wife, that's why he left the madman outside. He tried to force me, tore at my clothes. He was strong, I had to fight.'

'So you took the knife?'

She nodded. 'I was shouting at him, telling him to go home to his wife. And that's when I saw what this filthy imbecile had been trying to do to the boy. Neil shouldn't have left him, he must have known.'

'You say Donald O'Hagon was waiting outside. Where then was the boy?' William Abercrombie was losing the thread of her tale.

'Out there with the smoker. He'd been smoking fish for our supper. Then this disgusting great brute cornered him, tried to force himself on him like Neil was trying to on me. They're rotten, the lot of them!'

'Enough! We must keep to the evidence. Your account of what happened, your true account.'

'Dylan rushed in, holding his clothes on with both hands. And behind came this – this – ' The word escaped her, but she speared Donald with a look that more than made up for that.

'And the knife? You were holding the knife?'

'I got the knife to protect myself. I wouldn't have killed Neil. It was to keep him off me. He'd almost torn the shirt off my back. He couldn't see that now he had a wife, things had to be different. I never thought to kill him, I swear I didn't. Then the boy rushed in with this maniac after him.' She turned to the crowd. 'What would you have done? What would any of you have done? Of course I went for the big devil, it was my son he was lusting after. But he's got the strength of a giant. He got the knife off me.'

Lottie tried to close her mind, but she heard every word; she tried not to imagine it, yet the picture was there before her.

'You may stand down for the present. I call Dylan – Kitashee – O'Hagon . . . '

'Dylan,' Jim avoided the confusion of a surname, 'say after me: "I, Dylan, do solemnly swear . . ."'

'I'm sorry, son, having to put you through this.' William Abercrombie pushed his glasses up his nose, unhappy with the turn of events. He'd expected the woman to have wept and confessed. 'You've heard what your mother says? Now about Donald O'Hagon, is what she tells us right? Was it like she says?'

Dylan clenched his lip between his teeth. His face twitched convulsively and all he could do was nod his head.

'All right son. Just tell me, just point if you know the answer – and remember you are under oath to tell the truth – did you see you who put the knife into Neil O'Hagon?'

Dylan shook his head. ' No. I didn't see.' Opening his mouth was his downfall. Until then he'd managed not to let himself cry. He was ashamed, here in front of all these people, but he couldn't stop crying. 'The room was dark, they'd not got a lamp lit. She – Rosie – was screeching at Neil like she told you, "Go home to your wife", and

172

she had the knife. *He* had it,' pointing at Donald yet avoiding looking at him, 'Neil was between him and Rosie, trying to get it. I didn't wait. I ought to have tried to stop them. He was so strong. I went to get help.' It was hard to understand his garbled words. 'I'd seen fights before. He's not like other people – '

'Good man,' Mr Abercrombie interrupted him, 'that'll be all we need from you. Just sit down again.' There were times when he wished this job on someone else.

'Call Donald O'Hagon.'

Molly was on her feet in an instant. For days she'd been withdrawn in a world of her own. Now suddenly she had something to fight for.

'You can't do that! William Abercrombie, you've known my Donald for pretty well thirty years. You know he ain't up to giving evidence.'

'Molly.' Sad eyes looked over the top of the half-moons. 'I don't take kindly to what I have to do, but it has to be done. You know if I could I'd just let you take him home without all this. But the law is the law. Your Donald was there, he was witness to a crime, and it's not for me to say who talks and who holds his peace.'

While Dylan had sobbed out his story the locals had been silent, not wanted to miss a sound. Now though, as Mr Abercrombie talked gently to Molly, they took the opportunity of whispering to each other, speculating, trying various pieces of the puzzle for size.

'Silence!' Again that roar of authority from the little Coroner. 'I'll not say it again, next time you're out! Now then, Jim, just call Donald O'Hagon.'

He'd not liked to see Molly O'Hagon so upset, but he didn't honestly believe that Donald would be too bothered by the questions. More likely he wasn't bright enough to be any use to them, watching life go by but never taking a part in it like he did.

'Put your hand on the book.' Jim guided him to it. 'Now say after me: "I, Donald – "' With his mouth open, Donald looked at him blankly.

'Do you, Donald O'Hagon, solemnly swear that what you tell us will be the truth, the whole truth and nothing but the truth?' The Coroner spoke gently to the big man. 'Just say "yes", that'll be enough.'

Donald's oversized head nodded. Mr Abercrombie didn't press the matter.

'Now, Donald, I want you to tell me what happened.'

Silence. There was no intelligence in Donald's eyes.

'Let me talk to him, let me come and stand up there by you.' Molly was on her feet. 'He'll tell me, won't you Donald?'

173

Until that moment he hadn't looked towards the body of the room. Now he saw Molly was with him, his mouth fell open into a smile of pure happiness.

William bit his lip. He'd never heard of such a suggestion. Here he was, an officer of the law, being asked to turn an official hearing into some sort of fireside chat. But it was apparent they'd get nothing out of this poor great hulk without her. So he nodded his head and signalled her forward. After his bellowed warning a moment ago, no one was risking being thrown out at this stage. The silence was electric.

'Now then, Donald boy, you just tell me about it. Neil and Rosie went inside, left you to wait with Dylan?' To Molly that didn't ring true. Neil would never have done that.

'They went inside. I watched them, lamp was on in there.'

'Were they arguing? Could you see if he touched her . . . tried to touch her?'

Lottie's eyes were closed, but the pictures she conjured up were worse than the scene before her. Easier to watch, try to detach herself, try to look at it from outside. She felt empty, old, her trust destroyed.

'Why shouldn't he touch her?' It was as if Molly had touched a 'start' button. Donald's shout took everyone by surprise. He had no control over the volume of sound, no control over the way his face worked. 'All ready for her he was, I was watching. They were on the couch there. I saw. Right up to when it went dark, I was watching. Bitch! My Neil didn't do no wrong. Course he wanted to have it with her! Why shouldn't he? She's been his woman long as he's needed one. Bitch! Get him pitched up right ready – tell you, I saw. Then it went dark, Moll.' He was crying now, his blubbering as uncontrolled as everything else about him.

'Ask him about the boy,' William whispered to her.

She didn't want to. She already knew the answer.

'Dylan was outside, with you? Did he see?'

'Tell you, we were all pitched up ready, Neil and me. Was the devil at me, Moll. I saw the boy and I – I – it was the devil at me.' Pathetically he looked at the sister who'd always stood between him and a world he couldn't understand.

'Try and tell me what you saw when you followed Dylan into the cabin. What were they doing, there in the dark?'

'Bitch, that's what she is, Mol.' His wild outburst over, he was crying quietly now. 'Screaming at him that he wasn't going to get it, that he got to go home to her – ' He pointed at Lottie.

'And the knife? You can tell old Moll, sure you can, Donald boy. Come on now, don't you cry, lad. It's all done now.'

174

'She was waving the knife, screaming at him. Screaming at me' cos of the boy. It was her that got us pitched up like it. I told you, I been watching them. My Neil . . . she got no right to turn him off like she did. She'd been there with her breasts all bare, pushing at him.' He wiped his great hands down his tear-drenched cheeks, but made no attempt at control. 'I took the knife off her. I was going to kill her. Yes, I was, Moll. I'd have killed her for my Neil. Easy as anything, I'd have killed for my boy.'

'All right. It's all right, boy. Just tell your Moll.'

His arm was up high, his fist clenched as if he held the knife.

'Hard as I could, I felt it go right in.' His voice broke as he re-lived the moment. 'The bitch! She gone ducked out of the way. It was my Neil . . . Moll, I done it to my Neil.' Then, in the instantaneous way Donald could turn, he did now. Without warning, he leapt at Rosie. 'You, that's who it was for! You! You bitch, you cow!' With all his might he shook her, his hands moving from her shoulders to her throat. Jim forget the dignity that went with the job of court usher and rushed to drag at one arm. Craig was on his feet pulling at the other. When Donald was roused to anger it took more than their strength to hold him.

'Donald!' Molly's voice cut through to him where force couldn't. His grip loosened, his head hung. 'You're a good boy to have told us. Indian Rosie'll get her punishment, don't you worry about her. You did what you could to help Neil.'

Of those four seats in the front row only Lottie's was occupied now. She heard Molly calm Donald and lie to do it. Behind her, muted whispering had broken out again, but by now William Abercrombie was beyond noticing. Lottie saw it all, heard it all, no emotion touched her. She was drained, empty. These people pandering to half-witted Donald, what had they to do with Neil and her? 'My Neil . . . my boy', Donald had called him. That wasn't *her* Neil. But he'd gone, her Neil had gone, just as surely as Donald's. Her Neil? Their Neil? As if he were two men. No, don't think. Just sit here. It's only words. Look at Molly, look what happens when you let it touch you. Don't think, don't look back, don't look anywhere . . .

'What is your verdict? Do you believe Donald O'Hagon here is guilty or not guilty of murdering his nephew?' William Abercrombie asked the ten man jury as they returned from considering their decision.

From the spokesman's worried frown it was clear the vote hadn't been unanimous.

'I think we all say, yes, he did it. But, Mr Abercrombie, sir, we don't feel a guy like Donald here can be put away for murder.'

175

'You're aware I cannot convict a man of murder, I can only commit him for trial at a higher court. The idea of your verdict putting him away for the crime doesn't come into it. Are you instructing me to pass him on to a higher court? Can you answer me that?'

'Not rightly we can't. Look at the way he got his hands round Rosie's throat just a while ago – we all saw it. No ordinary man would behave like it. But there's not a man in this court would say Donald O'Hagon ought to be brought up for attempting to strangle her. Just, he ain't got the same control as you and me when he gets roused. And he never meant to harm Neil. Guess he can't be held responsible. That's the way we see it.'

'Ah!' At last the Coroner appeared satisfied. He'd got what he wanted out of the jury. 'That being so, I propose that Donald O'Hagon be taken back to the town lock-up until doctors can be called in to examine him. It's my belief he ought to be in one of these psychiatric establishments.' Then, more quietly and directed at Molly: 'Best way, you know, Molly, he can't always have you to watch over him. There's this business with the boy too. Bad business. Very worrying. We've got to see that can't happen again.' He shook his head, wishing there was a happier way of sorting things out for the poor woman; but his responsibility was to the public, to other young boys. Who could know the repercussions Neil's death would have on a mind like Donald's? He stood up to leave the Courtroom.

'Rise!' Jim O'Hara bellowed, making the most of his last few seconds of officialdom. 'All stand.'

Then it was over. Rosie walked out of the Court a free woman but, in the eyes of most of those who'd packed in to hear and see, the cause of a lot of trouble that need never have happened. She didn't wait for Dylan and he made no attempt to run after her as she strode off in the direction of the settlement.

'Coming home with us, son?' Craig put a hand on the boy's shoulder.

Dylan didn't meet his eyes, didn't look directly at anyone. He shook his head and turned away, mingling with the crowd who jostled out into the street yet isolating himself from them as much as he had from the O'Hagons.

There were people who would like to have spoken to Molly, to have offered her the comfort of knowing how much they were feeling for her. She'd been part of the community for more than thirty years. But there was something about her that stopped them speaking. Lottie was known by sight, no more than that. While Craig had hung back to speak to Dylan, Molly and Lottie had made for the door. Neither seemed aware of the curious stares and whispers any more than they were of the wave of sympathy.

176

In the truck Molly sat hunched, arms folded; Lottie stared unseeingly ahead. The onlookers who'd crowded the Courtroom were breaking up into groups as they moved away, what they'd seen and heard on every tongue. Neither Lottie nor Molly could speak of it. They didn't speak at all. Craig climbed in and started the engine, they started the journey out of town.

Such silence isn't easy to break. Once or twice Craig almost made some comment, tried to think of something to dispel the nightmare of the last hour. But he felt that, if he did, neither of them would hear him.

'Cliff Hulbert was there, Cliff Hulbert from the *Clarion*.' It was Molly who finally broke the silence. 'Where was the news in it?' She raised her head long enough to glower first at Lottie then at Craig. 'Just tell me that. News is something that concerns other people. Entertainment, that's what Cliff Hulbert will be giving to them, at our expense. A family trouble, a family trag –' But she couldn't quite say 'tragedy', not yet. 'It's no one's business.'

'I guess he has a job to fill his paper, Aunt Moll.'

Another silence.

'Christ, there's a skunk somewhere about,' Craig muttered, a mile or two on, his mouth turned down at the corners as if that way the smell wouldn't be so strong. Lottie remembered the other time, she and Ramsey holding their noses, sharing the smell, sharing the laughter; she remembered the brilliance of the colours at the cut backs. Looking out today there was no sun, just a thin covering of iced snow. She bit hard on the trembling corners of her mouth.

'Reckon Old Pop was right.' Again it was Molly who spoke, more to herself than to them. 'Better if my lad had been killed a hero in the war. Can you imagine what Donald must be going through? He loved Neil more than any living creature. That's the hurt of it. If he'd killed that whore he wouldn't be suffering, not like he must be now.'

Better if he'd been killed during the war . . . but that was *their* Neil. Lottie remembered the rough khaki uniform, the bicycle rides, Madlock Hill, the English pubs full of tobacco smoke, songs and laughter. All of it a lifetime ago. She remembered the first night she'd met him, the first time he kissed her. *Her* Neil, memories that belonged to her and to him. Yet even then – no, don't think about it. Don't think at all.

That night, after Katie was in bed, Lottie could put it off no longer.

'Dear Mum and Dad, I didn't write last week. I'm sorry. Once or twice I started to but just couldn't seem to do it. There has been a dreadful accident. Neil has been killed . . . '

Katie's memories of England had long since faded, the present overtaking the past. In the same way her early resentment of Neil had turned into acceptance. It was nearly a year since he'd come home from the war, time enough at her age for the man she was told she had to call Daddy to slot into position. In the beginning she hadn't done much to endear herself to him, she'd clung to Lottie, tried always to push between them. Lately, though, the three of them had formed some sort of a group; when they'd ridden out together there had been times when she'd sat in front of him. Lottie was still the pivotal point of her universe, but Neil was important too. Katie was growing up and, hardly realising that she did it, she divided the family of O'Hagons into groups: herself with Lottie and Neil; the boys with Craig and Eugene; Grandma with Donald (who frightened her and who she tried to steer clear of) and Old Pop (who ignored her but gave her mother some looks that Katie didn't like at all).

It was more than a week ago that the men had ridden away and Katie had been told they'd be gone for a few days. To her that simply meant 'a long time', for each day was a crowded thing revolving around her own activities. Anyway, the men were usually out all day. Lately they'd been gone before she got up and still out when she went to bed.

Then things had changed in the house. She'd felt that the change had something to do with Craig coming home before the others. She couldn't seem to get anyone's attention, not even Mum's. The boys had noticed how different everyone seemed too. The grown-ups often stopped talking when the children came into the room. So they'd kept out of the way, pretended that nothing puzzled them and made them uncomfortable.

Yesterday's covering of snow had melted, the mid-day sun still held warmth, the air was clear and crisp.

'Where's my mom?' Coming in from the yard, Katie asked anyone who cared to tell her.

'In her room I think, honey.' She was glad it was Eugene who answered. Of them all, Eugene had been the easiest to look at lately.

'Coming to see you, Mom.'

Lottie heard her and opened the bedroom door. It was no use hiding from it, she must tell her. The days before the inquest had been a nightmare, but through them all she'd clung to belief in Neil. Rosie had asked for his help; he'd meant to talk to her about whatever it was that bothered her, to help her if he could, then to come home; and to reassure Craig, probably to reassure her too, that there was no more to it than that, he'd taken Donald. What she and Neil had shared was all either of them had wanted. She had to hang on to that. Craig had

178

been honest with her, he'd not hidden what had been between Neil and Rosie in the past. But that was all over, Craig had told her that too. Sometimes, lying awake in the darkness of their room, Neil's clothes hanging next to hers in the wardrobe, his boots standing in the corner, she'd been haunted of memories of their bad times, quarrels, violence. But always came the healing of what those bad times had led to: Neil begging her forgiveness, swearing that it was because he loved her too much, he couldn't bear her to care about anyone but him. The lonely tears she shed were for a Neil known only to her, a Neil who seemed close to her still in the silence of night. By morning light there'd be anger that he could have put Rosie's problem, whatever it had been, before the knowledge that at home she was waiting for him.

And by the light of day a devil would whisper to her: 'He refused to let you go with him. Was it because even then he knew he meant to go to Rosie?' Misery and rage fought within her, her soul felt ugly, scarred.

But all that had been before the inquest. Now there was nowhere to hide from the truth. She was glad to hear Katie looking for her.

'Hello, Katie, what have you been doing?' She opened the door at the sound of her footsteps. 'Playing in the yard with the boys?' Her voice was bright, but Katie wasn't fooled.

'Come to be wiv you.' And to prove she meant to stay she crawled on to the bed and sat with her arms folded. 'Where's Daddy and that Donald?' Her brow was too smooth to pucker, it was her eyes that spoke her unease. No one told her what was happening.

'They went to take the cattle – ' Lottie started, putting off the moment when she must say it.

'Craig did that too. Craig came back a long time ago.' Five days is a long time when you're only three and a half.

'There was an accident, Katie.' She waited. 'Donald's in a sort of hospital place, that's where he'll live now.' Still Katie waited. Anger tore at Lottie. How dare Neil do it! Katie, sitting there waiting, trusting. For one wild moment she wanted to say: 'Your Daddy lied to us, he cheated us.' But she didn't. Whether for Neil's sake or Katie's she didn't ask herself. 'Your Daddy won't be coming home. He's – he's gone to heaven.'

'Where's that? Didn't he want to live here any more?'

'Yes, of course he did, Katie, of course he did. But there was this accident – he got killed – ' There, she'd said it. All her attempts at softening it had been wasted. It had taken the actual words to tell her.

'But you just said he'd gone to some uvver place?'

'Heaven' Lottie sat down next to the little girl. Into her mind came memories of her own childhood. Had they ever taught her where to

179

pin her faith? It had just fallen into place without any effort or deep thought on her part, so she supposed they must have. She remembered Sunday mornings, she and the boys being marched off to church with their parents whether they wanted to or not, leaving Freda to cook the lunch; Ronnie with a face like thunder above his stiff Eton collar that was a requirement for the boys who sang in the choir; flowers in a silver vase by the side of Grandpa's photograph and her mother's assurance that he was in a 'better world than this'; her mother coming into her room to say goodnight, adding the rider: 'Have you cleaned your teeth and said your prayers?' Was that faith? Was that how you found a rock to build on? Then she remembered the day Katie was born, the day they knew Michael was lost.

By her side her daughter, that look of puzzled trust still on her face.

'Just like we all get born, Katie, the little calves, the babies, we all have our time to live in the world.' She wasn't a bit sure what shape her explanation would take, it was a voyage of discovery for both of them. 'Think how a tiny baby grows to be a person, someone who can think and talk, play – '

'And ride – ride too, Mom?'

'Yes, ride too. Everyone can't ride though, Katie. Some people live in big towns, never see horses, never look out at the big country like we do here.'

'I wouldn't like that.'

'If you were with the people you love, and they loved you, I expect you'd learn to do other things. You wouldn't ride, but you'd have a lot of fun just the same, you'd have friends.'

'Ginney can't ride. She's my friend.'

Lottie needed to touch the little girl. She took the small, soft hand in hers. Katie, growing up, learning to reason.

'No, Ginney can't ride. But she's learning to use her life just the same. We all sort of reach out to people we learn to love – '

Katie showed two rows of white milk teeth in the smile she turned on her. The puzzled, uncertain look was going.

'Like you did to me, Mom. Here.' She waggled the hand that Lottie held.

'Yes, like that. But even more. That's what we do with our bodies, we touch each other, we talk to each other. But even not seeing each other – like just now when you were in the yard and I was in here – we still love each other.'

Katie nodded wisely. So far she followed.

'Nobody lives as a person for ever, Katie. They get born as babies, they grow up, one day they grow old, but a time comes for every single person to die. That's when they go on to live in heaven. If you

180

love someone while they're alive, then you'll find you'll be with them again.'

'In heaven?' It was an awful lot to try and take in. 'Old Pop's ever so old, Mom. 'S'pect he'll soon go there, don't you?'

'I don't know when, Katie. We just have to wait till it's our turn.'

'Dad'll be glad to see someone he knows, won't he? But Mom . . .' Even that smooth brow furrowed at what worried her now: 'S'pose we *have* to go there, do we? But, Mom, will it be all full up with people like Pop?'

Lottie wished she'd done it differently. She wished Katie knew aged people other than Pop. Then she thought of Lavinia. Even now, so far away, she could draw comfort from that never failing support. If Katie knew *her* the thought of being with old people wouldn't fill her with dread. Still, it had to be up to her to allay the little girl's worries.

'People aren't always old when they die, Katie.'

Instead of easing one sadness, she seemed to have given the little girl an extra anxiety.

'You aren't going there, Mom? You won't go to see Dad there?'

'You and me have got years and years and years to be together, Katie. I shall watch you grow up, then one day you'll have children –'

Katie giggled. 'Silly Mom!' But the clouds were blowing away.

Katie had gone back outside to find the boys. Sean had slotted into place amongst them by this time, following along sometimes with his uncertain baby walk, sometimes resorting to hands and knees for speed. It was Earl who was the author of wisdom in their juvenile world; perhaps he'd know about this heaven place. It was no more real to Katie than the fact that Neil would never come home. At three and a half life is immediate, yesterday is a long time ago and tomorrow somewhere in an infinite future.

Watching them from her window did nothing to bolster Lottie's resolve. Katie and the boys were inseparable. Hadn't she lost enough without uprooting her from them too? But they couldn't stay here, it was impossible. But where to go? What to do? Lottie closed her eyes, shutting out the sight of the children, not wanting to see the earnest expressions on their faces as they tried to fathom the unfathomable.

'When life knocks you down – and be sure, it will knock you down somewhere along the line – make sure you jump straight back up again. Don't give yourself time to think, fix your sights on a goal and work at it.' Those words of Eva's had been dormant waiting for just this moment. She had known tragedy – she had fought back.

It was six days since Craig had returned from auction on his own, days that had taken their toll on everyone. Old Pop cried a lot, he

181

seemed shrunken, hopeless. Ramsey's words had done nothing to change his attitude towards Lottie, he felt no sympathy for her, she was an outsider and always would be. Young Neil should have used her same as he had all the others, not married her and brought her back to upset everything here. If he'd had no clinging wife warming his bed at home, he'd have gone with Rosie and no harm to anyone. He'd have been here now. Then there was Dylan. All these years Pop had had his ideas about who the child's father was. Anchored to his 'danged chair' he'd watched Neil approach adolescence, then a bit later he'd been pretty sure what was going on between the lad and the half-breed woman. Had Molly known? He thought she'd probably added two and two same as he had himself. But no one had said.

On that Wednesday after the inquest they were all gathered around the table for their mid-day meal. Molly toyed with her food; Pop was raising his fork to his mouth, chewing and swallowing, but without his usual relish. The only thing that remained unchanged was the lack of conversation.

'Craig, do you need the truck this afternoon? I'd like to go into Radley.' At Lottie's suggestion they all stopped eating to look at her.

'On Wednesday? I thought McFee brought the mail.'

'I want to send a cablegram home.'

'Hah!' This punctured Old Pop's apathy. So the red-lips was going back to where she belonged. 'You'll be fixing to go home? That's what I said. That McFee man, we talked about it. That's what I told him you'd be doing.' His voice a shade brighter, he made no attempt to hide from her that he wanted her gone.

Lottie shook her head. Suddenly she couldn't speak. The old man's attitude pushed her right outside the grief she supposed knitted the O'Hagons together. Home. No, it was impossible. At home they'd hated Neil, they'd scorned his family and the life here . . . and all the time she'd loved him, she'd trusted him. Looking across the table her eyes met Mollys and in them she saw a reflection of the discord in her own mind. How often it had been brought home to her that however long she stayed here she could never be the same as the Kilton Down women. Yet now she seemed to see beyond Molly's rough manner, her down to earth kindness, and recognised a loneliness of spirit akin to her own. None of them could share the path of Neil's mother, Donald's protector, but for just that second Lottie came close to it. Then she pulled herself back into her own tangled web. Molly had the right to grief, her sadness wasn't clouded with anger and suspicion.

Jump straight back up again, don't give yourself time to think. Find a goal and work for it.

Chapter Twelve

In an ante-room of the Trading Post were two Public Telephones. Silly to expect that Eva would be at home in the middle of the afternoon. The bell was ringing . . . she counted, one, two, three . . . nineteen, twenty.

'Hello?' At the sound of her aunt's voice Lottie seemed to lose her own. The hand that gripped the receiver was shaking.

'Hello? Say, I've been working all night. This call got me out of my bed! Is there anyone on the line?'

'It's me.' As she said it, she thought how stupid. How was Eva to know who 'me' was?

But she did. 'Lottie, honey?'

'Yes. Lottie. I wanted to phone you – I wanted to ask you – to tell you – '

'It's all right, Lottie. Nothing's so bad it can't get better. Just tell me.'

'I'm leaving Kilton Down. An accident – he's dead. He was killed. I can't stay here now. I don't want to stay. Aunt Eva, I'm sending a cable home.'

'Are you sure it's what you want – to go back home, now, like this?' No words of condolence but in Eva's voice Lottie heard understanding and sympathy. Eva's pity for her was because she'd lost him. But what about the lies, the deceit, what about the years she'd trusted him and pinned her faith on him? How hard it was to hold her own voice steady as she answered.

'I'm not going home. I'll take a job. I'll be fine, you mustn't worry. It's just I want to tell Mum and Dad to send letters to your address until I sort things out. I don't want them to go on writing here. You mustn't worry. I've still got some money left. I'll find – '

'Lottie, listen. I'll fix things at the hospital, get someone in to work my night tonight. Tomorrow morning I'll get off real early and drive up to get you. You hear me? Lottie?'

' . . . don't have to . . . ' It's hard to speak when you're crying. Suddenly she wasn't alone any longer, she wasn't an outsider. She and Eva belonged together.

'Wish I could get there tonight, but that's just not possible. You pack your bags. Try not to think about any of it, Lottie. When you get here is soon enough to talk – if you want to talk, that is. Lottie, this isn't an end, honey, it's another beginning. It has to be.'

Talking to Eva helped. She handed her letter to Digby Bint, steeling herself for the reference he might make to the inquest; but he took it without comment and gave her the form to write out her cable. 'Neil killed. Contact me with Eva. Lottie.' Digby read it through the first time for his own information, the second time to count the words and tell her the charge.

'Shan't be seeing you on Mondays for a while then? There'll be those who'll miss you.'

She gave him his money and left. Tomorrow she'd be gone, all this would be no more than a memory. This evening was the last time she'd see the sun go down over the wide range; tonight the last time she'd sleep in the room that had been hers and his; never after this afternoon would she drive the truck. She thought of the fun she and Katie had had together, the freedom, the baby voice chorusing with hers. Tomorrow was Thursday. Tomorrow they'd be on their way to Calgary, not Higley Creek. That's what decided her. As she came up to the junction, she turned eastwards.

Marthe saw her drive up to the house. Her welcome was warm, both cheeks were kissed. In her greeting she seemed to have forgotten she'd chosen to belong to Canada, and was pure Hungarian.

'My dear friend, you have been in my thoughts,' she said. 'I lit a candle and asked that you would be given the strength to bear all that has been put upon you.' She spoke simply. 'And I see that you have.' It was a statement of fact. It seemed to imply that having cast the burden on wider shoulders than her own, the weight had been lifted. In Radley there was no Roman Catholic Church, but Marthe's faith never faltered. 'Now, you will come inside from the cold. I see you have not brought Katie with you. She comes tomorrow?'

'No, that's why I've called now.' Lottie followed her into the sitting room where a log fire burned. 'I'm glad you're home. I was nearly here when I remembered Wednesday is one of Ginney's days for lessons.'

'Not today. Mr Haggerty is not well. You say you are not coming for your visit tomorrow?'

Lottie shook her head. These 'wisits' had been precious to both of them, and to the children too.

184

'I'm going away. Marthe, I can't stay there. There's nothing for me – and I must be a reminder to them. Aunt Eva is fetching Katie and me tomorrow. We're going back with her to Calgary. I'll give you her address. I'll write – and you will too, won't you? I couldn't go away without saying goodbye.'

Marthe had had plenty of disappointments in life, she'd learnt to take them on the chin. It was Ginney who couldn't accept; Thursdays had meant a lot to her.

There was no sign of Ramsey. Lottie knew it was silly to have imagined she might have found him at home. Tomorrow she'd be gone. She'd never see him any more, never hear his soft gentle voice, never sniff the smoke of his tobacco or hear his rare laugh that seemed to tell her they shared a secret joke. Already the sun was disappearing below the distant horizon, the day nearly over, her last day. The end of a chapter, the end of a dream.

She pressed her foot hard on the accelerator, her mouth set in a firm line and her chin held high. Tomorrow was the start of something new. It was up to her to see that it was something good. Just think how Aunt Eva had picked herself up, had come out here all alone and built a life. Well, *she'd* not be beaten! She was lucky. She had Katie, she had Aunt Eva. There must be work she could find in Calgary, a nursery school for Katie. And in Calgary there was Barrie.

It was Friday morning. They'd been with Eva since the previous evening, time enough to unpack what was necessary and spend their first night sharing the twin-bedded spare room – an arrangement that enchanted Katie. It seemed that Eva had switched her work shifts with a fellow Sister in her department which meant that she'd left the house this morning before the others were up.

New surroundings couldn't heal the wound, but they were a balm, they took away some of the sting. Just as with a physical injury a sudden movement can bring a rush of pain, so now memories would jump out unexpectedly: good moments, bad ones too, and worst of all doubts that even the good ones had been no more than a fool's paradise. But here, where everything was fresh and different, at least for some of the time the ghosts were kept at bay.

'Breakfast time. I'll lift you.' She hoisted Katie to a high stool at the breakfast bar in the kitchen, then sat by her side. Katie beamed her satisfaction.

'All by our own selves, Mom.' Her words brought back the picture of mealtimes at Kilton Down, the shovelling away of food. Had Katie hated it too? But she could remember nothing else except Thursdays at Higley Creek. So Lottie came to her first conscious moment of thankfulness that they'd moved on to the next stage. For one dreadful moment she faced the possibility that Katie might have grown quite naturally into being what she thought of as a 'Kilton woman'. They ate fruit and cereals, then she washed the dishes and proudly Katie dried them. It was a relief to have them stacked away with nothing broken, but she didn't hint that to the little girl. The shared job had been a big moment in her short life.

Yesterday evening's paper still lay folded on the table in the little hallway. She ought to see if there were any vacancies – work, apartments, nursery schools, everything had to be arranged. It was tempting today to do nothing, just take time getting to know the city. Jump straight back up . . . She opened the paper and spread it out on the dining table.

Before she'd checked halfway down the first column, the doorbell rang. With Katie close behind her she went to see who it was. Probably someone who hadn't known Eva had changed her work schedule.

'You're here!' Barrie had been prepared to see Eva. 'Lottie, I just read it – I came to see if Eva had heard anything from you. Never thought to find you.' She was left in no doubt of his pleasure.

'You're just the same.' The eighteen months had left no mark on him, but they were months that stood between them. The girl who'd said goodbye to him at Brimley could have reached out to him naturally; the woman she'd become held back.

'Here's one person who isn't just the same . . . Katie! My word, how she's growing up.'

'Come in, Barrie. Aunt Eva's at the hospital. She ought to have been off duty, but she switched around so that she could come to Kilton and fetch us. We came yesterday. She spoke fast. It was easier to keep talking and yet impossible to talk about the thing that had brought her here.

'I just read it this morning.'

'Here? In Calgary?'

'It's in the morning paper. Lottie, I don't know what to say. I don't know how you feel. You'd written to me, you'd never hinted – '

'Don't let's talk about it, Barrie. What's done is done. I don't want to look back. Not yet any rate. And, Barrie, promise me – '

'There was a promise you made me. Remember. Couldn't you have trusted me?'

'It wasn't like you're thinking.'

'Who's that, Mom?' Katie tugged at her shirt.

'It's Barrie. He used to come and see us when we were in England with your granny and grandad – my mum and dad.'

186

'In the picture.'

'That's right. They're in the picture.'

Barrie laid a hand on Lottie's shoulder.

'What is it you want me to promise?'

'I haven't read the paper, I don't want to read it. I've written home and told them there was an accident, but that Donald would never – and it's true, he would never, *never* have meant to hurt Neil. That's all I told them. I've not mentioned anything of what you've been reading. Promise me you won't either.'

'I promise, of course I do. But, Lottie, do you believe that I would –' 'He couldn't find the word he wanted. 'Would – gossip, tittle-tattle – about *you*? You don't have to ask for my word, you ought to know.'

'Yes, I do.'

Then his moment of seriousness was gone. He smiled. She'd almost forgotten that smile of his. It wasn't so much aimed at her as at his enjoyment in living.

'What about you girls getting your bonnets on and we'll go out on the town? I'll show you around, take you out to lunch.'

She laughed. His enthusiasm was infectious.

'When you rang the bell,' she told him, 'I was resolved to sort out our immediate needs – apartment, nursery school, job. I was just getting down to scanning last night's paper.'

'You owe yourself a day off. For old time's sake, eh? Today I'm free, tomorrow I'm flying. What do you say, Katie? Shall we make her come out? I'll show you the way to the play park, we'll find somewhere where they sell huge icecreams at lunch time. What do you say?'

Katie nodded with gusto.

'Come on, Mom. Let's go wiv him.'

'I'll try and improve my face, give me five minutes.' Lottie said it as naturally as if he were a brother. But there was nothing brotherly in the way he watched her as she went back to the bedroom, leaving him alone with Katie.

In less than the promised five minutes she was ready and came back carrying Katie's coat with her. From the living-room doorway she watched them, sitting side by side on the couch, Barrie with a piece of paper folded to make an aeroplane.

'Do it 'gain, show me 'gain.'

'Better than that, Katie, I'll tell you how and you make one yourself.'

Under his guidance, and with a little surreptitious help from fingers stronger than her own, the plane came off the production line. Like a dart he threw it, watching her expressions of wonder.

187

'Look, Mom! Did you see? I made it all my own self. What'll boys say! I did it, didn't I, Barrie?'

'You did, Katie. When I come next time you can make me another. We'll build an air force, humph?'

She didn't quite know what he was talking about, but if that was what he wanted she nodded eagerly enough. This new man was nice.

It was Tuesday of the following week when a letter was delivered addressed to Lottie bearing a local post mark. The business note-paper bore the address of a downtown branch of a bank, it was signed by the manager. Arrangements had been made in England for a sum of money to be transferred and an account opened in her name. Would she please call at the bank to finalise arrangements and to give specimen signature?

It was no use her pretending that it wasn't a relief to know there was money to cushion her. So far she hadn't found anywhere suitable for Katie – partly because of the intervening weekend but mostly because yesterday Barrie had been free again. It was a week today since the inquest. Only a week. She'd run away from her unhappiness. Even now she rushed into anything that presented itself rather than look the truth in the face. She wasn't proud of herself, it was cowardly. There were moments when a silent voice told her that she was being every bit as disloyal to Neil as he had been to her. At the memory of him she shied away, wanting to fill every minute. So when Barrie had telephoned yesterday and said: 'I'll pick you up in ten minutes. Where we're going will take all day. Bring stout shoes', she'd pushed all her problems out of sight and done as he said. Out of the city, heading northwest, towards the foothills. They'd even made up songs. It had been the sort of very special outing after Katie's heart.

Money . . . an account opened by arrangement in England. Dad must have done it. She was touched, yet resentful that her parents expected she should need help; she was angry that it was the truth, that in all her months at Kilton Down she'd had no money except the dollars she'd drawn as the wife of a soldier. She was grateful yet, knowing their feelings, gratitude was a hard pill to swallow.

She and Katie were just leaving to try and find the bank when a cable was delivered. 'Expect telephone call Tuesday 2 p.m. Alberta time. Grandma.' It was already ten o'clock. Less than four hours and she'd hear her voice.

'Come on, Katie, we'll get a cab.'

It wasn't a word Katie knew, but from the sound of her mother's voice it was a treat so she stepped out eagerly. When it turned out to be just a motor car it was something of a letdown but she wasn't going to let that spoil the morning; going out together just as if she was a proper grown-up person was great fun. Each thing she saw she tried to stamp into her memory to tell the boys.

At the bank Lottie learnt that the account had been arranged by Mrs Lavinia Matheson.

It was five minutes past two when the telephone bell rang, the longest five minutes Lottie had ever known.

'Grandma?'

'I have an International Call from England. Hold the line.' She held. Clicks, buzzes, silence as the line went dead, another click: 'Are you still there? Keep holding, please, call is coming through, sorry to keep you! Another click, another buzz, then: 'Lottie? Are you there?'

'Yes, Grandma, yes. You sound so clear, so near.'

'Now then, child, enough of that.'

How did the old lady know she was crying? That she did know was a relief, Grandma always knew things, she never had to be told.

'It's just hearing you. You sound so close.'

'And have you ever thought for a moment that I haven't been close? Oh, Lottie, child, what difference can miles make? Kate telephoned me, said she'd had a cable. Say just as much as you want to, my dear, it's too soon to want to rake over hot ashes. Why I phoned was this: that money I opened an account with, it's no one's business but yours and mine. Now I mean that – not a word to Kate or Rupert. You may not even need it, I dare say you've been left well taken care of. No, I'm not asking. I'm just saying whatever you've got, add that to it. If you want your fare home, then there it is.'

'Thank you. Grandma, I'm so glad it was you. Can I tell Eva It's just that she won't feel burdened if she knows I've got money. Not that she does – I think she likes us being with her. Anyway, I've fibbed a bit and not let her know how short I am. Grandma, are the leaves turning on the elms by the lake? What's it like there today? Is it sunny?'

'It's eight o'clock in the evening, I'm just going in to eat my dinner. The elms are hardly turning. We've been enjoying a beautiful Indian summer. I went down to the lake today – I went purposely so that I could tell you. Dear Lottie . . . Now, enough of this. Your mother and father are well, things don't change much in Brimley.'

'No. They never did.'

'From a distance you find that comforting.' Then, with a chuckle so unmistakably her own: 'Couldn't take it day in and day out, no more than I could. She's a patient soul.'

189

'Mum?'

'We all start off with our dreams, my dear. Well, you're young, too young to put dreams behind you. You've turned over a new page. Write a happy story on it, Lottie. Now tell me about that great granddaughter of mine.'

Lottie did better. She called Katie to the telephone. To say 'Hello' into that funny black thing that her mother held against her seemed most odd, but she tried and a voice told her it was 'Grandma'.

'In the picture. I kiss the picture bedtimes,' Katie told the mystery voice.

'It's all there waiting for me, it's as if I've only got to open a cupboard door and it will all tumble out. Such a mess . . . things I don't understand, things I can never know, things I want to forget and things I want to remember. All of them jumbled up and waiting to force the door open and swamp me. But being here with you, everything so different, is like stepping into another world.'

Both in night things and dressing gowns, Lottie and Eva were sitting on the hearthrug in front of an electric fire that tried to give the illusion of burning logs. Eva puffed at her cigarette. She didn't hurry to answer but Lottie knew she was weighing what was said.

'When your fiancé was killed, was it like that for you? Oh, I don't mean you had things you didn't want to remember – '

'Oh, but I did. Things I wasn't proud of. Perhaps there's no such thing as uncluttered grief. Perhaps if you love someone there are always regrets, things you haven't done, times you've failed. In my case I had one great consolation – or so I believed. I was expecting his child.'

'But – I didn't know. What happened? You mean it was adopted?' Her one consolation.

'It was stillborn.'

'Oh, Aunt Eva.' Lottie closed her eyes. She remembered the day Katie had been born. 'How did you bear it?'

'Looking back, it's like that cupboard you talked of. When I lost Matthew, I felt that in the baby I still had something of him. Then there was nothing. If I'd opened that cupboard, let it all tumble out, I don't think I could have survived. I say that, but of course it's not true. I should have survived, if surviving is getting up each morning, existing through each day. But that isn't what life is all about. And now, from this distance, I know that if that's all I'd done with my life, I would have failed Matthew as well as myself. So, like I told you once, many years ago, I picked myself up before the feeling had time to come back into my numbed mind. It's the only way, Lottie.'

190

'It's just that I feel I'm being disloyal – not just to him. I can't even start to think about that, not yet – but disloyal to all my own dreams. You were a nurse – I'm not really anything. I used to be a shorthand typist but I've forgotten how to be that by now. I'll find a job of some sort, I'll find a place for Katie. But is that what life is all about? Where's the goal in that.'

Eva lit another cigarette. 'A better goal than I had.'

And again Lottie was ashamed.

'Lottie, don't listen to me if you think it's rubbish, but it does occur to me that Katie has had an awful lot of adjusting to do in her short life. Through it all, being with you has been her one constant. What's happened now has stripped her of the security she knew at Kilton Down. "The boys" she keeps talking about . . . There might have been things you didn't feel comfortable with, things that were wrong, but at her age she would have accepted without question. To her it was home, it was security.'

'You think I did wrong to bring her away? Aunt Eva, even if you hadn't come for me, I'd made my mind up. I wouldn't have stayed there. I couldn't – '

'Steady on.' Eva laughed affectionately. 'I never said any such thing. What I'm trying to say is that you're here now, she is starting to feel at home. Can't you make her your goal for a little while at least? Give your time to having some fun with her, let her have time to get her breath back. In all the jostling about she's had, you've been her one bit of continuity. Are you desperate to go to work? Mrs Matheson's taken the pressure off, and you're more than welcome to be here. In fact, you've no idea how much I've looked forward to this since you were a scrap of a child.'

'My Canada box, remember? All the things you told me about your country, about Alberta, your land of the wild rose.'

'And so it is, Lottie. There's never a rose without thorns, but never a more beautiful one than this. Give it time.'

At Brimley nothing ever changed, Lavinia had said. To see them at the breakfast table was to prove her right, except that now instead of Lottie the third place was taken by Ronnie.

'I don't understand it. She doesn't mention any plans for coming home. We count for nothing! Just that note telling us that that wretched man has been knifed – and now this. No explanation of why she's staying in Calgary. Not that we need it spelt out to us. Hasn't she always been the same about your sister?' Kate conveyed without actually saying it that in bracketing Rupert with Eva he automatically shared the blame for what Lottie was doing. She passed the letter to

191

him, in her action managing to dismiss him, his sister, and the letter too.

'Doesn't she say how long she's staying there, Mum? Perhaps she's just gone for a break. Heaven's, she's certainly entitled to something to take her mind off what happened. She'll probably go back to Kilton Down.' Ronnie never had quite Michael's special brand of patience with his mother.

'Don't be ridiculous!' Rupert drew his brows together in consternation. 'Go back there? Whatever for? Her place is here. Your mother is quite right. A week or two with Eva and she'll come home. Anyway, I dare say she has legal things to get sorted out first. We must be patient.'

'I guarantee she won't come home! If she had any consideration at all for how I feel she would give some indication, give me something to look forward to. But what is there? Nothing! Not a word about Brimley, about her home. Eva this, Eva that. Katie is settling, she says,' and at that Kate's voice croaked threateningly, 'settling with Eva.'

'Well, personally, what I say is, a damn good job Aunt Eva is out there to give her support.' Ronnie rolled his serviette and pushed it back into its ring, then stood up. 'I must go. Shan't be home this evening, Mum. I'm taking Millicent to that concert at the Town Hall, remember?'

'How nice.'

'You and Dad ought to have got tickets. Why didn't you, Dad?'

'Oh, I don't think we want to go. I have a busy enough day ahead of me. I can well do without rushing out again in the evening.'

'Mum might have enjoyed it.'

Rupert looked genuinely surprised at the suggestion. 'Oh, I don't think so.' Then, as Ronnie shut the door on them: 'You didn't want to be taken to this thing at the Town Hall, did you, Kate? You should have said. You've got plenty to amuse yourself with at home, haven't you?'

She ignored the suggestion and took Lottie's letter back to re-read.

'I must go too. Have a nice quiet day, dear.' Meticulously he folded the morning paper, corners at ninety degrees, brushed his lips against the cheek she turned towards him, then followed Ronnie. Had he looked back he might have been shocked by the look of cold dislike on her face.

Nice quiet day! Damn him, damn him. A quiet day, a quiet week, a quiet month, a quiet year, and another and another. Why couldn't she have come back to me? I used to pray that this would happen to him. And now it has. How God must be laughing. He's given me what I wanted – and she's gone to Eva. She's taken my Katie to Eva.

Through the half open door, where the kitchen led to the hall, Freda saw her walking back up the stairs.

'I'll be off to Market when I've done the dishes, Mrs Bradley. Anything special you want?'

'Lock the door when you go. I'm going to lie down. My head's – ' She didn't finish the sentence. Closing her bedroom door she leant against it indulging in the relief of feeling her face contort, letting the tears come. Where was the justice? Ronnie didn't understand. All he thought of was Millicent. Lottie put herself first, herself and that damned Eva. Only Michael had been different, only Michael had really cared about her. She'd lost him, she'd lost Lottie, soon Ronnie would be gone. And what had she? Just Rupert. 'Have a quiet day, my dear.' Lying on the unmade bed, she wept.

'For us Thursday is a sad day. Monday, Tuesday and Wednesday Ginney has her lessons. Thursdays she has nothing. For me as well it is a day I do not enjoy.' Marthe's writing was more stilted than her speech. Mondays, Tuesdays and Wednesdays they had a routine, they were busy. Lottie read it and remembered the Thursday trips and what they'd meant to Katie and her. 'We're on our way to Higley Creek, We go there Thursday every week . . . ' But what about Mondays and the trips to Radley? Marthe might write that 'we are all well' – reading it Lottie heard that voice telling her 'vee are all vell'. That was the nearest Ramsey ever had to a mention.

Once or twice Ginney wrote to Katie, but there was nothing in her life to tell. Katie 'wrote' back, barely recognisable pictures of the hills, herself, Lottie and Barrie on a sledge; a Christmas tree, herself, Lottie and Barrie by the side of it. Occasionally a fourth figure was added with more enthusiasm than accuracy: Eva. Under the pictures Lottie wrote what they were while Katie stood proudly by. 'Us on a sledge', 'us by the Christmas Tree'.

The cupboard to Lottie's secret mind stayed firmly locked. Barrie's companionship helped her keep the veil over what was gone – and yet a niggling conscience reminded her that this was how it had been once before. To look at that other time would have been to let too much else tumble from the cupboard, it was easier to take each day as it came. She looked for his coming, just as she had in Brimley; he made no demands on her, their outings were always fun – it had been like that in Brimley; Katie adored him – and so she had in Brimley. All that was ages ago, Lottie told herself when her conscience prodded. These days it was different. There were plenty of evenings when he was out with other people, he'd made friends in Calgary. Barrie was good-looking, his personality was attractive, he had girl friends apart

193

from her. That's what Lottie reminded herself if the memory of their last evening in Brimley teased her mind. How he'd felt about her then had been her own fault, she'd let him give her too much of his time. They'd both come a long way since those days. They were friends, just friends.

Half-past one, the morning of the first day of January. A new year. Of its own volition Lottie's mind jumped back twelve months when she was with Neil. 'Our first full year,' she remembered whispering, so sure of all that lay ahead of them. She shut her eyes tight as if that could banish the hunger that filled her. Yet it wasn't the hunger she wanted to run from, it was the ghost of the other woman in his life that haunted her. Closing her eyes to blot out the moonlight that flooded the room, there was nothing but darkness, black night and a craving that consumed her. Damn Rosie! Damn, damn, damn her. Neil, what we had was right, it was wonderful. Wasn't it? Damn her, what did you get from her that we didn't share together? Nothing. It couldn't have meant anything to you, it couldn't have been like it was for us together. Damn her, she doesn't count, she never did. Forget her, just think of him, of us. Neil, be with me, help me . . . help me forget her . . . damn her . . . damn her . . . just us, just you and me. Her hands caressed her tingling breasts. Need and longing drove her. In the other bed Katie turned over, muttering in her sleep. Only for a second Lottie was still, nothing could stop her now. Forget Rosie . . . forget everything . . . just think of how it had been . . . reach out . . . reach out.

Minutes later, from the physical height she plummeted to the depth. Loneliness mocked her. The moonlight was cold. A moment ago there had been nothing but the force that had driven her, now she wanted just to forget it had happened. Think of Katie, of the gathering of people at the apartment this evening, friends of Eva's, Barrie. A new year had begun, nineteen forty-seven – she resolved that with it she would make something of her life. For weeks she'd taken each day as it came, frightened to look ahead or to think of the weeks that had gone. But they belonged to yesterday, to last year.

She propped herself on her elbow and peered across at the sleeping child. Katie was fond of Barrie. Being with him was always a happy thing, there wasn't an ugly streak in his nature. Again she lay back on the pillow. Was she being any fairer to him now than she had at Brimley.

Supposing just now – all that – supposing it had been him? How strange. Dear Barrie, kind Barrie, good fun, good company – yes, and good-looking, he's certainly that – but what sort of a lover is he?

I've only known Neil. That wildness, a sort of greedy passion. But that's what it should be, surely that's what it must be. Supposing I married Barrie not knowing, supposing he was a sort of Wednesday night man. She chuckled to herself at the idea.

'Mom! What you doing, Mom?'

'Happy New Year, Katie. I thought you were asleep.'

'Saw you sit up. You were looking to me. What that, Mom, that new year. What's it?'

'Today is the first day of a fresh year. Come and have a cuddle. Let's start if off with a squeeze, shall we?'

Katie wriggled out of bed, and trotted across the gap between them. In the moonlight Lottie could see her two rows of white teeth as she beamed her delight at this unexpected turn of events. Then she was in bed, warm and sweet, arms and legs wrapped tight around Lottie.

'Happy new time, Mom.'

'I'm glad Eva's working late. I want to talk to you.'

'You have plenty of chance to do that,' Lottie laughed.

'Not to say what I have to say to you. We get on well don't we, and Katie too? I mean, I think she quite likes me? This is difficult. I told you years ago how I felt about you. Maybe because you didn't think of me that way then, you still don't. But, Lottie, we do get on well – '

'I don't know what I would have done without you, Barrie, back in Brimley or these last months.'

He smiled, at her and at the world.

'Then don't do without me.'

'Wait!' She gripped his hand. 'Please. It's just that I can't look ahead, I can't see a pattern.'

'Can't I help you to see one?'

She shook her head.

'I have to find my own way. It would be so easy to let myself be steered, so temptingly easy just to shut my eyes to things I don't want to remember. But it wouldn't work, it couldn't. Tomorrow has to be built on today, on yesterday.'

'You mean it's too soon? Of course it is. I shouldn't try and push you. But, Lottie, I'm not expecting that you could be in love with me.'

'I'm not sure I believe in being in love. I know I like you very very much. No, more than like. I do love you. It's just I'm not sure, right now, that I'll ever be capable of that sort of intense feeling again. I think something inside me has sort of curled up and died.'

Raising her chin, he was only inches from her. It was Lottie who made the move, her mouth touching his. Until now no man but Neil

195

had ever kissed her, and with Neil it had never been like this. Sometimes his kisses had been an expression of his mastery over her, sometimes they'd been to arouse a need in her as urgent as there was in him, sometimes they'd been a sharing of the pure joy of being together: but never had he touched her with anything akin to reverence as Barrie did now. Another ghost pushed its way into her mind. Her mother telling her that one day some nice young man would come along and put her on a pedestal.

'Barrie, if I'm not sure, doesn't that mean it would be wrong – for you as well as for me?'

'No. It means I'm a fool to have said anything yet, you need time. And I'll give you time, Lottie. We'll forget all about it and go on just as we were. Until you're ready I won't say another word.' There was neither passion nor yet reverence in the friendly way he smiled at her. 'Old age won't be getting us in its grip yetawhile. I'll just say this – then no more, I promise. If you prefer, we could go back home, make a fresh start in England. I don't necessarily want to stay in Canada.'

Suddenly, and she didn't know why, she felt very lonely.

Chapter Thirteen

Through Lottie's first weeks in Calgary she'd taken the coward's way and tried to push thoughts of the O'Hagons out of her mind. By December, with the shops full of bright lights, the city in a fever pitch build-up to Christmas, she'd found her thoughts turning more and more to Molly. She'd hunted through the cards in the shops. 'Festive Christmas', 'Joys of the Season', 'Yuletide Happiness', all these she'd put aside. Then she'd found one with the simple wording 'May the Peace of Christmas be with you'. Only now, from this distance and her own mind losing the numbness of the early weeks, could she start to imagine what Neil's mother must be suffering. Molly's Neil, the baby she'd borne, the child who'd depended on her, the youth, the man; sometimes Lottie would find herself looking at Katie and in her seeing Molly's heartbreak. To write any of that would have been impossible, any hint of emotion would have distanced them even further. So she'd sent the card, adding to the simple wording nothing more than 'From Lottie and Katie', with a snapshot of Katie feeding a squirrel in the park.

In January a letter was delivered, addressed in that hand that Rupert had scorned.

'Having a card from you made Christmas easier. And I hope yours was not full of hard thoughts about the dreadful mess of it all. What happened wasn't what any of us expected – like when Old Pop had his fall, it spoilt the rest of his life. An accident can happen so sudden. The men rode out and who expected that would be the end of it all? Poor Donald, he's been put into a mental hospital, a lock-up. Some of the people in there have done real bad things. Young Donald would never have hurt a soul, he'd have given his own poor life for Neil. Makes me feel ill to think about how he's doing in that place, no one there to care about him. Old Pop he's got real miserable, cries for nothing. Eugene is having another, I think you'd gone when she said.

End of April. The kids often speak of Katie. With kind thoughts, your mother in law, Molly O'Hagon.'

Katie drew some pictures so that the boys would know all the exciting things she was doing.

For all Lottie's good intentions that she would stop marking time and make something of her life in this new year, it was Eva who opened the next door for her. Through contacts at the hospital she had heard that an assistant was wanted at a playschool on the south side of the city. Not the sort of job Lottie had envisaged, but in its favour was the fact that Katie would be included. So half way through January saw them setting out together each morning. They had to be at Mrs Harmsworth's house, where each day a dozen or so children were brought, before half-past nine. Katie felt this was a shared responsibility; she stepped out full of her own importance.

Being caught up in the morning rush hour was just as new to Lottie as it was to the little girl. Neither a cycle ride to Brimley nor the works bus from Kingstaunton House had prepared her for the jostle of crossing Calgary at this time of day. For the first few mornings it was an adventure. Perhaps had the weather of an Alberta January been kinder the excitement might have lasted longer. By the beginning of February she dipped into Lavinia's cushion of support and with Barrie to guide her bought a second hand car. Its acquisition was a great stride in her battle for independence. She took its photograph with Katie about to climb in, imagining how pleased they'd be at home to see it.

'And you tried to make me believe she'd only be there until that wretched man's affairs were settled! Would she buy a car if that were so?' Back in Brimley Kate looked at Rupert as if it were his fault. '"Katie – off to school", that's what she's written on the back.' She looked up, her eyes two blue pools of hurt.

'We've no choice but to be patient. At least let us be thankful for one thing. It seems he hasn't left her unprovided for, she has money to spend on this car. She'll come home when she's ready.'

'If I thought it was because of Barrie she's staying in Calgary, I wouldn't mind so much. But she seldom mentions him. He's a dear boy, I could see from the first how right he was for her.' Hope took an upward turn as Kate gave rein to her imagination just as so often she had in the past.

'She'd be just as far away in Canada with Barrie as she has been on her own – or with Neil O'Hagon,' Rupert reminded her.

'Nonsense! Why do you think Barrie took that job out there? You don't seem to have any idea about people! He went to Canada

198

because of Lottie. Not that he ever wrote of having visited that Kilton Down place. I dare say Lottie was ashamed of what he'd find there, and I can't wonder. But now, if at last they might come together, he'd bring her back to England, I know he would.' She picked up the snapshot and carried it to the light.

With a job and a car came new freedom. Lottie expected it would help her in the building of a new life. Often she'd driven with Barrie far beyond the city boundaries into a country held in the grip of winter. Now though the air was full of a new hope, it was more than 'that danged chinook', it was the promise of spring.

It was Saturday, no playschool today. Eva left home for the hospital at noon, she'd not be home until about ten o'clock; yesterday Barrie had flown east and wasn't returning until today. So that left Lottie, Katie and the freedom of the road. They headed northwards, it was the road she'd taken on the day they'd arrived.

'Shall we sing, Mom?' A song had always been part of their shared trips.

'Here we go in our very own car,
We sing to show how happy we are,
Far ahead is Kilton Down,
Long way away from Calgary town . . . '
She drifted into silence.

'Is that all Mom? Isn't there any more song?' Katie recognised their tune, but usually there was more to it than this.

'I don't know, Katie.' For was there? Where was she heading? It was nearly six months since Eva had collected them from Kilton Down, three months since Barrie had asked her to marry him. And what had she done with her time, except live through it?

She was conscious that Katie was looking at her with a puzzled frown. Again she burst into song and was rewarded by the sound of a chuckle.

'One day we'll visit Higley Creek,
We used to go Thursday every week,
We won't care if it rains or snows,
We won't care if the north wind blows,
Marthe and Ginney'll be waiting for us
And more than that we won't give a cuss.'
'Silly Mom. That's miles and miles and miles I 'spect'.
'One day we'll go there, Katie. To Kilton Down too, maybe. Perhaps then I'll find the last line of today's song.'

Katie had no idea what she was talking about, but she liked the idea of going to see her friend Ginney. She'd sent her a lovely drawing the other day of their new car.

199

For the first time in all these months Lottie felt the mist was lifting enough for her to see the straight of the road ahead. She could not yet tell where the bends were coming, what hazards were waiting to trap her, where the signposts would point, but the first stretch was as clear as this beautiful day touched with the magic of spring. And fortunately the fresh air made Katie tired. She was bathed and in bed before seven o'clock. Then Lottie waited another half hour to make sure she was sound asleep.

'Will you get me Radley 2424, please?' Her stomach was home to a hundred butterflies as she waited. This was her own decision. By the time Eva came home, by the time she saw Barrie, it would be arranged.

'Ha-lo', came the unmistakable voice of Marthe.

'Marthe, it's me, Lottie.'

'My dear friend. I have a letter just written to you, waiting for Monday.'

Suddenly it seemed more like yesterday than six months ago. Monday, Radley, the Trading Post, the hybrid car, the cut-backs, the sound of rain on the roof of Ramsey's car, the freedom of escape into the great outdoors with Katie, the freedom of escape into the great outdoors on her own. A kaleidoscope of memories crowded in as she answered: 'Marthe, I'm phoning to ask a favour. Things are fine here, there's nothing wrong, it's just that I feel I must see everything again – the range, Kilton, Higley, Radley, all of it. When I left I just wanted to put it behind me, not to look. I'm sure if I can do that now, look and really see, somehow I'll know the answer to what I should do next. Does that sound silly? Can you understand?'

'And what is the favour? You would like to come here to stay with us? Is that it?'

'That's what I hoped. Just for a few days. A week at the most. I'll arrange to get the time off from my job. Can you understand why I need to come back?'

'I do not need to understand, I am just happy that it is how you want it.' Hearing her, it was indeed just how Lottie 'vanted' it. 'And Ramsey will be delighted that my friend is to stay with me. You come soon?'

'Please. Now I know what I have to do, I want to do it straight away.'

So it was arranged.

'Don't stay away too long,' Eva told her. 'But, Lottie, you're right to go. It'll open the door on all your ghosts, but you won't be free of them until that happens. Have you talked about it to Barrie?'

Lottie shook her head.

200

'We'll only be away a week. You'll neither of you have time to miss us before we're back again.'

Eva lit another cigarette. Tonight there was a suppressed excitement about Lottie, she seemed to glow with an inner purpose. Eva understood her so well. She suspected that this trip would lay those ghosts she'd been frightened to face up to and leave the way clear for the next move.

'I guess he'll find it worth letting you go for one week, it'll clear your mind, let you free to take the next step,' she said.

'To Barrie? That's just it, Aunt Eva. I don't know. I'm sure it would work, we never quarrel, never even disagree, Katie loves him – and so do I. It's just . . . why do I hesitate?'

'My feeling is that when you get away you'll see things clearer. You'll probably come back ready to tell him what he wants to hear.'

'He talked of finding a flying job back home. He wouldn't if I said I didn't want to, I know I could persuade him to stay here. But that's what bothers me, Aunt Eva – he could leave here without a backward glance.' She looked at Eva helplessly.

Eva laughed affectionately. 'But then, honey, he never had a Canada Box to save his pennies in. He never had a dream.'

At Higley Creek the only thing their welcome lacked was a red carpet. Marthe was openly delighted. There were no flowers to be bought in Radley at this time of the year, but at the Trading Post she'd found small Japanese figures, artificial miniature trees, a bridge, a pagoda, pebbles and a shallow bowl. During the week she and Ginney had put all their artistic talent into making a Japanese garden to stand on the table by the window in the room Lottie and Katie were to share.

The first evening there was an air of festivity about the meal. Lottie and Katie had been here often to share a snack lunch, but always there had been just the four of them. The difference this evening was the extra presence of Ramsey – that and the fact that this was no mere snack. Beef soup, stuffed salmon, Pandosy apple cake . . . At Kilton Down food had always been plentiful and good, but how could Lottie help the comparisons that sprang to mind between there and this comfortable room with its cheerful drapes shutting out the night, the table laden with crockery that shone, with serving dishes, cutlery that Marthe took pride in polishing; but most of all what set this apart was the steady hum of conversation. Question, answers, interest, them in her, she in them.

Naturally she helped Marthe clear up afterwards, then she put Katie to bed. Coming back into the sitting room, she found Ramsey alone.

'Marthe is looking after Ginney.' How could she have forgotten that smile? Shared by no one but themselves. 'Lottie, you've no idea how good it is to have you here. It's been a long time.'

'Before it all happened. I went away without seeing you again.'

'The old man O'Hagon said you were going back to England. Of course, I knew you hadn't. Ginney told me you were in Calgary with your aunt. And now?'

'I don't know, Ramsey.' How easy it was to talk to him. 'That's why I wanted to come back. Can places really matter so much? I just feel that something of me belongs here in the open spaces. Yet because of – oh, so many things – I've tried not to let myself believe it.'

'And now you think you're ready to decide?'

She could tell by the way he asked it that his question went deeper. And just as she had before, so again she spoke to him about Barrie.

'You see, I'm not sure. It isn't that I'm not fond of him – it isn't that I find him physically unattractive – nothing like that. So it must be something to do with what happened at Kilton. Perhaps it's because Neil was so angry about it. Could that be what holds me back? I'd not even considered that until this moment.' She smiled, happy at the realisation. 'There! Already I'm seeing things that had been hidden. I knew coming back would be the answer.'

'It may take longer than a week. You know you are welcome here. I hope it takes longer.' He knocked the dead ash from his pipe into the open fire, then started to refill it. 'Now, don't you think it might be a good idea to telephone your aunt, tell her you got here safely?'

'You know something, Ramsey? You really are a very nice person.'

Bending down he lit a spill from the flaming log. She didn't see his face and couldn't read his thoughts. Nice person! So was her brother, so was the grandmother she was so fond of, probably so was Molly O'Hagon. Leaving her to make her phone call, he went to say goodnight to Ginney.

The difference between Kilton Down and Higley Creek was as marked as the difference between their owners. Kilton bred beef cattle; the thousands of acres of Higley Creek were given over to the growing of wheat. Lottie had visited here regularly, she'd seen the land change; the first hint of a carpet of green, then later the young shoots growing tall. She'd seen them turn gold under a summer sun, as far as the horizon an unending sea of ripened corn. Higley didn't stretch to that distant horizon, but Higley and its neighbour were identical, one merged with the other.

Astride the chestnut mare she gazed out over the empty landscape that gave no hint of vegetation.

'Well, what do you think?' She'd heard a rider coming. Without turning, she'd known it would be Ramsey. 'Barren? Empty?'

In a way, I suppose it is. But that's what's exciting, isn't it? I was going to say it's like a canvas waiting for a picture, but that's not true. The picture is already decided. Now you just have to wait for nature.'

He laughed. 'You make me sound a lazy sort of a guy, sitting back and waiting. Land has to be nurtured. Not often you can look across this stretch and not see work going on – feed dressings, sprays.'

'I didn't mean it like that. I was thinking what a miracle it is.' Then, with a teasing grin, 'With a little bit of help from man, of course.'

'Yeah, it's a miracle right enough. Be a poor sort of farmer who saw it as anything else. Different from the land you got used to though, Lottie.'

'At Kilton? They'll be turning the cattle on to the range. A new beginning. I thought this afternoon I'd drive over, take Katie to see the boys. Would Ginney like to come, do you think – that is, if I could take the "hybrid"?'

'Fix it with Marthe. I never interfere. I know she told Mr Haggerty that Ginney wouldn't be having any lessons this week, with you here.'

Lottie did as he said. There'd be no objection to Ginney coming with them, surely. But one look at Marthe told her she was wrong.

'I'll drive carefully, Marthe, you don't need to worry. And when we get there I know how the ramp lets down to wheel her out. I thought a change would be good for her.'

Marthe was tight-lipped.

'She's used to me. She would feel helpless, having to ask you to do what she can't manage. Even little things – reaching what is too far away, bending to pick something up. I never need her to ask, I always watch, try and see her needs before she knows them herself even. I know what is right for her.'

'Let's ask her, let her decide for herself. It would do her good to feel she can mix with other people.'

Marthe's already tight lips turned down at the corners.

'If you think that, then you ask her.'

'No, Marthe. Please you. If she senses you don't want her to come, it'll take all the pleasure out of it for her. So you ask her, let her see you don't mind.' It was the first time Lottie had ever felt uneasy with Marthe. Perhaps it was natural that she should be possessive of Ginney. But it wasn't fair, the child needed to learn independence.

'We're on our way to Kilton Down,
   We're going to see the boys,' Lottie started the song.

203

'We like the country more than the town . . . ' She paused for inspiration, something to rhyme with boys. It was Ginney who took up the strain:

'Let's sing and make some noise.'

The 'hybrid' was filled with the sound of song and laughter. If Marthe could have peeped at her charge, surely she must have agreed how right it was for her.

'Holy jeepers! What sort of car do you suppose that to be?' From his position by the open doorway where his chair had ben put so that he could make the most of the spring sunshine, Old Pop saw them drive into the yard.

Eugene waddled to his side to look.

'Why, that must be the McFee child. I've seen it sometimes in Radley. You remember Mr McFee, Pop? He called here with Lottie's mail.'

The old man cleared his throat and spat, taking long distance aim and almost clearing the verandah. Clearly it was meant as a greeting for the visitor he wasn't likely to forget in a hurry.

'Well, I'll be danged! It's that red lips chit of Neil's come back. See, it's not the McFee man, it's that Lottie wench. Look, Molly.'

Pushing past him she went down the three steps from the verandah to the yard.

Getting out of the car Lottie came to meet her, only now realising that, sure as she'd been that she needed to see Kilton Down again, she'd never imagined the moment when she and her mother-in-law would come face to face.

'I'm staying at Higley Creek for a few days.' I've thought about you, my thoughts have been full of pity for you. But she couldn't say any of that.

'You brought Katie? The boys'll be wanting to see Katie.'

'Yes, and Ginney too. Can I get her chair out, let her be with the others? It's warm enough for them to play outside.'

'Eugene,' Molly called, 'tell the boys they've got company. If they put their coats on, they'll be best out here.' Then to Lottie: 'I'll give you a hand with the chair.' Having something to do helped them both over the first moments.

'I suppose you're not going to come and say hello to me?' came Pop's whining voice. 'Why should you?'

'Of course I am Pop. In just a minute.'

'You go and talk to him. Poor old fella, not a bit his old self these days. We'll unload the chair then I'll get the children sorted on to a chore. Nothing like a job of work to break down the barriers.'

204

Lottie found herself reaching out and taking Molly's big hand in hers. There was so much she wished she could have said, but she knew Molly too well to try.

'So you decided to show up again,' Old Pop greeted her. 'Thought you would have gone back where you came from. What's keeping you from all the folks used to send letters you were always chasing to Radley after?' He chewed hard on his tobacco. 'Can't see what there is for you here.' So often when he made his sly remarks, playing his game of stirring up trouble, he'd not quite met her eyes. Now he looked at her direct. Just for a second he was ready to do battle, be as unpleasant as he knew how. He expected her to rise to his bait but what he saw as her gaze met his was pity. He slumped in his chair; the fight went out of him. 'Nothing for you here,' he repeated, a dribble of saliva on his trembling mouth, 'nothing for me, nothing for Moll. Even Eugene, look at her, ready to drop another. And what for? Don't know what any of it's for, danged if I do.' His lined old face crumpled, he made no attempt to hide his tears.

Behind his back Eugene shrugged her shoulders helplessly, sending a silent message to Lottie that this wasn't anything unusual. Dropping to her knees by his side Lottie took his hand in hers, a hand that once must have been as hard as leather but now, after years of idleness, was pathetically soft, the skin hanging lose and peppered with the brown blotches of age. He's aroused feelings of dislike, contempt, irritation or impatience often enough; just occasionally she'd enjoyed him when he'd been in the mood to recount tales of his youth. She'd never expected to feel so touched by his frailty.

'Poor Pop. I remember the very first evening I met Neil, he talked about Kilton Down, and told me about each one of you. "Then there's Old Pop," I can still almost hear him saying it.' And if she hadn't got the words exactly right, what did that matter, to Pop or to her either? Pop wiped the back of his hand across his cheek, he sniffed, his mouth was open slightly but now his expression was of hope. Neil's words. This was what the boy had said about him. Thousands of miles away in England, and Neil had talked about him. '"He's a great old guy, is Pop. Had to hang up his saddle long time since, but he's always been there for Craig and me."'

He didn't say anything. Her hand still held his and almost shyly he rested his other on it. Then, just as she'd heard him hundreds of times, he cleared his throat. She steeled herself for what she expected to come next. But no! He thought better of it. His mood could change as quickly as a child's. Now there was an impish twinkle in his eyes. He knew she'd noticed his change of mind.

'And so I have. Always been there for the boys.' Some of his self-esteem seemed to have come back. 'Hey, Lottie, I'm sure glad to have you tell me about what he said.' He nodded his head, muttering 'Neil's words' under his breath as if to imprint them on his mind to draw on later. Then a thought struck him. 'All this time you kept it to yourself. Went off without a care that I didn't know he'd talked about me there in England. Didn't matter to you what he said about me – but it mattered to me. Did you care? No. Waited all this time afore you got around to telling me.' This was the Pop she was used to. 'If you hadn't come here today I'd have gone to my grave not knowing how, all those thousands of miles away, the boy spread the word about me. It ain't right, ain't right at all. Things he said about me, no business o' yours, yet you kept them to yourself.'

'I expect he wrote things to you about me, and I'll never know them, Pop.'

'About you?' His hands were his own again now. He'd pulled them away as though ashamed of his moment of weakness. 'And why should he have written us about girls he picked up with? I suppose he said he was hitching up with a bride in England. Why, yes, he wrote and told Molly that. What were you expecting him to say? Prettiest wench he ever seen? Was that what you hoped for? Or that you'd got caught out this time, the both of you, that your folk were after him to make an honest woman of you? Maybe that would be it?'

Lottie got up and turned to go to the yard. For that one brief moment she and Pop had seemed to come close, and because of it he was intent now on making himself even more unpleasant than usual. As she went down the three steps he cleared his throat, took aim, fired, and missed her only by inches.

'I'm in here,' Molly called to her from the shed. The children were already busy. They seemed to be transferring a pile of posts from one end of the yard to a lean-to by the stable. 'That should keep them all busy.' Molly nodded in their direction. 'Won't hurt Ginney, will it, piling a load like that on her knee?'

'She's loving it. See her face. Even the chair has turned into an asset. She doesn't know any children, only Katie. Being part of a team is something quite new to her.'

Molly watched them ploughing up and down the yard, Earl and Katie balancing the load that Ginney carried as she propelled herself along. Mickey followed draging another pole, Sean staggered empty-handed but quite sure he was as busy as any of them.

'Does Dylan often come?' Lottie asked. He would be one way of breaking the ice, talking about what must be at the forefront of both their minds.

'Why should he?'

'I just thought – well, he seemed to fit in so well, the children loved him –'

'I don't want him! Neil's boy – and that woman's, that cow – I don't want to talk about it. If that's what you've come for, just go away!' Day after day Molly kept going. She cooked, she cleaned, she worked in the yard, she looked after Pop. but she seldom spoke at all and never of anything that mattered. Now Lottie had hit below the belt and winded her. She was a tall woman, she seemed to fold up as she dropped to sit on a bale of straw. Her large red hands hung limp between her open knees.

'Molly, I know how you must feel.' Lottie came to sit by her side.

' – don't know. How can you know?' With her mouth hanging open she cried, tears welling up and taking her by surprise. She'd fought them down for so long. Now there was no holding back as she blubbered, her gaunt face contorted, her nose red and her eyelids even redder. Into Lottie's mind sprang a picture of her own mother. There's an art in weeping. Kate could portray hurt, she could portray dignity, gentleness, even anger. Molly was no artist.

'Tell me. Surely you can talk to me? I loved him too.'

'You say about Dylan coming here . . . Neil's son. I know I ought to have him, I ought to let Craig go and make sure he's all right. But I've said no. Couldn't bear to look at him, frightened to think of all that they said there in that Courtroom. If he hadn't rushed away from Donald – if, if, if . . . When I heard Rosie was pregnant, right back then, I think I knew it was Neil's. I never doubted he'd had Rosie. She was teaching him and I'd known he was ready to learn. I was thankful. Thankful!' Sobbing, out of control, she had to fight for breath.

'About the baby? Thankful? Did Neil tell you?'

'I'm his mother, mothers know. Before that I was sick with worry.' She was gaining control. She wiped the palms of her hands across her cheeks. Now that she'd started, she didn't want to stop. 'You say you understand, but you don't, you don't even know what I'm saying. Neil and Donald – things were going on. Neil knew I had some idea. He told me not to worry, he could handle Donald. I expect old Pop could see too, he's pretty wise. So when I knew Neil had taken a woman, I said: Thank God.'

'Molly, if he said you shouldn't worry, then can't you try and put it out of your mind?'

Molly went on as if she hadn't spoken. 'Poor Donald, he couldn't help it. Had all the same urges as any other able bodied man. I used to watch, see him following Neil. No older than Dylan is now, but a well grown boy. Very fond of Donald too, always kept an eye on him, saw he came to no harm. Some people were frightened of him because he wasn't the same as other folk. Neil never was. I'd see them go off together. Worried me.'

207

'And what about all the years since? Perhaps you imagined it was worse than it was. For years Neil was away. Anyway, once he was grown up . . . ' She seemed to have lost her way.

'Never let Donald go off alone where temptation of young boys might have got him. I talked to him straight, told him it was a sin for men to touch boys. The devil at him, that's what he told me. But it wasn't the devil, poor boy, it was no more than nature driving him. Neil had plenty of women. Well set up man like he was, girls were easy to come by. And Neil helped Donald get himself sorted out. All the time the war was on, he came home each day from his work, good as gold.'

'Did he watch Craig?'

Molly gave a piercing look. 'Never. Was Neil he loved. Worried me when you came. He's a strong man, I didn't know how he'd take it that Neil had a wife. Got his own pleasures from you and Neil being together – see what I mean? That's the way I figured it was.'

Side by side the sat, they'd reached the end of all that could be said.

'So I can't have the boy here. Every time I looked at him I'd think of Donald. Chasing Dylan because he loved Neil, and then all that, all that dreadful . . . ' Her words drifted into silence. 'Why did you come back?' she asked after a while, not as Pop might have asked but out of genuine curiosity.

'I wanted to see it all again, to remember so much that I'd been frightened to think of during those last days here. And, Molly, I don't care what you say about Rosie, I know she'd been his mistress for ages. But I know that he didn't need her any more. I don't care what lies she tells. Neil didn't want her, not like that, not any more. He couldn't throw her off completely because of Dylan being his son.'

'If it helps you to think that, then just go on thinking it. As for me, I can't get comfort that easy. Been just once to see him, Donald I mean. He's out at Fort Edgcombe. Middle of nowhere, nothing save mountains around. Now spring's coming I'll take the truck and go again. His face when he saw me . . . You know something? Loving Neil and losing him ain't got the pain of having Donald taken off without me. Honest to God, I wish he'd fallen on that knife. Grieving for someone who's gone is clean, sort of neat. Ain't nothing but misery in having him locked away and pining.'

It was Eugene who followed her out to the 'hybrid' and helped load Ginney and the wheelchair.

'Mom never mentions Rosie. She told Craig she didn't want him to go see Dylan, so we left it at that. Kindest way most likely. But anyways, since then we heard that Indian Rosie's cleared out. We

208

never said nothing to Mom, seemed unkind to rake it all up again. Best forgotten. Just thought I'd tell you, seeing you're only here for a few days. You weren't thinking of going out to the settlement? Best forgotten for you too. But I'm glad you came, Lottie. Wouldn't mind betting before you head south to Calgary, I'll have shed this load, and I shan't be sorry.'

But for Lottie the image of Eugene that would always spring to mind would be like this, pregnant, surrounded by children, unruffled, her rule always fair.

It was driving back to Higley Creek that Katie surprised her mother by saying: 'The Dylan boy wasn't there, Mom. Pity the boy wasn't there.'

He'd been her hero for those few weeks of round-up. He'd made a lasting impression.

That afternoon while they'd been at Kilton Down, Ramsey had had to go into Radley. Lately the Monday trips hadn't been so regular, usually there was nothing urgent about their mail. So he'd looked in at the Trading Post to see if there was anything waiting for Higley Creek. A catalogue for him and a letter with a New York post mark for Marthe.

'I heard from Lazlo,' she told Lottie that evening as they were setting the table for supper. Now that Ginney was home and the wheels of routine turning smoothly again, her usual good humour was restored. 'You remember Lazlo, my cousin? He is to be married, had I told you that? Olga is somebody from our own town. Younger than me but I remember her, of course.'

'That's lovely. When?' Then, mouthing her words silently so that the children wouldn't notice: 'Are you going?'

'No, no, no, of course not. I told you so before. You ask me when. In two weeks' time. They will be the beginning of a family, an American family. A new start for them.'

'And in a way for you too, Marthe. An American family – your family.'

'I am quite well where I am.'

Ginney was cutting up coloured paper and sticking it into patterns, helped by Katie. It took all the little girl's concentration, but Ginney had room for listening too. Later on when, supper over, Lottie was seeing Katie to bed and Marthe was safely out of earshot in the kitchen, she put her suggestion to her father.

209

Chapter Fourteen

Seeing Lottie come out from the house, Ramsey called to her. She followed him until they were out of earshot and then he told her what she already knew. Lazlo was getting married, Marthe showing no sign of attending the wedding.

'I know what bothers her,' he said. 'She has never trusted anyone to look after Ginney. Maybe I've no right to ask it of you, you have a job waiting and a life of your own, but Lottie, she trusts you.'

'You mean, for me to look after things here? I'd not thought of it.' The days had been going so fast, suddenly she realised how she'd put off thinking about going back to town. 'I'd willingly look after Ginney, you know I would. But she was determined not to say anything . . . '

'She sure can be a stubborn woman.' But Ramsey said it affectionately. 'If you'll agree to stay, Lottie, I'll book her ticket, then she won't be able to argue. You know, she's not been away from us since Ginney's fall, getting on for six years ago.'

'I think she's happier here than she would be somewhere else away from you both.'

'These people are her own kin, she ought to be there. If Ginney hadn't heard her talking about it and told me, I'd not even have known this cousin Lazlo was getting married. It was Ginney's idea I should ask you.'

'You know I will, if you can persuade Marthe to go. She'll worry though, she won't have that much faith in my housekeeping ability.' Lottie's eyes teased him. 'One thing I can guarantee, she'll get a royal welcome when she gets back. You take her for granted – '

'That I don't.'

Lottie laughed. 'I mean, you take her cooking for granted, and the way she looks after Higley. I'll do my best, but it won't compare, so don't expect miracles. I shall have to telephone Mrs Harmsworth, say

211

I can't get back to work for a week or two longer.' Watching her, he could see from her expression there was something she wasn't happy about. 'You know, Ramsey, Aunt Eva has never hinted at it, but I have a sneaky feeling that she did more than hear of a vacancy there. I think somehow she persuaded Mrs Harmsworth to make a place for me. I'm not really necessary.'

'Then take your time here. Apart from Marthe's trip, don't hurry back to Calgary, not till you know exactly what you want, where you mean to be heading for.'

'It's more than half a year, Ramsey. The nearest I came to being sure of anything was when I went back to Kilton Down. Seeing them all, the house, the yard – that was just it – I was *seeing* it yet I wasn't part of it. That was surely a pointer?'

'To what?'

'I still don't know. Not Kilton, not home to Brimley – although I feel dreadfully mean, I know that's what Mum wants. I've got to follow what feels right.'

She looked at him earnestly, not prepared for the way his gaze caught and held hers.

'It's not Kilton Down that calls you, it's not Calgary – and all that that means – so could it be that your heart is telling you not to rush away from here? From us?'

Easier to watch the children playing on the grass than to look at Ramsey, and safer to talk about Marthe. Marthe belonged to Higley Creek, to him and to Ginney, Lottie must hang on to that.

'I'll tell Marthe I'm staying – '

'No, don't do that. I'll get her ticket, get it all fixed so that she has no decision to make. We won't say anything, even to Ginney.'

This time she did turn to smile at him, confident of the pleasure the shared secret would give.

It was two days later. Drawn out of doors by the clear blue sky Lottie and the girls had gone in the 'hybrid' to Wildwood Lake. They'd even taken a box of food with them, trying to make believe this was more than a flukey warm day in April.

Coming back up the ramp into the house, Ginney shouted: 'Hi, Marthe, we're back. We had a super time, you ought to have come.' Then as Marthe reached to help her off with her coat: 'It's OK, I can manage, just watch this.' On her knee she had a stick about three feet long with a Y-shaped joint at the end. They'd found it on their expedition. Now she wriggled out of her coat unaided, caught the hook in the Y and hoisted it to the clothes peg. 'There! I did it! It was Lottie's idea, she found the stick. There'll be lots I can do with this.'

'It seems you are to do without me for a week or two. Your father has arranged for me to go to my cousin's wedding. Purposely I said nothing.' She glowered at Lottie. 'I thought I made it clear I was saying nothing.'

'Did Dad fix it? Gee, Marthe, that's just great! It was me, it was my idea. I said to him that you'd go if we could persuade Lottie and Katie to stay here.'

Rather than mollify Marthe, knowing that Ginney had suggested it set her mouth in a tighter line than ever.

'You owe it to Lazlo, Marthe,' Lottie said. 'You're the only family he has out here.'

'He and Olga will be their own family. My place is here.' And with that she returned to the kitchen where she was creating a pie for supper.

'Marthe, you must be pleased. Deep down you must be.' Lottie followed her. 'I'll take care of things. Honestly, you don't need to worry. They won't get those sort of treats,' she pointed to the flakey pastry that was being rolled, turned, re-rolled, each fold guaranteeing it to puff that bit more lightly, 'but I'll see they don't go hungry. And you know I'll look after Ginney.'

She was unprepared for Marthe's answer.

'We are all right here, the three of us. Why do you interfere? I've seen the way he looks at you. Is that what it is you want? Is it not enough for you to have this Barrie you speak of? You and I were friends, that is what I thought. When I said yes, of course some and stay here, that was because we were friends and I knew Ramsey was glad for me to have someone here. But I have watched you together, always you are hanging around, and I've seen the way he looks at you – like – like – '

'Marthe, you're imagining things. Of course we're friends, you and me. And Ramsey's my friend too. But that doesn't alter what's between you and him.' She put her arm around Marthe's shoulder, prompted by a rush of pity for the woman. Older than Ramsey, no doubt afraid that she'd given him her best years, insecure. Even Eugene had wondered why it was they had never married.

'Is it because he's divorced? Because you're Catholic, because of your faith – is that why you didn't marry him. But, Marthe, I don't understand. It is less of a sin to live with him, love him – '

'In his bed? Ach! You are all the same, even you, Lottie. Can a woman not love a man without all that beastliness?' Her pastry was subjected to the full force of her rolling pin. 'Ach!' she said again. 'Ramsey has never thought of me as a woman for that sort of making love. Jeanette, his wife, she couldn't leave men alone. Ramsey must

213

have been as sickened by it as I was. I told you, she lay with first one and then another, even with people they both knew. She was like an animal on heat. In the end he said to her, "behave yourself or go." So she went. With a man who managed the elevator in Radley, a man who'd sat down to eat at their own table. Of course Ramsey must have been sickened. And you, even you who have come to the house as my friend, always have you been thinking of whether I share Ramsey's bed? Well, I do not and I never have. There is more to what holds a man and a woman together than bed or a certificate of marriage. Here at Higley Creek, we are the three of us. We do not need you, we do not need anyone else. But you have to come here, looking at him with those big brown eyes, upsetting the way things were. I have seen the way he looks at you – '

Lottie tried to hang on to that feeling of compassion, but there were other emotions battling to the fore. One of them was anger. She felt that she was being accused unjustly when she'd done nothing except be her natural self.

'You're talking nonsense. Let's forget it or we'll be saying horrid things we'll regret. A couple of weeks or so and you'll be home again and Katie and I will be off back to Calgary. You've no cause to think the way you do. You know why I came back here. You made me welcome, told me you were glad to have me.'

Her level tone gave no hint of the tumult that was in her mind. 'The way he looks at you.' But was it true? And if it was, was it simply the lonely void in her life that gave her this sudden surge of joy? He was her friend. He had been her friend almost as long as she'd been at Kilton Down. Marthe had made her own possessiveness plain, but louder and clearer than anything else she'd said, those few words echoed and re-echoed: 'The way he looks at you.'

'How could I know this was where it would lead? Me, sent away, and you taking my place here – with him and with Ginney.'

'He's been very kind to me, Marthe, very understanding.'

'That is how he is.' Anxiously Marthe surveyed her pastry, realising how during her impassioned outburst she'd vent her feelings on it with more force than was good for it. 'I have rolled it too hard.'

Lottie believed she'd allayed some of Marthe's fears.

'If it's not up to your usual standard, that'll break them in gently for what they'll have to put up with next week.' She hoped her laugh sounded more natural to Marthe than it did to herself.

'Yes, he is always kind. It is the reason that he made all my arrangements, gave me my ticket to New York. He knew that I would not have left them unless I was shown it was his wish. For years we have been together; in his bad times before he got rid of that woman,

214

in his grief over Ginney. Does he treat me like a paid housekeeper? No. We are bound as close as any family. Closer than you were with a husband in that house you shared with his relatives.' Her eyes defied Lottie to say differently.

The flat terrain of Higley Creek had been seeded, thousands of acres waiting now for that miracle of nature – with a little help from man, as Lottie reminded herself.

'Ramsey, I've got an idea. Can you spare an hour this afternoon – today Ginney has no lessons.' She had followed him to the long sheds where he kept his machinery and where this morning he was doing something to the engine of a tractor.

'Sure I can arrange to be free. Is it for something special you want me?' He wiped his hands on a rag and gave her his full attention.

'It's an idea I have for Ginney. The most important thing we can do for her is give her a feeling of independence. Right?' So far she wasn't on dangerous ground.

'Right.'

'I wondered how it would be if we went for a ride? I'd put Katie up front of me and Ginney could ride with you?'

'It's not possible. She's not been near a horse since – '

'Since the accident. I know how that happened. If she remembers it at all it will be something to frighten her, to make her feel that it's part of the way of life here that is lost to her. Oh, Ramsey, we can do better than that for her.' Squarely she met his eyes. She wasn't going to waltz around the edges, she was going straight to the heart. 'I don't know what sort of a rider her mother was, and it's too late for that to make any difference now. I do know she'd be safe as anything with you. I ride with Katie often enough. All right, I don't take jumps with her up in front of me and neither would you. But let's go out, let her sit tall on the back of a horse. It would give her a new view of the world.'

For a second he hesitated, then that slow smile gave her her answer. 'The way he looks.' Lottie tried not to think of Marthe's words.

Ginney was never to forget that afternoon. From her chair she'd looked up at everyone – everyone except Katie. On the occasion of that first ride Ramsey stood on a bench, Lottie lifted Ginney in her arms and passed her to him and he hoisted her to her place at the front of the saddle. From her high perch she surveyed the world from a new angle. People were suddenly smaller. Her face seemed set in a smile. As Ramsey swung himself to sit behind her, one arm on each side of her as he held the reins, his eyes met Lottie's. She'd been right, his

215

silent message was clear to her. Next Lottie stood Katie on the bench, swung herself to the saddle, then reached to help the little girl into position to ride before her. And so they set out.

The children were delighted with the venture. In years Katie, with her fourth birthday not long behind her, had lived about half the length of time of Ginney. But her life had been full, always there had been fun to be had, even riding like this was no new experience. So circumstances narrowed the gap of years. For both of them the afternoon was special. And for Lottie and Ramsey? Neither of them gave any sign of the wonder of the spring day, the rightness of being where they were.

They were into the second week of Marthe's absence when a message came from Mrs Haggerty, the wife of Ginney's teacher. For some time her husband hadn't been at all fit, but he'd not wanted to have to stop her lessons. Now he had no choice. He'd been taken into hospital.

'The school in Radley is a physical impossibility for her,' Ramsey told Lottie after the children were in bed. 'It's an odd building, you've seen it, built on three storeys. Quite impossible for her to manage in a wheelchair. Steps from the road up to the grounds where the children play, more steps to the building.' There was no sense of contentment in the way he puffed his pipe this evening. 'When first I realised she'd never be able to attend the school in Radley, I got particulars from a place the other side of Calgary. It's designed for children who are – children who, for a variety of reasons, can't go to the normal schools. That was before I thought of Mr Haggerty. He was heavensent. She's always been a happy child. Here in the home she has her own special place. I can't do it, Lottie. The only thing that's wrong with her is that she can't walk. I can't send her . . . ' Lottie couldn't bear to see that look in his eyes. Before she could stop herself, her hand reached out and took his.

'There must be another way,' she said. 'Ramsey, she's a bright child, she'd be so easy to teach – easier than one who could rush about and fill her mind with other things. Wouldn't the school in Radley let you collect work for her? Wouldn't they give her books to read?'

'She's not nine years old. She can't be expected to learn unless someone works with her. Marthe can't do it. She's mastered our language,' something that was almost a smile tugged at his mouth, 'but she has her own mode of spelling.'

Lottie nodded. She'd had enough letters from Marthe to know this was true. The incorrectly phrased sentences, the poor spelling . . . these things had brought Marthe close as Lottie had read. But it was true, she'd be incapable of helping Ginney with her lessons.

216

Ramsey's fingers held the hand Lottie had reached out to him, his gaze held hers. They were each thinking the same thing, they could each read the other's mind.

'If the school would agree to send her some work, if I could go there sometimes to talk to the head teacher . . . if you think I'd be any good . . . But, Ramsey, I'm not a clever sort of person. I've never been trained to teach, I'd only be one step ahead of her. But until you can find someone better – yes, all right, I'll do what I can.'

The grip of his fingers tightened. Did he realise he was hurting?

'I'll go and see the principal tomorrow. Lottie, I'm grateful. But more than that – you won't be rushing away, you'll still be here.'

'The way he looks at you.' Marthe's words prodded. She'd believed the housekeeper had imagined it out of fear for her own position. Now, though, she saw it for herself. There was no way she could look away from him.

'For a while,' she said with a forced brightness, pretending not to read his unspoken message. 'Mr Haggetry will soon be well, I expect. But, Ramsey, when you say I'll still be "here", I don't need to stay in the house. Summer's coming. Driving conditions are good again now. I'll take a room in Radley, come over three times a week.'

He was weighing her words, thinking before he spoke.

'You'll be putting off going back to Calgary. What about this guy Barrie? Does this mean that you've made your mind up?'

'I expect it means that an awful lot of my heart has settled in these parts – Radley, Kilton, all around here. But most of all it means that I don't want Ginney to be sent away. Especially now when she's learning to do so much for herself. Did you see the way she set the dinner table? And I hardly had to steady her as she wriggled to sit on the edge of the tub tonight, then lowered herself into the water. She and Katie sat in there together, they had a great time.'

'And you want to take Katie to live in rooms in Radley?'

'I didn't say I *wanted* to, I said that's what I intended.'

Now he held both her hands and leant towards her, defying her to look away.

'Lottie, I beg you, stay here. You must know how I feel, how I've felt about you since we used to meet in Radley? I had no right to love you, you were someone else's wife. But that made no difference to how I felt for you. If you'd come here telling me you were in love with this Barrie guy, if I could have seen you were dying to get back to him . . . but you can't bring yourself to leave here. And do you know why? Yes, you do know. You may run away from admitting it, but you know right enough. You can't leave here because this is where you belong. Here, with me.'

217

'Wait, Ramsey. Three more days and Marthe will be back. The three of you – you, Ginney and Marthe – are enough for each other here at Higley. This is madness. I've been here for less than three weeks. When Marthe comes back I'll look for rooms in Radley, we'll forget all this, we'll – ' His hand against her mouth, she was silenced.

'I'll never forget,' he said quietly.

Tonight Marthe was booked to start on her long journey back. Wasn't this just what she'd feared? Marthe, who'd been so sure that what she felt for Ramsey was enough for both of them. Imagine her arriving to find that her place usurped, Lottie was to be mistress of Higley, Lottie was to teach Ginney, in fact Lottie had stolen all that she prized most.

'Ramsey, I'm so mixed up, I'm trying to find my way.' How lame it sounded.

'Your way is my way.'

She shook her head. 'I don't know.' But she lied; she did know. At first she'd seen him as gentle, reliable, kind; then she'd come to appreciate his understanding, his sensitivity; tonight she'd recognised a hunger in him, and wanted to reach out in response. But it was madness. She'd been here less than three weeks, she couldn't base a lifetime on these few hours they'd spent together. And in the front of her mind was the thought of Marthe.

'Not yet,' she whispered. 'My way must be my own way. Ramsey, maybe it's just spring fever that's getting at us? In a day or two Marthe'll come back. Soon Mr Haggerty'll get better, and I'll go back to Calgary. We can't build a lifetime on just these few days.' But why not! And it's not a few days, it's months and months when I counted the hours until Mondays and our time together. That had nothing to do with how I feel now though, then he was just my friend, someone I could talk to, someone who understood. 'Let's just think of Ginney, of how we're going to persuade the school to help us. And, Ramsey, I've been thinking, is there any reason why we couldn't teach her to control a horse herself? Once she's in a saddle she's the same as anyone else. Think what it would mean to her. You could get hold of a really gentle pony, we could start her on a leading rein.'

'You think she could?'

Of course she could.'

They had steered back to a safer course, Ramsey noticed the 'we' and 'us' as part of the scheme, but he didn't refer to it and at that very moment the shrill bell of the telephone rent the air.

'Hello, this is Higley Creek . . . sure, put her on. Hi, Marthe, what's the trouble? Have you missed your coach?' Then a longer pause while he listened and Lottie waited. 'There's no need to feel

218

that way. Things have been happening here too. Lottie'll tell you . . . What? . . . To do with Mr Haggerty. You're to stay there just as long as it takes. Now, promise me, Marthe, you're not to give us a care. Honestly, we're doing fine. Here's Lottie.' He handed over the receiver, telling her: 'She can't get back yet. She's worried.'

'Marthe, Ramsey says you're worried. You mustn't be. Honestly, I haven't poisoned anyone.'

'It is Olga's aunt – or, how it is you would call her – her grand-aunt? I did not know that Olga had any person from Hungary here, but her Grand-aunt Helga arrived in New York just before the marriage. She has an apartment, very small and up two flights of stairs, but it is a place to live.'

'And you're staying with her?'

'I am telling you. The marriage was beautiful, they are so full of hope in their new country.' Hearing her, Lottie smiled. 'Someone has lent Lazlo his motor car, they have gone away for two weeks. It happened only this evening, I heard this crash and Grand-aunt Helga was flat on the floor. She has been to the hospital for two hours, now her arm is plastered. She knows only her own language. I feel I cannot leave her. Yet I worry. My place is at home.'

'Marthe, home won't run away. It'll be waiting just as you left it – perhaps the windows not so sparkling and the furniture a bit short on elbow grease – '

'Grease, what sort of grease? What has happened?'

Lottie laughed. 'That's just an expression: elbow grease. I'll explain when you get back.'

'Ramsey says that things have been happening. He said you would tell me. Lottie – oh, I should never have come away.'

'What has been happening is that Mr Haggerty is ill in hospital. Ramsey is going to try and arrange with the school in Radley that they supply the work and I teach Ginney.'

Silence. She could almost hear Marthe's thoughts coming down the line.

'You are not a teacher. Is there no one else? For myself, I like to have you and Katie at Higley. But you have work, you have friends, your aunt, the man you call Barrie. Can you just stay away like that? You have a life of your own to lead, people waiting for you in Calgary. You came to sort out your own problems, now you seem to be taking on the burden of ours.'

'I'm looking forward to trying to help Ginney. You're not to worry. I'll hand you back to Ramsey, I expect you want to speak to him again.'

While they talked she went to check that the children were asleep and covered.

Later, when the house was dark, Lottie re-lived all he'd said. Along the corridor was he lying like this thinking of her? Plumping her pillow she turned over, chasing sleep that was out of reach. Marthe wasn't his mistress, she would never be his wife; but she loved him, he and Ginney were the centre of her life, she had no one but them. Because of Marthe it would be impossible even to contemplate breaking up the ménage they'd had here. There were different ways of loving, she'd said. But was that to expect that Ramsey put a normal life aside? In the next bed Katie was dreaming. She laughed, burbled something that had no meaning, turned over and threw her arms out of the covers. Lottie lay still, willing the girl not to wake. She remembered each word he'd said, each nuance. Here in the silence of her room he seemed even nearer to her than he had earlier; then she'd held back, frightened to give rein to thoughts of what he was suggesting.

Ramsey wasted no time in visiting Brian MacMurray, the principal of Radley school. He'd expected a higher hurdle than this to overcome. It seemed the school master had heard of the English girl who'd been married to Neil O'Hagon, in fact he'd even seen her sometimes in town. Her accent set her apart from the locals and, when Ramsey told him that in England she'd been well educated and had examination certifications to prove it, he was duly impressed. The fact that those examinations were no more than the School Certificate she'd managed to scrape through at sixteen was lost on both of them. Brian MacMurray undertook to lend the books they required, to advise Lottie, and even to scrutinise Ginney's progress.

Lottie wrote to Barrie.

'I came here to try and lay my ghosts. Perhaps I have. I went to Kilton Down. I felt desperately sorry for Molly. Katie loved to be with the boys again – ' But could she hope that he would understand even if she tried to find words to explain? Taking the easy way out, she finished: 'And so she loves to be with Ginney. You remember I told you about Ginney McFee, the little girl who was hurt in a riding accident? She can't attend school and the person who gives her her lessons has had to go into hospital. Ramsey has arranged that I shall get guidance from the school in Radley and I've said I'll stay on for a while to help her until her teacher is well again – ' Reading it through she felt she was letting him down. Not only because she couldn't say yes to what he'd wanted, but because she gave him no answer at all, simply left him to guess at what was unsaid.

To Eva it was easier.

'Now that I've been to Kilton and am looking back on it, I wonder why I was scared. There were no ghosts. I looked at the house and

220

honestly I felt nothing at all. I didn't know where I was heading, where I wanted to be heading, and seeing Kilton again did help the fog to lift. It's so incredibly beautiful here – at least it is to me – but there would be lots of folk who'd look at it and see it differently. *You* will understand what I'm trying to say. Whatever the magic of this land is, it was you who led me to see it. Here at Higley I look across the prairie. Even in the short time I've been here the landscape has undergone a scarcely perceptible change. To start with it was bare earth, the seeding was only just done, in fact far away the drills were still scattering their loads. Now though, if you half close your eyes, you can imagine it's green – almost it is. I'll be here to see it grow. But then what? Ramsey says that at harvest time they work twenty-four hours a day. They have great lights fixed to shine their beam ahead of the combine. Shall I see it? Long before that, Mr Haggerty will be ready for Ginney. Aunt Eva, I wish we could talk, a proper deep down talk. Isn't that funny? All the time I was at Kilton I hid from you what the place was like, the fact that I could never be an "O'Hagon woman" like the others. Here is so different. Here I'm myself, I don't want to hide anything. Remember how we used to talk at bedtime, a few minutes slipping into an hour before we realised? Did you notice that?

'I said "used to", I wrote it before I even thought. You see, the thing is, I'm ready now to jump back up and make for the goal I want, but if I do I'm going to hurt people who don't deserve to be hurt. When Marthe comes I'll find somewhere to live n Radley for as long as Ginney needs me. That's as far as I've decided.'

It was the beginning of a new era. Each morning, without a thought to whether the windows shone or the furniture had forgotten the feeling of elbow grease, Lottie, Ginney and Katie sat at the dining-room table. Katie's presence was voluntary, but at least to start with the discipline made her feel very adult and important. She had a box of crayons and busied herself with 'letters' to Eva, Barrie, the boys at Kilton, her grandparents from the picture, even Mrs Harmsworth at the playschool was favoured. To Lottie schoolwork had often been something that interrupted more important pastimes. This was quite different. She was determined to make Ginney's lessons interesting and fun – and if sometimes she had to do her own homework the evening before to make sure that she was ready for the next morning's work, that was her secret.

Mid-day they ate a snack, something that was quick to prepare and almost as quick to eat. Ramsey dropped into the habit of joining them, sometimes even taking a tea towel and helping Lottie with the washing up. Then in the afternoons they were free of work.

221

'Its great Dad coming home lunchtimes,' Ginney said as she finished her self-appointed task of putting away the cutlery. Until Lottie took over the running of the house she had never helped. Marthe had worked quickly and competently, always making sure Ginney had something near at hand to amuse herself with while she waited.

'You know where things go better than I do, Ginney. Shout if you can't reach.'

'Sure I know. OK, Lottie, I can do it.' And from her voice there was no doubt she was keen.

'High up things you can't get to, but apart from that wheels get you around just as easily as legs.'

'Yep.' And a giggle of satisfaction at the new responsibilities coming her way.

It was almost the end of Ginney's first week of lessons when Lottie and the girls headed off in the direction of Radley, just as she used to she left the children in the 'hybrid' while she shopped. It was a glorious day. The sky was so high she felt she could see for ever.

'Let's not go straight home,' she suggested when she stacked her box of shopping next to the wheelchair. 'What about the cut backs? You've been there, Ginney?'

'No. I've heard people talk about them. I thought it was too rough for the chair. Marthe said so.'

'I think it'll be OK if we keep to the top path. It's a magic sort of place. Your dad took me there. It was in the fall, the trees were beautiful . . . '

'What's been cut back, Mom? What do you mean – cut backs?'

'It's by the river. The river cuts right along the valley, a long way below where we shall be. On the other side the bank is all trees. This side there are fewer trees, a lot of rocky boulders. You'll see. I shall want you to help me, Katie. The chair will be quite hard to push. It will take all our strength.' The high path was no place for Katie to take a fit in her head to wander off track.

'Sure, Mom. I'm strong as anything.'

Perhaps it had been a silly idea to come here. With Ramsey it had seemed an easy enough walk along the edge of the slope. The ground was sand and rock, the path on a slant, the left side of it some inches higher than the right. The going was hard. Katie pushed with all her might, but progress was slow.

'Look, Mom! See who's that. 'Tis, Mom! It's the boy, the Dylan boy! 'Tis, Mom!'

A little further up-stream the bank was sheer, a flat table of rock jutting into the river. It was here that a dark-haired boy was fishing. Could it be him? They'd left the district, Eugene had said so.

222

'I don't think it can be, Katie. It's just that he's got the same black hair.'

"Tis him.' Then, at the top of her voice: 'Dylan! Coming to see you!'

Without a second thought she was on her way down the slope, loose stones slipping under her small feet.

'Katie, stop! Katie, do you hear me? Come back!'

If she heard she gave no sign of it. Just once she looked round, her frightened face telling Lottie that she couldn't stop if she tried as she slipped and slithered ever lower.

'Dylan!' Now Lottie took up the shout. 'Katie's coming down. Dylan!'

At the sound of the shouting he turned. His reaction was immediate. He left his fishing and started to rush around the bank of the river towards Katie.

'Tis him, Mom!' Her fear forgotten, she started to run. Dylan had the agility of a mountain animal. Katie wasn't so blessed. It all happened in seconds. There was nothing for her to grab, nothing to stop her as she reached the water. And in that same instant Dylan plunged in after her. Ginney screamed, Lottie screamed. That somebody heard they shouts they hardly noticed. Gripping the chair Lottie stared unblinkingly at the water.

'He's got her,' a man's voice said. Dylan was swimming with Katie to the flat surface of the rocks where he'd been fishing. 'He's getting her out. Sounds like she's just frightened.' Katie's screams echoed across the cut backs as Dylan pushed her on to the rock then pulled himself up after her.

Other people had gathered, they must have been with the man who was watching.

'Can one of you keep a firm hold on the chair for me?' Lottie said. 'I must go and help her back up.'

No one tried to stop her, it was clear from Katie's screams of 'Mom' that no one else would do. From tree to tree she felt her way until she came to the last stony drop that had been Katie's downfall. Then, away from the trees, she bore to the left, steadily working her way diagonally downwards until she reached the rock.

'She came before I could hold her back,' she greeted Dylan. 'Thank heavens you got her.'

'Saw Dylan,' Katie hiccoughed, starting to recover now, except that her clothes were heavy with icy cold water.

'Do you have far to go, Dylan? I'll take you home. You must get those clothes dried. Where are you living?'

There was no answering smile. 'Around,' he mumbled, avoiding her eyes. The last time they'd seen each other had been in the

223

Courtroom; that, and all that had led up to it, seemed to stand between them. He looked so thin, so young.

'Pack up your fishing things, I'll take you.'

'No. I don't need taking. I can look after myself. You see to her. Go away and leave me alone. I'm all right.' Still no smile.

Picking Katie up, Lottie started to insist that he came, but he wasn't listening to her. From high on the cliff behind them he recognised the rattle of falling stones.

'Quick, move her.'

He pushed Lottie off the rock, back on to the stony bank. It happened so quickly, before she was aware of the danger.

Chapter Fifteen

Radley was proud of its hospital, built only three years before. Certainly it was small, with one ward for men and one for women, but it possessed examination rooms, a surgery, and a general appearance which set it apart from anything else in town: startlingly white, flat-roofed and looking as if it had dropped down in Main Street by accident, having been intended for Sunset Boulevard. It was as out of place amongst the timber buildings as the ornately decorated brick frontage of the bank.

A nurse pushed Ginney's wheelchair up the ramp while Lottie carried a very cold and wet Katie: behind followed two attendants bearing the stretcher on which Dylan had been strapped to be hauled back up the slope. In the ambulance the wound to his head had been cleaned, but he was still unconscious.

'Katie isn't hurt, she's just cold and miserable that's all,' Lottie assured the nurse. 'If I can go somewhere to get her clothes off her, can you lend me blankets to wrap her in?'

'Doctor Marshall will need to check her over, Mrs O'Hagon. We'll get her into a good warm bath, then we'll wrap her up. I guess maybe he might let you take her home.'

'Of course I shall take her home! She wasn't hurt at all, only wet and frightened. We were right out of the way when the rocks fell.'

'The boy, Mom. Where they taking the Dylan boy, Mom? He won't wake up. I keep calling him and he won't wake up.'

The nurse had heard the gossip at the time of the trial. Who in Radley hadn't? This was a sequel she hadn't expected, the bastard half breed boy out with the murdered man's widow and her golden-haired girl who was his half sister.

'They've taken him to get him dry and warm, then the doctor will make his head better,' Lottie answered as she started to peel off the still-dripping coat.

225

Katie didn't like it here at all. Even a hot bath wasn't fun in this strange place, not like it was at home. Ginney had been left sitting in a room with a row of empty chairs and no one to talk to, the lady in a stiff white overall was telling them all what they had to do, she was even telling Mom. Now there was a man she didn't know coming to lean over her as she sat in the bath.

'Now then, and who's this young lady?' Dr Marshall spoke in the voice he believed small people expected of him. 'What have you been doing with yourself, then? Not the time of year for taking a swim, eh?'

Wide-eyed and silent, she stared at him unsmilingly. She wasn't used to entertaining strangers from her bath-tub.

'Who's him, Mom? Is he the one making Dylan boy better?'

Lottie recognised the doctor from the Courtroom, just as he did her.

'It's Dr Marshall, Katie. Yes, he's looking after Dylan too. If you hurt anywhere, you tell him.'

'Want to get out, Mom. When can we go home?'

Eddy Marshall lifted her arms one at a time, then bent her legs, while she viewed him with the same expression.

'While Nurse Bishop dries the child and finds her something to keep her warm, perhaps you'll spare me a moment or two, Mrs O'Hagon?' Then, leading the way to his consulting room: 'The boy who was with you . . . er, I should contact his next of kin. Are you able to help? His mother, do you know her whereabouts?'

'Of course I don't.'

'No, no, it was stupid of me to hope perhaps you might. The fact that you were with the boy . . . yes, stupid of me.'

'You'll have to ask Dylan. Has he come round yet?'

Dr Marshall's face creased into worried lines. He'd pinned his hopes on Lottie.

'He's conscious, but I can get nothing out of him. Nothing at all. I hoped he might have told you where they were living. Are you sure he said nothing. I've visited at the settlement recently. I heard that they'd left.'

'Yes, I was told that too. I don't know where they went. "Around", that's what he said when I asked him where he was living. That was when he was soaking wet and I wanted to get him home. Then the rocks started slipping – '

'He'll be here for a day or two anyway. Word of the accident will get around, be sure of that. When she hears she'll turn up. But why the boy has to be so secretive, I can't think.'

'He's going to be all right soon? It's not serious?' Never mind about Rosie; suddenly she wasn't important. Lottie remembered the days

Dylan had spent at Kilton Down, his gentleness with Katie, the way she'd shadowed him and hero worshipped him. She remembered that Molly couldn't bring herself to have him in the house. And all the while, like a shadow in her mind, memories of Neil. His two children, his son and his daughter.

'Not serious, no,' the doctor answered. 'But certainly I shall keep him here for a few days, whether we can trace the Indian woman or not. With a head wound he'll be in no state for the sort of life these people lead. I see you have the McFee child with you.' It was a statement, although he hoped she'd hear it as a question. He had his natural share of curiosity, but the confidential nature of his profession put gossip out of his reach.

'May I use your telephone, doctor? Her father will be wondering where we are.'

So it was that not much more than an hour later the 'hybrid' arrived at the door of the hospital. One of the men from Higley Creek had driven Ramsey to collect it. From then it was only minutes before the wheelchair was aboard, and they were on their way home. Katie, clad in a winceyette nightgown inches too long for her and wrapped in blankets, was cuddled on Lottie's knee while Ramsey drove.

'Why didn't they let me go see Dylan, Mom? Is he going to sleep all night in that nasty place? Can we go and see him tomorrow? Can we, Mom?'

Morning followed its usual pattern, with Katie none the worse for her cold dip in the river. Today Ginney was introduced to multiplication sums in dollars and cents, followed by Lottie reading the first chapter of *Who Has Seen the Wind* aloud to both of them.

'I'll rustle up some food, you girls set the table,' she said as she stacked away the books and papers.

'We are going, aren't we, Mom? 'Safternoon, we are gong to see him?' At regular intervals, Katie needed reassurance.

'You sound like a gramophone record stuck in the groove.'

Katie frowned, put off by an answer she didn't understand.

'But we are? You said we could.'

'Then get the knives and forks on the table. Do your share to help Ginney.'

In the kitchen she switched on the grill, turning it high. Gammon steaks and tomatoes for lunch, something that cooked quickly and cooked itself. Thinking of the hours Marthe spent making their meals that little bit better than ordinary, she wasn't proud of her culinary efforts. She wondered why Ramsey bothered to come home at midday. A smile tugged at the corners of her mouth, and she forgot the less than tidy kitchen.

227

'Lottie, push that door shut, I want to talk to you.' It was Ramsey, coming in from the yard.

'What's the matter?'

'Maybe nothing's the matter, maybe you won't mind hearing where I've been and what I've found out.'

She switched the heat low and turned to look at him, her heart seeming to miss a beat. Where he'd been, what he'd found out . . . was he ill, had he had confirmation of some awful disease? Forgetting all her resolutions she came close to him, her hands on his shoulders.

'What is it? There's nothing wrong with you?' He read the fear in her eyes. Their expression was enough to put his morning's mission out of his mind.

'I've been to the hospital – '

'Oh no!'

'I've been to see Dylan.' In her relief she rested her head against his shoulder. 'I don't know how you feel about him.' And even without looking at him she knew he was smiling as he added: 'But it's no secret that Katie has lost her heart.'

Lottie moved away to sit on the edge of the kitchen table.

'If he were any other boy, not Neil's I mean, and especially not Rosie's, then – Ramsey, he's a dear. You remember I told you when he used to come to Kilton during round-up, I could trust him completely to see no harm came to Katie? Well, you could see that yesterday. Even apart from that, I felt drawn to him.'

'And perhaps that's not so surprising. He is Neil's son. He is Katie's half-brother.' He watched her closely as he said it.

'But he's *hers*. Even yesterday when he jumped in after Katie, I could see Rosie in the way he moved. Before all that happened – I don't mean yesterday, I mean last year – before I realised about Neil and her, I thought I was truly fond of Dylan. Yet now, all I can see is Rosie. In all my life I've never known the sort of hatred I have for her.'

Yet in her own heart she knew it wasn't as simple as that. Hatred and fury for Rosie, yes, and jealousy too that a woman twice her age possessed the sort of grace that belonged more in the animal king-dom, the sort of grace she could never have; anger and shame for herself and for the failure to be all he wanted; contempt for Neil that tainted her memories. Now as Ramsey stood with his back towards her, making the excuse of busying himself with the food, she ought to have realised what he read into her words. But she didn't.

'Lottie, she's cleared out. Left the settlement.'

'Yes, I knew they had, Eugene told me.'

'No, not both of them. Just her. The boy said he didn't want to go. It seems from what he told me, she's always believed in giving him a free hand, never worried if he's strayed off for days at a time. Once the snows had gone she told him she was going west. He told you he'd been "around". That's about the truth. I guess he has folks back at the settlement where he could go if he hit real trouble, but he seems to have been fending for himself. Do you think they know at Kilton? He's Molly's grandson.' Then: 'I'm sorry, Lottie, this is tough on you. I figured that Molly might be glad to have him there.'

Lottie shook her head. 'All the trouble stemmed from what happened with him and Donald, that's the way she sees it. I know it's not just, she knows it's not. But we can't sit in judgment. Imagine what she must suffer. But if Rosie's left him – that makes everything different.'

'He's been sleeping in any shelter he could find, catching fish, setting his traps. It can't go on. He's still a child. He tells me the authorities used to get after Rosie to see he went to school. Now of course he's slipped through the net, he's running wild.'

He'd turned the heat up too high, the gammon was splattering, small flames shooting as it hissed. She watched, fascinated, making no effort to move the pan. Dylan living rough, Katie's 'Dylan boy' sleeping under the stars while summer was still no more than a promise, Dylan perhaps hungry, Dylan's pale blue eyes so like Neil's. But were they the only legacy Neil had left him? Surely he had a right to be at Kilton.

There was no one but her to fight his battle. She was being trapped. Her past wouldn't let her go. Rosie's son, Rosie's and Neil's. Now he had no one but her. She'd have to tell them at Kilton that Rosie had gone, that he had no home. Not that he'd welcome her interfering. She remembered how he'd avoided her eyes yesterday, how he'd told her to go away and leave him alone. Soaking wet, cold, probably hungry too – yet he'd refused her help. Katie was looking forward to the hospital visit with innocent eagerness; for herself she was less sure.

A long tongue of flame shot out at them, followed by a cloud of smoke. The fat that had dripped in to the pan ignited. For the next few seconds rescuing their lunch took all their concentration. Then Ramsey picked up the conversation.

'You'll talk to him this afternoon? I wanted you to be prepared. None of this was his doing, he can't be left to suffer for it.'

Picking up the dish of gammon and tomatoes, she faced him.

'You are a truly nice man. Somewhere there must be a flaw I haven't come across yet.' It would have been so easy to say much more, so gloriously easy. But she didn't. 'You've heard of smoked bacon?' With a determined laugh she changed the subject. 'Well, this

229

is pretty well cremated! Can't think what Marthe would say to my efforts. Bring the loaf and butter, can you?'

Ginney didn't go with them to the hospital. Instead Ramsey hoisted her to sit in front of him and rode out to see the progress of the young shoots that were making a light green haze over the land.

Apart from Dylan there were two other patients on the ward. One, of course, was Mr Haggerty, looking very old and frail propped up by three or four pillows. First Lottie went to speak to him, partly prompted by courtesy for his age and weakness and partly so that Katie could have the first moments with her "Dylan boy". Making an effort to give an impression of studiousness that nature had never intended, she tried to reassure him that Ginney was in safe hands, and even talked to him about the work they were doing.

'You know, my dear, they always say that when one door closes another opens.' His voice was so weak she had to bend near to hear him. Then he let his eyes shut, a sign that he'd had enough.

She crept away from his bed, going to join the children. Katie had been so excited to come. Now she was standing by the side of Dylan, gazing at him in mute wonder. Today his eyes looked startlingly blue. With a complexion as swarthy as his he could never be pale, but there was a drawn look about his face and he was too thin. Lottie thought of what Ramsey had told her. If Molly could see him now she would forget everything except that he was Neil's son and needed her protection.

'We brought you some candied fruits, Dylan. Hope you like them.' She perched on the edge of the bed, watching the door for authority to approach clad in a starched white apron. The visitor's chair seemed too formal.

'For me? I guess that was kind . . . ' He didn't know how to accept generously, especially from the woman Neil had married. He took the lid off the box. With unchildlike dignity he offered: 'Katie, would you care for one of my fruits?'

Beaming with delight she took one, unwrapping it and nibbling it delicately, wanting to make it last. Candied fruits were gorgeous at any time but, given her by Dylan, this was the sweetest she'd ever tasted.

'What you did yesterday, Dylan . . . "thank you" doesn't say a fraction of what I mean. The way you just dived in, didn't hesitate. If you hadn't been there – '

'But, Mom, if he hadn't been down there, I would have been pushing the chair 'long with you. I went down 'cos I saw him.' Then to Dylan: 'I been looking most everywhere we go, trying to see you.'

230

Another nibble of the sugary coating of her plum, then a shiver of excitement as she remembered. 'Then I saw, didn't I, Mom? That's him, didn't I say, Mom?'

Dylan turned his face away, but not before Lottie had seen the sudden tears that filled his eyes.

'What we found out last autumn – last fall, I mean – was a shock to you and me too, Dylan. But it gives us something to hold us together, doesn't it? Neil. Katie's father, and yours too.' He kept his eyes cast down. If he looked at her she might read the fear. He was never without the dread of what would happen when fall came, when the ground was covered with snow. Now the concern in Lottie's voice was almost too much for him. 'Do you know where your mother has gone? Or when she's coming back?'

'Said she was heading out towards Blue River. Said she'd done with these parts.' He was mumbling, it was hard to understand him. 'I could have gone too. Just there were things here I didn't want to leave.'

'Kilton Down?'

He didn't answer. His mouth set in a hard line and still he looked at some point at the foot of the bed.

'I'll be around for a while. Dr Marshall wants to keep you here for a few days yet. I'll be in again.'

'I told you, you don't have to worry, I can look after myself. I got traps need looking to right now – '

'If you go out too soon you won't be as well able to look after yourself. Let Dr Marshall keep you until he knows you're quite fit again.' While she talked to him Lottie's mind was jumping ahead. If Molly realised that Rosie was gone, that Neil's boy was alone, that he'd stayed because he knew he belonged to the land here, then surely she would come and see him? And to see him would be to want to take him back to Kilton Down. Neil had gone but she'd still have his son.

Promising to come again tomorrow, they said goodbye. It was Katie who turned at the doorway to the ward, then concerned at what she saw, rushed back to Dylan.

'Is it 'cos you've got a sore head?' Her face was puckered at the sight of her hero's tears.

He nodded, too proud to tell the truth.

'Me'll make it feel better.' She touched her lips to his bandaged forehead. 'Gotta go, Mom's waiting.'

Lottie knew just what she meant to do. She'd drive straight to Kilton Down. But almost as she turned out of the hospital gate she recognised the O'Hagons' truck. Her naturally optimistic nature took an upward leap. What else but fate could have brought one of them to town today? She drew in near the parked truck and waited.

'Craig!' she called as he came out of the bank building.

'Why, hi there, Lottie. Aunt Moll said you'd visited a while back. I was sorry to have missed you. I thought you'd be back in Calgary long before this. Eugene'll be tickled I've met you, she'll be wanting you to know. We got a girl. Justine, she's going to be called.'

'That's wonderful! Hear that, Katie. You've got a baby cousin.' The news gave Katie plenty to think about. When Lottie got out of the car and told her to wait where she was she didn't complain, she was used to being left while the shopping was done. 'Craig, I was just going to drive out to Kilton. It's providential meeting you like this.'

'What's the trouble, Lottie?'

She was so sure of Craig, he'd never failed her. They moved away from the car. She didn't want Katie to hear what she had to say.

'It's Dylan.' Did she imagined his guarded expression? 'Rosie's gone, you knew that. She's left Dylan. He's been sleeping rough, got nowhere to go. It's because of Kilton Down that he wouldn't go with Rosie, I'm sure of it. I know how Molly felt about him, she told me – but with Rosie gone, surely it's different?'

'Hell, but it's no different at all. Listen, Lottie, that boy's got no place at Kilton. He came there a couple of weeks ago. Walked in just like he had a right.'

She hadn't expected this tone from Craig.

'And hasn't he? He's Neil's son.'

'Whose side are you on, for Christ's sake? You don't owe them any favours. His mother's a whore. Who can say who his father was? He might be anyone's. And you think he has a right to come and work on our land, make it his? You just listen here. If Katie had been a son, then that I would have had to accept. You were Neil's wife. But I got boys of my own, three sons, they'll grow into the job just the way I did, just the way Neil did too. I'll not have that half breed's offspring coming in to Kilton, the eldest boy, thinking he can have equal rights with my sons.'

'If you saw him you wouldn't talk like this. Yesterday Katie fell into the river at the cut-backs. In a second Dylan jumped in and got her out. She wasn't hurt, but she might have been drowned. Then there was an accident, a fall of rock. His head was hit, he's in the hospital. That's where we've just been. Craig, if you saw him, he looks so thin –'

'We're all right as we are at Kilton Down. Don't you think Aunt Moll has had enough? Even if I didn't see things the way I do, I tell you honest to God, Lottie, I've never known her so against anyone as

232

she is Dylan. The way she sees it, if there hadn't been the boy, Rosie wouldn't have had a hold like she did on Neil – '

'Ah!' Lottie jumped in, finding a crack in his argument. 'But just now you said you didn't believe he was Neil's child.'

Ignoring her, Craig went on: 'And Donald wouldn't have gotten the devil tempting him. I'm telling you, I never seen her blow her fuse like she did when he came riding into the yard like he had a right to be there. We each of us got our reasons, but neither of us is going to have him there. So, the sooner he goes chasing after that bitch of a mother of his, the better for everyone around these parts.'

He'd always been kind and fair, Lottie wouldn't have believed this of him. The two day growth of stubble, untidy hair hanging around his collar, these things she'd become so used to she hardly noticed them. Now, though, she saw hostility in his eyes.

'You were always kind to me. Why? I was an outsider, but you never spoke to me like Pop did.' Her voice was steady. It seemed she asked him because she really wanted to understand.

'You? Well, you were wed to Neil, guess we had to make a place for you. Anyways, he'd soon have seen to it if he figured you weren't being treated right.'

'Don't you believe that Neil still see's what's going on at Kilton Down even though he isn't here any longer? Surely you must know that he'd want you to make a home for his son?'

'Do I believe that? Hell, no. We get our problems to sort out while we're alive. Ain't that enough for any man? You trying to tell me we got to keep a watch out even when we're dead? You're wasting your time, Lottie. Far as the boy's concerned he's as welcome at Kilton Down as that whore of a mother of his would be. I got no time to hang around, I must get on.' Then, just as if their conversation hadn't taken place: 'I'll tell Eugene I've seen you. When you got the time, drop by and meet Justine, she's swell. Bigger than any of the boys. Weighed in at ten pounds.'

'Tell Eugene how pleased I am she's OK.' But Lottie didn't say she'd be visiting.

'You can't live in the past, Lottie.' Packing tobacco into the bowl of his pipe seemed to take an unwarranted amount of Ramsey's attention. 'I thought you came back here to lay your ghosts.'

'Ramsey, he's only a child. He has no one else. Molly isn't a woman to harbour hatred and especially for someone who doesn't deserve it. It's because she's so upset, so miserable and worried about Donald. It's not really to do with Rosie that she won't have him. I'm sure I'm right. If Donald were home, then she'd make a home for Dylan, and

233

take it on herself to watch there was no trouble. But with him shut away in this mental place, it would seem like an added disloyalty. Can you understand?'

'Sure I can. Just one thing I want you to tell me, Lottie, and to tell me the honest to God truth. You came here trying to free yourself of the past, to find a way forward. Now you talk of finding an apartment, giving the boy a home. Neil's son, a reminder of how you got hurt. Why, Lottie? Is it for Neil? I don't believe you want to live in yesterday.' He seemed to have forgotten he'd asked her a question. He put his still unlit pipe on the table and took both her hands in his. 'Today, tomorrow, all the time there is. This is where you belong.'

The space between them was less, only inches now. She nodded her head.

'Here – wherever you are – ' She raised her face to his. His mouth covered hers. There was nothing else but this. They drew apart just far enough to look at each other, their eyes saying more than any words. Then close again, rocking gently in each other's arms, his chin against her hair, her lips on his neck. Whatever question he'd asked her, in this he had his answer. Lottie had hers too. The mists had cleared. There was only one possible way forward.

When he saw the handle of the door turn he knew it was her. She hadn't told him: 'I'll come to you.' When she'd gone to the room she shared with Katie there'd been no excited preparation for something they'd arranged. She'd undressed, she'd stood by the side of the single bed where she'd lain so many nights thinking of him – and she'd known just what she meant to do.

'I hoped you'd come,' he whispered. 'I prayed you'd come. Lottie, I've loved you for so long, wanted you . . . '

This was really happening to her. Through the thin material of her nightdress she could feel the warmth of him as he pulled her gently to his knee on the edge of the bed, held her close against him. She could feel the beating of his heart. His hand that caressed her breast was firm, just as she'd imagined. This was really happening. Tonight it was no dream. Such an easy movement, and she was lying, he kneeling over her, his eyes telling her the truth of what he'd said. 'I've loved you for so long . . . wanted you.' Ahead of them stretched the hours of night, but in these minutes there was nothing but this, the union of two people. One in body, one in heart, one in spirit. Afterwards Lottie knew a great peace. 'Now you're mine, branded, my woman.' Out of nowhere came the memory of that other time. She could still recall the wonder she'd felt there on an English hillside, the rightness that she'd become Neil's woman. In the dark

234

she half smiled, remembering. She felt cleansed, the hatred and bitterness wiped away. All that had gone before had been stages on the way to where she was now.

'Did I sleep in, Mom?' Clad in her nightgown Katie ran out to the living room where Lottie was setting the table for breakfast.

'No, we're not late. Get your things and we'll go along to Ginney's room.' It was habit that Lottie was on hand to give any help either of them needed.

'Your bed's all tidy. I must have slept.'

'Oh, I see. Well, maybe you just didn't hear me when I made it.' Lottie didn't like lying, she wished she could have told the world, but Katie and Ginney lived by set rules, on these their standard would be based. So a white lie was necessary. But not for long.

'You look all smiley, Mom. Are we going to see Dylan today? We are, aren't we? Can Ginney come too?'

The first cloud appeared on Lottie's horizon. Dylan. What could she do about Dylan? Yesterday she'd made up her mind that she'd find somewhere to live in Radley, somewhere for the three of them. But that was yesterday.

She wouldn't let herself see the cloud. Ramsey came in for breakfast. She let herself imagine life would always be like this for the four of them. She could feel that he was watching her, she looked towards him confident that in the glance she would see a reflexion of the hours they'd shared. Instead, although his gaze was on her, whatever it was that his mind's eye saw was drawing his brow into a worried frown. It must be Marthe. Ramsey was always sensitive to other people, he must be as aware as she was herself that Marthe's security had been built on the trio at Higley Creek.

Bringing his thoughts back from wherever they'd wandered his eyes met hers, that slow intimate smile touched the corners of his mouth. As they ate their cornflakes the children chattered. Their world was built so much on an atmosphere created by the grown-ups. Today was a happy day, they could feel it. Lottie would let no clouds cast their shadow. Just think of now, she told herself, this moment, this place; only fools believe they can see into the future, and even worse fools let fears of what might happen spoil the perfect moments.

As afternoon and their visit to the hospital grew nearer, so the cloud over Lottie darkened. It was inconceivable that Dylan would be released with nowhere to go. Perhaps the authorities would track Rosie down and bring her back to collect him. In her heart she knew there could be little chance of that – 'somewhere in the direction of

Blue River' might mean anything. So what was the alternative? Would he be made a ward of court? Would he be sent into some institution? He had no one but her . . . but that wasn't true. He was Neil's son. Whatever Craig said about Molly, if she could just see him, see the fear in the eyes so like Neil's . . .

In the yard a car door slammed. A second or two later, another. Had Ramsey brought a visitor? Easily distracted from her plasticine Katie wriggled down from the table and went to the window.

'It's him! Mom, Ginney's dad's brought the Dylan boy.'

At the hospital his clothes had been laundered, probably for the first time. The water might have been too hot for them, perhaps that's why they looked washed out, shrunken and uncomfortable. The description suited Dylan too, Lottie thought, watching him sit at the lunch table. At Kilton Down he'd fitted 'sweet as a nut'. Here he looked miserably out of place.

'I'm riding out to North Down, the top end of Higley, this afternoon,' Ramsey told him. 'Why don't you come along? Time you got in the fresh air. You can go out with Lottie and the girls, of course, if you'd rather. But I figure if you're going to be here for a while, you'd best get to know the land.'

Only Katie looked crestfallen. Ginney was relieved. Except for Katie, who was so much younger, she knew no children. Now suddenly her father appeared with a boy, someone able to ride, to run, to do all the things she couldn't do. Her chair became a prison. If anyone but Ramsey had brought him to the house it would have been easier to bear. Lottie had noticed the way she'd not quite looked at Dylan. Perhaps if they all went together this afternoon . . . but there was something about Dylan that prevented her suggesting it.

'Maybe you can give me a job?' The skinny lad sat that bit taller. A glimmer of hope had shown itself on his horizon. 'I can work real hard.'

'Guess that's what we all do here at Higley. You'll get plenty to do. Eat a good meal, you've got a long afternoon ahead. What about Lottie helping you to another spoonful of this macaroni cheese?' Then to Lottie: 'And me too. It's good.'

'Something must have happened to inspire me,' she laughed. And this time he was on the same wavelength.

'Bodes well for the future.'

It went over the children's head. Her clouds were rolling away, the sun getting brighter by the minute.

Inspiration stayed with her as afternoon passed. In true English style

236

she even attempted Yorkshire pudding to serve with their roast beef for supper. Every hour brought her closer to when she'd be just with him again. This morning the problems of Dylan had seemed insurmountable. Yet Ramsey had lifted it from her shoulders. She'd go again to Kilton, she'd talk to Molly, once she knew the true facts everything would work out right. But for the moment there was no need to rush. She hummed a cheerful tune as she whipped the Yorkshire pudding, scattering the floor and splattering the batter even on to the wall of the kitchen that Marthe had made her pride.

Lottie had plenty of enthusiasm but little experience, so somewhere a guardian angel must have been on her side. The beef was tender and rare, the pudding rose to dizzy heights. Mealtime had about it an air of celebration. Only Lottie and Ramsey understood the reason, yet it touched each one of them: Katie, bursting with pleasure at the way events had turned; Dylan as he shovelled his food in true Kilton Down style; Ginney who, seeing her father wasn't paying undue attention to their visitor, felt more at ease. Here at the table she sat at a chair the same as the others, she could feel the excitement in the atmosphere, she wanted to be part of it. They were a noisy crowd, never had there been chatter and laughter like this amongst the O'Hagons.

So it was that none of them heard a car pull up in the yard, nor even the door of the house open. Marthe was home.

'This is as it always was, Ginney, just you and me.' And as if to put emphasis on how well she liked it that way, Marthe polished the window with extra gusto.

'You mean you don't like Katie and the others being here? But, Marthe, she and Lottie used to come over most every week. Don't you remember how we used to look forward to it?'

'And so of course we did. They are our friends. But, Ginney, they are visitors. Just you and me together, that is how our lives are. When they came to stay for a week I was pleased to welcome them. It won't be long before they return to Calgary. As soon as Mr Haggerty is well again. Then we will fit back just as comfortable as ever we were. Is that not so?'

Ginney frowned. 'I wish they didn't have to go. Do you suppose they'll take Dylan?'

'I'm surprised she brought him here. Did she say why?' Marthe had arrived home only the day before, there was a lot she didn't know about.

'Lottie didn't bring him. It was Dad. He went to the hospital and fetched him just yesterday morning.'

237

'The hospital?'

Duster poised in mid air Marthe stopped polishing and listened to Ginney's account of the visit to the cut backs and what followed. Knowing the child as well as she did, she could read every expression. And when the story reached the point that Ramsey brought the boy to stay at Higley Creek, she recognised that here was something she could use to her own advantage. Not that she knew exactly why she felt threatened by the changes she'd found.

'You do not surprise me. I saw how he enjoyed having the boy here. Ach! But men are always the same if they have a young boy to train. You see, now even, Dylan has ridden out with him. But when Lottie goes, surely he will leave? Did your father bring him here because he has connections with Katie's father or because he means to find a permanent place for him at Higley Creek? The child has a mother, did he arrange this with her?'

'I don't know. They never said anything about Katie's dad. I don't see what you mean. Don't look cross, Marthe. Aren't you glad to be home?'

A hearty kiss on Ginney's brow, then back to the windows with renewed vigour.

'Did I not say so to you? You and me here in our own home. Better than all the travelling, better than all the bright lights and big cities. Now, can you see any smears? No? Then I will push your chair to the kitchen and you can talk to me while I wash the spots from the walls.'

'I can work my chair along by myself, Lottie always leaves me to do it. And, Marthe, I set all the meals now, and I put things away – except what's too high. I can almost get myself into the bath, she just sort of steadies me.' Such pride in her blue eyes. 'And I get nearly all my own clothes on.'

'If I'd have known all that had been happening, I should have been from my mind with anxiousness.'

'You mustn't worry, Marthe. Dad knew. Now you just watch me, how I whizz along.'

'Careful! Oh, for Godsakes, Ginney, careful. you'll catch your little fingers in the wheel!' Marthe's agitation seldom got sufficiently out of control for her to call on her Deity, but when she did she always pluralised His 'sake'. For the composed and efficient Marthe to cry our 'vor Godzakes' was a sure sign she'd reached her limit.

'Honest, I'm careful. I keep my fingers right clear. Just you watch how I whizz down the corridor.' Then as she took up position in the kitchen and Marthe ran a pail of water to attack the walls that bore evidence of nearly four weeks of Lottie's enthusiastic efforts: 'Marthe, I don't want to sound mean and horrid, but it would be very nice

238

if Mr Haggerty decided he wasn't going to give lessons any more. I don't want him always to be ill or anything like that – but he's ever so old, isn't he? Perhaps he'd like it better not to have me coming.'

With wordless vigour Marthe rubbed her soapy cloth on the yellow paint of the wall.

At Kilton Down the only thing that had changed was that it was a different baby hanging from Eugene's breast.

'Wait here for Mom to get back.' With Justine supported on one arm and taking succour with true O'Hagon concentration, Eugene stood at the stove stirring soup, while Old Pop's rheumy eyes watched and he said nothing. 'Katie likes being out there with the boys, what's your rush?'

Lottie had planned on seeing Molly alone, perhaps out in the shed where they'd talked last time. That was half her reason for refusing to wait, the other half was that she wanted to get away. For nearly a year and a half this had been her home. If she opened the door into the corridor, ten steps would take her to the room that had been hers. Memories had no place in bricks and mortar – or, in the case of Kilton Down, in the timber building of a house. This kitchen was where the family spent most of their waking hours. Home? To Lottie it was a reminder of things she wanted to wipe from her mind. Out there under the open skies, whether here or at Higley Creek made no difference, those were the moments when the Neil she'd loved was near to her. Eugene was talking, something about Craig and the fencing of a new corral, no more than words that needed the occasional nod to keep them flowing.

'I said I'd not be long,' she lied. 'If Molly's gone in to Radley I'll probably meet her on the road.'

'She's got buying to do in town, she's putting up a parcel to take to Donald. Tomorrow she and Craig are off for a visit. Always upsets her when she sees him in that place. He'd be better back here, that's what Mom thinks. But Craig believes we'd have more trouuble now than before all that business.'

Old Pop worked his tobacco into a juicy mess, took aim at the smoulder log and fired. Then he looked directly at Lottie.

'If it's that boy you're wanting to settle a home for then I'll tell you straight out, you're wasting your time coming here.'

'Pop you always said he fitted so well here. "Sweet as a nut", that's how you put it.' Lottie couldn't understand their change of attitude. 'DDidn't you mean it? Was it just one of your ways of trying to upset me, was that why you said it?'

The old man's tongue appeared, trembling with delight. His eyes twinkled. Just occasionally when he'd tried to stir up trouble for the fun of doing it, he and Lottie had shared the joke. He expected her to share this one. But she didn't.

'His mother's gone, Craig must have told you. Pop, don't you all owe it to Neil to give him a home?' Earnestly she appealed to him. 'He's Neil's son, you can see he is. Where else do you think he got those blue eyes?'

'Don't you take that preacher's tone to me. What makes you think you can come back here telling us what's right and what's wrong?' Again he spat – into the fire, but his glower telling her that it was meant for her. 'Couldn't even satisfy the one man who was tied to you by marriage lines. What could you understand of a wench like Indian Rosie?'

She ignored the jibe, surprised how little it hurt.

'Damn Rosie. It's Dylan we have to think of – and Neil.'

'The boy fitted here well enough, I'm not denying that, but then so would a good many others. And don't start on that blue eyes bunk, reckon there's plenty o' blue-eyed men besides Neil who bedded Rosie. You trying to tell me that we can be sure the brat was planted in her by a fifteen year old who was only learning what it was all about? And do you think a kid with no experience could have satisfied a woman with the lusts she got? Course not. While she was teaching young Neil, you be sure she was getting her share from plenty more besides. Wake up, girl, just you try using that high class English brain! Dylan might be anyone's off-shoot. And he ain't coming here laying claim to what should belong to O'Hagon men. Reckon that's what he expected, letting Rosie clear off without him. Still in that hospital place, is he?'

'No. Ramsey brought him home to Higley Creek.' Her tone implied that one man at least knew the right way to treat a child. 'And there's another reason I came today, apart from Dylan. It's me. I'm going to marry Ramsey. News soon gets around. I wanted to tell Molly myself, I didn't want her to hear from someone outside.'

Eugene turned to look at her so suddenly that Justine lost her anchorage and let out a whimper. A quick re-adjustment as she was bundled onto the other arm and her second course thrust into her mouth.

'What's happened to the foreign woman? Has he finished with her?' Eugene wanted to know.

'Marthe is home again, she only went to her cousin's wedding. You were wrong about her, Eugene. She belongs at Higley – but it's not the way you supposed.'

Eugene's sniff seemed to say: 'If you believe that you believe anything!'

240

Lottie was glad to get away.

'Ramsey has been telling us your news,' Marthe greeted her when they got home. 'Ginney is over the yard with him, watching him do some sort of thing to an engine, I did not understand what. She is pleased, of course she is, these last weeks she has been let to run wild. The way she bumps around in that chair frightens me for her safety. Of course she wants for it to go on like that. And who am I to say my say? This is just the thing I might have expected. Not so soon, but I knew his mind was on you.'

Katie was puzzled. Her brows drawn down, she looked from one to the other.

'Mom? What's she say? Mom, what's making her cross?' She tugged at Lottie's skirt as she whispered.

'Nothing's wrong, Katie. Marthe isn't cross, she's just surprised. You and I, we're going to stay here at Higley Creek.'

Katie's eyes were wide. 'Always, Mom, or for more holiday?'

'Always, Katie. You and Ginney will be like sisters. I'm going to be married to her dad.'

It wasn't often Katie couldn't think of anything to say! Her smile broadening into a grin, she let go of Lottie's skirt and ran outside to find Ginney.

'Marthe, please be glad for us. I know how much you've meant to Ramsey – '

'I am hoping you will make him happy, and that you will give him a good marriage. Not like *she* did. But you are different, not her sort of woman.' Still no smile accompanied her words.

'Marthe, thank you. You are pleased? Truthfully, you don't mind us being here?'

'Mind? But what place would I have to have an opinion. You are to be the Mrs McFee; me, I look after the house, it is not for me to mind.' Her accent was more pronounced even than usual. It reminded Lottie of Marthe's position. Coming from Hungary, knowing only Higley Creek and the family there, building her life around them – 'The three of us, we need no one else.'

'The children are pleased.' As soon as she said it, Lottie saw her mistake.

'Yes. You will be a very happy family, the four of you. The five of you, for it seems your step-son is to live here too.' Marthe turned away. 'I do not know what to do. To stay or to go away. A house does not have the place for two women. I have looked after Ginney since she was born. I have cared for her, reared her. But I am the house-woman. And a foreigner. You who are so clever, you always know

241

the right words to speak, you can teach her. Already you undo the caring I have given. I am away only a few weeks and I see her guiding her own chair, bumping over the rough ground of the yard, even sitting on the saddle of a horse. A horse – after the way she fell! There is no bigger fool than a man blinded by a new woman.'

'He isn't blinded, his eyes are wide open. And so are mine. Marthe, I love him very much. Please.' She reached to take Marthe's hands in hers, surprised even as she did it that she could feel no anger, only a need to restore the older woman's security. 'Please, be happy with us. Surely there's room for all of us here? We each play our own part.'

'I am happy for you. At this time I cannot find how to be happy *with* you. If you love him as you say, then it must be what I want for him. Ramsey and Ginney have been my – my – purpose.'

Lottie nodded.

'At Higley Creek one can feel it. The atmosphere is full of a sort of contentment. I sensed it the first time I came here. Remember Thursdays?'

'You were my friends. I was happy to have friends visiting me.'

'So can't it be even better now that we're going to live here? Oh, come on, Marthe, smile. These things happen. I didn't come here realising how I felt about Ramsey. But think of the future, Ginney and Katie growing up together. And perhaps there'll be other children. Let's look forward, make sure it's all perfect.'

Marthe nodded, but still her mouth was set in a firm line with no hint of a smile. She avoided Lottie's eyes. How many times was one supposed to re-make the shape of one's life?

A high wire mesh fence surrounded the grounds of the hospital. The porter opened the double gate to let the truck through and Craig and Molly drove up the long driveway.

'Wait! Look!' She pointed. 'Over there! That's Donald, can't you recognise him? He's digging. Leave the car. We'll go right over and surprise him.'

'Let's go talk to the doctor first. You know last time how it bothered him when the doctor took you off to his office. If we get through with that first, then you've nothing to do but talk with Donald.'

'Maybe you're right. He's working, Craig, now isn't that about the best we could have hoped?'

An interview with Dr Hoffman gave her spirits an extra boost. In the winter Donald had come into his own, snow clearing; now that even here in the foothills of the mountains the snow had gone, he was kept busy every day working outside. He was eating well, sleeping well. Give him a job to do and he worked at it, seeing nothing else.

242

Now that was the Donald they knew!

'I'll go out and surprise him,' she said. 'Give me just a few minute with him, Craig, before you come.' If those first minutes threw Molly off balance she didn't want anyone to see it.

'Sure, Aunt Moll. I'll take a walk around.'

He saw Donald look up as she came near; he saw him throw down his spade; as far away as this he didn't see the way the empty eyes suddenly lit up. He gave them ten minutes together before he went over to join them.

'She's gone. Moll says that bitch Rosie has gone,' Donald greeted him. 'Cleared out. Moll been telling me.'

'Yeah, cleared out, and a good job too. The boy ain't gone though, did Moll tell you that?' Molly shook her heat at Craig but it seemed he didn't notice. 'He's living with Lottie over at Higley Creek. Seems she's getting hitched to Ramsey McFee and he's taken the boy too.'

Donald's mouth opened and shut as he tried to keep up with Craig's words, only bit by bit could he assimilate each piece of news.

'Neil's boy. He's Neil's boy.' Then, as the news filtered in: 'What's that other bugger got to do with Neil's boy? Ah, and her, she was Neil's too – and the girl.'

'Katie?'

'Ah, Katie. All of 'em, Neil's.' His knees sagged under him and he knelt on the loose earth he'd been digging. 'He's gone, my Neil.' His mouth trembled, a dribble of saliva hanging from the bottom lip. 'That's what they think – they don't know.' Wide-eyed he looked at them – or through them, for there was no real intelligence in his expression. 'They think he's gone. He don't come seeing them p'rhaps, not like he does me. I see him, I see him all the time. They think he's gone. Her, that bitch Lottie, she wants him gone so she can have this other bugger. You tell her – you tell her I know he ain't gone, he's right here with me. McFee, I remember him. You tell him he can't have Neil's folks. He ain't gone . . .' The rest was lost as he started to cry, blubbering loudly.

'Stand up, lad.' Molly reached out to him as if he were still the little boy she'd always cared for. 'You'll get your knees all wet down there.'

He did as she said, standing with his legs wide apart, his shoulders hunched. The noise he made was half cry and half moan, as he looked down at his legs and watched the dark patch spread. Donald had wet himself.

'Never mind, lad, we'll soon get you changed.' Molly could have cried too. He'd never done this at Kilton Down; but there he'd been happy. Even with Neil overseas at the war, Donald had gone his daily way, doing as he was bid, smiling that open-mouthed smile whenever he caught her eye; she could still seem to hear the monotonous hum of contentment as he'd chewed his way through a plate of food. He was so changed. What he'd done that dreadful night at Rosie's cabin had taken more than the life of the person he loved above all others, it had destroyed his own slim hold on reason.

A male nurse was coming towards them.

'It was an accident. He's upset – ' Molly started.

'Sure, lady, don't you worry. It's all in a day's work, these things happen all the time. Come on, Big Boy, let's get you some clean pants.'

His head down Donald shuffled off with the nurse, turning only once to shout: 'You tell that bugger – he can't take what's my boy's.'

It sounded so easy: Dylan taken into the home at Higley Creek, given a room more comfortable than anything he'd known before, well fed, his clothes washed and pressed. As Dr Marshall told him when curiosity brought him on a 'follow-up' visit: 'You're a lucky young fella. Not many boys placed as you were have been given your opportunities.'

Ah, but that was only half the story. The school authorities had chased Rosie with regular persistence, and after each visit Dylan had returned to the classroom just until temptation took him in another direction – maybe his traps had something waiting, or with the salmon rising the call of the river couldn't be resisted. Now the authorities didn't have to come seeking him. Living at Higley Creek put certain responsibilities on him and going to school was one. Sometimes in the 'hybrid', sometimes in the car, occasionally even on horseback with his bag of books on his shoulder, each day he made the journey to Radley. Summer was coming. In the forest beyond the settlement this year his traps were lying unbaited. His swarthy face was never a mirror to his soul; so often, seeing his inscrutable expression, Lottie would remember Rosie.

Chapter Sixteen

Alone at her breakfast table, Lavinia Matheson read her letter. So many emotions jostled in her heart. Lottie would stay in Canada. This was the end of any thought of her coming back to live in the old country. But was that such a surprise? Life at Kilton Down hadn't been as rosy as she'd tried to make them believe. Lavinia had been given a hint or two, and when she hadn't been told was sufficiently in tune with Lottie to be able to read between the lines. Yet never once had there been any suggestion from her that she wished she'd not gone there. After Neil had been killed and Eva had fetched her to Calgary, still she'd not proposed coming back here, even though she'd had the money for her fare.

Ramsey McFee . . . Ah, now, he'd figured in her letters for most of the time she'd been with the O'Hagons. There was a woman, a Hungarian woman, who had been Lottie's friend. But surely she'd been the McFee man's wife? Where was she now? Gone away to stay in New York and Lottie had moved in to take care of Ginney, that was what they'd been told. Something that was very nearly a smile tugged at the old lady's mouth. She pictured Lottie giving Ginney McFee her lessons! What was the saying about the halt leading the lame?

The smile disappeared before it had quite got a hold. Had Lottie fallen for this man on the rebound after what had happened? At the thought of all that she'd read Lavinia gave up all pretence of breakfast and got up from the table. She'd take her letter and walk to the lake, call up the spirit of the little girl who'd been so close. Dear Lottie.

Please let her be doing the right thing this time. Was last time wrong? I suppose it was. But we can't make the rules for people just because we love them. This man now, he's always sounded understanding. Is that why she's turned to him? Often enough she's mentioned him . . . showed him her pictures, talked to him about

Bullington, went to his house each week. Yes, but that was to see her friend Marthe, the woman who went off to New York. Could Lottie have come between them, broken the marriage?

Her thoughts went round and round. The other things in the letter she wouldn't let herself dwell on, not until the could sit quietly and give it her full attention.

'A telephone call for you, Madam.' Jackson, the elderly butler knocked, entered and made his announcement all in one. 'It's Miss Kate.'

'I'll come, Jackson. Thank you.' Oh dear, Kate must have had a letter this morning too. I'd like to have had time to straighten out my own mind before I had to take hers on as well! 'Kate, my dear, you're an early caller.'

'Mother . . . oh dear, I'm so worried, so miserable.'

'Hush, Kate. Carrying on like that will get us nowhere. You've had a letter from Lottie this morning, is that it? And so have I.'

'I was so sure she'd come home, bring Katie back.' Her mother didn't need to see Kate to know that she was crying in that way she could, her face set in sad resignation, tears spilling to roll gently down her cheeks.

'You surprise me!' Purposely Lavinia ignored the tone. 'I understood you to have had hopes of her making her future with Barrie Miles in Calgary.'

'In Calgary? With that woman getting the love that should be mine? You know that's not what I wanted. Barrie, yes, he would be perfect for her. If she married him he'd bring them home, I know he would. And I've said so to her in letters. More than once I've told her I was sure that's what took him to Canada. But this man, Ramsey McFee . . . ? Mother, we know nothing about him, he's another of her wild cowboys. And, oh, the disgrace, the things she's been dragged down to by that dreadful O'Hagon man, I feel quite ill. I suppose she told you too? A child, that hateful man's illegitimate son – did she mention him in your letter?'

'Kate, steady a minute, just listen to me. It's time you had a break. Don't wait alone all day worrying. Telephone Rupert now, the minute you put the phone down from talking with me, tell him you're coming away for a few days. Find out the time of your train and I'll see you're met at Newton Dingley Halt. You understand me?'

'Just to get away, forget it for a few days.'

Lavinia had no intention of their doing that but she didn't argue. 'Has Rupert read her letter?'

'Yes – and Ronnie. I'd have kept it from him if I could, just told him Lottie was thinking of marrying this Ramsey McFee man. As if that

246

isn't bad enough! But all the degradation she has suffered . . . imagine it being bandied about the dinner table amongst Millicent's family.'

'It takes a very empty mind to have nothing more to amuse it than other people's misfortunes. Millicent's family didn't impress me so unfavourably.'

'That's not what I meant at all. You know it isn't. But, Mother, what Rupert says is quite right. If Ramsey McFee were a whit better than Neil O'Hagon, do you imagine he would harbour the illegitimate child in his house? A half breed! To think that uncouth lout took Lottie for his wife after – after – sleeping with a woman like that! My poor head . . . throb, throb, throb. I can't tell you. I feel quite sick.'

'Perhaps you'd better not consider a journey today if you're not well.' The twinkle in Lavinia's eyes held no unkindness.

'It'll do me good. Coming to Bullington always does. Away from the cares of running a home, being at the beck and call of a family.'

'Yes, well, it seems you're not going to get the chance to be at the beck and call of Lottie and Katie. So just do as I say. Telephone Rupert and tell him you'll be away for a few days so it's no use his beckoning and calling.' A man with an ounce of spunk about him would look at the situation and if he thinks it that bad then he'd try and do something about it. What help is it to anyone grizzling to Kate that this new man is no better than the old? What does he know about it? Stupid ninny. Always was. No chance of changing him at his age. 'Don't forget to find out the time of your train and let me know.'

At Bullington Manor and at 14 Sycamore Avenue telephone receivers were replaced. Lavinia sighed. She'd do as she'd planned, she'd sit by the lake and get her thinking done. It would be no use hoping for any decisions from Kate, nor yet from that husband of hers. Kate wiped her tears, and asked for Rupert's number. The throbbing of her head was almost forgotten. Once she got to Bullington everything would be all right.

It was tea time when she arrived. Lavinia had never been a woman to hesitate. If she had a problem she faced it, viewed it squarely, decided the best action – and took it.

'Mother, just being here takes all my worries away. It's like being young again. We were all so happy.' Watching her mother pour tea from the same silver pot was like slipping back down the years. Kate, the youngest of the family, the delicate one, everyone's pet.

'There have been plenty of happy times since. I was thinking about them this morning. By the lake. I like to do my thinking by the lake!'

'It's not fair, Mother! What have I ever done to deserve the way life has used me? Other women have their daughters near enough to visit

247

– like I've come to see you now – and their grand-daughters too. Even when she lived at home she was always restless, dreaming of the day she could get away.'

'Mercy me, Kate, would you want her to be the sort of person who never had a dream, never wanted to know what was beyond the horizon? Would you want her different from what she is? No, of course you wouldn't. And neither would I.'

'Yes, I do want her different. I want her to be sensible, find herself a good husband, one we can learn to love too.'

'Ring the bell and let's get rid of this tray. Then we have some talking to do. I've had a busy day.'

'Poor Mother. I shouldn't burden you with my troubles, you have plenty to see to here on the estate. Charles telephoned the other day. He says you're having the stable block re-roofed.'

'They've managed to get the tiles at last. But never mind the stables, we've more important things to talk about. Thank you, Betsy,' as the parlourmaid appeared, 'you may take the tray. I don't want anything to disturb us for the next hour or so. If by chance there are any telephone calls, just take messages.'

'You see, Mother, this morning you were quite snappy with me when I suggested people would gossip about the scandal. But you know I'm right. Even you want to make sure no one hears a whisper of it.' Kate's face prepared itself for the onslaught of gloom.

'I've got a lot to tell you, that's why I want no interruptions. This morning I sat by the lake and read Lottie's letter again. There were things I didn't understand. This woman Marthe, did you not think she was Ramsey's wife? I certainly did. I've always kept Lottie's letters, you know, so I read them again this afternoon. She never actually told me they were married.'

'You mean he was living with her! Mother, I told you, he's no good. I feel so helpless.' Kate was twisting the lace corner of her hand-kerchief in her hand. Lavinia imagined she was holding it in readiness for the tears that would soon overspill.

Sympathy would be no use at all. 'You'll do her no good that way. As soon as it was decently late enough, bearing in mind the difference in time, I had a telephone call put through to Eva.'

'You brought *that* woman into our troubles! What's it go to do with her? I suppose she's laughing, scoring again at my expense. *My* daughter and you have to ask *her* advice.'

Lavinia ignored the outburst.

'Fortunately Eva had just come home from the hospital. She'd been working all night. I asked her how much she knew of Ramsey McFee and of this woman, Marthe. Don't look like that, Kate. For

248

goodness' sake, do you intend to carry a grudge to the grave? Doesn't it ever occur to you to look at all you have and then at her and, for once, count your blessings?'

It was too much for Kate.

' . . . wouldn't have come if I'd known you were going to be like this . . . ' These tears didn't roll gently down a sad face. Now her mouth trembled and she cried as she might have done as a child. 'Thought you'd understand. But how could you? You can't know what it was like? The only real happiness I've ever known. What do you expect me to do? Make a friend of her? Think how she must crow when Lottie always puts her before me.'

'It may well be quite the other way round. If it's having something to crow about, don't you ever consider that she may have looked at you over the years, you with a husband, you with three children.'

'Two. That's all I have left. Perhaps I loved Michael too well. I ought to have learnt.'

'Kate, my dear, let it go. All the old bitterness, all the hurt. Let it go. It was such a short time to cast its shadow down the years like this.'

'Happiness isn't measured in hours and years. It was mine, I thought it was mine for always . . . ' Bitterness that had stayed with her for nearly thirty years was more than a shadow, it was something deeply ingrained into her life. Kate's memory was no more reliable than anyone else's. With time some moments must have dimmed, some become more vivid even than reality. But she was sure every word, every thought, was true, recalled with the clarity of yesterday.

It started the day the authorities came to look around Bullington Manor, to decide on the number of beds to be brought in, where the nurses would sleep, which would be the matron's room and the bedrooms for the two resident doctors. In this summer of 1916 the numbers of casualties being sent home from France was putting a strain on hospital resources. Bullington was only one of many houses that had been taken over for the duration of the war.

This room had been Kate's since she'd moved out of the nursery. Now it was stripped of her personal belongings, nothing remaining but the bare furniture. She turned round from looking at the familiar scene from her window, excited that suddenly life was being turned upside down. At nearly nineteen she felt that now at last life was opening up for her. The rest of the family had already left home, but Kate was the youngest, the 'runt' her family lovingly called her, delighting in spoiling and protecting her. As a child she'd been slight, timid, shy with strangers; it was as if the Mathesons' three elder children had used up the quota of self-confidence, none being left for little Kate. 'If Kate goes with you, take care of her.' 'Slow down, Kate can't keep up.' Remarks like that had been part of life. Had she been a spiteful child, the other three would have resented it, but she hadn't been. She'd been gentle. So they'd all taken 'looking after Kate' in their stride and loved her dearly.

Hester was the eldest. In 1913 she'd married Toby Marks, a young army subaltern, third son of Sir Julian Marks. She had a baby son, Alistair, and lived in London where he was looked after by a nursemaid while she spent her time organising the running of canteens. Toby, now a Major, was serving in France. Jonathan and Charles were both in France too. Kate missed them, each night she asked that they'd be kept safe; but that was as far as the war had touched her life. Now, happening so suddenly in a matter of weeks, she and her parents, with the decreased number of staff left to them, had moved into the East Wing. The war was coming to Bullington Manor, bringing an excitement to Kate that she'd not realised she'd lacked.

Lost in thought she hadn't heard anyone coming until her door was thrown open and she was confronted by a powerful-looking woman dressed entirely in navy blue. She must be a nurse, Kate decided, a senior nurse. Behind her followed an Army Major. Like so many shy young people, Kate lived on dreams. And never a dream more handsome than this.

'And who might you be?' The voice fitted the general appearance of the navy-clad intruder. 'I understood the staff were to have left before I arrived.'

'Yes, they have.' In an attempt at dignity Kate held out her hand. 'I'm Kate Matheson, this was my bedroom. Please, do come in.'

'Matheson, you say?' The large lady was thrown off her stroke. 'Are your family still here?'

'We've moved into the East Wing. I'll go, I won't stay and be in your way. I meant to be gone before anyone arrived.'

It was the dream in khaki who answered her.

'You mustn't let us frighten you away.' His blue eyes smiled, she could even hear the smile in his words, his voice held all the music of his native Ireland. 'This is a lovely home you are lending to us. To be in surroundings like this will be the medicine the men from the front need. Let me introduce Bullington's Matron, Miss Henderson.' Knocked a little off balance that so perfect a vision could have a voice to match, Kate forgot she and the Matron had already shaken hands. Again she held hers out, then remembering her mistake when Miss Henderson didn't respond, went to drop it to her side. Instead it was taken in a friendly grasp, setting her senses reeling. 'And I'm one of the resident doctors. Matthew Harkin is my name.'

'How d'you do?' she muttered, suddenly shy and gauche.

'You say you're living in East Wing? Are you already doing war work somewhere, I wonder? Or are you going to help us here?'

She suspected that he knew exactly how hard her heart was hammering, that he was taking pity on her. She wanted just to be gone. Yet what was he saying? Work here . . . *he* was to be here.

'I'm not a nurse.' She turned to Miss Henderson, trying not to see the major out of the corner of her eye. 'I'm not really anything, not trained I mean, but I'm willing to do anything I can to be useful to the patients.'

The Matron was pulled in two directions. She had no time for pretty little flipperty girls who fancied their chances plumping up the pillows and fluttering their eyelashes. On the other hand this girl belonged to the family here. Until the hospital got established she didn't want antagonism with the Mathesons.

'When we start to get our patients in, I'm sure there will be a place for you.'

Kate's world took on a new dimension. Hurrying back to the East Wing with her news, even the handsome major was of secondary importance.

Not for long though. In April the hospital beds were set up, by May military ambulances were a regular sight in Newton Dingley. Bullington Manor Hospital was already full. Each day, wearing her starched white apron, Kate wrestled with the white kerchief that hid her golden curls. With or without her hair to frame it, her face was beautiful. With never failing patience she wrote letters for the wounded, read to them, pushed them around the grounds that had always been home to her. And with each day she fell more deeply in love with the Irish doctor who never missed an opportunity of seeking her out.

Lavinia had always loved company. In the East Wing – and with wartime restrictions – grand scale entertaining was out of the question. But the door was always open to the medical staff from the hospital. She and Clifford, Kate's father, could see the way things were going between their young daughter and the Irish doctor. To know him was to love him, that's what Kate thought, confident that her parents would welcome for her the path she was hurtling down. Summer of 1916 was a magic time, something that would live for ever. That's the way she wanted it to be.

It was Christmas when Matthew asked her to marry him. She had no doubts, the promise of marriage was the promise of a future that would be perfect. This was the first year she'd not been to church with her parents on Christmas morning, sitting in the family pew, listening to her father reading the lesson. But this year was different. Instead she'd been to the hospital. Someone had pounded the grand piano which had been left in the one time drawing room, now day room. They'd sung carols. Then in her father's study which had become a doctors' office she'd drunk two large glasses of sherry. And when Matthew had kissed her she'd floated on air – or was it sherry? He loved her, he wanted always to be with her. If her life had ended at that moment she would have asked for nothing more.

'She's had no experience. I've nothing against you, my boy, nothing at all. Indeed, you seem to have the ability to make Kate happy and to me that's all that matters. But nineteen years spent as hers have been hasn't equipped her for married life.'

'But I am ready. Please, father. If we wait a while. But please, please let us have it to look forward to. So that we can plan, talk about it.'

She looked so innocent, her eyes brimming with tears. Her father put his arm around her. What a child she was.

'You are nearly twenty. All right, I agree that Matthew may give you an engagement ring – you can plan and talk about it.' Indulgently he patted her shoulder, touching her hair with his lips. 'I do insist that you wait a year, though. You'll still be under age, but if things are the same this time next year, then I'll agree. If the war is over before then, we'll think again.'

For Kate that was enough, in fact it was perfect. Matthew brought her a sapphire and pearl engagement ring, telling her it was but a poor copy of the blue of her lovely eyes. At the hospital she was sure every nurse must envy her. Matthew was her god. Every spare moment she had she sewed for her bottom drawer: embroidered table linen, lace edging for her underwear, and with each stitch she dreamed of the future. 'Come home with me, I'd love you to meet my wife,' she imagined him inviting some faceless friend, or even jump further ahead, see them with children, a boy and a girl.

If Kate was happy to wait indefinitely for their wedding, Matthew saw things differently.

'Have you tried to persuade him? Kate, I may not be here for ever. Supposing I get sent overseas?'

'Oh, don't,' she held her hand across his lips, 'it's like tempting fate even to suggest anything so dreadful. But I'd wait for you, a month, a year, a lifetime, I'd be waiting when you came back.'

Winter evenings with her family or sometimes in the doctors' office at Bullington had given way to spring and now at last to the first soft

252

warmth of a summer evening. All this time he'd been gentle with her, from his first tender kisses to a hint of his need to arouse the same passion in her as he felt. She was so beautiful. One day she would be his. So he kept telling himself.

Tonight there was no moon, the black sky was studded with golden stars. And here, on the seat by the lake, she sat by his side, her hand in his. Blissfully happy in what she had, she was taken by surprise when with one movement he pulled her to lie across him. In the darkness he could just see the pale disc that was her face. Surprise, excitement, fear, which was uppermost in her mind as his hand moved on the outline of her body? She lay quite still, hardly breathing; she might have been a statue.

Only when his hand moved inside her blouse did he feel her start. She sat bolt upright.

'No, you shouldn't. Matthew, it's not right.'

'Not right for a man to want to touch the woman he loves? Not right for her to want him to touch her? Sure and it's right, isn't it the way man and woman were made? Don't you feel anything?'

She swallowed. Her voice seemed to have left her.

'Haven't you the same ache, here,' he guided her hand and pressed it against him, 'in your loins? Aren't you crying out for me just like I am for you? Katie, you're trembling.'

'Soon we'll be married. I want everything to be perfect for us when the time comes.' And into her mind came the thought of the delicate silk of the nightgown she'd been making, the narrow band of lace around the neck and wrists. For her father had said they were to wait a year, that meant it would be a winter wedding. So often as she stitched she imagined Matthew's eyes lighting up in admiration as she took off her dressing gown and stood before him in her lovely nightgown.

'Soon! Six months!' He stood up. 'Sometimes I don't think you're flesh and blood, sometimes I don't believe you even care!'

'For you? Oh, Matthew, how can you say such a horrid thing? I'm so in love with you that I see you in my mind every minute of the day; I go to sleep thinking of you; I wake up thinking of you – '

He pulled her into his arms.

'Bless you, my Kate. My beautiful cruel Kate.'

She didn't understand what he was talking about, but then she often didn't. It was the Irish in him, she fondly believed. But standing up she felt safe, and raised her face for his kiss.

There had been one or two other occasions similar to that, there had been times that hadn't ended in a way Kate had felt to be happy. Matthew had been withdrawn, silent, had made excuses that he had work to do at the hospital.

One teatime on a gloomy day in October she ventured to his room, the bedroom that used to be hers. Her excuse was to carry his tea tray to him. Perhaps he really did misread her purpose, certainly he looked forward to a cosy hour with her in the warmth of the rather smelly gasfire that had been put in since the house had become a military hospital.

'Never mind tea, come and sit on my knee, my Kate.'

Willingly she came.

'I've been making up a list of people to invite to our wedding.' She snuggled contentedly against him. 'We have such lots of relatives. You must give me your list too. Mother ought to have it by the beginning of November if we're going to arrange the wedding for the turn of the year.'

'Sure and I will, but there's only two people matter at a wedding. You and me.'

She nodded in agreement, not for a moment taking him seriously.

'You and your Irish blarney,' she chuckled. 'I love weddings, don't you? So many people aren't able to have proper ones, all dressed up I mean. I'm lucky. Mother is going to have Hester's gown made smaller and the veil is the same one the Matheson brides have worn for simply generations.'

'And then you'll be mine. Not a Matheson bride but a Harkin wife. But sure sometimes I don't think you love me at all.' His accent was purposely pronounced, she thought that he was teasing her for fun. 'Only weeks now, and you won't send me starving away any more? Don't you trust me? Is that why you ration me your favours like an inmate in a workhouse?'

'That's a dreadful thing to say. It's not true. I just don't see why we can't wait. Waiting, looking forward, anticipation . . . can't you see how much it's all part of the joy of a wedding? That sort of thing is for married people, it's not right to make it furtive. It's a sort of holy thing. And I'd be frightened. Wouldn't you?'

'Pour my tea, Kate. I have a ward round to do.'

'Matthew, I'm right, I know I am. Afterwards you'll be glad that we didn't spoil things.' She turned away to the tea tray, but he could see her heightened colour, even her neck had a red patch on it. 'Supposing it wasn't what we expected? It might not be an easy thing to do – oh, it's so hard to talk about – but if I'd agreed, it would be rushed, furtive – we don't know what to expect – and even if it was easy it would be spoilt for us because we'd feel guilty. When we're properly married and have time to – to – well, have time – I'd hate us to have bad memories. Oh, Matthew, I don't know how to say it, it's such a hard thing to talk about.'

254

'You're such a babe, Kate. Sometimes I wonder about it all – us – the future.'

'That's mean and beastly.' Her eyes brimmed. 'You're being unkind just because I won't go to bed with you.'

He tilted her face and kissed her gently.

'Time you went home. And time I was on the ward.' He picked up his teacup and she felt herself dismissed.

'Just a moment.' Matron's voice boomed at her as she came down the stairs to the large stone hall. 'I want you to take Nurse Bradley up and show her where she's to sleep. You might help her make up her bed before you go home, too.' Miss Henderson took pleasure in her position of authority in Kate's erstwhile home.

'I'll carry one of your cases, shall I? We have to go up to the second floor.' However Kate felt about Matron's manner, her own welcome was friendly as she turned to the tall girl who waited with two leather suitcases.

'Thanks.' In the one word and the twinkle in conker-brown eyes that so exactly matched the shade of her hair, Eva Bradley let Kate see they shared the same opinion of their oversized superior.

Leading the way up the wide shallow staircase it was so natural to feel a sense of responsibility here at Bullington and, as if she were welcoming a guest, she told the new recruit: 'I do hope you'll like being here. I'm afraid they've crowded an awful lot of beds into the room, but I suppose they have to.'

'Do you sleep in here too?'

'Me?' She sounded surprised at the question. 'No, we've moved into the East Wing.'

'Oh, I say, I've never had a dormitory with bars at the window before. What is it, a prison or a lunatic asylum!'

Kate laughed. 'I never even thought of it. It was the nursery. This bed must be for you. I'll help you make it up, shall I?'

There was nothing about those moments to suggest that their lives were to run so closely together; certainly there was nothing to hint at the hurts, the resentment, jealousy, hatred. In fact it was Kate who said, as she turned to leave Eva to unpack: 'We've moved into the East Wing, that's our entrance door over there, do you see? You won't be on duty before tomorrow I don't expect. If you've nothing better to do, why don't you come across this evening? My parents love to have company. The medical staff from here are always welcome. My fiancé, Dr Harkin, will be there and there are sure to be other people too. Do come. It's so much nicer in a home atmosphere than in a rest room here.'

255

'That sounds a good idea, thanks.'

She came that evening, and others too over the weeks of autumn. 'The jolly chestnut' was the nickname Clifford Matheson gave her. Tall with long slender legs, the impressions she gave of suppressed vivacity . . . perhaps these things put him in mind of the frisky chestnut mare he so often rode; or did he name her simply for the colour of her hair and those eyes that were her one real claim to beauty? Of all the staff who came over from the hospital, Eva was the one who added a sparkle. And it was the same on the wards. The patients looked forward to her coming on duty. Everyone liked Eva Bradley, Kate as much as anyone else. When she said her brother Rupert had been posted to a nearby army base where he was in the Pay Corps, it was Kate who extended East Wing's invitation to include him.

'Not what I would have expected my "jolly chestnut" to have for a brother,' Clifford said after Rupert's first visit. 'Still, I dare say a young sister like that could be a bit of a handful. What a contrast, eh, Vini!'

'Not scintillating, but too careful of putting a foot wrong ever to be anything but harmless,' Lavinia laughed. 'Perhaps he'll unbend when we know him better.'

It was Kate who came to the defence of Eva's elder brother, who'd managed to wear his Captain's uniform as if he were part of the window dressing at a military outfitters.

'He was probably uncomfortable, out of his depth with medical people.' For in Kate's eyes any man must be aware of his own failings when he stood against Matthew.

Weeks of autumn leading to evenings when the first frost of winter nipped the blacked-out darkness of the gardens at Bullington. And in the East Wing Kate stitched happily, half listened to the laughter, the singing around the piano where Matthew showed himself master of yet another talent. There were plenty of evenings when he couldn't come, when he had rounds to do, was concerned about a patient he didn't want to leave; plenty of evenings when Eva wasn't free to be with them too. But such was the open hospitality of the Mathesons that Rupert – tailor's dummy, all too careful not to put a foot wrong, dull, out of his depth among people of the medical profession – spent much of his time there. He seemed content to sit next to Kate, to watch her small hands busily at work. He sensed a shyness in her, perhaps because he was familiar with it himself. While the hum of conversation went on, gradually she opened up, told him about the plans for her wedding, how her brothers were hoping to arrange leave. The date would depend on when they could be here, she hoped

256

around Christmas time, but it was important for her that they should know Matthew, even if it meant waiting a little longer. Now that the time was drawing near he was being so kind and understanding – but those last thoughts she kept to herself, with a smile of contentment.

Christmas came and went, the bans were called, Hester's wedding dress had been made smaller and was hanging draped in a sheet ready for the big day. Then everything changed, the plans were thrown into chaos: Matthew received a posting overseas, he was to go to report to a Field Station in France on the 28th January. It took a lot to beat the Mathesons. Johnathan and Charles couldn't be here, but the rest of the clan rallied. The wedding was to be on the 18th January. News of it spread like wildfire around the village. Kate had been everyone's darling, even as a little child she'd been as sweet as she was beautiful, now she'd be the loveliest bride ever to walk up the aisle of Newton Dingley church. In her excitement and joy she smiled at the change in Matthew's manner; he was more tender, he treated her gently, now that they'd so soon be married he no longer frightened her with demands she knew were wrong. Thinking back, realising how wary he'd become, she smiled lovingly. Darling Matthew. For all his talk he was as frightened by it as she was herself now the day was coming near.

The Bullington carriage had been polished until it was fit to take Cinderella to the palace. Already it had made three journeys to the church, the first two with aunts, uncles and cousins, the third with Lavinia and Hester, who was Matron of Honour.

'Be happy, my little Kate. I hope he knows what a lucky man he is.' Clifford's gaze rested lovingly on this youngest fledgling, so eager to rush into marriage, yet to him such a child, such a precious child. The carriage had already come for them, next time she came into the house she would be another man's wife. More than three years ago he'd taken Hester to her wedding, but he'd not felt like this. Kate was so innocent, so unready for life's knocks. 'The door bell again,' he smiled. 'Poor Millie Craddock is having a busy time with your telegrams at the post-office today. We'll see who it's from before we leave.'

They heard someone go to open the door, they heard voices. Then unannounced Rupert came into the drawing room.

'I don't know how to tell you,' he blurted. 'Here, you read it.' He passed a letter to Clifford. 'Kate . . .' he held both hands out, took hold of hers. 'I should have seen. She's my sister, I should have been able to see . . .'

How was it that the family returning from the church, the nightmare

257

of a wedding breakfast disguised into a meal to sustain guests who'd travelled, somehow it was Rupert who was there to dry Kate's tears? Eva's brother, the one person she might have been expected to avoid above all others.

Changed out of her wedding gown, dressed in boots and fur coat, she escaped unseen, or so she thought. But she was wrong. He'd been watching from the shelter of the trees in the drive. Seeing her half running and half walking in the direction of the lake, he chased after her.

'Kate, wait!' Only when he caught up with her and grabbed her arm did she realise what he imagined. Of all people she was glad it was him. He knew the whole story, he wouldn't ask questions. She saw the concern in his eyes. Somehow it was natural and easy to cry. With him she didn't care if her eyes were bloodshot and her nose red. This was her wedding day and she'd never been so miserable in all her life.

In the days and weeks that followed, his devotion was the balm her wounded pride needed.

'The man's a doormat!' Lavinia's opinion of him didn't improve. 'Clifford, she mustn't let him salve the wound that wretched Matthew Harkin left.'

'He'll never play her false. Doormat he may be, but he'll be gentle with her. He's patient – and he loves her, be sure of that. He'll protect her.'

When in the spring Kate walked up the aisle of Newton Dingley church on her father's arm the villagers watched with the same pleasure as they had for the wedding that hadn't taken place. Seeing Kate, serene, beautiful, the whisper went round that she'd refused to marry the doctor because she was in love with this army captain.

Such a short time to cast its shadow, Lavinia had said. Sitting here with her Kate remembered it all, the halcyon days that in her memory were all sunshine; then despair and humiliation; afterwards the beginning of her life with Rupert. From this distance she could see that it was pride that made her so willing to accept the love he lavished on her, love that was undemanding. Eva was his sister, yet in those months before the wedding he'd never once mentioned her. Kate had taken some sort of comfort from that. Eva had stolen Matthew, but she'd lost her brother in doing it. That had been important. Only later had she found that it wasn't the truth.

Rupert was neat and orderly. Even his lovemaking had been in keeping with his appearance and personality. Then or now, there was nothing wild and abandoned about him. She'd told herself she was glad, and yet as she'd subjected herself, his movements following their regular pattern, his weight taken on his elbows, she'd known a feeling of disappointment. Then had come a joy that must have been sent to compensate her for her suffering. She was to have a baby. But what a cruel fate that just as she began to look forward with hope, to pick up the pieces of her broken world, she should have found out that Rupert had kept in touch with his young sister. It had robbed her of the point she'd felt she'd scored, and destroyed the respect she'd been trying to build for him. She'd seen it as weakness that he'd not been prepared to stand up and be counted, let the world see whose side he was on.

'Sometimes, Kate, you make me very cross. You seem to take a delight in feeling yourself ill-used. It can't go on for ever, you know, it's sheer nonsense. If that young Irishman had run off with anyone but Rupert's sister, you would have put it out of your mind long ago.'

'You don't understand. Anyway she is Rupert's sister, the precious aunt Lottie's always been so besotted with! Now we even have to ask for the truth about Lottie and this man through Eva!'

Lavinia felt a twinge of pity. She remembered the sunny little girl Kate had once been, she thought of Clifford and how he would have hated to see her so warped with hatred. Only an unhappy person could bear a grudge all these years. In her heart she didn't blame Eva nor even Matthew, she blamed Rupert. He'd been Kate's husband all this time, yet had he ever come near to knowing the spirit that guided her?

'Kate, child, you've had nearly thirty years of marriage. Except for a few months of hope what has she had but a career? Cold comfort, I'd say, for the sort of girl I remember Clifford's "jolly chestnut" to have been.'

'Living without a man you mean? And who says that she has? Father's "jolly chestnut", as you call her, would hardly be faithful to Matthew's memory all the years I've kept my marriage vows.'

'There's more to marriage vows than running off to bed with a man. You've never done that.' Then, with a grin that took years off her, 'And perhaps you'd have been all the better for it if you had! If there's no more push in him lying down than there is standing up, then I can see why you look at him like you do sometimes.' She reached to take Kate's hand. 'But for your own sake, forgive and forget. You and Rupert are a couple, time has made that of you, and she is bound to be part of his life, just like Charles and Hester – and Jonathan, I dare say – are part of yours. Yes, and like Ronnie and Michael will always be part of Lottie's. When you paint a picture you make the background first, it doesn't change just because of what you choose to put on top of it.'

259

Her grip tightened for a second then she withdrew her hand and went on in a businesslike tone that had no place for introspection, 'It's Lottie we are thinking about – and how we can see she sets off on the next stage with her family firmly behind her. So now let me get the list I've been making and you'll see what a busy time I had on that telephone before you arrived.'

Chapter Seventeen

Lavinia made all the arrangements – and that they entailed two more telephone conversations with Eva was no one's affair but her own. They were to sail on 1st June, then follow the same route as Lottie and Katie had just over two years before.

'It's a long time for me to be away from the business.' Rupert, now senior partner of Craddock, Bradley and Merchant, Chartered Accountants, had never absented himself for longer than two weeks at a time and, even then, the family had always been aware that he'd fidgeted through the second, sure that chaos would be waiting on his return.

'You've a good staff, Rupert. They're as qualified as you are yourself.' Kate wasn't going to let anything stand in the way of the trip.

'I dare say. But qualifications aren't the same thing as experience. I've never left the business for anything like this span of time. It'll be on my mind – '

'My dear man,' Lavinia sat that bit straighter as she surveyed the ninny, 'if you've taken partners so useless, then you've no one to blame but yourself! However, I intend to be at Lottie's wedding and I'm sure Kate does too. You must make your own decision.' One word from Lavinia and Rupert saw things from her viewpoint, he always had. She had no more respect for him now than she'd had when he'd first visited the East Wing; she'd disliked his ingratiating attitude then, and she disliked it still. The only emotion he aroused in her was sympathy not liking, and it was that sympathy that made her add: 'But you'll disappoint her if she sees herself playing second fiddle to somebody's annual accounts. You're her father, she'll want you there, and she'll be anxious that you meet Ramsey, get a picture in your mind of what her life is.'

'Yes, yes, of course, you're quite right. Richard and George Merchant are both good men. I wouldn't have taken them into the business

261

if I'd not had faith in them. Indeed, Mother, I'm extremely grateful to you, it's most generous of you – '

'Rubbish!' Lavinia's face lit up when she smiled. 'It's going to be a holiday such as we've never had.'

'But, Mother, you and Father travelled so much. Even when I was small I remember being left with Nanny while you were off in Europe.'

'Venice, Rome, Paris . . . oh yes, we travelled. Vienna too.' Her mind drifted back, the smile softened with memory, then she brought herself back to the plans for today. 'Ah, but what I said was we've never had a holiday like this will be. Neither have we.'

'Certainly *we* haven't. For us it's always been a fortnight in Cornwall, until the war put a stop even to that, with Freda to help with the cooking just the same as at home.' Kate's words were loaded with pent up criticism. Yet if Ronnie or Lottie – or Michael if it were possible – were asked, they would have said those weeks in Cornwall had held all the wonder of childhood and given them memories that stayed with them all their days. 'But this . . . Mother, I feel that at last, and I've waited so long, but at last I'm going to really *live*.'

'Sometimes you talk more nonsense than even Rupert does.'

But to Kate it wasn't nonsense.

From the day they steamed out of Southampton Water she felt that she'd stepped out of her old identity. They were invited to the Captain's table; she and Rupert danced together; she knew the coupons Freda had insisted on giving her had been put to good use, in her new clothes she was the prettiest woman on board. Somewhere at the end of this wonderful journey they would be met by Eva. But for now, forget it, enjoy every wonderful moment, then look beyond Eva to Lottie and to Katie. Some people were seasick – but not delicate Kate. Her head didn't throb. She was grasping at life, eager to make the most of each second. Even the long train journey didn't daunt her. This was Canada, the country she'd resented ever since Eva had given Lottie that stupid money box. But now the sting had gone, it was something she was seeing, sharing. Sycamore Avenue was no more than a shadow at the back of her mind; this was Excitement.

Excitement for her and for Lottie too as she counted the days until their arrival. Eva was to meet them in Calgary and to drive them on to Higley Creek. That was to be on the 3rd July. An evening there, then rooms had been booked for them at Radley's one and only hotel. On the 4th Lottie and Ramsey were to be married in the chapel at the top end of Fourth Street. Then the family were to stay at Higley with the children while Lottie and Ramsey drove to Banff for their honeymoon. The days of June went by, a telephone call from Montreal told Lottie that they were on Canadian soil and were making a holiday of their cross country journey.

262

Everything seemed to be falling into place. Lottie could see ahead of her clearly, no longer was there any fog of doubt and uncertainty. One small shadow was a a new aloofness in Marthe, the old warmth had gone. Lottie told herself that time would heal, Marthe would realise her place here wasn't changed; her confidence would be restored and with it her good humour. And Dylan? It was hard to read what went on in his young mind. Each day he went to school, but he told them nothing about he hours he spent there. He lived behind the shelter of his impassive expression. Lottie swept all her worries under the mat. Her family were coming to see her! And even more paramount in her mind was the future she was so certain of with Ramsey.

Today as she drove into Radley she was alone, Katie had stayed behind with Ginney. Had Molly not noticed her coming and sounded the horn of the truck, she might have passed without realising. But, glad to see Molly, she drew to a halt and got out of the car.

'I just been to the Trading Post,' Molly greeted her, 'though what I could have heard by mail I don't know.' She looked at Lottie with eyes that were bloodshot from lack of sleep. 'I'm worried out of my mind. It's Donald. Went to see him again a few days back. Sometimes I wonder whether I'd be kinder not to go, whether seeing me upsets him, makes things worse for him. Each visit he seems to have drifted further from reach. Talks about seeing . . . I tell you, he's in a world of his own – and it's not a happy place – cries like he was a little boy still. Seems to be haunted by devils, poor boy. He's got no future. Nothing. He's not like you knew him. I tell you, he's gone right down. If they'd let me keep him at home I could have taken care of him. Craig says I ought to keep away, that it's seeing me that stirs up all his memories. But I can't! How can I? He's only got me cares about him.'

She wasn't so much talking to Lottie as just saying aloud the anguish that was in her mind. Probably as she'd driven along on her own, she'd talked just the same. 'I don't know what to do. Don't know what to think. Old Pop goes on the same day after day. There's Neil gone, now Donald . . . I ain't got no purpose for any of it any more.'

'Don't say that, Molly.' Lottie touched the long, bony hand that rested limply on the steering wheel. 'It's you who makes Kilton Down what it is.'

Molly shrugged. 'I hear you're to wed the McFee man. Never saw you as a girl who would have stayed around these parts. Used to wonder how things would pan out for you and Neil. Never though it would go the way it did, that's for sure. Well, I wish you well. And I mean that, Lottie.' Suddenly she smiled. 'Remember the day my

263

Donald saddled up Sherry to test you out? I knew then you had plenty of spunk. You can tell Ramsey McFee that Molly O'Hagon says he's a lucky guy. If my Neil had still been here, he wouldn't have had a sniff of a chance. Still, that's the way life shapes out. I tell you, Lottie,' the worry of Donald was constantly at the forefront of her mind, 'they've broken him. He was good as gold with me.'

Lottie watched her drive away. She was filled with pity for her and for Donald too, lost in the labyrinth of his poor muddled mind. But one thing that Molly had said stood out: 'If my Neil had still been here he wouldn't have had a sniff of a chance.' She got back into the car and sat a long time, remembering Neil, and the girl who'd loved him, the girl who would always love him. And now? If he were to ride by now? Her excitement for the future was clouded by a sense of shame. She'd married Neil confident that what they had would last for ever. Yet here she was, nine months after he'd ridden out of her life, looking ahead with certainty, knowing that beside what she felt for Ramsey everything else paled into insignificance. The love she felt for him had a depth, a breadth, that she hadn't known possible. Supposing Neil had come straight home from round-up, suppose this spring they'd started building their own home? She was ashamed. Even if physically he'd been unfaithful to her, was what she'd done any better? Ramsey had been her friend through all those months at Kilton Down, she knew now he'd been her life line.

Barrie had been her friend too. She smiled, thinking of him. Of course he'd been her friend, she hoped he always would be. But in her feelings for Barrie there was no disloyalty to Neil, there could be no disloyalty to Ramsey. 'Until death do us part . . . ' In her mind she stood again before the altar at Newton Dingley, the family gathered to give her support. How far she'd come since then. Not just in miles, not even in months and years.

Kate was as excited as a young girl. From Brimley to Newton Dingley, with an occasional day's shopping in Oxford, had been as far as her world had stretched since the pre-war days. But this Kate was a born again traveller, she'd missed nothing as the train had sped westward. Unlike Lottie who'd found in it the realisation of a dream, to Kate the journey re-kindled a spirit that had been almost extinguished. And, although logic had no place in what she believed, she felt that she was sharing all that was new with Michael. She was certain he knew where she was, that he was glad for her happiness – and because she was so certain, so her happiness knew no bounds.

In the first few moments of being with Eva she bordered on the brink of 'one of her heads'. But she held her chin high and stood to her full five foot three. Here she was, a married woman, travelling first class half way across the world. What had she to fear from Eva?

'You've managed to get time off from the hospital for the wedding?' She heard the patronising tone in her question.

'Sure, and to stay on a while after. I'm due on the ward again on the 11th.' If Kate had been talking down to her, Eva hadn't noticed. 'We ought to make Higley by about six this evening. There's a motel and eating house around half way, I thought we'd stop there for a snack. Unless you're starved right now?'

There were much too anxious to get on their way. Lavinia sat in the front with Eva, Rupert and Kate behind.

'You're all right?' he whispered anxiously. 'Sure you don't want to rest before we go on?'

'Don't be silly! If you mean you're wanting a break, then say so. I'm fine.'

He looked puzzled. What had he said to make her snap at him like that? That it had something to do with Eva he didn't doubt, but he couldn't follow the way women's minds worked. To escape he closed his eyes. Five miles later he slept.

Five hours and a stop for steaks of a tenderness cattle at home didn't produce, even if the rations would allow such extravagance, and they turned through a gap in the wooden fencing where a painted board announced they were at Higley Creek.

Katie ran straight to Eva, glad to shelter behind someone she knew as these strangers swamped her.

'My Katie!' The lady with curly hair and a hat on with lots of flowers on it squatted down in front of her. 'Oh, Katie, you remember Gran, of course you do.' Even Eva's presence didn't hold Kate back.

Katie nodded unconvincingly, peeping from behind the aunt she was used to. 'Got a picture,' she agreed.

'And we'll take lots more pictures. Pictures of you, pictures of us. Oh, Katie, I'm really seeing you.' Kate pulled the child towards her, her hug bearlike. Katie wasn't at all sure she cared for it, but she didn't want to seem rude so let herself be squeezed.

'Hi, Mum, what about me? Don't I merit a hug? And this is Ramsey.'

In the quick glance that was all Kate had allowed herself she'd seen a man in what she would call working trousers and a check shirt. What a way to welcome his future parents-in-law! Why, even after all these years, Rupert would have too much respect for Mother to keep his gardening clothes on if she were expected. Now Kate gave the stranger her full attention, prepared not to like what she saw.

'Welcome to Higley Creek.' His voice was soft, in her mind she called it 'rounded'. There was nothing soft about his handshake. His

265

eyes smiled at her before his mouth followed suit. She forgot the working trousers.

'We're glad to be here. So very very glad, Ramsey.'

How could Lottie help remembering that other time? But today she didn't want to think of anything but the here and now, it was like a dream seeing them. Mum and Dad both looked out of place, he in a dark suit, collar and tie and grey homburg hat just as if he were off to Brimley, she in a smart summer coat and a hat that would make all heads turn in the Chapel in Radley. Only Lavinia, the same here as always, seemed to fit the scene; but then, tall and with that aristocratic bearing, she could be dropped down anywhere and she would always look right. Ramsey was taking them all into the house, Ginney suddenly the centre of attention.

'Marthe, they're here. Come and meet everyone. What are you doing hiding out here?' Lottie found Marthe cleaning spoons and forks at the kitchen table.

'I am not hiding. They are your family, you need time with you and with Ramsey before I make an intrusion.'

Lottie laughed. 'What bunkum! Come on. Mum, Dad, this is Marthe. Gran, you remember I've told you about Marthe, my first real friend here?'

It was all going so well, even Marthe was unbending as she talked to Rupert. Standing close to Lavinia, Lottie reached to touch the thin hand. She felt the long fingers grip hers, the rings the old lady always wore pressing tight. Katie was forgetting to be shy, Ginney was showing Eva some paintings she'd done, Ramsey was talking to Kate, Rupert to Marthe. It was perfect, just as Lottie had dreamed.

Through the window she saw Dylan ride into the yard as if all the devils in hell were chasing him. At the sight of Eva's car he reined in and stopped quite still. He seemed to hesitate, unsure what to do. Lottie opened the window and called to him, but he seemed not to notice; certainly he didn't look her way as he brought his heels hard against the horse's flanks and disappeared back through the gap in the wooden fence with the same speed as he'd arrived. One quick look up the narrow track as if to reassure himself and he was gone.

Whether pride or hospitality spurred Marthe was her own secret, but whatever drove her she produced a celebration dinner such as they'd not experienced even during their first days in Canada, and certainly not through the years of rationing at home. The table wasn't weighed down with silver, but the linen was white and crisp, the crockery gleamed and the cutlery sparkled. Kate started to relax, she no longer looked around consciously ready to find fault. How could she, when sitting across the table from her was Katie, her small fingers stretched manfully to grasp her knife and fork?

The wine had been sent by Barrie.

'Dear Barrie, he must miss you, Lottie.' It was Kate's final salute to her dream.

'We thought he'd be coming to the wedding. He wrote and said he hoped to. Then Eva brought the wine and a message that he wasn't able to get away, he was flying.'

Kate looked at her over the top of her glass. Was happiness dulling her understanding of other people's feelings?

'Why's Dylan not having his dinner, Mom?' Katie asked.

'Maybe he's forgotten the time.'

'Wherever he was off to, from the speed he rode out of the yard he wasn't wasting time.' Ramsey didn't approve of the boy's absence on this important evening, but he was determined nothing should spoil things for Lottie.

'It is likely he is unwishing to sit with so much family, it will make him feel uneased.' Marthe's understanding of people went much further than her vocabulary would allow. 'I will serve his dinner and put it to keep warm. Later, when he thinks the high time is over, he will come back.'

Kate for one was glad the boy's place was empty. He was a shadow of Neil O'Hagon that this evening could well do without. Now Katie was his child every bit as much as the boy, yet she brought no reminders of her father. Katie had been *theirs*. Even now as their eyes met the little girl was learning to hold her gaze, forgetting to be shy. Tomorrow Lottie and Ramsey would go off on their honeymoon, and for a whole week Katie would be hers to care for.

'Katie's bed time, Mum,' Lottie said. 'Are you coming to see her tucked in?' Ever since they'd sailed out of Southampton Kate's life had been full of wonder; but nothing could compare with this. 'Tomorrow you'll be in charge, so best you get used to where things are, don't you think?'

'Katie can show me. Let me help her to bed. We'll call you when we're ready. Shall we do that, Katie?' It was a gamble. Was she going too fast for a four year old who knew her as no more than a picture in a silver frame?

Katie considered. For a moment she was undecided. Then she slipped her hand into Kate's.

'Come on,' she said.

Another hour went by and still there was no sign of Dylan. Daylight was at its longest but dusk was falling fast when the departing party packed into Eva's car to drive back to the hotel in Radley.

'I've never heard of a bride and groom setting out together for their wedding! You shouldn't even see each other in the morning, it's courting bad luck,' Kate the traditionalist worried.

'When folk are as sure as we are of what they're doing, they don't need luck, Kate,' Ramsey told her. Neil had called her nothing at all, Ramsey called her Kate. She felt young, attractive; a man of his age could hardly think of her as 'Mother'.

'Then we'll be at the Chapel for eleven o'clock. Your father will wait for you outside so that he can bring you in when all the rest of us are seated. It really does seem a funny way . . . '

Only Lavinia saw the half wink that Ramsey gave Lottie. She settled back in the front seat of the car. No need to worry about those two. She was tired, all this journeying was a reminder of how the years were slipping by; not like the effect it had on Kate, so full of life that her neighbours in Sycamore Avenue wouldn't think her the same woman. A blessing they came. It seemed to have set the score straight, washed away the sour taste of uncertainty they'd all had for Lottie. Lovely to see the child again. Marrying a man with a crippled daughter, a housekeeper who liked to rule the roost, and a half breed legacy of her first husband . . . Lavinia's head drooped forward. The others pretended not to notice that she was asleep.

'We can't just leave him out,' Ramsey said. 'He'd got no friends around, I can't think where he can have been rushing off to.'

'Perhaps he's started setting traps again. He never really tells us what he does.' Lottie wouldn't put into words what she knew: at Higley Creek Dylan didn't fit 'sweet as a nut', he didn't seem to want to.

Darkness came and there was still no sign of him. Marthe went to bed, the last hour of the day ticked by.

'We can't go to bed and forget him,' Lottie worried. 'Ramsey, perhaps he's been thrown from his horse? Perhaps he's lying hurt? Supposing by tomorrow we haven't had any word of him? Being shy of meeting strangers couldn't have kept him out as late as this.'

'I'll take the car and drive around. Perhaps the young fool went fishing . . . or to Kilton Down. Do you think they would have taken him in if they thought your family were here?'

'More likely his traps. Perhaps he went to look at them and got hurt.' She walked with him to the car. 'Let me come, Ramsey. Let's look for him together.'

'No, you wait back here, maybe he'll get home before me.' Then he tilted her chin. 'You know what time it is? Two minutes past midnight. Today you and me will be married.'

It would have been easy to forget the missing Dylan, she wanted to forget him as she clung to Ramsey.

'You remember what Mum said?' she chuckled. 'About it being bad luck to see the bride before the wedding.'

'Seeing you could never be bad luck.' He rubbed his chin against her rumpled hair. 'Please God I'll see you every day for as long as I live.'

She nodded. 'Me too, that's what I want.' Her face buried against his neck, she sniffed deeply. 'You smell lovely. Even in the dark I know it's you.'

'And who else would it be?'

'I'm so happy I could burst.'

But she didn't. Instead she watched as he drove out and the tail lights grew faint in the distance, then turned to walk back across the yard past the sheds to the house.

'Over here!' someone hissed the words.

She stood stock still, frightened to move, almost frightened to breathe. Silence. Perhaps she'd imagined it. She waited, her confidence returning as the seconds went by.

'Dylan?' Her own voice was soft. She was crazy, out here alone in the night talking to herself. Of course it wasn't Dylan. Of course it wasn't anyone. She started forward. What was that? If only she had a light. If only she weren't at the far end of the yard. The implement sheds were between her and the door. Well, what if they were? They were familiar, there was nothing to be frightened of there. Probably there was a nocturnal animal on the prowl.

'Ah!' In the moonless night an arm stretched out and a hand covered her mouth, then she was pulled into the shelter of a shed where the seed drills were housed. She bit as hard as she could, but she was pulled closer to someone, her back pressed against him, someone whose left arm imprisoned her while the right hand seemed impervious to her teeth.

'He told me to come. He ain't gone, my boy ain't gone.'

Donald! Her first reaction was relief. Poor demented Donald. But how had he got there? He was miles away, locked up in a mental hospital, getting more and more confused . . . She'd never felt safe with Donald, even at Kilton Down, yet now his words took away some of the fright. He must have felt her relax. He removed his hand that silenced her.

'Who told you to come?' she whispered.

'Neil, he told me. You think he's gone, they all think he's gone. But he hasn't. I see him most all the time. Reckon you never see him no more. But he's there right 'nuff, I see him. He knows I come here. Sent me, he did.'

269

Her mind was working overtime. She knew she couldn't argue with Donald, reason was out of the question, and if she opposed him and he got angry she'd be powerless against strength like his. How long would Ramsey be? She had to keep Donald talking until he came back. But he might be an hour, two hours. Her mouth felt dry with fear.

'Why did he send you? Were you unhappy in that place?'

'Eh?' It was as if he had no idea what her question meant. His mind could only cope with one thing at a time and that thing was – she belonged to Neil. 'He sent me to stop you. Moll, she said you were going to get wed. But you're not, you can't. You belong to my Neil. He told me I gotta come and stop you. I seen through the window, I seen you with him back there at Kilton, an' I heard the two of you.' She tried to pull away from him but his hold was firm as steel. 'Now you think he's gone, you think you'll get all that from that other bugger. I used to listen. I know what you want.'

'You don't. You don't know anything about it.'

'You're *his* woman, same as Rosie was. And the boy. Moll, she told me that bastard's got Neil's boy too, and the girl. If I take you back with me he ain't gonna want a couple o' kids.'

If only he'd loosen his hold. How long would Ramsey be? Where had he gone in his search for Dylan? It seemed hours ago that she'd watched him drive away but it was no more than a few minutes, he'd hardly have reached the Radley road yet.

'We'll talk about it Donald.' She kept her voice low and steady. 'There's no rush. Let's talk a while. Does Molly know where you are?' She spoke quietly, keeping her voice friendly, hoping to relax him. Of course Molly didn't know where he was.

'Come for you like Neil wants.' She couldn't see him but she knew just how his mouth would be hanging open, she could tell it from the sound of his heavy breathing.

'They must have sent to tell her you've run off. How do you think she'll feel? She'll be sick with worry, Donald.' His stomach rumbled emptily, giving her her next cue. 'Remember the huge pot of bean soup she usually keeps on the stove? She'll have food all ready for you.'

His grasp wasn't quite so tight. Then at the thought of food another drum roll echoed its way from the depth, ending in a hard belch.

'Jeez, ain't fed since Christ knows.'

'I'll take you. Bet the soup'll be waiting, just like when you used to come in from the range. It won't take us long and you'll be home with Molly. She'll feed you.'

Like a child he let her lead him to the 'hybrid'. She opened the door on the passenger side and helped him in. In the house the only light

270

was in the sitting room, she didn't see Marthe's bedroom curtain pulled to one side. A minute later they were on the way towards Kilton. By her side he slumped in the seat, making no more attempt to talk. Perhaps the thought of steaming bean soup had made him forget his mission.

They'd just turned on to the road that led from Radley to Kilton Down when he sat up with a start.

'Down here, down this track,' he spluttered.

'No, it isn't. Kilton's straight on. What are you doing? Donald, don't pull the wheel, it's straight on – '

'There!' He was wrenching the steering wheel from her hands, trying to turn on to a track that led to the range. 'Neil boy, I got her back for you. You gotta see him! Why can't you see him? Over there on his horse, riding back off the range.'

She jammed on the brake as the 'hybrid' swerved out of control. The engine stalled. She mustn't let Donald know how her heart was pounding as she answered: 'Yes, I saw. He'll be back at Kilton by the time we get there.' Switching on the engine she prepared to reverse back on to the road.

'You never saw my Neil. You're lying to me. Why don't you listen, proper listen, to what I'm telling you?' The big man sagged, his hands hanging limp between his knees. He was crying quietly. 'He's only got me to see someone else don't get his woman and his kids.'

Just as suddenly as her fear had come, so it left her. She switched off the engine. Poor broken Donald, he could love with a dedication not given to many with their full powers of reasoning. People would call him a half-wit, perhaps that was why his mind was uncluttered with anything but the purpose that drove him. As long as she'd been at Kilton Down she'd been uncomfortable with him, frightened of what she'd not understood, hating the way he'd watched and listened. The court case had given her the answer to so much, but the fear was still here. One thing she did know though, he could never be hurried, his mind had to go slowly down its own chosen path. So for some minutes they sat in silence except for the snuffling sound of his weeping.

Presently she turned on the small interior light and for the first time they looked at each other. She was shocked by the change in him. Still as huge, nothing could alter that, but even with two or three weeks' growth of beard she could see how gaunt he was. Protruding from the pocket of his dirty and bloodstained shirt was a pair of secateurs, presumably his only 'weapon'. The blood must be evidence that somewhere on his long journey he'd robbed from traps. The hospital would never have allowed him matches. So how could he have made a

271

fire? Or had starvation driven him to eat raw meat? She could have cried for him. To take a life must haunt one all one's days; to bring about the death of the person one loves above all others must be to be in unending purgatory.

'All right, Donald,' she spoke gently, 'yes, I lied. Just now I didn't see Neil. But I do believe what you say. For you he's there, he wants you to be with him like you were right since he was a little boy. He's trying to tell you that he understands about the dreadful things that happened, he knows you would never hurt him – you were trying to help him. Don't cry, don't be unhappy. Neil would hate you to be miserable, you know he would.'

He didn't answer, just rocked backwards and forwards in the seat, a picture of helpless misery. The minutes ticked by. She knew she was walking a tight rope. They were miles from anywhere, he had enormous strength; even after living as he must have done as he'd made his way home she would be powerless if his mood suddenly changed. Best to be still, to treat him quietly as the minutes went by.

She had lost all track of time. Had Ramsey found Dylan? By now would he have arrived back at Higley to find that she was gone and the 'hybrid' missing?

'If I close my eyes I often see him too, Donald.' Gently softly, her voice soothed him. 'Not just now, when you did, but at odd moments. Perhaps when I'm riding I feel he's there with me, or when the wind blows strong I can hear his voice.' His mouth open in a half smile, Donald was watching her now. 'Some people might not know what I'm talking about, but I believe you do. I remember the Neil I met in England. The girl I used to be will always be his . . .'

But Donald wasn't listening. Far away along the straight road they could see the headlights of a vehicle coming towards them. He gave no warning, but threw open the door and pulled himself out, then without a backward glance he stumbled away into the night.

'Donald, come back! I'm taking you to Kilton!' She got out too, she mustn't lose him in the dark. Once he was at Kilton Molly would look after him, hers would be the heartbreaking task of passing him back into custody. Lottie knew the reason for his fear as he went blundering into the night. How was he to know any more than she did that the headlights belonged to the truck from Kilton Down?'

'What have you done with him?' Molly greeted her. 'The foreign woman telephoned. She said she'd seen you drive out with him, she was sure it was him.'

'He's there, somewhere. He ran off when he saw the lights of the truck.'

'Donald! Come on, lad, it's Moll. Donald! It's Craig and Moll. Come back to the car.'

Standing still, they listened. There was a movement, they sensed it rather than saw it. He would probably have come to them, but at that very moment another vehicle was approaching from the opposite direction, following the route Lottie had been taking.

When she recognised it she forgot Donald, she forget everything but her relief. Ramsey pulled up. Until he was with her, holding her against him, she hadn't realised quite how frightened she'd been. Now it was over. Molly and Craig had moved off in the direction of where they thought they'd heard a movement.

'I'll turn the van for you, then you head for home. I'll be right behind you. It's all over, sweetheart.' Such an old-fashioned endearment; she felt loved, protected, her fears wiped away.

'Dylan – did you find him?'

'He was back at the settlement. He saw the lights of the car, recognised it was me. Guess he was worried at what he'd done, couldn't sleep. Next shack to where he used to live with Rosie, that's where he'd headed. The guy there told me he was the one came to fetch you the night of the trouble.'

'But why? Why did Dylan go back to them? You'd been good to him, he'd settled at school – '

'Had he? I doubt it, Lottie. He told me that this afternoon he was riding around looking at the traps he used to use, that's when he came upon Donald O'Hagon. Seems Donald started telling him he'd come from – well, never mind.'

'I know. From Neil.'

'Said he was going to take him, and you too, take you to Neil. He's crazy as hell, Lottie.'

'I know. Poor Molly.'

'Anyway, there's only one proper place for Dylan. He knows it, I know it too, and so I guess do you. With his mother. When he rode off from Higley he went straight to those Indian folk back at the settlement. Lillian, that's what the woman called herself, is kind. He feels safe with them. And her guy, the one who said he'd fetched you from Kilton, he's going to set off with him tomorrow, to take him to Rosie.'

Lottie nodded. Deep in her heart she must always have known that she'd never make a home for the Indian boy.

Almost lost in the night they could still hear Molly calling: 'Come on Donald, lad, it's Moll and Craig come to fetch you home.'

273

Epilogue

These days the mail came in by air, Radley had its own single runway airport. Instead of folk anxious for their post waiting to take it from Digby Bint the moment the truck arrived, now he had time to peruse the few envelopes or cards brought in each morning. Today he had quite a bundle in an elastic band waiting for Higley Creek: to Mr and Mrs McFee from Brimley, that came regular as clockwork every week; a trade catalogue for him; a mail order book for her; a letter from New York for Marthe Koparomy; and five for Katie O'Hagon, four of them from England.

It was the afternoon of the 28th March when Lottie and Ginney came into town. The year was 1961. No 'hybrid' vehicle for Ginney and her chair these days; or, more accurately, no conspicuously 'hybrid' vehicle. The car she drove had been adapted but no one would know that to see it, nor yet the pretty girl at the wheel.

'There's plenty of parking outside the Trading Post. Are you going to wait in the car or are you coming in?' Lottie asked her as she checked her last minute shopping list.

'Neither. I want to go along to Handy Crafts, I need more paint. Morey said he'd see me in there after school.'

Lottie unfolded the chair and opened the driver's door. But she didn't offer any help. Ginney knew just the way to transfer herself into her next means of transport.

'School should be just about out,' Lottie said. 'The boys'll be along soon. How long shall we be? I'm in no great rush, but all I've actually got to do is get a few extra treats for tomorrow and pick up the post. I do hope there's some waiting for her.'

'Of course there will be. You folk never get late with any of our birthdays – and eighteen seems kind of special. But, Lottie, I want to look as if I'm not just hanging about. I mean, I wouldn't want him to feel he was lumbered with me. Shall we say half an hour?'

'That's fine,' she laughed, 'leave him panting for more.' When she saw the way Ginney flushed, she was sorry she'd teased.

'I wondered – if – only *if* I can suggest it without him feeling he hasn't an easy excuse to refuse, would it be all right to suggest he comes tomorrow? It was Katie's idea. She said I should tell him that she suggested it if I wanted.'

'Of course ask him. Make the boys mind their p's and q's, having a teacher from school for the party!'

Watching the chair disappear up the road she sent up a prayer of thankfulness. Ginney might have been resentful of the way fate had used her, she might have been withdrawn, jealous of Katie. She was none of these things. Always she'd been the same, each hurdle she'd overcome had given her pride. But now? Was she falling in love with the young teacher who'd come to Radley back in the fall? Morey Darwin, teacher of history and art. It was that, the painting, that had given them their first common ground, meeting in Handy Craft one teatime last October. He'd shown genuine interest in her work, had come to Higley Creek to see the canvasses she had stacked in her room. If she was falling in love with him, would it be a cruel reminder to her of her own failings? Or would he see beyond, feel love and pride as they all did at the life she built?

Looking not a day different from when she'd first seen him, Digby Bint greeted her: 'Plenty o' mail here for your young Katie.' He pushed his spectacles down his nose as he looked at her, curiosity getting the better of him. 'Must be birthday time come round?'

'That's it. She's eighteen tomorrow.'

'Darned if it seems that long . . . ' He didn't say exactly what, but both of them knew.

Fourteen and a half years since the town had buzzed with gossip of the court case. It was like looking back to another life. The thought of Molly stabbed her. Would she feel it another life? Or had it brought about the end of the only life that mattered? Donald would never come home to Kilton Down, Molly had even stopped saying how at every visit he seemed to have slipped further away from them.

Lottie put Katie's mail into her pocket, it wouldn't be given her until the morning.

'Hi, Mom. Ginney said you'd be in here, we just saw her up the street.' That was Paul, just twelve, the elder of the two.

'We figured if we found you here, right by the chocolate bars, then our chances were pretty good.' And that was Nick.

The McFee boys had only one thing in common, their brown eyes, the same rich colour as her own. So often, watching them together, she'd look at Paul and find herself remembering Michael. He had the

276

same thoughtfulness, the same care of other people's feelings. Yet in appearance he was like Ramsey. In truth he was like him in character too, it was simply that to see the two boys together rolled back her years. It was memories of Michael and Ronnie that had prompted her to persuade Ramsey into having an area of the yard made into a tennis court.

Nick was ten, the wiry curls of his auburn hair suiting his vivid character. Now he grinned at Lottie, his eyebrows raised hopefully. How could she refuse?

It wasn't until after she arrived home that she opened her own letter from her parents and learned what one of Katie's birthday presents was to be.

'Oh, boy! Gee . . . ' Katie stared at the letter she'd just opened. She opened her mouth to speak, shut it again. 'Gee.' No more than a whisper. She was talking to herself.

'Well, come on, tell us! Don't sit there looking like a guppy fish! What do they say?' Nick couldn't understand it. She looked as though they'd sent her a million dollars but there was nothing in the envelope except a letter.

'Mom, it's from Grannie and Grandad.'

'We know that, silly – ' Again, impatient Nick.

'I'm to have my birthday present later – in England!' She looked at Lottie and Ramsey, her blue eyes shining with excitement. Then she tore open another enveloped, one addressed in Lavinia's bold hand. It was from that one that she took a small folder. 'This is it. Look, from Grandma, an open ticket. All we have to do is fix the date for me to travel! To fly to England! Listen to what Grannie says – we're to get my present from Grandad and her in London – we'll watch them changing Guard at Buckingham Palace, we'll take a boat on the Thames, we'll go to the Houses of Parliament . . . and, oh Mum, there's a great list of things we'll do. All the places I've got pictures of in my scrapbook, I'm going to see them – '

Lottie felt the prick of unshed tears. In Brimley her parents would be picturing the scene here as Katie read her letter; at Bullington Manor Grandma would be thinking of them too, now this very minute . . .

'But, Mom, you mustn't worry, I'll be all right on my own. Tell her, Dad, tell her I'll be fine. I'm old enough.'

'Sure you are. I guess she wishes she could change places.'

Lottie blinked and smiled. 'Then you guess wrong. One of these days maybe we'll take a holiday there, you and me. But I wasn't thinking of that. I was picturing Grandma, she was always the organiser.' To her it made sense, even if the others didn't follow her reasoning.

In April they took Katie to Calgary Airport. When her flight was called they watched her disappear into the departure area. Even then they didn't go home. They waited until her plane took off, watched it rise into the clear blue sky, higher, further, smaller . . . smaller . . . no more than a speck that occasionally sparkled in the sunlight. Then an empty sky.

In May she wrote: 'How could you ever bear to leave it, Mom? The bluebells are like a carpet, and you never told me that springtime would smell like it does. Grandad says it's the rain makes things smell so good. We've had a lot of rain, but it's different from back home – gentle and damp, hardly raindrops you can see at all, yet you get real wet in it. I stayed at Bullington Manor with Grandma last week. Isn't it strange? I felt I knew it already, yet I couldn't have remembered from before, I was only a baby when I was here. Same as being with Grandma. She said it took her back twenty years, to when you used to stay in your school holidays, Mom. You know how some folk make you feel real comfortable in your spirit – she and I got on just like that.
  'Grannie and Grandad still kept your bike, Mom. It had a little seat on the back. They said that's where I used to sit! I took that off and I've cycled for miles since I came back from Bullington.'

In June: 'Uncle Ronnie, Aunt Millicent, John and Cliff came. My real cousins! Of course they're only kids, but they play pretty good tennis. With Uncle Ronnie and them, I played doubles. Dear old Freda got quite weepy.'

It must have been August, school holiday time, when she joined the family party at Bullington. How it brought back memories for Lottie to read her letters: 'I've had a wonderful time at Bullington. I never knew I had so many relatives. The place was teeming with cousins, second cousins they said they were, Great Aunt Hester too. Summer holiday time they all seem to go there. Isn't it funny, this feeling I get of living it all before? I walked down to the lake one morning early, all by myself to the seat. Grandma said it's her thinking place. She said you used to go there, Mom. The ducks came out of the water to inspect me. Next time I took bread. I rode quite a lot, mostly with second cousin Nigel (he's your first cousin Christopher's eldest)! My word, one of these days I'll have to draw a family tree. He and I got along well. He rides OK too – for an Englishman!'

278

They'd planned on her staying for six months, five of them were gone already. It was towards the middle of September, an afternoon when Lottie and Ramsey had driven in to town together.

'While you go to pick up Nick's shoes I'll check if any mail's come in,' Ramsey told her. 'It's early yet to get the boys, we'll have time to drive out to the cut backs.' At any time of year it was a favourite spot, but especially now when the trees were a glory of gold and amber.

There was a letter from Katie, but like a child saving the best until last, Lottie didn't open it until they were on the high bank by the river. Then they read it together.

'You must be expecting to hear when I'm coming back. I know we said six months, but I've been wondering – and I've talked about it to Grannie and Grandad – would you mind very much if I stayed on for a while? You see, I could easily get a job in Brimley. When I suggested it they were so pleased. I don't want to sound boasty but I know they do like having me here. And – oh well, guess I'll be honest, Mom, the thing is – I met this guy . . . '

'She'll fall in love lots of times yet, darling,' Ramsey said. 'When she's ready, she'll come back.'

Lottie nodded. Yes, of course she'd come back. Or would she?

'Remember I told you about my Canada Box? She never had a money box – or if she did, I didn't know about it – but there was her scrapbook. On my box I had pictures of the Maple Leaf and a wild rose. In my mind Alberta was a sort of wonderland. On the front of her England Book she pasted a scene of a lock on the Thames and, on the back, a thatched cottage. Photos, those flowers Mum used to press for her . . . all the time was she weaving her own web of dreams?' Lottie rubbed her head against his shoulder. 'It's sad, isn't it? We've no real idea what goes on in our children's secret minds.'

'I guess no one ever has. We just have to hope that they'll reach whatever it is they strive after. And did you, Lottie, so far from the gentle Thames and the thatched cottages of home?'

'Home? For me this *is* home. Words aren't any use – Aunt Eva said that to me ages ago and it's true – you've got to see it, you can still seem to feel the – the courage of the old pioneers. You know what I think?' There was a twinkle in her brown eyes as she went on: 'I think that when God made the world this was the last bit to be done. All the practising was over, so this was about perfect.'

He didn't answer. At the touch of his lips brushing against her hair she looked up at him, teasing him, loving him. 'All that, and you for a bonus!'

279

You have been reading a novel published by Piatkus Books. We hope you have enjoyed it and that you would like to read more of our titles. Please ask for them in your local library or bookshop.

If you would like to be put on our mailing list to receive details of new publications, please send a large stamped addressed envelope (UK only) to:

Piatkus Books, 5 Windmill Street
London W1P 1HF

PIATKUS

The sign of a good book

7